Florine Thayer McCray

The life-work of the author of Uncle Tom's cabin

Florine Thayer McCray

The life-work of the author of Uncle Tom's cabin

ISBN/EAN: 9783743377219

Manufactured in Europe, USA, Canada, Australia, Japa

Cover: Foto ©Andreas Hilbeck / pixelio.de

Manufactured and distributed by brebook publishing software (www.brebook.com)

THE AUTHOR'S ACKNOWLEDGEMENTS.

THE authenticity of facts given in a work of this kind is of paramount importance. The writer having received assistance which it would be ingratitude, not to say presumption, to leave unacknowledged, wishes to return thanks to the numerous persons who have kindly aided her in her work, and, first of all, to refer with special tenderness to the friendship which the great author accorded to a young friend, and the cordial assistance given by her and her immediate family, to this history.

Having for several years cherished the friendship of Mrs. Stowe as one of the precious things in life, having been a frequent visitor at her house and a welcome companion in her walks, and one of the last acquaintances whom the famous woman recognized in the coming shadow of the clouded mentality which so sadly obscured her last days, the subscriber has been frequently called upon to write of the author of Uncle Tom's Cabin, which she several times has done, though never without the knowledge and consent of Mrs. Stowe and her family.

When, about one year ago, the publishers of this work, made a proposition for a history, of The Life Work of the Author of Uncle Tom's Cabin, the writer, though strongly inclining towards such an effort had no thought of undertaking it, without the full knowledge and consent of those most nearly interested. There were several cogent reasons for this proviso, chief among them being a sense of honor,

which must prevent any breach of the hospitality and confidence accorded to a personal acquaintance. Therefore the writer called upon Mrs. Stowe at her home, told her of the proposition and asked if it would be agreeable to her to have the work done. She replied, "Certainly, my dear friend. You are quite the one for it. If a history of my life work will interest or benefit any one, I shall be glad."

A few hours later her maid brought to the writer the note which here appears.

Realizing, however, that her son, Rev. Charles E. Stowe. who was also a personal friend, would naturally be her legal and literary executor, and that he might possibly demur at his mother's authorization, as she was at that time rapidly becoming weakened in her mind, the writer sent to him a long letter, giving a full account of the proposed work, her feeling of restriction as a friend to whom many facts had been given without reference to such a work as this, at the same time citing some ideas of her publishers and Rev. Dr. J. M. Sherwood their well known literary critic of whom she had asked advice. In reply came the following letter which sufficiently indicates the import of the one to which it replies, as well as previous confidential conversations upon Mr. Stowe's own projects for the future.

HARTFORD, DEC. 12, 1887.

MRS. FLORINE THAYER McCRAY :

Dear Madam :—I appreciate highly the delicacy of feeling which you have displayed in the matter of the work which you are contemplating ; yet at the same time I am of **Dr. Sherwood's** mind in the matter.

In the first place even if I did object you would have a perfect right to go on, as it is public property.

In the second place, your work will be of direct advantage to me pecuniarily, by acting as an advertisement, it will increase the sale of her works and stimulate public interest in her and her writings.

The work which I am doing, will be likely to be all the better received for the work which you are about to publish.

So I say go on with it, and I will do all I can to assist you.

Very sincerely yours,

C. E. STOWE.

In confirmation of this consent and promise, Mr. Stowe at various times afforded considerable assistance, courteously loaning an artist's proof engraving from the famous portrait made by Richmond, in London in 1853, for the purpose of its reproduction in this volume, and spending a long afternoon with the writer at the Safety Vaults wherein are stored the magnificent pieces of silver plate, which were given as testimonials to the author of Uncle Tom's Cabin, on the occasion of her first visit to Europe. To him we are further indebted for conversations upon the religious and psychological experiences of his father and mother.

To the Misses Stowe, we are under obligations for information not otherwise to be obtained, and views of souvenirs of their mother's wonderful career.

To Mrs. Isabella Beecher Hooker, Mrs. Stowe's youngest sister, for descriptions of her famous sister's personal appearance, and numerous important actions from the time before Mrs. Stowe's marriage, to the last, when she remained her devoted and trusted companion.

To Mrs. Mary F. Perkins of Boston, Mrs. Stowe's older sister, for reminiscences of Harriet's childhood.

To Dr. Edward Beecher of Brooklyn, and his wife, for

conversation upon her school days and her subsequent dealings with domestic, religious and literary problems in life.

To Rev. Joseph H. Twichell, of Hartford, Dr. Edwards
A. Park, of Andover Theological Seminary, Francis H.
Underwood, founder of the "Atlantic Monthly," and to
many other sources, the author makes acknowledgements
for valuable information, affording much interesting matter
both personal and historical.

PREFACE.

THE design of this work is not to trench upon the ground of strict biography. In treating of THE LIFE-WORK OF THE AUTHOR OF UNCLE TOM'S CABIN, the writer has undertaken a labor of love which finds its excuse in the desire to present to the young people of the age, and particularly the young women of America, a list of the literary works of Harriet Beecher Stowe, with an outline of each, and an unpretentious running commentary, such as is naturally suggested in their reading.

The main facts of Mrs. Stowe's life are given, with such reference to her personal experience as seems to explain the motives, the conception, and the prosecution of the great works, which have made her our most famous author.

To these, are added personal reminiscences, in which the writer claims not only the ownership which all admirers have in the authentic reports of the personality of a well loved author, but also the special right accorded to a witness and a friend.

What under other circumstances, might seem to be catering to idle curiosity, is sanctioned and dignified by the feeling of human sympathy it engenders, between the great author and her vast army of readers, and the possibilities it opens to others, who are, as they suppose, ham-

pered by physical conditions and the demands of domestic life.

The achievements of Mrs. Stowe are an example of the power of genius and will, to overcome obstacles which, doubtless in many cases have deprived the world of beneficial ideas.

If this history of THE LIFE-WORK OF THE AUTHOR OF UNCLE TOM'S CABIN incites fresh interest in her reader and yields a tithe of the profit and deep satisfaction experienced by the writer in its preparation, it will have amply demonstrated its right to be.

While the natural bias is always in favor of a dear friend and venerated author, the writer has tried not to ignore the limitations which are inevitable to human nature. It is hoped that all references to the personal peculiarities which eminently characterized the subject of this work, making her original and interesting above all the persons that the writer has ever known, will be received in the spirit in which they are set forth. To her, they appear infinitely engaging, and, mingled as they were, with the ineffable sweetness and fine humor, which deepened in Mrs. Stowe's later years, most tenderly appeal to the affectionate memory cherished by

FLORINE THAYER McCRAY.

HARTFORD, CONN., July, 1889.

CHAPTER I.

HARRIET BEECHER STOWE was born at Litchfield, Connecticut, June 14th, 1812. She was the seventh child of
Dr. Lyman Beecher, who with his eleven sons and daughters who grew to maturity, comprised a family which is
perhaps more widely and favorably known than any other
in the United States. The father and seven sons were clergymen, and three of the four daughters, have made themselves powerful factors in the progress of civilization as
authors and reformers. With the shades of difference
which always obtain between individual characters, they
bore a striking resemblance to each other, not only physically, but intellectually and morally. The father was perhaps a trifle below average size, and some of the sons a little
above it, neither stout nor slight, but compactly and
ruggedly built, with a certain abruptness and want of grace,

11

common to New Englanders of the past generation. Their
features were large and irregular, but with a strength of
bearing, which made the men almost handsome, while the
faces of the daughters, all but one of whom were plain,
were illumined by an expression of bright intelligence, and
wit which sparkled in the bluish grey eyes.

All of them had the energy of character, restless activity, strong convictions, tenacity of purpose, and deep sympathies which are requisite to the character of such propo-
gandists. The father and sons were ever in the thickest
of the religious battles of their time, always however,
dealing with questions which were full of vitality, rather
than dwelling upon metaphysical abstractions which were
so anxiously considered by most members of the Presbyterian church to which they belonged. Temperance, foreign and home missions, the influence of commerce on public morality, the conversion of young men, the establishment of theological seminaries, colonization, abolition, and
the political obligations of Christians, engaged their energies.

In order to understand and appreciate the springs of action in the life-work of great men and women, one must
not overlook their inherited characteristics, for "character
is destiny," or their social and intellectual education, for
these influences are so potential as to have received recognition in the social scientists' terms,—heredity and environment. The father of this family, so remarkable in their
personality and achievements, so distinctly individual in
their nature and utterances as to be generally known as a
" tribe," and to call forth the celebrated saying attributed
to Dr. Leonard Bacon, of New Haven, an eminent New
England divine and literary critic, that there were "only

three kinds of people in the world; the good, the bad and the Beechers"—was a descendant of an English family who came to America sixteen years after the landing of the Pilgrims of the Mayflower. He was the son of a New England blacksmith, who was one of the best read men in the country, being particularly well versed in astronomy, geography and history. Lyman Beecher was taught the trade of his father, and like a couple of intellectual Titans, they discussed science and theology to the deep blowings of the forge and the beat of their clanking hammers. The son received a solid education and graduated at Yale college at the age of twenty-two.

Having passed through a profound religious experience he made choice of the Christian ministry, as his profession, and with three classmates entered the Divinity School at New Haven under Dr. Dwight. From this he graduated with honor, and at once assumed charge of the Presbyterian church at East Hampton, Long Island. He had found time however, during his vacations at Old Guilford, to fall in love with sweet Roxana Foote, the daughter of Eli Foote, of Nutplains, a genial and cultivated man who, though a royalist and a churchman, was universally respected and honored in a puritan and revolutionary community. She was the queen of a coterie of young girls at Nutplains who used to sing hymns, spin, read Sir Charles Grandison and Miss Burney's "Evelina," talk about beaux and have merry times together, bewitching the hearts of the many bashful swains who respectfully gathered about them. Young Lyman Beecher went into love as into everything else, at full speed, and with resistless enthusiasm, and soon became engaged to marry Miss Foote. Dur-

ing the two years previous to their wedding he studied hard, observed intelligently, and formed those habits of original thought which characterized his work in after life and were transmitted to his children.

When Harriet was born, her father, then pastor of the First Congregational Society at Litchfield, Connecticut, was thirty-six years of age, in the full vigor of his early manhood, a man of fine physique, great power of mind, of indomitable force, high ambition, and electric eloquence. He was withal, genial in his manners, possessing a healthy appreciation of the humorous, and pre-eminently endowed with that faculty of philosophical deduction from experience, which we call common sense.

There were already five brothers and sisters in the parsonage at Litchfield, who filled the house full of noise, and their parents hearts with pleasant trials. There was Catherine who was in her twelfth year, already developing a powerful intellect and a high-strung ambition, which made her the favorite companion of her father, and filled her mother's heart with mingled pride and solicitude; William a sturdy lad of nine; Edward a curly haired fellow two years younger, full of boisterous fun, and constantly in chase of adventures at home and afield; Mary a child of three; and George who had to be weaned to make way for the new-comer. There had been an infant two years before, a girl named Harriet, whose death in the first few weeks of existence is touchingly referred to as the first bereavement of the parents and the affectionate sister and brother, who were old enough to mourn the speedy taking off of the little one. When another baby girl opened its eyes to the light that mid-June day in 1812, it was named for the one who was lost, and

soon became the object of the tender affection of the adult family, and the victim of the enthusiastic caresses of the lusty boys, who had already begun to assist their father about the house and barn, and to share his angling and hunting excursions, and his tramps through the woods.

Harriet, however, was quickly deprived of her royal prerogative as baby queen of the household, by the advent in a year, of a brother, who was named Henry Ward Beecher; and the last of the nine children who had come in quick succession to the arms of gentle Roxana Foote was Charles, who was an infant when she died Sept. 27, 1816. She was physically worn out; but it is the testimony of her children that she never lost the beautiful calmness and sweet serenity of manner, with which she moved on through the crowding duties of an arduous life. They pressed heavily upon her, not only as the wife of a young clergyman with straitened means and as the mother of eight living children, but also as a teacher, having with the assistance of her younger sister, Mary Hubbard, carried on a school, in which she taught the higher English branches, besides French, drawing, painting and embroidery, in which her own children received instruction with several young ladies, who were members of the large family circle.

The mother of the celebrated "Beecher family" was a woman of rare virtues, cultivated, highly educated and accomplished, and an artist of no mean ability. She took up the work of life with unshrinking devotion and was indeed a help meet to her husband, visiting, riding, walking, reading and talking with him, stimulating him to his marvelously productive work, and acting as anchor and balance to his less well-poised temper, which sometimes ap-

peared in erratic performances, of which many amusing stories are told.

The disciples of Fröebel maintain that the influences upon human character which are most lasting, are those which are brought to bear upon the mind of children before they are six years of age. Little Harriet Beecher took in refinement and culture with her mother's milk and, in the atmosphere of her infantile home life, breathed strength and purity of thought, and daily opened her baby eyes upon objects and scenes which contributed to a wide culture, seldom to be obtained in New England at that time. Dr. Oliver Wendell Holmes, being asked when the training of a child should begin, replied "A hundred years before it is born." The same cultivated American is modestly boastful of the fact, that he as a child built houses of quarto volumes, of a rarity and literary value quite out of the reach of persons of less culture and means than his grandfather.

There were no children's books for the young Beechers, no pictures adapted to an infant's comprehension, none of the modern dilution of things worth knowing, to fit them for immature intellects. The younger children studied what they must, listened receptively to the conversation of their elders, and imbibed strength and force of character in the very atmosphere of home.

An important element in the literary and domestic history of the Beecher family, was found in the society of their aunt, Mary Hubbard, and an uncle, Samuel Foote. Mrs. Beecher's tastes were rather for subjects of a scientific and metaphysical cast, while Mary Hubbard, the charming young widow, whose fascinations drew a throng of law students and young professional men about her, inclined pre-

dominantly to polite literature and works of the imagination. She was a delightful reader, and the older children have a most vivid recollection of the impassioned tones in which her favorite authors were given to the family circle. Uncle Samuel Foote was a sea captain, a man of great practical common sense, united with large ideality, cultivated taste and wide reading. On his return from each voyage, he came to the home at Litchfield, each time making his advent as a sort of brilliant genius from another sphere, bringing gifts, and tales of wonders, and descriptions of far countries, which seemed to wake new faculties in them all. Sometimes he came from the shores of Spain, with mementoes from the Alhambra and the ancient Moors; sometimes from Africa bringing Oriental head-gear or Moorish slippers; again from South America, with ingots of silver, or strange implements from the tombs of the Incas, or hammocks wrought by the South American Indians.

Moreover, Uncle Samuel Foote possessed a species of good humored combativeness, that led him to attack, sometimes jocosely and often in earnest, the special theories and prejudices of his friends. As a result he and Dr. Lyman Beecher were in continual skirmishes, in which all the New England peculiarities of character, and especially their trend of theological thought, were held up in caricature, or for serious discussion. There were long arguments, to which the children listened absorbedly, in which he maintained that the Turks were more honest than Christians, bringing very startling facts in evidence. They heard his tales of the Roman Catholic bishops and archbishops which he had carried to and from Spain and America, whom he affirmed to be as truly learned and pious and devoted to

2

the good of men, as any Protestant to be found in America. His account of the Jews in Morocco was most curious; their condition appearing, even to his skeptical mind, the strongest verification of Hebrew prophecy. The new fields of vision which he presented, the skill and marvelous adroitness of his arguments, and the array of facts which he brought to bear upon these topics, taxed to the utmost the intellectual powers of Lyman Beecher, and the brilliant conversations made an impression never to be effaced, upon the plastic minds of the young people who listened.

In the literary circles of Litchfield, and especially among women of culture, Captain Foote appeared in the most heroic and romantic light. He spoke the polite languages with ease, and had a fair knowledge of the various dialects in the foreign countries he had visited. Best of all, he always brought a stock of new books when he came to Litchfield, which he and Aunt Mary Hubbard read aloud. This was the time when Scott, Byron, Moore, and that bright galaxy of contemporary writers, were issuing their works at frequent intervals, and the childrens' minds were stored with the wierd tales from Scott's Ballads. The Lay of the Last Minstrel and Marmion became household lore, The Cotter's Saturday Night, and the touching verses of the Ayrshire ploughman who had burst into song, as well as the heroic poems and rhythmical complaints of Byron, shared a place with Mother Goose, in the affections of that group of receptive boys and girls.

Harriet was between three and four years old when her mother died. The few remembrances that Mrs. Stowe had of her are most pathetic. Her last look at the cold body; the funeral, which Henry was too young to attend, remain-

ing at home frolicing in the sun; his ignorant joy with his toys, and the halo of golden curls ill according with his little black frock; the scene at the grave, and the childish failure to understand that her mother was in Heaven, while yet she saw her body laid in the ground, have been frequently recalled in conversation with her friends.

Mrs. Stowe told how Henry was discovered one day not long after her mothers' funeral, digging earnestly under sister Catharine's window, and when she called to him to know what he was doing, he lifted his curly head with the utmost simplicity and answered, "Why, I am going to Heaven to find Ma."

Among the vivid reminiscences of Harriet's early childhood were her visits to her grandmother Foote at Nutplains. She wrote:

"I think, in the recollections of all the children, our hours spent at Nutplains were the golden hours of our life. Aunt Harriet had precisely the turn which made her treasure every scrap of a family relic and history. And even those of the family who had passed away forever seemed still to be living at Nutplains, so did she cherish every memorial, and recall every action and word. There was Aunt Catharine's embroidery; there Aunt Mary's paintings and letters; there the things which Uncle Samuel had brought from foreign shores; frankincense from Spain, mats and baskets from Mogadore, and various other trophies locked in drawers, which Aunt Harriet displayed to us on every visit.

"At Nutplains our mother, lost to us, seemed to live again. We saw her paintings, her needle-work, and heard a thousand little sayings and doings of her daily life. And so dear was everything that belonged to grandmother and our Nutplains home. that the Episcopal service, even though not well read, was always

chosen during our visits there in preference to our own. It seemed a part of Nutplains and of the life there.

"There was also an interesting and well-selected library, and a portfolio of fine engravings; and, though the place was lonely, yet the cheerful hospitality that reigned there left them scarcely ever without agreeable visitors; and some of the most charming recollections of my childhood are of a beautiful young lady, who used to play at chess with Uncle George when he returned from his work in the wood-lot of a winter evening.

"The earliest poetry that I ever heard were the ballads of Walter Scott, which Uncle George repeated to Cousin Mary and me the first winter that I was there. The story of the black and white huntsman made an impression on me that I shall never forget. His mind was so steeped in poetical literature that he could at any time complete any passage in Burns or Scott from memory. As for graver reading, there was Rees's Cyclopedia, in which I suppose he had read every article, and which was often taken down when I became old enough to ask questions, and passages pointed out in it for my reading.

"All these remembrances may explain why the lonely little white farm-house under the hill was such a Paradise to us, and the sight of its chimneys after a day's ride was like a vision of Eden. In later years, returning there, I have been surprised to find that the hills around were so bleak and the land so barren; that the little stream near by had so few charms to uninitiated eyes. To us, every juniper bush, every wild sweetbrier, every barren sandy hillside, every stony pasture, spoke of bright hours of love, when we were welcomed back to Nutplains as to our mother's heart."

The first event that followed in the year of the great family sorrow, was the removal of Grandma Beecher and Aunt Esther to the parsonage at Litchfield to take charge of the family. Grandma Beecher was a fine specimen of the

Puritan character of the strictest pattern. She was however naturally kind, generous and sympathizing, and had a special fondness for animals. She was the perfection of neatness and order; but her love for her motherless grandchildren opened the door of her room to them, and little Harriet was her favorite. Her stock of family traditions and neighborhood lore was wonderful, and among her precious books were chiefly, the Bible and Prayer-book. Lowth's Isaiah, she knew almost by heart; Buchanan's Researches in Asia, Bishop Heber's Life, and Dr. Johnson's Works, were also great favorites with her. These books her grandchildren were called upon to read, while at frequent intervals she explained passages. Under the regime of honest, conscientious Aunt Esther, the family lived on comfortably for a year, when a new mother came to govern and guide at the parsonage.

She was a Miss Harriet Porter, of Portland, Maine, a lady of gentle birth and personal accomplishments, whom Lyman Beecher had met upon one of his professional visits to a brother pastor. Harriet Beecher's first impression of her was of a beautiful lady, very fair, with bright blue eyes and soft auburn hair, who came into the nursery where Harriet slept with her two younger brothers, with an eager, affectionate smile, kissed them and told them that she loved little children and would be their mother. They wanted forthwith to get up and be dressed, but they were pacified with a promise that she would be there in the morning. Probably never did step-mother make a prettier or sweeter impression. The Beechers were noisy, red-cheeked, hearty country children, and they looked at the delicate, elegant lady whom their father had brought home, with awe. She

seemed rather like a strange princess, than their own mamma; her ways of speaking and moving were very graceful; she was peculiarly dainty and neat in her personal appearance and belongings; she had beautiful white hands, adorned with handsome rings, and Harriet used at first to feel breezy and rough in her presence.

While Harriet worshipped her with a childish devotion, it appears that she at least once, was stung with a momentary jealousy of her high place in her father's affections, and the little girl poutingly said, to the great amusement of every one: "Because you have come and married my Pa, when I am big enough, I mean to go and marry your Pa." But the feeling was fleeting, instantly superceded by the love which endured during their life together.

But, as transpired, the second Mrs. Beecher's nature and habits were too refined and exacting for the bringing up of so many children of great animal force and vigor, under the pressure of straitened circumstances. She became the mother of four children, who were Isabella, Thomas, a babe who died, and James, but to the last had little sympathy with the ordinary feelings of childhood. Mrs. Stowe has said of her religious training of the little ones, with whom she spent an hour of intense and positive exhortation and prayer every Sunday night: "She gave an impression of religion as being like herself, calm, solemn, inflexible, mysteriously sad and rigorously exacting." Lyman Beecher used to declare that his second wife, who was converted from a lighthearted petted beauty into a serious Christian of extreme severity, adopted her minister's dyspepsia at the same time she did his Calvinism!

In these early years were made those impressions of the

old meeting house in which her father preached, so graphically described by Mrs. Stowe in one of her sketches:—

"To my childish eye, our old meeting house was an awe-inspiring thing. To me it seemed fashioned very nearly on the model of Noah's Ark and Solomon's Temple as set forth in the pictures in my Scripture Catechism—pictures which I did not doubt were authentic copies; and what more venerable architectural precedent could one desire?

"Its double row of windows, of which I knew the number by heart; its door, with great wooden quirls over them; its belfry projecting out at the east end; its steeple and bell, all inspired as much sense of the sublime in me as Strasbourg Cathedral itself; and the inside was not a whit the less imposing.

"How magnificent to my eye seemed the turnip-like canopy that hung over the minister's head hooked by a long iron rod to the wall above, and how apprehensively did I consider the question what would become of him if it should fall? How did I wonder at the panels on either side of the pulpit in each of which was carved and painted a flaming red tulip with its leaves projecting out at right angles! And then at the grape-vine in bas-relief on the front with exactly triangular leaves. The area of the house was divided into large square pews, boxed up with stout boards, and surmounted with a kind of baluster work which I supposed to be provided for the special accommodation of us youngsters, being the 'loop-holes of retreat' through which we gazed upon the 'remarkabilia' of the scene."

In the same article appears a description of the singer's seat, which is only equalled by Washington Irving's inimitable word picture of the choir in the loft of the little church at Bracebridge Hall.

"But the glory of our meeting-house was its singer's seat, that

empyrean of those who rejoiced in the mysterious art of fa-sol-la-ing. There they sat in the gallery that lined three sides of the house ; treble, counter, tenor and bass, each with its appropriate leader and supporters.   There were generally seated the bloom of our young people, sparkling, modest and blushing girls on one side, with their ribbons and finery making the place as blooming and lovely as a flower garden ; and the fiery, forward and con-fident young men on the other.

"But I have been talking of singers all the time and have neg-lected to mention the Magnus Apollo of the whole concern who occupied the seat of honor in the midst of the second gallery, and exactly opposite to the minister.   With what an air did he sound the important fa-sol-la in the ears of the waiting gallery, who stood with open mouths ready to give the pitch preparatory to the general *set to*.   How did his ascending and descending arm aston-ish the zephyrs when once he laid himself out to the important work of beating time.

"But the glory of his art consisted in the execution of those good old billowy compositions called fuguing tunes, where the four parts that compose the choir take up the song, and go racing around one after the other, each singing a different set of words, till at length by some inexplicable magic, they all come together again and sail smoothly out into a rolling sea of harmony!

"I remember the wonder with which I used to look from side to side when treble, tenor, counter and bass were thus roaring and foaming, and it verily seemed to me as if the psalm were going to pieces in the breakers ; and the delighted astonishment with which I found that each particular verse did emerge whole and uninjured from the storm."

The girl was mother to the woman, whose keen observa-tions and discriptive powers were of a remarkable order,

and whose sympathy for the suffering and oppressed rose into the sublime eloquence of her great book.

An older sister thus describes an incident which displays the affection of the child for her pets, and the earnestness with which she paid to one, her tribute of sympathy and regret.

"There was a very old yellow cat in the house in Litchfield, to which my father moved when I was about five years old, and in which Harriet was born. Tom, for that was his name, must have been an old cat at that time, and when Harriet was about eight, it was evident that he was about to die. Harriet came to her step-mother one morning and said, poor old Tom is lying on the bank all alone, and he's going to die, and I can't bear to have him die alone, mayn't I stay at home and sit with him? Her step-mother gave her leave, so the little girl gave the old pussy company and comfort for the little of his life which was left.

"The other children appear to have been so excited by this devotion of hers that they made a funeral for Tom, at which her sister Catherine read an epitaph which Harriet with the 'sweet invocation of a child; most pretty and pathetical,' had implored her to write."

From the same pen we receive another reminiscence, which further illustrates her instinctive fondness for cats, which with other animals were always her pets, and frequently mentioned in her writings.

"Harriet was very fond of reading the Arabian Knights, which she found at her grandmother's house, at Nutplains. It happened that a stray cat attached itself to the grandmother, who took no fancy to it, and rejected its affectionate attentions. This grieved the little girl, who conceived the idea that the cat was really the old lady's daughter, who had lost her human form, by some magic

art, and was hopelessly trying to make her love known to her
mother. She, remembering how those magic spells were broken,
in her favorite book, used to take her opportunity in private, and
throw water over the poor cat,—saying, 'If this is thy natural
form, retain it, if not, resume the form of a woman.' But the imprisoned daughter was never set free."

Another cat story is worth reproducing here, having a
special interest, as it was doubtless Mrs. Stowe's last contribution to the press. It was given by her to the writer who
was then editing the *City Mission Record* of Hartford, Conn.,
for publication in that magazine, of Feb., 1888.

"When I was eight years of age I had a favorite cat, of whom
I was very fond. Puss was attacked with fits, and in her parox-
ysms flew round the top of the wall, jumped onto our heads and
scratched and tumbled up our hair in a frightful way. My father
shot her, and when she was cold and dead my former fondness returned. I wrapped her nicely in a cloth and got my brother to
dig a grave and set up a flat stone for a monument. Then I went
to my older sister, Catherine, and asked her to write me an
"epithet" (epitaph) to put on the stone.

She wrote:

> Here lies poor Kit
> Who had a fit
> And acted queer;
> Killed with a gun
> Her race is run,
> And she lies here.

I pasted this upon the stone and was comforted."

Harriet Beecher grew into girlhood a hearty, rosy, strong
child, with flying curls of sunny brown, and sweet, keen
blue eyes, always ready for fun and play ; a happy frolicsome
creature, rejoicing in this life, yet already weighted with the
prospect of the life which is to come—a subject which in

all its theological bearings was never ignored or neglected in that hill-top parsonage. She says of herself,—" I was educated first and foremost by Nature, wonderful, beautiful, ever changing as she is in that cloud-land, Litchfield."

She ran wild among the trees and hills. She heard with rapture the pipe and trilling of the birds; she made friendly acquaintance with the small game aflight or afoot in the fields; she followed winding streams to their source; she sailed boats; listened to the rippling of the water over the bright shallows; watched the sunlight in the shimmering depths of the deep pools, or the shining fish which darted out of sight or lazily floated in the sun. She gathered the first sweet wildlings of the spring; had her secret places where luscious strawberries, equally gratifying to the æsthetic and gustatory sense nodded upon their stems; gathered gorgeous lilies and blazing poppies and the blue corn flower in the hay-field in the quivering heart of June, and went nutting in the delicious haze and leafy brilliance of October. There was nothing foreign or unknown to her in the kindly fruitage of the earth; and she learned, close to Nature's heart, those unspeakable lessons which she whispers to her devout children.

But coming from what Oliver Wendell Holmes has termed " the Brahmin class of New England," whose instinctive refinement of feeling and natural aptitude for learning seem, to use the genial doctor's own words, " hereditary and congenital," Harriet Beecher early promised to be a scholar. When she was five years of age, she had been to school, learning to read very fluently, and having a retentive memory, had committed twenty-seven hymns and two long chapters in the Bible.

Her eagerness to read, which grew and increased with
every year of her life, was constantly stimulated by the
bracing intellectual atmosphere of her home, which as we
have seen, was characterized by an unusual degree of activity. The light literature, which now floods every household, was a thing unknown, and after revelling in the Arabian Knights, she used to spend hours in the attic, desperately searching among the sermons, treatises, tracts, and
essays, which she surreptitiously dragged from a barrel, for
fresh food for her active mind. Once turning up a dis-
sertation on Solomon's Song, she devoured it with a relish,
as it told of the same sort of things she read of in the in-
exhaustible tales of her beloved Scherherazade. She was
at another time rewarded for several hours toil in what she
called, "a weltering ocean of pamphlets," by bringing to
light a fragment of "Don Quixote," which was fraught
with enchantment and read with a frantic disregard of the
possible objection of her parents. At this time the names
of Scott, Byron, Moore, and Irving, were comparatively
new. The "Salmagundi Papers" were recent publications
though making a literary sensation among intelligent people. Byron had not quite finished his course, and Aunt
Esther, a woman of strong mind, ready wit, and the best
of critical perceptions, one day gave to Harriet a volume
of his works, containing "The Corsair." This she read
with wonder and delight, and thenceforth listened eagerly
to whatever was said in the house concerning Byron. Not
long after, she heard her father sorrowfully observe, "Byron is
dead,—gone." She says, "I remember taking my basket
for strawberries that afternoon and going over to a field on
Chestnut hill. But I was too dispirited to do anything;

so I lay down among the daisies, and looked up into the blue sky, and thought of that great eternity into which Byron had entered, and wondered how it might be with his soul."

Harriet Beecher was then a child of eleven, but was sufficiently precocious to appreciate the genius in Byron's passionate poetry and to share the enthusiasm which his works had everywhere created.

Scott had written his best poems, and "The Lay of the Last Minstrel," and "Marmion," were familiar to the Beecher household, as to intelligent people the world over, but a novel, was regarded by most pious people as a thing detrimental, if not unclean, having become so generally depreciated in the hands of the writers of the previous generation.

"The Tales of my Landlord," and "Ivanhoe," had just made their appearance, and great was the joy of the household when Dr. Beecher, after careful perusal of one or two of them, gave his son George permission to read Scott's novels. In the summer, Harriet and George, who was a year or two her senior, read "Ivanhoe" seven times, and learned many of the scenes so that they could recite them from beginning to end, rehearsing them as dialogues each assuming several characters in the most versatile manner, suiting voice and action to the words, in a style which they deemed dramatically effective.

One of the events of the year in the parsonage at Litchfield was the apple cutting, when a barrel of cider apple sauce was to be made and the boys and girls were pressed into service as assistants. The work was done in the kitchen, an immense shining brass kettle hanging over the

fire in the deep chimney, and the whole family of children
and servants, gathered around, employed on the great
baskets of apples and quinces.   Dr. Beecher presided at the
apple peeler, turning the crank with great expedition, and
one evening said to George, " Come, I'll tell you what we'll
do to make the evening go off.   You and I'll take turns
and see who'll tell the most out of Scott's novels."   So
they took them, novel by novel, reciting scenes and incidents, which kept the children wide-awake, and made their
work fly, while Harriet often made a correction, or supplied
with joyful eagerness, some point they had omitted.

Before Harriet could write, she had printed many of
these and other stories from memory, making little books
which her sisters sewed together, and often used to entertain her little brothers, Henry and Charles, by reading to
them portions which she had reproduced almost verbatim.
Henry Ward Beecher has said that a verbal memory such
as hers, would have doubled his powers.   She shared the
bed in the nursery with these two little fellows, and her older
sister recalls often hearing her adapt condensations of her
reading to their comprehension.   She used to lay flat upon
the floor, poring over the great family Bible, committing
entire chapters to memory.   She studied Paradise Lost in
the same manner.

Dr. Beecher constantly encouraged his children to intellectual joustings.   In the words of Charles Beecher :

" The law of his family was that, if any one had a good thing,
he must not keep it to himself; if he could say a funny thing, he
was bound to say it ; if a severe thing, no matter—the severer
the better, if well *put ;* every one must be ready to take as well
as give.   The Doctor never asked any favors of his children, nor

stood upon his dignity, in encounters of wit or logic. When they grappled him, he taught them to grapple in earnest, and they well knew what they had to expect in return."

The conditions of young Harriet Beecher's early school life were particularly favorable to sound learning and thorough culture. There were situated in Litchfield at the time, the best school in Connecticut. Nominally under the direction of Miss Sarah Pierce, a well educated and superior woman, its real head and moving spirit was her nephew, John Pierce Brace, a teacher who left his impress upon many now celebrated minds, and, afterwards became famous as the principal of the highly reputed Hartford Female Seminary. No teacher can have better " educated " his pupils in the true sense of the word. While not a martinet or drill master, in the modern sense of the term, he yet possessed a subtle intelligence in reaching the intellect of his scholars, an instinct for all that was best in them, and an appreciation of their individual tastes and mental bias, which was as rare, as it was an enviable quality. The Academy in Litchfield became one of those pure wells from which the hidden strength of New England character was drawn. Pupils had gathered to it from as far as Boston. There were one hundred students about equally divided between boys and girls. There was a class of young men preparing for college, and the greater number of the boys had the same ultimate object. The girls however had no restrictions as to their course, except such as were the result of personal preference, and this clear-headed daughter of Dr. Lyman Beecher took up the classics and higher mathematics with her brothers. Mr. Brace was always stimulating the girls to such undertakings and felt a special

pride in this alert, fun-loving child. She held a natural admiration for the doubtful works of art which came under the supervision of Miss Titcomb, and possessed of a fair proficiency in reproducing the embroidery and feminine accomplishments of the Hannah More and Johnsonian school. These consisted mostly of mourning pieces, with the family monument in the centre, a weeping willow drooping sadly over a black robed woman, whose face was invariably covered with a pocket handkerchief, and pastoral scenes, with fair shepherdesses sitting on green chenille banks, tending bunchy animals of uncertain species, which were by faith received as sheep. But she had a stronger predilection for book lore, and pursued her Latin and Greek verses with the same persistency and disposition to win, that she followed a bee to its lair or sought the first sweet blossoms of the spring in the cool wet nooks under the forest leaves.

The fact was John P. Brace during his early life had been a sailor, and in the ports of the Mediterranean and the churches of Spain and Italy, had seen the old masters, knew what Murillos and Titians were like, and glanced with scarcely concealed amusement at the marvelous artistic productions, then held in such reverence by New England housewives. Cicero and Ovid, Greek authors, Shakespeare, Milton, Johnson, Bacon, Spenser, Goldsmith and Dryden, geography, history, rhetoric and higher mathematics, were the daily exercise and recitation of his pupils. Mr. Brace was accused of using his teachings as a mental gratification for himself. If there was a subject he wanted to investigate, a classic author that he wanted to unearth, or a knotty point to unravel, he would put a class

upon it and come out with scorn upon any poor body so
bound down by routine as to suggest that it had nothing to
do with the coming college examinations. Mr. Brace was
sparing of praise, took delight in puzzling his pupils and
setting all their faculties at work by unexpected questions,
and could not endure the mechanical methods which then
obtained, and have not even now, become desirably obsolete in schools. He understood perfectly that mere cram-
ming of the memory with facts was not education, and
realized that to fit the intellects under his charge to grasp a
new question, to view it from all standpoints and judge
accurately of its merits, was better than to pack away much
undigested learning, upon the shelves of the mental store-
house. He used to say—"Learn to use your own heads
and you can learn anything." And "Learn to read Greek
perfectly, and it's no matter what you read."

As may be imagined, there was little idling or shirking
in a school conducted on such principles, and the result of
his training has been shown in the lives of his pupils, many
of whom became prominent and luminous in the intellectual history of New England.

When Harriet was very young, her own simple lessons
were neglected and forgotten as she sat listening intently,
hour after hour, to the conversations of Mr. Brace with his
older classes upon moral philosophy, history and rhetoric.
Particular attention was given in this school to the writing
of compositions. Harriet was but nine years old when
roused by the inspiration of her teacher, she volunteered to
write one every week. One of the first themes given was
"The Difference between the Natural and the Moral Sublime," a subject sufficiently formidable to have appalled

3

many an older pupil; but she found herself laboring with
the subject, felt sure that she could make some clear distinctions, and before she could write legibly or spell correctly,
brought forth her first composition, upon this ponderous
theme, receiving judicious praise. Two years later she
received the appointment to furnish one of the articles
to be read at the closing exhibition and took the
negative of the following question :—" Can the Immortality of the Soul be proved by the Light of Nature." This
argument was read before the *literati* of Litchfield who
crowded the town hall upon that distinguished occasion,
and so interested Dr. Lyman Beecher, who knew nothing
of the effort, that at the close he said to Mr. Brace, " Who
wrote that composition ? " " Your daughter, sir," was the
the answer, which plainly filled the father with pleased
surprise, and Harriet has said, it was the proudest moment
of her life.

Most favorably supplementing the advantages of inherited character, home and school influences, and education, was the social environment, the high literary and historical atmosphere, which pervaded the society which
recognized the Beecher's as among their most capable
leaders and inspirers. Few country towns in our land have
so beautifully diversified topographical features as Litchfield, Connecticut, and still rarer are the localities, which
have so many interesting incidents and associations, patriotic, literary and religious, connected with their history.
The home of the Beechers was upon a wide and breezy
hill, from which can still be seen a long stretch of characteristic New England scenery. Distinguished people made
their home in this picturesque township, near the centre of

the county, and Lyman Beecher preached in the meeting house of the Congregational Society to persons whose careers have made them famous in history. There was Ethan Allen, a native of Litchfield, whose professed infidelity did not prevent his honest admiration for Lyman Beecher, whose church he regularly attended. There was the gallant Colonel Tallmage, of Herculean frame and a face like Washington's, who once rode three miles with a defenceless girl behind him on horseback, carrying her to a place of safety. There was Gov. Oliver Wolcott, a member of Washington's cabinet; Hon. John Allen, a member of Congress celebrated for his uncommon stature, being nearly seven feet high and large in proportion; Hon. Frederick Wolcott, a distinguished lawyer; Hon. Uriel Holmes, a lawyer of note, member of Congress and Judge of the County Court; John Pierpont, the poet, and Dr. Sheldon, one of the most celebrated physicians in the State. Most intimate in his relations with the family, was Judge Reeves, who was for over a half a century a citizen of Litchfield, and founder of the celebrated Law School, which for forty years was sought by young men of talent, from nearly every state in the union. Judge Reeves was distinguished for his piety and interest in all benevolent operations, as much as for his learning. In him, Dr. Beecher found a kindred spirit, and one who stood nearer to him than any other, in Christian intimacy. His first wife was a grand-daughter of President Johnathan Edwards, and a sister of Aaron Burr, who for six years made Litchfield his home. The influence and lasting impress of these associations upon the girl, is to be easily traced in the work of the woman who became America's greatest reformer.

It was fashionable in Litchfield to take long walks to the
hill tops to see the gorgeous sunsets, to make observations
of the constellations which starred the heavens by night, and
watch the changing phases of the moon, with an astronomical
enthusiasm quite apart from the sentimental observations,
peculiar doubtless then, as now, to young lovers. Tea
parties were then as now social occasions, but varying
from what has been cleverly characterized as the " creme
de la creme uneventfulness " of the four o'clock receptions
of the present day, in a manner reflecting most favorably
upon the intelligence of that time.

It was the rule to discuss the current literature of the
day, the last articles in the English Reviews, the latest
Waverly novel, the poetry of Scott, Burns, Byron, Southey,
Moore and Wordsworth.

Frequently one of the learned Judges, who was an admirable talker, would hold the attention of the drawing-room,
while he ran a parallel between the dramatic handling of
Scott's characters as compared with Shakespeare, or gave
an analysis of the principles of the Lake School of poetry.
The students in the law offices and school, and the young
ladies of the best families, had reading circles and literary
partialities, and there was much polished allusion and
quotation and spouting of poetry, and some youths who
tied their open shirt collars with black ribbon after the
fashion of Byron, and professed disgust at the hollow state
of human happiness in general. Compassionate young
ladies found them all the more interesting, for this state
of mysterious desolation, and tried with surprising success to console them. Frequently, literature was forgotten in the intense interest in politics; and one evening

when enough had come to light to make it apparent that the state of Connecticut had gone over from the Federalists to the Democrats, the triumph of the lower orders, the reign of " sans-culottism," was felt to have begun, and the prediction, by a social magnate, that they were all dwelling over a volcano which would burst and destroy all their institutions, was heard with fear by Harriet Beecher, who was yet a little comforted to observe that the judge selected a particularly choice piece of cake, and took a third cup of tea with much calmness in the very midst of these shocking prognostications.

CHAPTER II.

A CHANGE of base was coming for little Harriet Beecher,
not yet in her early teens. Catherine, the oldest of the
family, then a thoroughly educated, intellectual and dignified young lady, was engaged to marry Professor Alexander M. Fisher, of Yale College; a man already distinguished,
and of great promise in his profession. He started for
Europe in April, 1822, where he purposed to study and
travel for a year before his marriage. The ship Albion, in
which he sailed, was lost, and only one of all its passengers
and crew, came back to tell the tale. The brilliant girl,
lately so full of joy and hope, lost heart in everything in
life, and fell into a sort of rebellious melancholy, from

38

which it seemed for a time that even her helpful spirit and practical education, could not rescue her.

With the lapse of time she rallied somewhat, but felt that she must fly from the scenes which spoke so constantly and eloquently of her lover and her lost hope, and seek relief from crushing thought, in active work. She went to Hartford, Connecticut, and with the assistance of her younger sister Mary, afterwards Mrs. Thomas C. Perkins, she opened a school for girls, which became famous and was known under the name which it still preserves, of the Hartford Female Seminary. This school, which was in a way a successor to one kept by Lydia Maria Huntley, afterwards Mrs. Sigourney, was soon standing on a par with those of Mrs. Willard at Watertown and Troy, New York, and Miss Lyon's and Miss Grant's academy at Ipswich. Their brother, Edward, then at the head of the Hartford Latin School, boarded with his sisters in the household over which Aunt Esther Beecher presided. The older members of this family, were even then coming to be famous for their intellectual force and scholarly attainments, attracting to them the best of the cultured society of the town. Harriet was confided to her sister's care, and, leaving all the freedom and varied joys of child life in the country, she settled seriously to work and remained at Hartford six years. During the latter part of the time she became an assistant pupil, teaching Latin and translating Virgil into English heroic verse, mingling her teaching, studies and social diversions in the most delightful and profitable manner.

While Harriet was not thought, by any means, the equal of her elder sister in mental weight and power, and of a rather

careless and unpractical turn of mind, she was amiable and
endearing in her ways, and was recognized as a decidedly
clever young lady, of rare sincerity and plainness in speech,
with a vein of humor and a sleepy sort of wit, which
flashed out in the most unexpected manner.   No seer perceived above the ringleted head of the absent-minded
young teacher, a dark attendant spirit, benignant yet
mournful, "poor, grand, old world-wept, polyglotted Uncle
Tom," the brightness of whose character will forever illu-
mine her name; but the pupils, who in after years recalled
with pride their acquaintance with Harriet Beecher,
never remembered aught of her that was not generous and
kind.

Göethe has said that much may be known of a person's
character by observing what things excite his laughter.
Though Harriet Beecher's sense of the ludicrous was keen
practical joking was not to her taste. No strange or amusing
combination of happenings could excite her mirth, if thereby,
another was made uncomfortable. She was richly possessed of humor—that charming faculty which enables one
to be amusing without a sting; the quick perception of the
ludicrous in life, which is so expressed as to leave no
smart behind. The difference between wit and humor has
been cleverly defined by George W. Bungay. He says:
"Wit laughs *at* everybody; humor laughs *with* everybody."
Harriet Beecher began in her earliest childhood to laugh
with everybody with most enviable good nature and it was
only upon rare provocation, that she exercised her power of
trenchant repartee.

In 1826, after long and anxious self examination, Dr.
Lyman Beecher came to the conclusion that he had no

longer a right to live in debt, for want of a sufficient salary.
He was the father of eleven children, and the problem of
educating, feeding and clothing the large family who
remained upon his hands, was a dark one. Eight hundred
dollars a year, had it been promptly paid, which was not
usually the case, was not a princely income. Many of the
ministers of that time in New England were forced to eke
out the small salary given them, by farming on week days, by
writing school or religious books, or even by taking agencies
and selling popular articles. Dr. Beecher's sense of dignity
and clerical duty would not permit this, and without con-
sulting any one, he resolved to leave Litchfield as soon as
he could find a more remunerative parish. By a singular
co-incidence, in twelve hours after this decision was
reached, a letter arrived, inviting him to the Hanover
Street Church, of Boston. Here for six years he waged an
earnest war for Orthodoxy against Unitarianism, preaching
upon various themes in so trenchant and powerful a manner that his fame spread all over the land. His Boston
career was the acme of his life.

Dr. Beecher united the logical faculty with the imaginative and the emotional, in a very high degree. His preaching, as has been said of another, was *logic on fire*. He
preached the fundamentals of Christian doctrine, and not
the philosophies or the nice distinctions of the schools;
and he preached them in a light so clear and convincing,
with convictions so irresistible, with appeals so fervid, and
with such persuasive attraction, that his ministry in Boston
and elsewhere, was one of singular power and success. He
likewise took a prominent part in the famous theological
and ecclesiastical controversy which agitated New England

ILLUSTRATIONS.

CHAPTER XIX.

CHAPTER X.

CHAPTER XI.

CHAPTER XII.

CHAPTER VII.

CHAPTER VIII.

CHAPTER IX.

CHAPTER IV.

CHAPTER V.

CHAPTER VI.

CONTENTS.

In the Office of the Librarian of Congress
at Washington, D. C.

THE

LIFE – WORK

OF THE AUTHOR OF

UNCLE TOM'S CABIN.

BY

FLORINE THAYER MCCRAY,

Author of "ENVIRONMENT; A STORY OF MODERN SOCIETY," ETC.

———

FUNK & WAGNALLS

NEW YORK: LONDON:

1889

18 AND 20 ASTOR PLACE.   44 FLEET STREET.

Florine Thayer McCray

The life-work of the author of Uncle Tom's cabin

49 Forest St
Dec 11. 1887

Dear Friend
        You are quite
welcome to write the Sketch
you propose I believe
that all the material for
such an one is quite
at hand & at your disposal
        Yours Very truly
                H B Stowe

and several branches of the Church, and which resulted in the division of the Presbyterian Church in 1837, and of the Methodist Episcopal Church in 1844.

Slavery as well as doctrinal differences, entered largely into this fierce conflict. Lyman Beecher was a man of great originality, boldness and robustness of character, openly and vehemently denouncing intemperance, dueling, and other social evils of the times. His six sermons against intemperance, prepared and preached while at Litchfield, were a trumpet blast that shook the world and produced a prodigious excitement and impression everywhere. Although among the first to speak and write on the subject, those sermons on the evil and guilt of drunkenness, in the matter of argument, fact, invective and appeal, have not been surpassed in the whole history of temperance literature. He was withal a profound student of theology, and was selected by the voice of the Church to establish a Theological school for the training of men for the ministry in the great and rapidly growing West, where for twenty years he did grand service. He was called to a professorship, and later the presidency of Lane Seminary, Cincinnati, in 1832, and the whole family followed him. Catherine and Mary Beecher resigned their school in Hartford to the able management of John P. Brace, under whose teaching they had been, and following whose precepts given them years before, they had made it a gratifying success, who carried it on for twelve years after their departure. Mary having married, Catherine and Harriet, together founded a school, in Cincinnati.

For several years following, the social life of Harriet Beecher was of the most stimulating and beneficial kind. The intelligence, and general culture, which pervaded the atmosphere about the region at Walnut Hills, upon a high point of which stood the Seminary; the charming associations which embraced the professors, their wives and families, theological students and visiting graduates; the transition to the broader life of the then far West, which enabled her to look back upon New England life and customs with a discriminating eye; and the inspiring conversation and inquiries which called forth description and opinions, all tended to cultivation, and freedom of thought and expression.

The literary guild into which Harriet Beecher was happily drawn, had no little influence in awakening in her a consciousness of her powers, and furnished opportunities and encouragement in the exercise of those faculties which have made her famous. Out of the sympathy and good fellowship of many of the men and women of that vicinity, there grew a desire to associate themselves in literary work, and a series of social reunions were established, under the name of "The Semi-colon Club."

At these meetings, essays, sketches, reviews, stories and poems were read, and discussions and conversations carried on, enlivened and diversified with music. Among the people who participated in the meetings who have since become distinguished, may be mentioned Judge Hall, editor of "The Western Monthly Magazine," Miss Catherine Beecher, Professor Hentz, and his graceful and accomplished wife, Caroline Lee Hentz, a novelist of popularity; E. P. Cranch, the humorist, whose delicious fancies flowed with equal ease into word pictures or pencil drawings, Charles W. Eliot, the New England historian, three Misses Blackwell, two of whom have gained distinction as physicians,

Professor Calvin E. Stowe, then already widely known in Europe and America as a scholar and author, and Professor, subsequently General, O. M. Mitchell, whom the nation remembers as one of its most accomplished scientific men, and mourns as one of the noblest martyrs in the cause of liberty.

In this brilliant circle, Harriet Beecher's genius soon began to shine conspicuously, and her articles descriptive of the peculiarities of New England life and character, were met with tremendous applause. One called "Uncle Lot," written for the Semi-colon Club in 1834, made the greatest impression, and when Judge Hall offered fifty dollars for the best story for his magazine, and Harriet Beecher having revised the sketch sent it to the judges, she received the prize—an accession to her private funds, which was by no means to be despised. She became an occasional contributor to the *Western Monthly Magazine*, and to *Godey's Lady's Book*, writing a number of sketches which made a favorable impression, drawing her out of the immediate circle of inspiring and enthusiastic friends into the wider criticism and approval of the reading world in American cities and towns. These sketches will be noticed later on in the discussion of their publication in book form, under the name of "The Mayflower."

Among the intimate friends of Harriet Beecher, at this period, was Eliza Tyler, the daughter of Rev. Dr. Tyler, of Andover, Mass., the wife of Calvin E. Stowe, the scholarly professor of Biblical Criticism and Oriental Literature in Lane Seminary. Mrs. Stowe was several years older than her chosen friend, Harriet Beecher, but found in her energetic mind and brisk manners, the natural complement to her own gentle personality, which was somewhat depressed by a delicate physique.

Mrs. Stowe died during the first year which her husband spent in his capacity of Professor at Lane, and his intimate acquaintance and regard for the daughter of President Lyman Beecher, was augmented and deepened during the next three years, at the end of which they were married. Harriet Beecher was twenty-four years of age when she became the wife of a man in every way fitted to guide her in the life work which yet lay folded in the veil of the future. He was nine years her senior, a man of fine presence, a graduate of Bowdoin College and of the Andover Theological Seminary, where he became assistant professor of sacred literature, and later, had been professor of languages in Dartmouth. In 1833 he was chosen professor of Biblical literature at Lane Seminary, and remained in that chair seventeen years. During the year of his marriage he spent several months in Europe in behalf of the Legislature of the State of Ohio, studying the public school system of Europe, particularly that of Germany. He prepared a valuable public document on " Elementary Education in Europe," and other papers treating of the Prussian school system. These were reprinted from the Ohio state documents by Pennsylvania, Michigan, Massachusetts, North Carolina and Virginia, and were circulated through those states, free. His conclusions were the key-note for much of the educational work in the United States. This, however, was by no means his first achievement in literature. He had been editor of the *Boston Recorder*, afterwards merged into The Congregationalist, immediately after his graduation at Andover, and had contributed liberally to many

leading periodicals of the day. While at Andover as
assistant professor of Sacred Literature, he translated Jahn's
" History of the Hebrew Commonwealth," which was published at Andover and in London. His " Lectures on the
Sacred Poetry of the Hebrews," were of the same period.
He published one volume of "An Introduction to the
Criticism and Interpretation of the Bible " at Cincinnati,
in 1833, the year of his advent there.   So his attainments
became a stimulus to his young wife, and the first to en-
courage and appreciate her efforts in her literary career was
her husband.

Harriet Beecher Stowe never lived in Kentucky, but during the years spent at Cincinnati, which is separated from that
state only by the Ohio River, which, as a shrewd politician
once remarked, was dry one half the year and frozen the
other, she traveled, accompanied by her father, somewhat
extensively in the northern belt of slave holding territory,
and became acquainted in the families of her pupils, whom
she visited, with some excellent slave holders, for whom the
Shelbys served as a type. She saw many counterparts of
the humane, conscientious, just and generous people who
regarded slavery as an evil, and were anxiously considering
their duties to their chattels. Her life on the banks of the
Ohio River—the boundary line between the slave and free
states—opened to her a new field of experience, observation
and sympathy. Her life was full of pleasant cares, sympathetic anxieties, loving pride, and there was a widening and
awakening of her powers of mind and heart, which came from
wifehood, maternity, and an active concern in the affairs of
the various types of humanity which throbbed closely about
her. All of her faculties and feelings were called into

active play. No neglected capabilities wasted away from disuse. Every impulse of her strong, comprehensive nature was stimulated, strengthened and encouraged in the atmosphere of her environment.

Children came, and a double blessing and care promptly presented itself in the form of twin daughters. Mrs. Stowe has since laughingly remarked that the first child is always a poem, but those who follow are often most unsentimental prose. This tiny couplet was welcomed with all the fervor of young maternal affection. The babies were, with one exception, exactly alike; one had curling rings of soft hair, and the other appeared quite satisfied with her silken halo, which under the brush of the nurse laid more circumspectly upon the little head. The proud father soon decided upon the names, to which his wife gave pleased acquiescence. The one was called Eliza Tyler, after the beloved wife and dear friend, gone to Heaven, and the curly head was named Harriet Beecher. A boy made his advent within the next year, another son came while these little ones yet toddled about the floor, another daughter, and a baby boy who died in his wee childhood, in all six who came upon the stage during the fifteen years at Cincinnati.

In 1845, during an epidemic, which spread through the city, and by the illness and sudden death of a number of students, spread consternation in the community at Walnut Hills, Mrs. Stowe narrowly escaped death by cholera. In three hours after her attack she had run into a collapse, with spasms, burnings and cramps, with the stamp of death upon her face. But it was not to be. Her work was not done, and she recovered.

Professor Stowe's salary was small, and their means straitened, so that his wife kept but one assistant in household affairs, "Miss Anna," the young woman who for years was a faithful nurse to the children and has ever been kindly remembered by the whole family. It is related by a sister-in-law, that one morning, when this girl had been sent out upon an errand, Mrs. Stowe was trying to get through some household work, and three babies, none of them yet able to walk, were crying upon the floor. Mother Beecher, the Doctor's third wife, who had been a Mrs. Jackson, of Boston, came in just then and after helping to pacify the screaming twins, and the sobbing boy who vociferated for his mother was taken in her arms, Mrs. Beecher suggested to Mrs. Stowe that she might employ her talents to better effect, than in doing housework. "Try writing for the magazines again. I am sure you could succeed, and by far less labor and much pleasanter occupation, you can earn enough to pay a woman to do the work." Mrs. Stowe acted upon the advice and soon found acceptance for her pen creations, which helped wonderfully in lightening the burdens of her daily life.

*In 1846, having selected some of her earlier sketches and added thereto others with the prize story "Uncle Lot," Mrs. Stowe issued her first book under the name of "The Mayflower."

It had but a limited circulation and for some years was out of print. After she became famous, the articles were republished in the present volume known under that name, which also contains miscellaneous writings which have appeared in different periodicals.

---

*The date upon a title page of a volume from the first edition fixes the time of this publication three years earlier than that given by Allibone.

" Uncle Lot " opens with a breezy paragraph which calls forth the interest and sympathy of the reader, the more so, if he happens to be a native of the good old New England, of which she speaks so proudly. It proceeds into graphic description and a delineation of indigenous characters which holds out a bright promise of her future wonderful work. Uncle Lot Griswold, the personified chestnut burr, full of prickly points without and substantial sweetness within, with his cross-grain of surly petulance, and his strong fibre of right feeling and action; his wife, a respectable, pleasant-faced, God-fearing, and domestic matron of the real New England type; his pretty daughter Grace, just returned from school, radiant with magical brightness, pretty in person and pleasant in her ways, with native self possession and a good humored but positive mind of her own; are drawn with a few clean strokes, which evince skill and rounded ideas. The effervescing personality of Master James Benton, the lover of Grace Griswold, who was not altogether favored by Uncle Lot, chiefly on his principle of contrariety in all things and pride in not succumbing to an universal favorite, is so clever and full of vitality that one may be pardoned an extract.

" Now, this James is to be our hero, and he is just the hero for a sensation—at least, so you would have thought, if you had been in Newbury the week after his arrival. Master James was one of those whole-hearted, energetic Yankees, who rise in the world as naturally as cork does in water. He possessed a great share of that chacteristic national trait so happily denominated " cuteness," which signifies an ability to do everything without trying, and to know everything without learning, and to make more use of one's *ignorance* than other people do of their knowledge. This quality

4

in James was mingled with an elasticity of animal spirits, a buoyant cheerfulness of mind, which, though found in the New England character, perhaps, as often as any where else, is not ordi-
narily regarded as one of its distinguishing traits.

" As to the personal appearance of our hero, we have not much
to say of it—not half so much as the girls in Newbury found it
necessary to remark the first Sabbath that he shone out in the
meeting-house. There was a saucy frankness of countenance, a
knowing roguery of eye, a joviality and prankishness of demeanor,
that was wonderfully captivating, especially to the ladies.

" It is true that Master James had an uncommonly comfortable
opinion of himself, a full faith that there was nothing in creation
that he could not learn and could not do ; and this faith was maintained with an abounding and triumphant joyfulness, that fairly
carried your sympathies along with him, and made you feel quite
as much delighted with his qualifications and prospects as he felt
himself. There are two kinds of self-sufficiency ; one is amusing,
and the other is provoking. His was the amusing kind. It
seemed, in truth, to be only the buoyancy and overflow of a viva-
cious mind, delighted with every thing delightful, in himself or
others. He was always ready to magnify his own praise, but
quite as ready to exalt his neighbor, if the channel of discourse
ran that way : his own perfections being completely within his
knowledge, he rejoiced in them more constantly ; but, if those of
any one else came within range, he was quite as much astonished
and edified as if they had been his own.

" Master James, at the time of his transit to the town of Newbury, was only eighteen years of age ; so that it was difficult to
say which predominated in him most, the boy or the man. The
belief that he could, and the determination that he would, be
something in the world had caused him to abandon his home, and,
with all his worldly effects tied in a blue cotton handkerchief, to
proceed to seek his fortune in Newbury. And never did stranger

in Yankee village rise to promotion with more unparalleled rapidity
or boast a greater plurality of employment.   He figured as schoolmaster all the week, and as chorister on Sundays, and taught singing and reading in the evenings, besides studying Latin and
Greek with the minister, nobody knew when; thus fitting for
college, while he seemed to be doing everything else in the world
besides.

"James understood every art and craft of popularity, and made
himself mightily at home in all the chimney corners of the region
round about; knew the geography of everybody's cider barrel
and apple bin, helped himself and every one else therefrom with
all bountifulness; rejoiced in the good things of this life, devoured
the old ladies' doughnuts and pumpkin pies with most flattering
appetite, and appearing equally to relish everybody and thing
that came in his way.

"The degree and versatility of his acquirements were truly
wonderful.   He knew all about arithmetic and history, and all
about catching squirrels and planting corn; made poetry and hoe
handles with equal celerity; wound yarn and took out grease spots
for old ladies, and made nosegays and knick-knacks for young ones;
caught trout Saturday afternoons, and discussed doctrines on Sundays, with equal adroitness and effect.   In short, Mr. James
moved on through the place

'Victorious,
Happy and Glorious,'

welcomed and privileged by everybody in every place, and when
he had told his last ghost story, and fairly flourished himself out
of doors at the close of a long winter's evening, you might see the
hard face of the good man of the house still phosphorescent with
his departing radiance, and hear him exclaim, in a paroxysm of
admiration, that 'Jemeses talk re'ely did beat all; that he was
sartainly most a miraculous cre'tur!'

" It was wonderfully contrary to the buoyant activity of Master James's mind to keep a school. He had, moreover, so much of the boy and the rogue in his composition, that he could not be strict with the iniquities of the curly pates under his charge ; and when he saw how determinately every little heart was boiling over with mischief and motion, he felt in his soul more disposed to join in and help them to a frolic, than to lay justice to the line, as was meet. This would have made a sad case, had it not been that the activity of the master's mind communicated itself to his charge, just as the reaction of one little spring will fill a manufactory with motion ; so that there was more of an impulse towards study in the golden, good-natured day of James Benton than in the time of all that went before or came after him.

" But when ' school was out,' James's spirits foamed over as naturally as a tumbler of soda water, and he could jump over benches and burst out of doors with as much rapture as the veriest little elf in his company."

It is not difficult to believe that Master James succeeded in " getting around " the old man, and, having won the heart of the maiden became her happy husband at the end. In this sketch there becomes apparent the writer's great love for nature, as seen in trees and flowers and in the conventionalism of the old-fashioned country garden. She speaks of the tiny blooming beauties as if they were beings with souls, and conveys to the reader the keen enjoyment of the humorous side of common things, for instance, the chasing of a flock of sheep out of the garden, with the rare gift of expression which has distinguished her character drawing, and irradiates all her writings. The inimitable scene where Master James plays himself and his obnoxious flute into Uncle Lot's good graces by means of "Yankee Doodle," and through the gamut from patriotic feeling to religious sentiment in "Old Hundred," stands in pleasant relief against the pathetic scenes which precede the death of George Griswold, the minister-son of the old man, upon whom his heart and hopes were set. The devotion of the son-in-law, and the touching confidence which the broken old man at last reposes in his daughter's husband, who was also his son's friend, bring the story to a symmetrical close.

Other pertinent and well written articles are, "Let every Man mind his own Business," a pithy temperance tale, full of telling points and healthful sarcasm; "Mrs. A. and Mrs. B., or What She Thinks About It," a sketch which hits off in the most telling manner, some of the social peculiarities of her own sex, one which has the enduring quality which attends a true reading of human nature, and is just as applicable and forcible to-day as when it was written; "A Scholar's Adventures in the Country," which humorously sets forth the difficulties and annoyances suffered by a learned man without "a faculty," who essays to live economically in the country; and the sketch of "The old Meeting-House," which is a faithful description of the old church at Litchfield, with her childish impressions of the service and the actors in it, from which excerpts have been made.

These, and other sketches, cannot be unread by the one who desires to make a fair estimate of Harriet Beecher Stowe's culture and quality of mind, at the period of her life which preceded the writing of that great work which sprang full-armed, burning with fiery strength, brave with conviction and mighty with right, from this quiet woman's brain, straight into the arena of politics, and the full light of the world's criticism.

It was not the characteristic of the Beecher mind to deal with dead issues or musty questions. They all had abundant sympathy with the human failings and vicissitudes of existence, and kept an outlook upon the aspects of the race as the world moved on.

At Cincinnati, Harriet Beecher Stowe was in the very rush and turmoil of the stream of public opinion upon the Slavery Question, as it wore and broke into seething currents, against the still water of indifference or apathy, or dashed madly against the rocks of diverse opinion, which here and there interposed. On the other bank of the Ohio River, men were bought and sold, tortured, dishonored, murdered, with no hope of rescue or redress in this world. On her side they were nominally free, but only so in name, for the hunters of escaped slaves forced the laws to their side of the question. The people were forbidden under heavy penalties to harbor fugitives, and not until their feet touched the soil of Canada, were they safe, and really free.

At this time Lyman Beecher and his family were on principle, in favor of gradual emancipation, and the President of Lane Seminary ordered that the question of abolition should not be discussed. The result, which was the departure of three-quarters of the students, was a sore trial to him and his children, and especially so to Catherine, who published a volume in 1837 entitled, " Miss Beecher on the Slave Question." It was evident that her feelings against the Abolitionists had been intensified by recent occurrences, and this book was received with much favor by the slave-holders and their apologists. But facts were more persuasive than theories, and the younger members of the family, Charles and Henry and Harriet, as well as Professor Stowe, were so moved by the outrages which constantly came to their knowledge, that they threw politics and expediency to the winds.

Whenever opportunity offered, they gave aid and succor to their colored brethren escaping from bondage. They sheltered them, gave them food and clothing, planned to send them on their way to the Canadian border, and Charles Beecher and Calvin Stowe rode nights to further them on their journey under the friendly cover of darkness. Harriet Beecher Stowe, clasping her own little children to her heart, saw and heard the agonies of dusky mothers separated from their darlings. Living secure, and proudly resting upon the protection and guiding care of her noble husband, she saw wives torn from their husband's arms and sold away to shame, and lonely death. Fondly associating with, appealing to, and rendering helpful love to her father and brothers, she saw black brothers and sisters taken from their parents and scattered to the farthest ends of the states which staggered under "the system."

She educated her own children, and in the elasticity of her affections, which embraced all new appellants for mercy or kindness, she had taken into her little school, several colored boys and girls, who under the social ostracism obtained in Cincinnati, were without instruction. When, one day, the mother of a bright little boy, who had become one of her charges, came weeping, to tell her that he was a slave, and was about to be dragged back to ignominious servitude, Mrs. Stowe promptly put on her bonnet and canvassing the neighborhood, raised enough money to pay his ransom and returned him to the ownership of his over-joyed mother. These cases many times repeated and multiplied, with the constantly recurring tales of sorrow and hardship which would come over the border, made a deep impression upon the uncalloused mind of the incipient author of "Uncle Tom's Cabin."

Furthermore her brother Charles, who had betimes been most enthusiastic and reckless of his own safety in co-operation with Professor Stowe in spiriting some terror-stricken slave out of reach of his pursuers, not yet prepared to enter the ministry which he afterwards assumed, had gone to live in New Orleans. He was engaged as a collecting clerk in a large mercantile business house near the wharves and river docks, where slavery loomed up, showing in a horrid light the degredation of chattels, drivers, traders and owners. Society there was permeated through and through with its pollution, and Charles Beecher saw it in all its enormity, and the hideous deformity of human character and institutions which resulted from it. His letters to his family at Cincinnati were read with ever increasing horror and indignation, as he cited in his impetuous manner, case after case which came under his observation at New Orleans.

In the meantime, Cincinnati began to ferment in agitation against and in defense of the "institution," and even the more conservative souls were painfully disturbed by the question. The president, the leading professors, and a great proportion of the students at Lane Theological Seminary, in fifteen years had become avowed Abolitionists. Theodore D. Weld, then a student, raised his persuasive voice in exhortation and prayer against the terrible evil. Mobs raged in the city. "Fanatics" were threatened with death

at the hands of the aroused thugs and bullys who, without
any particular principle in the matter, welcomed any chance
for violence, and one day a riotous crowd started for the
Seminary, which was situated a mile or two out of town,
with the purpose of burning it over the heads of the Abolitionists, whom they further declared they would string to
convenient trees. But their ardor, which rose high at the
prospect of congenial entertainment, flagged perceptibly in
meeting natural obstacles to their progress, and a trudge up
the long hill, which was knee deep with mud, was too much
to undertake, even for the anticipated pleasure of mobbing
the Seminary. They therefore subsided and turned back
to town, where rioting had fewer drawbacks. The excitement and fury which came to the surface and scum of society in these demonstrations showed how deep and intense
was the tide of feeling underneath. Dr. Gamaliel Bailey,
"a wise, temperate and just man, a model of courtesy in
speech and writing," came to Cincinnati, set up an anti-
slavery paper and proposed to discuss the question upon a
public platform in the city. He was mobbed, and finally
driven from the place, by a horde of Kentucky slave-holders
and their inflammable sympathizers, who attacked his
office, destroyed his printing press, and threw his type into
the Ohio River. As will be remembered, he went to Washington and afterwards published an anti-slavery paper
called the *National Era*, in which subsequently appeared
Mrs. Stowe's first great work.

The Cincinnati respectability, in church and state, deprecated this disturbance, and severely condemned the impru-
dence of Dr. Bailey in thus "arousing the passions of our
fellow-citizens of Kentucky." The supreme irony of the

situation did not fail to be appreciated by the comparatively small band of Abolitionists, who resided in the vicinity. The general policy of the social aristocrats was the same in Cincinnati years ago as it exists everywhere to-day. Professional reformers were considered "bad form" and avoided as nuisances. The Abolitionists were an unfashionable set and few in number. Like all who uphold the principle of abstract right, as applied to human affairs, they were regarded as a class of monomaniacs, and a disturbing element which had become an annoyance to society. It was the general impression, even among those who felt some qualms of conscience as to the justice of certain phases of slavery, that the question was a dark labyrinth, into whose mazes one must penetrate at extreme peril. It appeared to be so full of obscurity and tortuous turnings, difficulty and pain, and so utterly beyond human adjustment or help, that it was worse than useless to distress one's self about it.

It was considered a subject of such delicacy that the people of the free states, who thought to interfere, were branded as meddlers troubling themselves in a matter in which they had no proper concern, the management of which should be left to the slave-holders.

This state of public opinion served for a time to smother the growing indignation of those who saw the abuses and inherent dangers of the system, in their true light. But when the servants of good families were pursued to the very doors of their employers in Ohio, and were threatened, maltreated and frightfully abused, even on free soil, their feeling against slavery deepened. Righteous indignation at the outrages which followed fast upon its march, contempt for the conservatism of society, which shut

its eyes to the evil, because it had not the moral courage
to come out against it, rose higher. Pity for the hunted
beings who came to them for shelter, and the almost
forlorn hope that somehow, sometime, this all might be
done away with, grew, intensified, and concentrated in
the mind of Harriet Beecher Stowe, although she as yet
felt no call to write. The fate of Lovejoy, who for printing an anti-slavery paper was shot at his own door in
Alton, Illinois; the circulation of rumors that Edward
Beecher, known to be associated with Lovejoy, was also
killed; the persecution of young John G. Fee, a Kentucky
student in Lane Seminary, who liberated his slaves and
undertook to advocate emancipation in Kentucky and was
in consequence disinherited by his father and driven from
the state; the bravery of Salmon P. Chase, who dared to
appear in defense of a man who was imprisoned, his property attached, his life threatened with utter ruin for harboring
runaway slaves; and hundreds of other glaring instances
of the fury of the people who upheld slavery, and the
courage and martyrdom of those who condemned it, are
familiar to all who have studied this political epoch.

CHAPTER III.

AFTER a residence of seventeen years in Cincinnati, as
Professor of Biblical Literature at Lane Seminary, Calvin
E. Stowe resigned the chair and returned to New England.
He was influenced in this change by ill health, finding it
impossible to longer endure the rigors of the climate at
Cincinnati. He immediately received the appointment of
Divinity Professor at Bowdoin College in Brunswick,
Maine.

It was in the Fall of 1850, at the period of the greatest
excitement over the act of September 18, which amended,
and to a considerable extent superceded, the less effective

BOWDOIN COLLEGE, BRUNSWICK, ME.

Fugitive Slave Law. This measure, to which Webster consented in his celebrated speech of the 7th of March, was particularly humiliating to the North, making at the behest of the Southern masters a slave catcher of every free-man.

This Bill not only made it a penal offense to aid or harbor slaves who had escaped to the free states, but enforced their seizure, demanding under severe enactments their return to their former masters, to be followed by a life of bondage under, if possible, increased miseries. While at Brunswick, Mrs. Stowe was in constant communication with Dr. Edward Beecher and his wife in Boston, who wrote her from day to day of the terror and despair, the law and its enforcement, had occasioned to industrious, worthy colored people, who had escaped from the South and had for some time lived in peace and security in that city. She heard of midnight captures; of the seizure of defenceless women on the street, or while going about their household duties; the abduction of little children at play or on their way to or from school; of families broken up and fleeing in the dead of winter to the ice-bound shores of Canada. And what was to her and is still to succeeding generations, inexplicable and dreadful, was the apathy of the mass of the usually right minded, just and conscientious New England people, on the subject. In New England, as at the West, the Abolitionists were a despised band, with comparatively few adherents, and subject to the contempt of the self-denominated "best society."

There were a few strong voices in the pulpit, that denounced the institution, but to her excited mind the church and the world appeared to join hands against the oppressed.

In Oct., 1887, George W. Cable gave the Congregational Club of New York City a talk on " Cobwebs in the Church." "Speaking as a Southerner," he said, " I do believe we have to thank the Protestant Church of America for the war that drenched our land in blood, for it fell into condoning conventional sin and into approval of a national crime."

This denunciation is doubtless unjust to the many conscientious Christians who hesitated not upon the desirableness of abolition, but were sadly troubled to know how to bring it about. It was not that they were apathetic, as the history of the church militant will show, but only that seeing all sides of the controversy they appreciated the risks incident to a violent disregard of constitutional law. It should not be forgotten that in 1818, the Presbyterian General Assembly passed stringent resolutions against slavery, but in 1837 slavery found many apologists in the Southern bodies on account of commercial influence. As is well known, the institution had then become so utterly abhorrent to the Presbyterians of the North, particularly in New York State, there was a division, which separated the Southern brethren from their remonstrating friends, who were almost a solid body in the North. But in spite of the earnest objection of many Christian people, the nation still presented to the world the sorry spectacle of a Christian republic upholding slavery.

And now it seemed as if the system, heretofore confined to the Southern states, was gathering itself for irruption into new fields, preparing to extend its folds all over the North and West, and overlap and choke the dearest principles of free society. With growing astonishment and distress Mrs. Stowe heard on all sides, from humane and Chris-

tian people, that slavery was a constitutional right, and
that opposition to it was treason, and endangered the national Union. Under this conviction, she saw many earnest and tender-hearted Christian people close their eyes,
ears, and hearts to the harrowing details of its practical
workings, silence all discussion of its wrongs, and act as in
duty bound to assist the slave owners to recover their *property*. She felt that these good people could not know what
slavery was. They had no comprehension of the thing
they were tolerating.

It was impossible for Harriet Beecher Stowe, so born, so
reared, and so married, not to have been opposed to slavery. With her family and friends, like Webster, Sumner
and Emerson, she at first advocated the purchase of the
slaves and gradual emancipation, but the encroachments of
the slave power in the passage of the Fugitive Slave Bill
in 1850, opened her eyes, and she became aggressive in her
opposition. Hers was not alone the objection of the eminent politicians, whose jurisprudence controlled their feeling, that slavery was detrimental to the progress of the
nation ; nor that of the great transcendentalist, who based his
opposition on the fact, that it degraded the manhood of men.

She saw the question in its various relations and fully comprehended its complex aspects, but her heart was greater
than her head. The woes, the terror, the suffering of human
beings, roused her to action even while ulterior reasoning
seemed to counsel patience. It was not that she failed to
comprehend the political situation; it was that justice,
pity, and righteous indignation rose above, and made them
secondary. She had an innate appreciation of how far
nobler it was to maintain the right than to defer to unjust

established laws. She placed her feet upon the rock which upheld Epictetus when he wrote, "It is better by agreeing with truth to conquer opinion, than by agreeing with opinion to conquer truth," and she gave Americans the credit of assuming, that if they could see slavery as it existed they would rise for its extermination.

Dr. Gamelial Bailey, who had been driven from Cincinnati under such aggravating circumstances some years before, had in 1847 established a journal, "*The National Era*," at Washington, D. C., which became one of the leading organs of the anti-slavery party. He was a man of literary predilections and was wise enough to secure for his magazine the influence of the best writers. He had associated with himself as assistant or corresponding editor, John G. Whittier, a young man who had served his apprenticeship in the poet's corner of Garrison's "*Free Press*," in Thayer's Philadelphia "*Gazette*," and as editor of the "*American Manufacturer*," and the "*Gazette*" of Haverhill, Mass. He had suffered for his opinions as expressed in "*The Liberator*," and spoken in ringing in tones in his poems, which are properly called "Voices of Freedom," in several Journals and at all needful times. In the first volumes of "*The National Era*," may be found many of his grandest poems, and also the poems of the Cary sisters, Lucy Larcom, and the bright and witty articles of Grace Greenwood, whom Dr. Bailey had early called to his aid.

In perusing this magazine, Mrs. Stowe noticed the incident of a slave woman escaping with her child across the floating ice of the river, from Kentucky into Ohio, and it became the first salient point of her great work and is seen in the history of Eliza. She began to meditate and dream over a possible story that should graphically set forth the bare ugliness, and repulsive features of the system of negro slavery. The black husband who remained in Kentucky, going back and forth on parole and remaining in bondage rather than forfeit his word of honor to his master, suggested the character of Uncle Tom. Once suggested, the scenes of the story began rapidly to form in her mind, and as they are prone to do in the practical forces of energetic character, emotions and impressions instantly crystalized into ideas and opinions. The whole wonderful scheme was defined, before the author of " Uncle Tom's Cabin " put her pen to paper. She has related that the closing scene, the death of Uncle Tom, came to her as a material vision while sitting at the Communion one Sunday in the little church at Brunswick. She was perfectly overcome by it, and could scarcely restrain the violent emotion that sprang into tears and shook her frame. She was carried out of herself.

Aristotle wrote, " No great genius was ever without some mixture of madness, nor can anything grand or superior be spoken except by the agitated soul." It was the fire of outraged feeling which inspired this memorable work. She hastened home and wrote, and, her husband being away, she read it aloud to her older children. Her burning sentences so touched their young hearts that they wept with her, and cried out that slavery was the most accursed thing in the world. Some days afterwards Professor Stowe, having returned, was passing through her room, and noticing many sheets of closely written paper upon his wife's table, he took them up and began to read. His casual curiosity soon merged into interest and deepened into astonishment., He sought his wife with words of enthusi-

5

astic praise and said, "You can make something out of this."

"I mean to," was the quiet reply of his wife.

From this time on, Harriet Beecher Stowe was possessed by the theme; it dominated all other concerns, and held her a willing captive until it was done. She said to the writer a year or two before her death, " I did not think of doing a great thing, I did not want to be famous. It came upon me and I did as I must, perforce, wrote it out, but I was only as the pen in the hands of God. What there is good and powerful in it came from Him. I was merely the instrument. It is strange that He should have chosen me, hampered and bound down as I was with feeble health and family cares. But I had to do it."

A glance at her domestic situation may give an idea of what it was to undertake the writing of a book at this time. Mrs. Stowe was the mother of six children, the youngest of whom, now the Rev. Charles E. Stowe, pastor of the Windsor Avenue Congregational Church, of Hartford, Conn., was then a babe of a few months. He was born in the spring of 1851, and it was during the following summer and fall that this great labor was performed. Mrs. Stowe, in addition to her own little flock, had a number of pupils whom she had taken into her family, and her father, the Rev. Lyman Beecher, had come on from Cincinnati, and was occupied with the revision and publication of one of his books, and he and his step-daughter, Mrs. Laura Dickinson, who acted as his amanuensis, became members of the Stowe household. Catering to and caring for the comfort of this large family, which comprised more than a dozen members, of all ages, from the venerable Doctor to his tiny, helpless grandson, would seem to be quite enough for one frail little woman to do. In her position as Professor's wife there were also various duties as hostess and entertainer constantly incumbent upon her, but she was not discouraged. Her vocation was upon her and most nobly she assumed it. She has said, "I knew my work must be done, my children cared for, dinner prepared and put upon the table and a thousand and one things seen to, but this was always uppermost in my mind, and it got itself done, somehow."

Scenes, incidents and conversations rushed upon her with such vivid clearness and strength that they could not be denied. During her varied domestic and maternal duties, the idea ran on, an undercurrent of logical argument illustrated with suggestive incidents, and she could hardly wait to get at her pen and fix it upon paper, as she sat with her portfolio on her knee by the kitchen fire, in the moments snatched from her domestic duties.

Harriet Beecher Stowe had none of the dependence upon small accessories, which was a peculiarity of authors as great as Wordsworth, who when writing, habitually fingered the button of his coat; Ben Johnson, who inhaled clouds of his beloved snuff, and Schiller, who could not get inspiration without the aroma of half-decayed apples which he kept in the drawer of his desk, to the discomfiture of his friend Goëthe, who was made extremely ill when once attempting to write thereon.

Her theme was sufficient stimulus, and no particular conditions were necessary to the easy working of her mind. A friend who had an intimate knowledge of her literary methods recently said to the writer concerning the author of Uncle Tom's Cabin. "When the inspiration came and she was in the midst of a thrilling or pathetic scene, she sat with her MSS. on her knee and wrote, no matter what were the distractions." This power of self-withdrawal is a rare gift even among the greatest of novelists. Silence comfort, and seclusion are the indispensable conditions for most writers. As Lowell says:

> "Thy work unfinished, bolt and bar thy door;
> Where they see *two* the sky-gods come no more."

"The book," as Professor Stowe once said, "was written in sorrow, in sadness, and obscurity, with no expectation of reward save in the prayers of the poor, and with a heart almost broken in view of the sufferings which it describes and the still greater suffering which it dared not describe."

When two or three chapters were written, Mrs. Stowe sent a letter to Dr. Bailey of the *National Era*, telling him she had projected a story which might run through several numbers of the paper and offering it to him if he desired it. He instantly applied for it and the weekly installments were started. The *story*, and her *duty* on this subject were so much more real and imperative to her than any other things in life, that the copy was always ready for the type-setters. In shaping her material Mrs. Stowe had but one object; to show the system of slavery as it existed. No idea of sensational success would permit her to exaggerate or pervert facts. She had, however, the tact to perceive that its presentation in unrelieved gloom of sadness, would not command readers. She therefore summoned all her experience of the wit and drollery of the African race, at the same time developing a sincere desire to show that the evils of slavery were the natural outgrowth of a bad system which retaliated upon its victims, and its administrators many of whom were not to blame, with almost equally baleful force.

Mrs. Stowe knew what she was braving. Public opinion had long before made itself unpleasantly emphatic in personal attacks on the persons of women who had the temerity to harbor anti-slavery views. Almost twenty years before, the distinguished Englishwoman, Harriet Martineau who had committed herself to anti-slavery principles in her book "Demerara," and, against her wishes found herself forced by circumstances to avow her settled aversion to it during the early part of her visit in Boston, became subject not only to annoyance and insult, in free, Puritan New England, on this account, but had been the object of obscene abuse in newspapers and pamphlets. Mrs. Stowe knew that Miss Martineau's expressed desire to view the institution of slavery as it existed in the United States had aroused such feeling against her, that traveling became a peril, and her entertainers in various cities were jeopardized by her presence. In the ferment in which society was then working, she ran the risk of personal violence and endured a large share of the virulent abuse which everywhere fell upon the Abolitionists. Mrs. Stowe knew of the public hatred of this Englishwoman who had dared to say, in recounting her experience in this country, "I was not then aware of the extent to which all but virtuous relations are found possible between the whites and blacks, nor how unions, to which the religious and civil sanctions of marriage are alone wanting, take place wherever there are masters and slaves, throughout the country. When I did

become aware of this I always knew how to stop the hypo-
critical talk against ' amalgamation.' "

Americans would not stand this sort of meddling in their
political and social affairs, and when displeased they had
proved they knew well how to punish the offender. The
fact that an Abolitionist was a woman, did not protect her
from the fury of the chivalric southerners and their northern sympathizers. Letters threatening to "cut out her
tongue and cast it on a dung hill," to hang her, and to commit her to imprisonment and disgrace, assailed Miss Martineau. Abuse of her ran through almost every paper in
the Union, and a certain sheet of New York, published an
article so filthy that it will not bear mention. She was represented as a hired agent, and floggings, tar and feathers, and
other receptions then popular in the hospitable South, were
promised her. On more than one occasion she found herself surrounded by an infuriated mob.

Maria Weston Chapman had also been subject to similar
outrageous treatment on account of her expression of anti-
slavery opinions.

Mrs. Follen was another social martyr to the cause.

The brave, sweet, gentle Quakeress, Lucretia Mott, had
at this same period addressed a meeting of anti-slavery
women, with the house surrounded by rioters, and brick-
bats frequently crashing through the windows. She had
walked the streets of Boston threatened with instant death,
pressed upon and jostled by a crowd of howling ruffians,
and preserved her gentle dignity even amid a shower of
eggs and other offensive missiles.

Many of the eminent scholars and thinkers of the country,
though occupying a position which made violence impos-

sible, had revealed themselves no less clearly upon the
question. As a class, the *literati* of Boston and Cambridge
sneered at the controversy as "low," and too utterly repug-
nant to fine feeling to be touched upon by cultured persons.
"Edward Everett, the man of letters par excellence," says
Harriet Martineau, was "burning incense to the South, in-
sulting the Abolitionists because they were few and weak."
Boston had seen Garrison flying through the streets in imminent peril of the hot tar barrel that was making ready
for him. The controversy had branded Wendell Phillips
and Theodore D. Weld as fanatics; it had aroused the
whole country and "put Boston in an uproar," and now this
brave woman under the stress of indignation and righteous
feeling at the probable extension of slavery, was about to
throw herself into the breach, with the prospect that her
small personality might in consequence, forever sink in
ignominy and public scorn.

While it is true that names that now are honored, such
as Garrison, Whittier, Phillips, Emerson, Gerret Smith,
Edmund Quincy, Theodore Parker, Sumner, Baird, Lucy
Stone and Sallie Holley, were enrolled as Abolitionists, the
solid phalanx of society in Boston, (with but few exceptions) the bench, the bar, the clergy, merchants, bankers,
politicians and the "best citizens" generally, felt the utmost
scorn and detestation for these advocates of philanthrophy
and justice. No one of the present generation can have a
realization of the manifestations of contempt which every
where met the Free-Soilers and Abolitionists. In the words
of an observer, "Phillip's oratory and Whittier's poetry
were mere whispers against a hurricane." It was a curious
fact, though one not unparalleled in the history of reforms,

that the people who raised their voices against a tolerated wrong became the objects of the hate and derision of the community. At this epoch it really appeared to many easy-going good people of the country that Abolitionism, and not slavery, was the sum of all villainies.

But all these considerations weighed as nothing, before Mrs. Stowe's sense of justice and her calm intention to uphold the right at any peril. She had never considered expediency as distinguished from justice, and the fact that society now gave it the preference, was no concern of hers. Her husband nobly upheld her, and the story went on, and speedily began to be heard from. The little woman, wife of Professor Stowe in the plain house up at Brunswick, performed her household duties, nursed her baby, trained her inefficient servants, taught her scholars, ministered to her husband, entered into his life's work with an intelligent sympathy and appreciation which were a rare inspiration to him, and wrote the weekly installments of what in spite of all critical and literary estimates, stands to-day as the greatest American novel.

It seems from all personal testimony to have been an inspiration, the action of a mind of which complete possession has been taken by internal influences. The theme held her as the ancient mariner held the wedding guest. She however, reinforced her writing by facts from various sources outside of her own experience, visited Boston, went to the anti-slavery rooms, culled from Theodore D. Weld's "Slavery As It Is," and the lives of Josiah Henson and Lewis Clark, circumstances of both of whose experiences are interwoven in the characters of Uncle Tom and George Harris.

Goethe says that " a great poet must be a citizen of his age as well as of his country." The power which was inherited from the father of the Beecher family and has always been observed in his children, of discovering and espousing the best interests of the hour, made Mrs. Stowe especially fortunate in the period of this writing. The first wave of furious resistance to the idea of abolition had subsided, and now that the waters were swiftly receding and gathering for greater strength to engulf the commonwealth, she threw her work upon the incoming tide, and by its force it was cast upon solid ground, where it rested as firm and incontestable as the rocks themselves. The tale which the writer thought would run through a few numbers, continued on through months, and as scene after scene unfolded, and the picture, dark and flashing with lurid light unrolled, messages, and letters came from the little band of sympathizers who read the paper, and rumors began to get abroad that a strange and powerful story was coming out, and the subscription to the *Era* was largely increased thereby.

While " Uncle Tom's Cabin " was in course of publication in the *Era* Mrs. Stowe proposed its publication in book form, to Messrs. Phillips and Sampson of Boston. They respectfully declined the proposition, but about that time a young Boston publisher, Mr. John P. Jewett, recognizing its strength and possible future as a bone of contention, made overtures to her for its publication. He remarked to Prof. Stowe that in his opinion it would bring his wife " something handsome." Upon hearing this Mrs. Stowe replied, with a twinkle in her eyes, she hoped it would bring her enough to purchase what she had not had for

a long time, a new silk dress.   Mr. Jewett reminded her that
it was an unpopular subject, and while a small volume might
sell, he should not feel warranted in bringing out a large
work.   Mrs. Stowe tersely answered that he must act his
own judgment in the matter, that she could not abridge or
curtail her work.   That the story made itself and when it
was finished, she would stop.

In view of the impression made by this book and the
resultant popularity which crowned its author as the most
honorably famous American woman, it will be well to
examine "Uncle Tom's Cabin" with the reader, and if possible, place ourselves back thirty-seven years, and try to
realize what the message was to that age, and thus appreciate its courage and persuasive force in relation to public opinion.

"Uncle Tom's Cabin" was not written like any other
successful story that the world ever saw ; it had no re-writ-
ing, scarcely a revision ; it was dashed off at white heat,
and sent forthwith to the printer.   No wonder that its
unities were not perfectly preserved.   Rather, is it not a
marvel that it came forth free from the little slips and over-
sights, which the greatest novelists have had to confess ?   As
for instance when Thackeray having killed off a character in
one number of his serial publication of a novel, unconcernedly continued his conversation in the next, and under
similar conditions Mr. Hardy after bringing a person to the
summit of a hill, in the next installment of the story
incontinently started him *up* again.

Let us take it for granted that every reader, certainly
every American reader, has read "Uncle Tom's Cabin"
and only ask that he will go again cursorily over its pages

with us. Let us notice how the characters, waiting for no introduction or explanation, enter upon the stage and by their words explain themselves as no description could do. Within ten lines the attention is arrested, opinion challenged, and the tolerated usages of the slave trade vividly portrayed and held up to the broad light of common sense and decency.

Haley, the type and epitome of all slave traders, earns hearty detestation in his earliest remarks. He is instantly seen to be a man whose flesh has hardened to leather under the unnatural circulation of the salts of cruelty and avarice through his veins, a man alive to nothing but trade and profit, cool and unhesitating and unrelenting as the grave, who would have sold his own mother at a percentage.

Mr. Shelby appears a refined and merciful man, one of the slave owners who were born to the system and who suffered from its moral workings in degree, as did his unconscious chattels, who lived under an uneasy dread of things that were permitted by it, though not inflicted by him. A picture is drawn of the fairest side of slave-holding as it existed in Kentucky and had been witnessed by the author. The good-humored indulgence of some masters and mistresses, of which the Shelbys stand the personified embodiment, with yet the awful contingencies which constantly waited upon pecuniary embarrassment or the death of the owner, are shown in all the fairness of the writer's honesty and the cruel ghastliness of truth. The brooding, portentous shadow of a law which regarded all these human beings with beating hearts and loving affections as so many heads of plantation stock belonging to their mas-

ter, is seen darkly hanging over what had been so often
falsely defended, as "a patriarchal institution."

The conversation of the two men, so full of highly
charged meaning, gives in few words, a strong outline of
the thing the author means to attack.

The irruption of bright-eyed, glossy-haired little Jim
Crow, his childish antics and amusing imitations of
various plantation characters; the entrance of his mother,
the beautiful yellow girl, Eliza, who is looking for the
child, the trader's offer to buy the lad, overheard by the
mother, and her distress and appeal to her mistress, rapidly
lead the reader into the intense story and fasten the interest,
which never flags to the end.

The character of George Harris, Eliza's husband, a bright,
talented mulatto " boy," who was a valued hand upon a
neighboring plantation, has become an overseer in a bag-
ging factory, and subsequently invented a machine for the
cleaning of the hemp, is like most of the other characters,
drawn from life and facts, and, it is needless to say, was a
revelation to northern readers, unaccustomed to regard
negro slaves as having souls and minds and intellectual
faculties worthy of respect. The original of the character
was an ex-slave, who for six years was an inmate of the
house of a family connection of the author, Deacon Safford,
of Cambridgeport, Massachusetts. He ran away from his
masters in 1840.

The exhibition of the jealousy of the master which
induces him to degrade George to the most menial farm
work, embittering his life, arousing deep and ineradicable
hatred for the man and the institution which made such
injustice possible, quickly follows, and the strange tale

takes deeper significance in every line. The flight of George inevitably ensues upon this unbearable treatment.

Mrs. Shelby is moved by her own religious convictions, her uneasiness as to the right of slave-holding and her sympathy with Eliza, to remonstrate with her husband, and their conversation brings out in strong effect the circumstances which may occur to all slave-holders, enforcing the sale of their people. In making this point the author dealt a heavy blow at the stronghold of the system, and powerfully refuted the assertions of Southerners, that things had been exaggerated by abolition fanatics.

The fact that a slave could not be married—that the most sacred of all ties, even though solemnized by a clergyman and witnessed by master, mistress and friends, might be ruptured any day at the whim of the owner, the husband forced to take another mate or live in bestial polygamy, the wife given to any man her owner selected, or reduced to a life of shame as the mistress of any uxorious white man who chose to buy her—is developed with power, and the world began to see slavery as it was in social detail.

Palpable truth waits on all the author's situations and common sense proved her standpoint to be the right one.

In chapter four we are introduced to Uncle Tom's cabin, and receive a bright picture of it, overrun with scarlet bigonia and a native multiflora rose, entwisting and interlacing until scarcely a vestige of the rough logs was to be seen.

Here is Aunt Chloe, the reigning queen of the culinary department of "the house," as the master's dwelling was called. Poor, faithful, kind, sensitive, brave Aunt Chloe,

with her "round, black, shining face, which suggested that
it might have been washed over with the white of eggs
like one of her own tea rusks."

Here too is Uncle Tom, Mr. Shelby's best hand, large,
broad-chested, powerfully made, with a full, glossy, black
face, in whose truly African features, shine grave happiness and steady common sense, combined with an air of
benevolence, self respect and dignity, which characterizes
all that he says and does. His earnest attempts to learn
to read and write under the tuition of young master George
Shelby; the sympathetic interest of Aunt Chloe in the
matter of education, which was quite foreign to her useful
lore; the rollicking of the children on the floor and their
subsequent sitting down to a feast of Aunt Chloe's delicious batter cakes, fills out the picture of plantation life which comes upon the canvas. A dark and sorrowful picture it is, but illumined with high lights and
bits of warm color which give it a richness, a brilliancy,
evolved from startling contrasts which takes the senses by
storm, and carries feeling captive.

The chapter ends with a graphic delineation of a religious meeting of the plantation negroes—a scene then new
and strange to readers who had no knowledge of Southern
life, but which has since become so familiar through the
scattering of the freed slaves over the country and the
dramatic representations of this peculiar phase of religious
manifestation. It has however, never been equalled in
verbal description, especially in the tender respect with
which the author illustrates the force and effect of Uncle
Tom's prayers.

While the meeting is going on in the cabin, Uncle Tom

is sold to Haley, the slave trader, to enable Mr. Shelby to pay his debts!

Eliza, finding that her child has also been sold, resolves to fly, and if possible, reach Canada. She makes ready at night and appears at the door of Uncle Tom's cabin, to bid them farewell. The dramatic situation—the black man with the candle, Aunt Chloe stricken with sympathy and terror at her own misfortune, Eliza, clasping her sleeping boy to her breast, wildly saying her few words of adieu and hastening away into the darkness—is familiar to the whole reading world. The flight of Eliza with her child has become a classic in every country of this round earth. Who shall describe it better or more tersely than the author's burning words, every sentence of which quivers with high wrought sensibility? Millions of readers have followed the slave girl fleeing with her babe, tens of thousands of play-goers, have felt their heart beats lessen in painful suspense as her shivering form has been seen flying across the treacherous cakes of floating ice which covered the river between her and freedom, and have burst into tumultuous applause and weeping, as with one last frenzied leap she has reached the shore and thanked God for safety!

CHAPTER IV.

CONTINUATION OF THE OUTLINE OF "UNCLE TOM'S CABIN."
SLAVE LIFE IN NEW ORLEANS. UNCLE TOM THE COACH-
MAN AND STEWARD OF THE ST. CLARE ESTABLISHMENT.
HIS GUARDIANSHIP OF LITTLE EVA. THE DEATH OF THE
SAINTED CHILD. THE CHARACTERS WHICH ARE FAMOUS.
THE BREAKING UP OF THE HOUSEHOLD. TOM IS PLACED
UPON THE BLOCK AND SOLD TO SIMON LEGREE. SCENES
UPON A RED RIVER PLANTATION. THE DEATH OF UNCLE
TOM. HIS EXPERIENCE AN EPITOMIZATION OF EVERY
POSSIBLE ARGUMENT AGAINST "THE INSTITUTION." "UN-
CLE TOM'S CABIN" AS A WORK OF LITERARY ART. A
STORY WITHOUT A LOVER. IS IT A NOVEL?

WITH fine understanding of the limitations of the reader's sensibilities, the author perceived that too long a tension of outraged feeling would be wearisome. She therefore presented counter situations, which appeal all the more acutely to the feelings, by contrast with what is in the background. In the chapter descriptive of the excitement on the Shelby plantation when it is discovered that Eliza has fled, the wrath of the slave trader, the secret gladness of Mrs. Shelby, and the unproductive preparations for catching the runaway girl, are most entertainingly depicted.

The clownish hatred of Sam for the trader, his irrelevant and confusing suggestions as to the means of Eliza's capture, his simulated wild anxiety to make ready the horses, which results in detention, and confusion thrice confounded

80

are described with great humor. The throwing of Mr. Haley over the head of the spirited mare whom Sam had alarmed by his twitchings and shoutings and irritated almost to madness by placing a sharp beech nut under her saddle; the escape of the horses into the grounds; the hurrying and scurrying here and there; the snorting of the horses who fail to comprehend the method in Sam's madness; the barking of the dogs who partake of the excitement; the impotent rage of the trader and the vociferous joy of the pickaninnies, who scream, giggle, run and roll over each other upon the earth; is all given with such rare wit and picturesqueness that one must perforce, lay back and indulge in a hearty ha-ha, with tears of amusement wetting the eye-lids which lately had been weighed with heavy drops of bitter sympathy.

Eliza's refuge with the good Ohio people, and her safe arrival on the Canadian shores, is a satisfactory outcome of her terrific experience. The dilemma, and generous action of the good man, the Senator, who theorizes that the law should be obeyed, but acts upon the feeling that this woman needs help, is a reproduction of the triumph of the heart over the head, which had been the frequent experience of the Beecher family at Walnut Hill.

In the meantime Aunt Chloe at home in the little cabin, irons Uncle Tom's shirts, moistening them with her fast falling tears. She packs his clothes neatly, after putting all in order, the sad farewell is taken, and Tom goes away with the trader towards the Mississippi River. The description of the dismal ride, which is pleasantly interrupted by the arrival of George Shelby, who has ridden after them to bid his dear old servant good-bye, and the attitude of Mr.

6

Haley towards his "property," is drawn with masterly strokes.

Where had Harriet Beecher Stowe, the daughter of a New England divine, reared in the innocence of life upon the breezy Litchfield hills, shielded by gallant whole-souled fellows who would not that their sister should know of the low possibilities of men, united to a learned professor of theology, and associated with masculine friends of noble character, refinement and cultivation, learned how to depict the scene that follows? Where had she been that she could so graphically describe the aspect, actions and conversation of a company of coarse men in a bar-room? The scene in chapter eleven, where George Harris appears as a gentle-man accompanied by his servant, is drawn as if from sight. Could it have been so accurately described from hearsay, the very spirit and flavor of the atmosphere permeating it? It was an inspiration, a psychological insight, which amounted to clairvoyance. And how the effects of "the system" stand forth as reflected upon these white men who were the administrators of it!

Then comes the sale. The scene in the slave market aroused thousands to vehement indignation and doubtless did more to liberate the American slaves than any other effort put forth by the talented and eloquent band of aboli-tionists in this country. Read it, Americans! Read it again, and thank Heaven that this blot is removed from the face of our fair land.

See again, the half blind, lame old woman, who is not salable, torn from her youngest son, a lad of fourteen, upon whom she hoped to lean in her decrepit old age. Hear her groans and piteous pleadings to be bought too!

See "the article enumerated as John, aged thirty," whose face quivers an instant as he tells Uncle Tom he has a wife who knows nothing of his departure from her.

See the black mother, who finds herself with her nursing child on the boat going "down river," when she hears that, instead of going to Louisville as a cook at hire, she has been sold, and forever separated from her husband. See her, when she awakes from a fitful sleep to find that her baby boy, a pretty fellow of ten months, has been taken from her arms and sold to a trader who chanced to fancy him! See her, as she hurries to the side of the boat when all is still at midnight, and leaps into the dark water and buries her troubles in death.

Who can read it calmly, even to-day when it is all past? Think what it must have been at the time when society was torn by conflicting opinions and the government had just decided to uphold the system, upon constitutional grounds. When the law sanctioned the invading of free states to reclaim "property," and leases were written to run ninety-nine years, which transferred slaves into the holdings of proprietors over the lines, thus carrying slavery *into free soil*.

We must not forget what a tremendous force and solidity of custom this slight woman battled with her delicate hands. There were strong arguments against interference with vested political rights. There were reasons of weight sufficient to deter our greatest statesmen from doing more than attempt to confine slavery within its old limits, social considerations which might well have had weight with one of a family who were superior to the fanaticism which clamored for a principle, without regard to the peril involved in the sudden disruption of laws which were based upon constitutional rights. These considerations not strangely placed the extreme abolitionists under a ban which it is easy to understand, when we look at their vehemence, and their rash haste which appeared mere incendiarism to those cooler heads, who viewed the question from an intellectual rather than an emotional standpoint.

Harriet Beecher Stowe might well have hesitated, but the wrongs of the blacks were upon her heart. Her soul was burning with an overwhelming pity and righteous indignation which brooked no restraint and made her cry out in so piercing, thrilling, and persuasive a voice, that it reached the world around, and resounded even to Heaven.

Yes, to Heaven, for this work was a prayer, and was doubtless one of the several providences which resulted in the emancipation of the slaves in America. For in spite of the augmenting power of the South in the government; in spite of the increasing value and usefulness of the slaves, which the invention of the Cotton Gin had brought about; in spite of the feeling among politicians, and conservative people everywhere, that constitutional rights must be protected until the frame work of the government could be reconstructed—the cause of freedom advanced.

Differences between the North and South widened, and the War which commenced upon other issues, and was fought to maintain the Union or disrupt it, brought about the Emancipation of the Slaves, because the hour had come.

Before Lincoln's proclamation Mrs. Stowe's ideas had permeated all society and had done much to work public opinion up to the support of the measure.

Without such support, no law can be other than a dead letter. The clear sight and courage with which she upheld her convictions, in that time when history was rolled in the scroll of the future, is a marvel. As we read it all now, it is with approval, with acquiescence, which yet is strengthened and augmented, with the flow of her highly charged, electrically eloquent, sentences. As we attempt to realize the state of feeling, which in the North permitted, even while it did not sympathize with, Slavery, and in the South rested upon it as the foundation of the political and social system, it becomes plain how this great book, appearing at that epoch, wrestled with the custom of the western world, and turned the eyes of all nations to the "deep damnation" of our institution.

But to return to the story. Uncle Tom was to see more bright days. He was purchased by a gentleman of New Orleans, to please his little daughter—an angelic child who had made acquaintance with Uncle Tom on the river steamer, and been rescued by him from a watery grave, when in her play she had fallen into the stream.

Augustine St. Clare took him home for a coachman for his wife. In Augustine St. Clare we see another phase of the character of a southern gentleman. Of distinguished appearance, grace of manner and intellectual culture, indulgent and light in his moods, as was to be expected from the strain of French Huguenot blood in his veins, he presents in his fascinating personality, as he himself declares, a victim of the institution of slavery. He says that masters and slaves are generally divided into two classes—the Oppressors and the Oppressed. He half satirically poses as one of the Oppressed, and indeed his patience and indulgent for-

bearance under the small impositions of his pampered servants, chief of whom is his impertinent valet Dolph, seemed
to bear out the anomalous situation.

Certain it is that he is the victim of the whims and
caprices of a pettish, frivolous wife; but his own airy
nature, and the love of his beautiful child, seem ample com-
pensations.   Into this luxurious southern home, decorated
and beautified with all the elegances that wealth and culture can bring together, with its richly dressed and aristocratic inmates, with its uselessly large retinue of servants
and the wasteful extravagances and indifferent management
which pertained to such an establishment, there comes Miss
Ophelia, a mature maiden cousin from Vermont. She is the
personification of New England thrift, common sense, orthodoxy and practical mindedness, a sort of composite pho-
tograph of the peculiarities and excellences of all the spinster dwellers east of the Hudson River.   She is the strongest possible foil to the ideas and characters of her southern
cousins, and finds a discouragingly uncultivated field for
her works of reform.   Miss Ophelia became at once the
recognized and accepted type of a Yankee woman.

Marie remains still a remembrance of what southern
women naturally became when not upheld by any sense of
duty, personal responsibility, or the innate right feeling
which is born to those who happily have to bear their part
in life and, by realizing their own privileges, appreciate the
rights of others.   In the experiences of this family, with
its diverse characters, in the conversations between Miss
Ophelia and her cousin St. Clare, as she sits fiercely knitting
and he reposes smoking upon a sofa, we are most naturally

shown the various aspects, and results of the system of slavery.

But while the author's ideas are thus cleverly promulgated the story advances. Uncle Tom becomes the most trusted factotum and the steward of the St. Clare establishment. Tom regards his handsome, volatile, young master, with a strange mixture of fealty, reverence and fatherly solicitude. His insecure religious standing troubles the good black servant and he speaks respectful words of warning and remonstrance. St. Clare receives these admonitions with kind tolerance, which however, on occasions deepens into a momentary self-condemnation and tender appreciation of the impulses which prompt Tom to make them. He promises his faithful servant not to tamper further with the wine which several times has sent him home in an unsteady condition. Miss Ophelia having undertaken to superintend the running of the house, begins to suffer the tribulations and to endure the manifold vexations and vain attempts to adjust irreconcilable differences, which can only be realized and appreciated by a housekeeper's mind. Her awful review of the condition of the hidden recesses of the house, and particularly the kitchen; her overhauling and re-arrangement of the store rooms, linen presses and china closet, her conflicts with Dinah, the deposed regent of this realm; the righteous indignation with which she regards such careless opulence and the waste of the provisions, and the vivid realization of all the circumstances calculated to wring a good house-keeper's heart, are inexpressibly amusing, and perhaps to some minds quite as convincing of the discomforts of the system of slavery as the most pathetic representation of the sufferings of the negroes could be.

When Miss Ophelia is tried past bearing, she goes to have it out with St. Clare, and their talks, begun in indignant remonstrance on her part answered by light persiflage from him, proceed into earnest discussion of the entire subject, and end in his return to his cigar, while Miss Ophelia with a softened face, goes out to her duties. In these discussions there is concentrated the essence, the beginning and end of slavery as it had never before been presented to the world. In St. Clare, Mrs. Stowe develops her possibilities in the analysis of a character, quite distinct and diverse from the several clear cut types in the tale. Modern portrayals of the person, motives, actions and varied tastes, and capabilities of a gentleman, have in no way detracted from this excellently well-painted picture. St. Clare is a born aristocrat, who is yet so far able to extricate himself from his environment, as to see it with unprejudiced eyes. Some of his comments and subtle insights into the distinctive moving springs of his class, are delicious. As for instance when he says,—" An aristocrat has no human sympathies beyond a certain line in society." Again, in speaking of his father, he says, " religious sentiment, he had none beyond a veneration for God as decidedly the head of the upper classes." The passage where he describes his mother's blessed influence is a worthy description of Harriet Beecher Stowe's mother's influence as it was felt in her family.

About this time Topsy comes upon the stage.—Topsy, the black imp, hardly to be known as a girl or boy, Topsy with the bare legs and arms, the pig-tails sticking up all

over her head, the bead-like eyes always seeking new mischief! She, of the unexpected and curious gambols, of the
warped conscience, and the total lack of responsibility to
any being! Every street child, every day laborer, every
huckster, thief, colporteur, parson and burglar, knows
Topsy. They have all seen her, time and again upon the
stage and in memory of the book and its dramatization.
She was a revelation, an unimagined personality and character, (not however without precedent as the original was a
girl named Celeste, who was known to the family in Cincinnati). But her actions so constantly appealed to the
various strings of the human heart that she remains, a
synonym for incarnated mischief, incorrigibility, irresponsi-
bility, fun and impish heartlessness. Quite without an idea
of her personal relation to the principles of social rights,
insensible to beatings, remonstrances, or any punishment
yet devised, she became Miss Ophelia's contradiction and
stumbling-block, St. Clare's proof of total depravity,
Marie's strong aversion, and the torment of all the house
servants.

Only sweet little Eva, the angelic child who gently
faded from earth because she had not enough gross material to stay, overcame the black child's stolid indifference to kind, well-meant reproaches, and by the melting
force of love, touched the calloused heart, pleading effectually with smiles and tenderness, by friendly hand-clasp and
the breath of flowers, where stripes and bruising blows had
failed. Gentle Eva, the immortal child of the author's
brain, had found the answer to the question, "What is to
be done with a human being that can be governed only by
the lash, when that fails?" Whipping and abuse are like

opiates, you have to double the dose as the sensibilities fail and decline. It was and is,—for we need the lesson still in this strange, queerly assorted life,—the power of love. It is the only power that can move the heart, heal wrongs, incite noble action and bring us a final "Well done."

In this bringing together of the two children, representative of the extremes of society, what dramatic force and sense of telling situations did the author display! It was as a tableau which flashed in one comprehensive scene, the effects of heredity and environment. The Saxon, born of ages of cultivation, the African, born of ages of oppression. There was a world of argument in the combination. It speaks most strongly for itself. Comments are not necessary to show between the lines volumes of deep meaning. We can apply it to various situations in life.

Two years go by, and Uncle Tom lives on comfortable and comparatively happy. By means of a letter from George Shelby, a line of communication, given as well, to the reader of the story, we easily return to the Kentucky home, where Chloe works with the hope of sometime buying her husband back, and Mrs. Shelby keeps the place running with her enviable executive faculty. It is but a glimpse, and we take a seat upon the magician's carpet and are again in New Orleans where we see Eva making Uncle Tom her chief companion and confidential friend, riding with him, talking upon many interesting and improving themes, exchanging her knowledge of polite society for his religious perceptions, reading to him in her melodious voice from the Scriptures, while he explains and expounds passages in his own simple and clear-seeing manner. Great,

black, earnest Uncle Tom, sings hymns in his heavy
sonorous voice, while Eva listens, sometimes joining her
clear piping treble.   It is to him, her best friend and most
appreciative companion, that Eva confides her feeling that
she was going to die, soon.   It is with him that she
talks of the happiness she feels in   leaving this earth
where she is always tired, and pants for breath, and suffers
with fever and a hectic burning in her cheeks; with him
that she longs for the rest and perfect happiness of the new
life which she is approaching; with him that she talks of
the glories of God and of the angels.   And he, with his
great, loving, honest heart, pierced with anguish, prays that
it may not be so, not yet, that she may stay to minister to
them all, where kindness and mercy and love are so sadly
wanting.

Have we not sobbed in uncontrollable emotion over this
story?   Have we not seen it portrayed by living actors
upon the stage, when no failure to rise to its possibilities,
could mar the effect of the sentiment, when even slow
music upon a melodeon, in provincial performances, could
not destroy its inherent strength and beauty and pathos?

Shall we discuss the literary merits of this tale ?   Shall
we talk of *art*, when its intensity of sweetness and sadness
make tears stream from our eyes, confounding the most
unimpressionable, and, having knocked the stilts of conventionalism from under us, let us down to the true basis of
feeling, sentiment and truth ?

The death of Eva, with the events clustering about the
time, the giving of Topsy by St. Clare to Miss Ophelia, his
intention of also freeing Uncle Tom which was unfortunately postponed too long, and his own death by accident,

follow in quick succession, and Uncle Tom and all the slaves of the household are left unprotected. Uncle Tom is finally sent to the warehouse and sold; not back to the Shelbys, for they know nothing of his changing fortunes, not to Aunt Chloe, for she, singing over her work in the hope of soon making him free, lives on in happy unconsciousness of his fate. Again the reader witnesses the scenes of a slave mart. Again the auctioneer places human beings upon the block, discusses their good points as animals, pats the glossy brawn of the male field hands and lays rough hands upon the tender flesh of modest women, discanting upon their beauties. Emeline and her pretty daughter Susan are introduced and Legree, the fiend in distorted human shape, the type of all that is naturally brutal, warped and degraded by his trade, appears upon the scene. Here is his picture.

" A little before the sale commenced, a short, broad, muscular man, in a checked shirt considerably open at the bosom, and pantaloons much the worse for dirt and wear, elbowed his way through the crowd, like one who is going actively into a business ; and coming up to the group, began to examine them systematically. From the moment that Tom saw him approaching, he felt an immediate and revolting horror at him, that increased as he came near. He was evidently, though short, of gigantic strength. His round, bullet head, large, light-gray eyes, with their shaggy, sandy eyebrows, and stiff, wiry, sun-burned hair, were rather unprepossessing items, it is to be confessed ; his large, coarse mouth was distended with tobacco, the juice of which, from time to time, he ejected from him with great decision and explosive force ; his hands were immensely large, hairy, sunburned, freckled, and very dirty, and garnished with long nails, in a very foul condition."

Simon Legree with the slaves he had bought at several auctions, among whom were Tom and Emeline, departs for his plantation on a Red River boat. The transformation of Tom, as far as wearing apparel could go, from the sleek, respectable coachman in white linen and broadcloth, to the plantation hand in rough clothes and disreputable hat and shoes, here takes place. Uncle Tom manages to retain his Bible while his other belongings are emptied from his trunk upon the deck, and amid much hilarity, sold to the highest bidders. In the character of Legree, the passage to his neglected and broken-down plantation, the fate of his abused slaves and the regime of terror and crime which he maintained, there is exhibited the most fearful possibilities, the most shameful probabilities of the institution which permitted the absolute holding of human beings, by a so-called owner. In this new situation is plainly demonstrated the pernicious workings of a system in which there is absolutely nothing to protect the life of a slave, but the character of the master.

It has been claimed that the character of Legree is a frightful imagination of diabolism in human form, an exaggeration of malignity which could never be realized. Legree has been declared as unreal as Caliban or an ogre in a nursery tale. But Bill Sikes and the Thenardiers furnish as distinct and successful literary types; and alas, have we not known in the flesh, of Wirz, another result of cruel conditions, the calloused keeper of the prison den at Andersonville! That personification of ingenuity in torture, who while utterly devoid of mercy or sensibility to suffering, yet showed a strange fertility in cruel expedient and an enjoyment of human terror and agony, quite out of keeping with those benumbed sensibilities. Such a fiend was Legree.

Charles Beecher wrote of a man like him upon the wharves of New Orleans who exhibited his fists, with knuckles enlarged and calloused in "knocking niggers down."

The story grows more intense as we follow Tom through the new experiences of his life on Simon Legree's plantation. The picture deepens, grows darker and sadder, and the figures of the down-trodden slaves stand out distinctly against the gloom of the surroundings. The heavy labor of the field hands, the weary, soul-crushing round of work, work uninterrupted or relieved by one hour of pleasure or peaceful rest, the night grinding of the corn by tired men and women, who impatiently wait their turns at the hand mills, or in utter despair abandon the attempt to prepare food, preferring death to such a struggle for existence and only longing for the end; the character of the woman Cassy, once a petted favorite of a rich and indulgent master, later the mother of fair and lovely children, then the abandoned mistress, who came to the block and saw her children sold into slavery, at last the desperate creature whose apparent insanity had made her the dread of drivers and her companions in slavery, and the consort of the fiend Legree, who was yet an abject coward before her terrible temper, and unconquerable spirit; the shameful life in prospect for Emeline, unless some kind fate shall interpose in her behalf; the brutal orgies of the degraded master, with his two still more degraded slaves and drivers,—all are depicted with ever increasing strength and graphic power—for the

climax of the tragedy draws near. Legree hates Uncle
Tom as is natural when he discovers his superiority, and
feels his unspoken disapproval. For as the author says:
"So subtle is the atmosphere of opinion that it will make
itself felt without words; and the opinion even of a slave
.may annoy a master."

Legree realizes, by some unseen but none the less palpable thought transferrence, that Tom despises him. This
arouses all his vindictive passions, and he resolves to sub-
due the man. With a just appreciation of the fine feelings
of the creature whom he legally owns, he perceives that
more degrading than punishment inflicted upon his person,
would be compelling him to flog another, and a woman!
This Tom refuses to do, by his calm but decided refusal
eliciting expressions of terror from the listening slaves, who
know too well what the result will be. Legree, at first
dumb-founded at the disobedience, then driven to fury by
the evidence that he has no power over the indomitable
courage and high spirit of the bondman, orders him to be
whipped by the brutal fellows who have been often
employed in this shameful office.

Again, when Cassy and Emeline disappear, Legree
demands of Tom their whereabouts. He declines to
speak of them, and at his repeated refusals to disclose
their retreat, the fiendish master orders him to be flogged
and without mercy. He could indeed hold and torture the defenceless body of the poor slave but his spirit
he could not degrade. A good Vermont Judge once
ordered a slave hunter who demanded "his property"
to "show a bill of sale from the Almighty." Legree had
no such warrant and his baffled ferocity expended itself

upon the poor tenement of the great free soul. One dreads
the denouement and yet perforce must read on. The consequences, the fatal injuries of Uncle Tom, whose spirit never
faltered even under the terrible cutting lash of the whips—
his hours of pain and mortal anguish as he lies on the floor
in a shed—the ministrations by night of Cassy, whose
unquiet soul had been moved to sweetness and hope by his
brave suffering, and spiritual insights—and—at last, his
death, bring the intense tale to a climax.

While from the first page, this story has been a startling
revelation, a marvelous sight as through a glass, of the various aspects of life under the system of negro slavery, it is
not until we stand over the dead body of Uncle Tom; not
until we feel the sublime pity of it, the tender regret and
rising indignation of it, the swelling sense of cruel wrong,
and the irrepressible rush of divine rage, aversion, and
unquenchable denunciation for what made this possible—
that the work reaches its highest power.

In the scarred, swollen, bleeding form of the noble black
man, now lying in the stillness of death, which is unlike
any other stillness in nature; in the holy love and trust,
which have been the consolation and dependence of this
poor dead creature, there is summed up, the possibilities, the capacities for joy and suffering, the patience, faith-
fulness, docility, great hearted kindness, the noble simplicity, devotion to duty, self sacrifice and determination to do
right, the deep religious faith and earnest Christian feeling
of the whole African race.

In his disfigured and excoriated body there is epitomized
every possible argument against the institution, which for
political reasons, for a mistaken sense of honor, on account

of a dim sighted valuation of principles over living issues, conservative souls hesitated to condemn hastily! For had it not had the sanction of custom, almost from the foundation of our colonial existence!

The arrival, too late, of young George Shelby, who has come to buy back his old friend, adds an exquisite touch of pathos; and his burial of the remains of Uncle Tom in his own cloak, presents a ceremony in which the reader feels as a sympathetic mourner. The short interview of the impetuous young man, whose soul is filled with sorrow and regret, with Legree who makes invidious remarks as to the sense of making such "a fuss over a dead nigger," and the sudden accession of wrath which excites George to promptly knock him down—affords an immense satisfaction to the reader, who involuntarily finds himself in young Shelby's place. The story draws to a close, with the sad return of George Shelby to Kentucky, the breaking of the intelligence to Aunt Chloe and the family of Uncle Tom's good master. The account of the happy situation of George Harris, Eliza and their child in a Canadian town, and the exposition through a letter from George of the author's idea for the colonization of Liberia, complete the work.

One commences to re-read this wonderful story with a view to its merits as literary art. But criticism, artistic standpoint, even the vehicle itself, is forgotten as one is swept away from all conventionalities and literary tenets upon the surging current of mighty feeling. Uncle Tom's Cabin has seldom been discussed as a mere work of art. Human interest and sympathy so transcend the machinery of the work, that one quite unburdened with susceptibility

7

to the weal or woe of the characters, the exquisite tortures
of mind and body, the sacred rights of living beings, must
be the cool headed, cool hearted critic.

It must be a technical mind which can learnedly discuss
the work as tested by the criteria of modern art criticism;
a mind which can describe with a nicety, the laws of novel
writing; which can assert that this book is not a novel
because it has a practical motive; because the end is outside of itself, because it carries in parallel lines the lives of
two heroes which have no essential relation each other.
And while we bow and say "Yes," "Yes," to these learned
and nice analyses, we still feel that it *is* a novel, that it *is*
artistic, that it is a work of great originality, genius, and
perception of actual possibilities, which are worked out
with rare discrimination and dramatic power.

It has been the verdict of some critics who place less
value upon the matter than the manner of a literary work,
that the characters in Uncle Tom's Cabin are all too extreme. That they resemble, in their respective antipodal
manifestations, (if one may be pardoned the flippancy in
thus digesting their wise conclusions,) the historic little
girl, with the curl on her forehead. This may be true from
a coldly artistic reasoning, which demands that the lesser
values shall have their representation, and which in the
attempt to round out and fill characters, often merely suc-
ceeds in leveling them to a dull, uninteresting plain, where
heroes and cowards, villains and noble actors, are so alike,
that it requires the minutest analysis to separate them from
each other. It was not the fashion forty years ago to de-
tract from the force of a representation, by an undue consideration of its drawbacks and limitations. Neither were

characters emasculated as they are often to-day, by a finical
anxiety as to their minor and contradictory traits.   Neither
was it at all to the taste or disposition of Harriet Beecher
Stowe to weaken her own, or the reader's convictions, by
citing all the possible modifications of her case.   She had no
inclination to reduce her strong points to the polished level
obtained by many writers.   Their indecision (which they
mistake for liberality) prevents them from making an enduring impress upon the age.   Her work was that of the
astronomer who looks at fixed stars through his telescope,
as compared with the microscopic nicety, which induces the
purveyors of details to call our attention to unessentials in
the modern novel.   And yet Mrs. Stowe's characters are
very like people we know, whose ruling passions quite obscure their minor traits, whether good or bad.

One fact is quite remarkable, it is, that this story is entirely
without a lover.   No tale of youthful passion holds it together
with delicate threads of sympathy, no hint of the old yet ever
new spring time of virgin love, is presented.   Of pure and
holy affection there is a fullness ; of marital, filial and brotherly love, most beautiful instances; but no sweet lady is
introduced to be the reward and pride of young George Shelby, and no dark-skinned lover complicates the situation
where pretty Emeline is concerned.   In Uncle Tom's Cabin
Mrs. Stowe regarded life, not in the light of hope or pleasant
anticipation.   She wrote of a terrible wrong as it existed,
and with the earnest purpose, to make others see it as she did.

It is indeed a nondescript work of fiction.   No rules or
canons which apply to average and mediocre creations, in
any way fit it.   Some works and actions are too low and
common for conventional criticism ; this is too high and

apart to be brought under usual comparisons. But granting its literary limitations it must be conceded that, aside from its powerful moral purpose, which obtained where thousands of works of polished rhetoric had failed, and "moulded" the heart of millions into one," the unprecedentedly popular impression it made, was due to the true art with which facts and impressions were assimilated, fused and set forth.

It was slave life: not something it was like, but the life itself, shown to us through the clear medium of this grand woman's intellect. Can art do more?

It is true that this work had the advantage of a new field of exploration, and that it was an unfolding to the world, of a phase of political and social life, into which the novelist had not penetrated, nor leveled and mannerized the actions and characters. The broad poetic features of life upon which romance relies, were the same, but the situation was peculiar, and the treatment fresh, vigorous, and entirely free from conventionalism.

The state of political feeling which prevailed at the time of the writing of "Uncle Tom's Cabin," can hardly be appreciated by the present generation. The lapse of years, and the anxiety then felt, being relieved by the adjustment of the difficulty, has (in a way) blunted the sensibilities of modern readers to the evil which its author dared to attack. But there is nothing ephemeral in her thoughts and methods. The sentiment of "Uncle Tom's Cabin" will be as true and moving one hundred years hence, as it was forty years ago. Mrs. Stowe's fun is intrinsically humorous. The comicality of her situations endures. It is not dependent upon style, time, or nationality.

Her pathos touches the deepest springs of human sympathy, moving the heart to tenderer throb for all humanity, because she so warms it for the weal of woe of her characters.

Her philosophy is based upon tenable ground, and withal, has a touch of indulgence for the error which she condemns, and a sense of the excusable mistakes of finite beings, emanating from her own generous spirit, which after all dominates her strongest conclusions. Her reasoning is masculine in its logic, a thing quite different from the woman's reason of "gentle Will Shakespeare" which "thinks him so, because, she thinks him so." Its sequence is convincing, building one proposition upon another, until a well constructed argument appears, which stands because well founded. Mrs. Stowe impressed the peculiarities of her personality upon her work. Honesty, directness, grasp of essential points, and good-humored toleration of human limitations, were remarkable, while yet she launched a thunderbolt against the system of negro slavery.

"Uncle Tom's Cabin" is full of thought which is deeper than speech. It glows with feeling which is deeper than thought. This work, had she written no other, would in itself be a sufficient passport to literary immortality.

While Mrs. Stowe was far from advocating disunion or a revolution—and hers was not a political effort but one put forth for moral suasion—it must be remembered, that common sense as well as the law, presumes that a person intends the natural consequences of his actions. Therefore in this soul stirring effort against slavery, Harriet Beecher Stowe proved herself an Abolitionist who looked earnestly to the end, let the means be what they might.

It proved to be an agent more powerful than Garris-

Liberator, more potent than the poems of Whittier, more persuasive than the speeches of Phillips and Sumner. As an eminent critic said; "It presented the thing concretely and dramatically, and in particular it made the Fugitive Slave law forever impossible to enforce."

Statesmen still think however, that neither the influence of this work—well calculated as it was to awaken the right feeling of the people—nor the speeches and writings of all the other moralists of the age, would have wrought the emancipation of the American slaves, had not the madness of the South upon various political questions, precipitated a series of events, of which Lincoln's proclamation was the glorious culmination. This question must remain a matter of personal opinion, as plainly, no one can measure or weigh moral force. Mrs. Stowe never expected to see the slaves free. It seemed impossible in view of the situation, that emancipation could come so soon. But "God disposes."

Men lived years in each day during that pregnant period, and the thing was accomplished, while yet it was supposed to halt in the dimness of future years.

CHAPTER V.

NOT until the last chapters of "Uncle Tom's Cabin"
were written, and that eloquent appeal to the people of the
United States which ends the book was finished, did Mrs.
Stowe falter in her task. Not until the last sheets were

folded and sent to the Post Office by a trusty messenger, did she realize how great had been the strain upon her body, heart and mind. It was only when the last page of proof was examined and corrected, that the exaltation and creative fire which had for so many months possessed the author of " Uncle Tom's Cabin," fell and died out, leaving her in despair, trembling and quite cast down. Because she feared the results to her personally, because she dreaded impending events, because she lost belief in the truth and justice of the cause which she had thus presented? Not for an instant. It was that it seemed so hopeless to reach the hearts of the people, so futile to remonstrate and urge a turning to the right, so impossible to break down the greed, prejudice and conventionalism which hedged in this system. For some days she lay with closed eyes, inert and plunged in reactionary feeling which destroyed hope and courage. But not for long. Her spirit rose. She felt that she must give her work, if possible, a hearing with the best minds of the age. She must leave nothing undone, which even remotely promised to further the success of her book.

Consequently, she occupied her time for several weeks writing letters, and when the book appeared sent a copy of it with her letter to the English Royal Consort, Prince Albert. There was another to Thomas Babington Macaulay, whose father, Zachary Macaulay, she knew to have been an anti-slavery laborer, of whom Mrs. Stowe afterwards said, " whose place in the hearts of the English Christians was little below saintship." Her book was sent, with the hope that the son might sympathize.

Charles Dickens had more than once expressed his sympathy with the slave, and to him she wrote, sending her book. She addressed another appeal and copy of "Uncle Tom's Cabin," to Charles Kingsley, and another to Lord Carlisle, who had been influential in giving freedom to the blacks in the British colonies.

"Uncle Tom's Cabin" was published in book form in March, 1852. The despondency and uncertainty of the author as to whether any one would read her book, was soon dispelled. Ten thousand copies were sold in a few days, and over three hundred thousand within a year. Eight powerful presses running day and night for months were barely able to keep pace with the demand for it. It was read everywhere, by all classes of people. Talk of it filled the atmosphere. Heated discussions occasioned by it, resounded in cottage, farm-house, business offices and palatial residences, all over the land. The pity, distress, and soul-felt indignation in which it had been written, were by it transferred to the minds and consciences of her readers, and the antagonism it everywhere engendered, threw the social life of this country and England, into angry effervescence through all its stratas.

Echoes of its clarion tones came back to her in the quiet home at Brunswick, returning as they had struck, the world with clashing dissonance or loud alarum or low sweet tones of human feeling.

Letters, letters of all sizes, colors, direction and kinds of chirography, astonished the Post Master at Brunswick, by their countless numbers, and the author began to feel the nation's pulse. Friends applauded, remonstrated, or vociferously deprecated her course. Literary associates praised the technique of the story, but thought

the subject ill chosen.   Abolitionists wrote with irrepressible enthusiasm, and praised God that she had been raised
up to do this thing.   Politicians angrily expressed their
amazement, that her husband should permit her to commit
this incendiarism, which might burst into a conflagration
that would dissolve the national union.   Slave-holders
heaped reproaches and contumely upon her, and badly
spelled productions, evincing cowardly ruffianism, were
taken with tongs by her husband and dropped, almost unread into the fire.

On one occasion Prof. Stowe opened an envelope which
contained a negro's ear, pinned to a bit of card-board.
Accompanying this sickening thing, were a few words
scrawled, which hinted that this was one of the effects of
her would-be defense of the "D—n niggers."   This was
never seen by his wife, as it, with all other offensive letters
were speedily destroyed by him in his anxiety to shield
her from the unpleasant results of her noble work.

A friend of Mrs. Stowe's favorite brother, has recently
said that Henry had threatened never to read "Uncle
Tom's Cabin," but couldn't help it, cried over it and wrote
to her: "If you ever write another such book I will kill
you, if I have to go around the world to find you.   You
have taken more out of me, than a whole year of preaching.   I wish that all the slave-holders in the South, and all
their Northern sympathizers with them, were shut up for a
century, and obliged to read about 'Uncle Tom.'"

In May, 1852, Mrs. Stowe, very much in need of rest and
recreation, visited New York.   It was at the time of Jenny
Lind's second visit to this country.   She was the idol of
the hour.   Women listened to her matchless voice with

THE HOUSE IN WHICH UNCLE TOM'S CABIN WAS WRITTEN, BRUNSWICK, ME.

tears, men were moved to irrepressible enthusiasm, which found vent in dragging her carriage, heaped with flowers, from the Academy of Music to her hotel. Tickets for her concerts were bought weeks in advance, and Mrs. Stowe found that seats were not to be had at any price. But somehow the young Swedish vocalist heard of Mrs. Stowe's application, and immediately sent her tickets for two of the best seats in the house, accompanying them with a charming letter, in which she very ingenuously and gracefully, thanked her for the pleasure she had felt in reading her wonderful book. The letter, with its delicate hand writing, and charmingly fluent, if unconventional English, remains one of the valued souvenirs of the woman and the time.

The cheering testimony came in from fugitive slaves, that people were more kind to them, after reading "Uncle Tom's Cabin." In one respect, however the author's expectations were amusingly controverted by facts. She had represented slave-holders at their best, had taken cognizance of their difficulties and limitations, had admitted their noble traits of character, and really believed that while the radical Abolitionists might think the picture altogether too tame and mild in its dealings with slave-holders, her book would be, as a friend in the South assured her it must be," a great pacificator; which will unite both North and South." To her astonishment it was the extreme Abolitionists who received it with acclamation, and the solid South who rose up against it ; and so far from leveling and smoothing away the differences of opinion between them, it drew an impassable line, fixing a barrier of facts upon either side of which must all the people array themselves.

In May, 1852, Whittier wrote to Garrison:—"What a glorious work Harriet Beecher Stowe has wrought. *Thanks* for the Fugitive Slave law. Better for slavery that that law had never been enacted, for it gave occasion for 'Uncle Tom's Cabin.'"

In a letter from Garrison to Mrs. Stowe he said, that he estimated the value of anti-slavery writing by the abuse it brought. "Since Uncle Tom's Cabin was published" he adds, "all the defenders of slavery have let me alone and are spending their strength in abusing you."

Harriet Martineau wrote sentenciously "I am glad to find Mrs. Stowe is held up to execration in the South, along with myself and Mrs. Chapman."

Alternating with and accompanying packages of letters from the illustrious, the celebrated, and the wise of the world were irate and abusive epistles from the brutal traders and slave-holders of the South. Some of these were a disgusting mixture of blasphemy and obscenity, and all rang with cruelty and brutal invective.

Responses came from over the sea. Mrs. Stowe was informed that Prince Albert and the Queen had read her story with the most intense interest. Charles Dickens wrote from London in July, and while courteously suggesting that she went too far and sought to prove too much—a natural criticism from one who had not seen slavery as it was in America—he closed by saying: "Your book is worthy of any head and any heart that ever inspired a book. I am your debtor, and thank you most fervently and sincerely."

Macaulay wrote, thanking her for the volume, assuring her of his high respect for the talents and for the benevolence of the writer. Four years later the same illustrious author, essayist and historian wrote to Mrs. Stowe: "I have just returned from Italy, where your fame seems to throw that of all other writers into the shade. There is no place where 'Uncle Tom,' transformed into 'Il Zio Tom,' is not to be found."

From Lord Carlisle she received a long and earnest epistle in which he says he felt that slavery was by far the "topping" question of the world and age, and that he returned his "deep and solemn thanks to Almighty God, who has led and enabled you to write such a book."

The Rev. Charles Kingsley, in the midst of illness and anxiety, sent his thanks saying, "Your book will do more to take away the reproach from your great and growing nation, than many platform agitations and speechifyings."

Said Lord Palmerston, "I have not read a novel for thirty years; but I have read that book three times, not only for the story, but for the *statesmanship* of it."

Lord Cockburn declares: "She has done more for humanity than was ever before accomplished by any single book of fiction."

In December of the same memorable year, 1852, the Earl of Shaftesbury, a man who spent a lifetime in endeavors to lift the crushing burdens from the laboring classes of England, and had redeemed from the slavery of the collieries and the mines, hundreds of women and children, who were degraded almost below belief, in the horrors of their situation and labor, introduced himself by letter to the author of "Uncle Tom's Cabin," commending various good points in her story, and testifying to his realization from experience, of the truth of certain characters. He waived the particularization of the various beauties, "singular, original and lasting, which shine throughout the work," and assured her of his sincere admiration and respect.

About the same time Mrs. Stowe received a letter from Hon. Arthur Helps, accompanying a review of her work written by himself, for *Fraser's Magazine.*

Her reply to this letter, having been shown to Archbishop Whateley, elicited a letter from him, complimenting her, and informing her that he had negotiated for articles from very able hands upon the same subject for the "Edinburgh" and "North British" Reviews, both of which had a wide circulation and potent influence.

This was surely most welcome evidence that the book had found powerful friends and sturdy support on English shores. Mr. Sampson Low, afterwards Mrs. Stowe's English publisher, wrote of its success in England, saying that from April to December, six months after its publication, forty editions had been issued, in all forms, from the handsome, illustrated one, at fifteen shillings, to the sixpence pamphlet. He estimated that the number then circulated in England and its colonies, would aggregate one million and a half.

Meanwhile the book had found its way to the North of Europe, and among the precious assurances of its worth was a letter from sweet Fredericka Bremer at Stockholm. It was written in her own charming style, and every sentence seemed to have been fused in the genial warmth of her woman's heart.

The Paris *Temps* has recently said: "Even if we go back to Alexandre Dumas's 'Musketeers' and to Eugene Sue's

'Mysteries of Paris' we still find that 'Uncle Tom' surpassed them all in the intense interest awakened. Every paper and publisher in Paris wanted it, and three of our dailies published it simultaneously. So great was the popular excitement that a reader of the *Siecle* would hurry out and buy a copy of the *Presse* in the hope that it might give more of the unfinished chapter."

We have ministerial authority for the statement that the reading of Uncle Tom's Cabin in Paris created a great demand among the people for Bibles. "Purchasers eagerly inquired if they were buying *the real Bible—Uncle Tom's Bible*. The same result was produced in Belgium and elsewhere. Could the most eloquent preacher do more than this?"

Henrick Heine, whom no one could suspect of such predilections, after describing his gropings and flounderings amid the unsatisfactory speculations of German philosophy, tells us how he at length come to quit Hegel and to read the Bible with Uncle Tom, finding in the simple faith of the poor slave a higher wisdom than in the great philosophers' dialectics.

Madame George Sand, a woman of rare intellectual strength, presented it to the reading public of France in a glowing review, which is doubtless one of the worthiest tributes to the author and the work, which has ever seen the light. It was vital with spontaneous enthusiasm, and while recognizing certain artistic defects, with true judgment as to the essentials, Madame Sand regards these as nothing, in comparison with the persuasive force and compelling strength of the story. George Sand declares that the children "are the true heroes of Mrs. Stowe's work."

Reviews and critics everywhere were speedily busy with the book, discussing it from standpoints as various as human opinions, in lights as many and different as the imperceptible gradations of the prismatic colors or the shades between black and white which Goëthe ingeniously, if erroneously, took to be the scientific explanation of color.

Within a year "Uncle Tom's Cabin" was scattered all over the world. Translations were made into all the principal languages and into several obscure dialects, in number variously estimated from twenty to forty. The librarian of the British Museum, with an interest and enterprise which might well put our own countrymen to blush, has made a collection which is unique and very remarkable in the history of books. American visitors may see there, thirty-five editions of the original English and the complete text, and eight of abridgements and adaptations. Of translations into different languages there are nineteen; viz., Armenian 1; Bohemian 1; Danish 2 distinct versions; Dutch 1; Finnish 1; Flemish 1; French 8 distinct versions and 2 dramas; German 5 distinct versions and 4 abridgements; Hungarian 1 complete version, 1 for children and 1 versified abridgement; Illyrian 2 distinct versions; Italian 1; Polish 2 distinct versions; Portuguese 1; Roman or Modern Greek 1; Russian 2 distinct versions; Spanish 6 distinct versions; Swedish 1; Wallachian 2 distinct versions; Welsh 3 distinct versions.

Of the "Key to Uncle Tom's Cabin" there are seven editions in different languages, of works on the subject of "Uncle Tom's Cabin" there are eight, separately published. Of reviews of it there are forty-nine. But this list is by no means complete. Many editions and translations have been impossible to procure, but the English speaking world owes thanks to Mr. Bullen and his coadjutors for their successful collection of so many versions.

In Italy, "the powers that be" published an edition in which all allusions to Christ were changed to the Virgin Mary, "a piece of craftiness," says our authority, "that argues better for the book than for its mutilators."

Many foreign publishers and translators sent their reproductions to the author and in the library of Mrs. Stowe's house at Hartford, the writer has seen many most interesting and curious editions. At intervals since the publication of "Uncle Tom's Cabin" the author has received editions of her work from the most unexpected sources, and the more interesting ones have been preserved, though with that characteristic lack of appreciation of her own greatness, and the carelessness which familiarity and close associations with a famous author, seem to make possible, neither Mrs. Stowe nor her children appear to have invested them with high value, and when asked for by the present writer, a few of them were found after some search on the shelves in the back of a closet, scattered about and in imperfect preservation.

Among them were specimens of several of the French editions, by various translators, and a few of the German issues. There were numerous Italian editions Spanish and Cuban, Dutch, Swedish and Danish. One from Abertawy, India, in the provincial dialect; one in Polish; and two which were found published on the island of Java in the Dutch language, an 18mo published at Sooraligia at the east end of the island, and an octavo brought out at Batavia. These were forwarded to

Mrs. Stowe by a missionary, the Rev. Samuel W. Bonney, who found them in this out-of-the-way place, with a letter written on the good ship "Comet" one hundred miles south of Java.   There was one which seemed to be all consonants, chiefly L's, W's and Y's in the Welsh. This was illustrated by George Cruikshank in his most peculiar style.   Those in the Russian, of which there were several, were pictured with the most astonishing and un-American negroes and drivers, imaginable.

There is one very rare and valuable, in Armenian, translated by one of the monks in the convent at Venice. The hieroglyphics which convey written ideas in this language, are most obscure and unfamiliar.

There was one, received from an unknown hand, which is in a language of which the family had no information. Prof. Stowe with his knowledge of philology could not guess at it, until some student of uncommon lore pronounced it to be one of the least known of the Hungarian dialects.

Some of the early English editions were quaint and interesting; one, a penny sheet, in print so small as to be ruinous to the eyesight.   Other cheap English editions were more attractive, but all had illustrations which were intensely English, and convey to the American reader no similitude of scenes in the South.   Many of these editions, numbering some seventy-five, came to the author with the compliments of the publishers, (it is not recorded whether in many cases their acknowledgments went so far as the paying of a royalty) and many were rich and costly, while others are in pasteboard or the penny sheet.

The Rev. Dr. Dwight, an eminent American missionary,

wrote from Constantinople to Prof. Stowe regarding the Armenian translation in September, 1855, three years and one half after the publication of the great book, as follows:

" Uncle Tom's Cabin in the Armenian language! Who would have thought it? I do not suppose your good wife when she wrote that book, thought she was going to missionate it among the sons of Haig in all their dispersions, following them along the banks of the Euphrates, sitting down with them in their towns and villages under the shade of hoary Ararat, traveling with them in their wanderings even to India and China. But I have it in my hands in the Armenian of the present day, the same language in which I speak and think and dream. Now do not suppose this is any of my work, or that of any missionary in the field. The translation has been made and the book printed at Venice by a fraternity of Catholic Armenian Monks perched there on the Island of St. Lazarus. It is in two volumes, neatly printed with plates, I think translated from the French. It has not been in any respect materially altered and when it is so, not on account of religious sentiment. The account of the negro prayer and exhortation meetings is given in full, though the translator, not knowing what we mean by people's becoming Christians, took pains to insert at the bottom of the page that at these meetings of the negroes, great effects were sometimes produced by the warm-hearted exhortations and prayers, and it often happened that heathen negroes embraced Christianity on the spot.

" One of your former scholars is now in my house studying Armenian, and the book I advised him to take as the best for the language is this ' Uncle Tom's Cabin.' "

Good Mr. Thomas Watts, the librarian next preceding Mr. Bullen of the British Museum, the one who first suggested making a collection of the various editions and translations, wrote Prof. Stowe many interesting facts regarding the book and said:

"The translation of the same text by thirteen different translators at precisely the same epoch of a language is a circumstance perhaps altogether unprecedented, and it is not one likely to recur, as the tendency of modern alteration in the law of copyright is to place restrictions on the liberty of translators. The possession too, of such a book as 'Uncle Tom's Cabin' is very different from that of such a book as 'Thomas a Kempis' in the information it affords to the student of a language. There is every variety of style, from that of animated narration and passionate wailing to that of the most familiar dialogue, and dialogue not only in the language of the upper classes but of the lowest. The student who has once mastered 'Uncle Tom' in Welsh or Wallachian, is not likely to meet any further difficulties in his progress through Welsh or Wallachian prose."

Thus it appears that this book was destined to stand pre-eminent as an educator, not only morally but technically.

It is related that during the season following the publication of "Uncle Tom's Cabin" a kind-hearted gentleman was staying over night at one of the New York hotels. After retiring to his room his attention was arrested by a sound as of some one in the next apartment, a strong man, sobbing and moaning. With occasional periods of quiet, the sorrowful sounds were prolonged even after he had gone to bed. At last moved to pity by the evident suffering of a fellow mortal, he arose, found it past midnight, and going to the wall rapped upon it and asked, "My friend, what is the matter? Are you ill or in any trouble that I can relieve? Shall I call for medical aid?"

After a slight pause the voice replied, though choked with convulsive sobs, "No. No, a doctor wouldn't do me any good. I am reading 'Uncle Tom's Cabin.'"

"Ah!" said the good man who was a friend of the slave, "I am sorry—no, glad. Weep on, my friend, and when the time comes, act upon what you are learning."

Rufus Choate, the brilliant lawyer, who, from his qualities, was naturally conservative,—even through his respect for the laws, a strong pro-slavery man—read "Uncle Tom's Cabin," as all needs must do who would be informed upon the latest and most powerful condemnation of the "system." He wept over it in spite of himself, and slamming down the book exclaimed angrily: "There! That will add two thousand more to the ruff-scuff Abolitionists." As it proved this estimate was a moderate one.

Seeing that the great desire of her heart, the awakening of the Christian people, had begun as a direct result of her work, and that various petitions and remonstrances had within a few months poured in upon Congress from the Middle and Western states, and that as many as one hundred and twenty-five remonstrances had already appeared from the ministers of the six New England states, Mrs. Stowe conceived the idea of a mammoth Memorial, so engrossed as to present the original signatures, and heading of each petition, protesting "in the name of Almighty God against the proposed extension of the domain of slavery in the territory of the United States."

She suggested it to Dr. H. M. Dexter, editor of *The Congregationalist*, through whose agency the heading was prepared at a meeting of the Boston ministers. The names of 3,050 New England clergymen were obtained and the memorial. a monster petition two hundred feet long, was presented to Congress.

Charles Sumner, then fresh in his seat in the Senate, thanked the ministers for their interposition, adding in his inspiriting voice, "In the days of the Revolution, John Adams, yearning for independence, said, 'Let the pulpit thunder against oppression' and the pulpits 'thundered.' The time has come for them to thunder again."

In the present age of the world and condition of literary criticism, it has sometimes seemed difficult to understand the phenomenal popularity of this work, but is only because in our supposed familiarity with it, we have forgotten its strength, its graphic power, its deep philosophy, its rare humor. While negro slavery has receded rapidly into the past, in the more than twenty years since the proclamation of Lincoln, and another generation has come upon the stage; while we are in our turn, absorbed with the burning questions of the present day, and naturally prone to undervalue those that are past, it needs but a re-perusal of this great work to carry us back into the very seeth and foam of the agitation of forty years ago. It is only in realizing how potent it is with its readers of the reconstructed Union of to-day—a Union which is fairer and brighter for the troubles and sadness of the past—that we can estimate the momentum which this intellectual work carried with it all over the civilized world.

A correspondent, writing of the tardy abolition of slavery in Brazil, which held its chattels after the sister republics of S. America had given them freedom, recently says: "Uncle Tom's Cabin" is a book that still goes marching on. Down in Brazil the emancipation of the slaves was mainly due to au editor who kept his paper red hot with abolition arguments. He did not have much success until finally he printed a translation of "Uncle Tom's Cabin." Then the people waked up. They cried over the story, and raised such a protest against slavery that the government was forced to abolish it."

Having freed her mind and heart of the weight of anxiety and responsibility which bore upon it, having eased her own sympathies in great measure by transferring from herself to her army of readers, the freight of woe which weighed her down and would not be lightened until she had spoken—Mrs. Stowe returned quietly to the duties of domestic life. Her baby boy then a year old, proceeded with the succession of small ailments which infantile man finds ready to meet him in this difficult world. The dreaded crisis of teething in the second summer was upon him, the older children demanded constant attention, and the mother's sewing was sadly in arrears. The two older daughters, nearly fifteen years of age, were entering young womanhood with alert and quickened senses, their evenings were spent in conversation and listening to readings from the best English authors by Professor Stowe, while the little mother patched, and darned, ripped, turned, pressed and made over innumerable garments and began to think of sending the twin girls to boarding school.

The author of "Uncle Tom's Cabin" knew with glad surprise, and a sort of awe of her own performance, of the wonderful sale of her book. She received and read hundreds of letters with a deep sense of gratitude that the good seed had fallen upon such unexpectedly rich places. With a singular modesty which she has ever since maintained—

a modesty which was superior to, and not to be lessened by the praise which poured in upon her, and has been poured in such precious measure at her feet even until now—Mrs. Stowe never thought of the work as a credit to her literary powers, but only with an humble thankfulness that she had been chosen the instrument by which God had unfolded the right.

At the end of the first six months, Professor Stowe one day tore open a letter from Mr. Jewett, the publisher of "Uncle Tom's Cabin," and found enclosed a check for ten thousand dollars, which the sender begged him to accept as the first installment of the author's royalty on "Uncle Tom's Cabin." "Why, Harriet," said he, "it is more money than I ever saw in all my life."

The sum which was now in their hands would indeed, if placed at the usual rate of interest, yield a yearly income which would largely augment the salary of Professor Stowe. It meant comfort, intellectual possibilities, æsthetic gratifications, which they had never dreamed of as for them. The next six months brought a similar sum, and for thirty-seven years the income from "Uncle Tom's Cabin" has not ceased, but brought not only the temporal good things of life to its author and her family, but the comforting assurance that the heart power, the spirit of love and good will to men which is embodied, still thrills responsive in human hearts, still carries a throb of pity and kindness to a million breasts, still works on, imperishable, as intrinsic goodness must ever be, sweetening and brightening the world.

In answer to an inquiry made by the present writer as to the number of copies of "Uncle Tom's Cabin" sold since its appearance, Rev. Charles E. Stowe wrote Dec. 28th, 1887: "I have no kind of a notion as to the number of copies of Uncle Tom sold since the first. Since last May, there have been twelve thousand two hundred and twenty-five copies sold.

"The edition is completely exhausted, so when new copies were wanted to sell at the Plymouth Church fair in Brooklyn the other day, there were none to be had."

A rough estimate shows that the steady sale of Uncle Tom's Cabin was, in 1887, at the rate of fifteen hundred copies a month. It will be understood that Mr. Stowe spoke of the American edition alone.

To the Hon. Francis H. Underwood, LL. D., at present United States Consul at Glasgow, we are indebted for the following account of Mrs. Stowe's first visit to a dramatic representation of "Uncle Tom's Cabin." Having been the projector of the Atlantic Monthly and then acting as managing editor, it fell to him and his wife to entertain its contributors, and Mrs. Stowe was the recipient of many courtesies from them.

In the winter of 1852 or 1853 a dramatic version of "Uncle Tom's Cabin" was performed at the National Theatre, Boston— a fine, large theatre, in the wrong place—that is to say, in one of the worst districts of Boston. It was burned a few years later, and never rebuilt. The dramatization was not very artistic, and the scenes introduced were generally the most ghastly ones of the painful story. Of the lightness and gayety of the book there was no sign. The actors were fairly good, but none of them remarkable, except the child who personated *Eva*, and the woman, (Mrs. Howard) who played *Topsy*. Mrs. Howard was beyond comparison the best representative of the dark race I ever saw. She was

a genius whose method no one could describe.   In every look,
gesture and tone there was an intuitive revelation of the strange,
capricious and fascinating creature which Mrs. Stowe had conceived.

I asked Mrs. Stowe to go with me to see the play.   She had
some natural reluctance, considering the position her father had
taken against the theatre, and considering the position of her husband as a preacher; but she also had some curiosity as a woman
and as an author to see in flesh and blood the creations of her
imagination.   I think she told me she had never been in a theatre
in her life.   I procured the manager's box, and we entered privately, she being well muffled.   She sat in the shade of the curtains of our box, and watched the play attentively.   I never saw
such delight upon a human face as she displayed when she first
comprehended the full power of Mrs. Howard's *Topsy*.   She
scarcely spoke during the evening; but her expression was eloquent,—smiles and tears succeeding each other through the
whole.

It must have been for her a thrilling experience to see her
thoughts bodied upon the stage, at a time when any dramatic
representation must have been to her so vivid.   Drawn along by the
threads of her own romance, and inexperienced in the deceptions
of the theatre, she could not have been keenly sensible of the faults
of the piece or the shortcomings of the actors.

I remember that in one scene *Topsy* came quite close to our
box, with her speaking eyes full upon Mrs. Stowe's.   Mrs. Stowe's
face showed all her vivid and changing emotions, and the actress
must surely have divined them.   The glances when they met and
crossed reminded me of the supreme look of Rachel when she
repeated that indescribable *Helas!*   There was but a slight wooden
barrier between the novelist and the actress—but it was enough!
I think it a matter of regret that they never met.

The *Eliza* of the evening was a reasonably good actress, and skipped over the floating ice of the Ohio River with frantic agility.

The *Uncle Tom* was rather stolid—such a man as I have seen preaching among the negroes when I lived in Kentucky.

It was afterwards put upon the stage at the Boston Museum in a more worthy presentation, and at the same period ran 150 nights in New York before packed houses. Dramatic versions, from those on the grandest scale to parlor dialogues, flooded the market, and thousands who might never have been reached by the book, were moved and thrilled by that potent educator, the theatre.

CHAPTER VI.

IN the summer of 1852 Professor Stowe accepted the
chair of Sacred Literature at Andover Theological Seminary as successor to Prof. Moses Stuart. The family
removed from Brunswick to that place in September. The
"Stone Cabin," which was tendered to Professor Stowe as a
residence, was a bare building, which had been used by the
students as a gymnasium and place for various kinds of

124

practical work and exercises, and, having never been used
as a habitation, it presented but a cold attraction to the
new Professor and his family.

Calvin E. Stowe was pre-eminently a scholar; a man
whose thoughts were ever full of his books, of his projected
themes, of his forthcoming lectures and literary works.
His wife was the practical manager of the affairs of the
house. She energetically undertook to make the stone
building fit for occupancy. She consulted carpenters and
arranged to have partitions put in, closets, cupboards and
shelves made, and in the meantime kept busily at work in
other ways, all tending towards the making of a home,
which the professor earnestly desired, and appreciated, but
knew little how to aid in preparing.

One of his brothers-in-law told with gusto how one day
he was going down the street, and meeting a man with a
load of lumber, asked him where he was going. The man,
not having known any masculine authority in the business,
replied in all seriousness, "I'm takin' it up to the Widder
Stowe's, she's going to have some partitions built."

Her mechanical ingenuity, which was strongly supple-
mented by the desire to make things about her comfortable,
and pleasant to look upon, incited her to buying wall papers, which she assisted to lay; to hanging pictures in various home-made frames; even to going so far as the construction of couches, improvised from long boxes, which
were cushioned and covered with chintz and gay cretonnes,
discovered in ancient chests among the family belongings.
She made chairs out of barrels, with the slat seat, stave
back, and flour-y bottom, stuffed, and covered with cushions

and frills of pretty cloth, which were indeed a triumph of upholstery.

Dressing tables of shallow boxes set upon the side, a shelf or two put in place, and the whole covered with pink or blue cambric and shirred with dimnity curtains, made her sleeping-rooms dainty and fresh. She worked with cheerful enthusiasm and frequent exclamations of satisfaction over any particularly pretty effect, for many weeks, until the house became a home, its bare, uncompromising ugliness, softened into tasteful convenience, and comfort.

Mrs. Stowe occasionally made trips to Boston to visit her brother Dr. Edward Beecher and his lovable wife, who who was a schoolmate of Harriet, at Hartford, and that lady testifies that her taste in millinery, was quite a marvel. She visited the shops and after making a few inexpensive purchases of straw braid and ribbon, returned to fashion most attractive head gear for herself and her daughters, giving the bonnets just the enviable touch which is commonly supposed to be only possible to the art of the trained milliner. This administrative and artistic ability was an inheritance from her mother, whose achievements in going to house-keeping in 1800 in the house at Amagansett, were thus described with characteristic Beecherian humor, by her father: —

"We had no carpets; there was not a carpet from end to end of the town. All had sanded floors, some of them worn through. Your mother introduced the first carpet. Uncle Lot gave me some money, and I had an itch to spend it; went to a vendue, and bought a bale of cotton. She spun it and had it woven; then she laid it down, sized it, and painted it in oils, with a border all around it, and bunches of roses and other flowers over the centre. . . She also took some common wooden chairs and painted them, and cut out figures of gilt paper, and glued them on and varnished them. They were really quite pretty. Old Deacon Talmadge came to see me. He stopped at the parlor door, and seemed afraid to come in. ' Walk in, Deacon, walk in,' said I. ' Why, I can't,' said he, 'thout stepping on't.' Then after surveying it awhile in admiration, ' D'ye think ye can have all that, and heaven, too?'"

Meantime Mrs. Stowe was not without annoyance from the attacks of the friends of slavery, and many friendly critics, questioned her grounds for the manifest she had made. In the winter of 1852–53 she therefore devoted her time to the compilation and writing of a set of arguments and recorded facts concerning slavery, which she called a "Key to Uncle Tom's Cabin," wherein were set forth her authorities for statements she had made. It was plainly and logically done, and carried conviction to many doubting readers, converting them from their idea of the work as a strongly sensational story, to the realization that every page was grounded in demonstrable truths and written with heart's blood. Mrs. Stowe declared that this "Key" was written with no pleasure but rather with real pain. She averred that in a work of fiction it is possible to find refuge from hard and terrible realities by inventing pleasing scenes and incidents; but no such resource was open to her here. It was to be the cold facts, the unvarnished truth, and necessarily very dreadful. But with her characteristic courage, she did it because she saw it was needed to make complete her great work. The book was selected out of a mountain of materials and contains documents and testimony furnished her by legal friends, north and south. She asserted that her object had been to present the truths regarding slavery to Christian people, to show what had been the action of the various denominations upon the question, and to place it in its true light, as a moral and religious question. In "The Key" she proceeds to give facts which crystalized into the various characters of the story, and takes into successive consideration, the personality and conduct of the types which are called "Mr. Haley," "Mr. and Mrs. Shelby," "George Harris," "Eliza," "Uncle Tom," "Miss Ophelia," "St. Clare," "Marie," "Eva," "Legree," and all the others, with the correlative facts, incidents and actions which make them probable existences. Mrs. Stowe follows this with a statement of conditions to which a large array of facts affirm, introduces a "Comparison of the Roman Law of Slavery with the American," continues, in a chapter entitled "The Men Better than their Laws," thus proving to the modern critic that what she began as a moral and religious exhortation, had intensified to a political *feuilleton* of prodigious strength and momentum. In answer to the good men who took refuge for their evil enactments under scriptural authority, Mrs. Stowe next draws a contrast between the ancient Hebrew slave law and the modern American one. In this exhaustive research she was materially assisted by her husband, Professor Stowe, who in all the laws, customs, languages and literature of the ancients was a close and erudite scholar.

The chapter, which is headed "Slavery is Despotism," would have no need to be written in this age of American civilization and moral right feeling. It is strongly significant of the change which has come about in the United States in forty years, to know that it was a vastly offensive statement to thousands of people in our land, in 1853. The book contains enough facts and testimony to condemn any institution, and there is little doubt that this work which is mathematical in argument and logic, following closely after the book which burned with feeling and meta-physical insights, clinched its arguments and ever afterward made slavery an anachronism in the civilized world. An enormous sale of this book naturally followed, for where "Uncle Tom's Cabin" was known, it was read with avidity. Ninety thousand copies were published in the United States in one month. For years, the call was scarcely diminished.

With the interest which naturally centres about a human being who has done a great good to the race, moral, esthetic or intellectual, people at home and abroad began to wish to know something of the personality of the woman who was becoming famous in every land. Among the letters coming from England, many of which had given rise to pleasant correspondence, were those of Mrs. Follen, the ardent anti-slavery lecturer, the contemporary of Har-riet Martineau, and of late, while sojourning in England, the intimate companion of George Eliot. George Eliot wrote early in 1853—"Mrs. Follen showed me a delightful letter which she has had from Mrs. Stowe, telling all about herself. She begins by saying—'I am a little bit of a woman, rather more than forty, as withered and dry as a pinch of snuff, never very well worth looking at in my best days and now a decidedly used up article.' The whole letter is most fascinating and makes one love her."

Without seeing the author of "Uncle Tom's Cabin," George Eliot felt the force of her genial personality, and to those who have known her well, how the humor of this letter appears, accompanied in the writing, as it must have been, by the smile in the bright gray eyes and the comical contraction of the mouth, which went with all her similar sayings! It was hardly excusable, however, this little laugh at herself, for Harriet Beecher Stowe had a face which, without any feminine prettiness, was frequently beautiful in the highest sense and she possessed various personal attractions which might well be envied by women. Her nose was shapely and indicative of sensibility and courage, her eyes were strikingly bright, intelligent, searching and honest in their expression, her hair was abundant and curled about her face and in her neck, where it escaped from the knot in the back. Her mouth, the most characteristic of all the features, was mobile, with full lips, which contracted into the funny expression just mentioned, when she saw the ridiculous side of any event or made ready some terse answer to an amusing sally. She was scarcely five feet high and spare, even to thinness. Her hands were small, and it needed no deep student of palmistry, to see in their shape and movements, clear evidence of the directness, capability and judicial qualities of her mind. A friend who knew her intimately during the years of her greatest literary activity, says:

Mrs. Stowe was, like all people endowed with genius, variable in her moods. She was sometimes so angelic in sweetness that her plain face was fairly transfigured; you seemed to see her already in beatitude. At other times she was depressed and moody. I do not mean ill tempered, but either dejected or apparently indifferent.

When the "Key" had been put to press in the spring of

1853, Professor Stowe suggested to his wife that in answer
to the many letters, cordially inviting them to England,
they should take a summer trip across the ocean for pleasure, rest and recreation. He wanted to witness her enthusiasm over the historical monuments of the old world and
to renew with her, his pleasant visit of seventeen years before. Their daughters were at boarding school at New
Haven, the two older boys were capable little fellows of
twelve and fourteen who would take pride in good behavior
under the charge of friends, and little Georgiana and baby
Charlie were placed in care of relatives.

Professor and Mrs. Stowe, with a party of four others, Mrs.
Beecher, widow of George Beecher, and her son George, her
brother Mr. Wm. Buckingham, and Rev. Chas. Beecher, sailed
from New York for Liverpool about the first of April, 1853.
After a voyage which was called "a good run," but which
proved rather unpleasant at least to Mrs. Stowe, who suffered the peculiar aggravations of sea sickness, and afterwards gave a most amusing description of it,—a description
that proves the whole world kin, under the unmerciful
action of the elements,—they came in sight of the Irish
coast and saw the reef where the Albion was wrecked.
This was the ship which was sunk carrying down every
passenger but one, a distinct memory in Harriet Beecher
Stowe's mind, having engulfed with her sister Catherine's
lover, all the hope and brightness of her father's household. Up the Mersey they sailed to Liverpool, in time to
hear the church bells of Sunday morning pealing their call
to service.

While they were making inquiries as to the best
hotel, they were accosted by a young gentleman who

introduced himself as the son of Mr. Edward Cropper of Dingle Bank. Mr. Cropper had been one of the most efficient supporters of anti-slavery in Liverpool. His wife was daughter of the great Lord Chief Justice Denman, who was also thoroughly devoted to the cause of freedom, and their whole social circle was composed of sympathizers in the cause which the author of " Uncle Tom's Cabin " had so powerfully espoused.

Their son's wife was a daughter of Dr. Arnold of Rugby, and sister to the eminent literary critic, whose works have become classic, and who a short time ago suddenly died while on a visit to her at "The Dingle." The acquaintance of Mr. and Mrs. Cropper had been made by correspondence, and Mrs. Stowe was gratefully impressed by their hospitable greeting and invitation to their home. Much to the astonishment of the Stowe party there was found quite a crowd of people on the wharf, who seemed to direct their attention to them, and bowed, saying " Welcome to England" " Welcome Mrs. Stowe!" and made a double line of eager figures and glad faces as they passed to the carriage. As a rule they stood very quietly, and looked very kindly, but with an evident determination to look, which was a matter of wonder to the Americans. The carriage was blocked for a time by other vehicles and the crowd pressed about the carriage, healthy, rosy, pleasant faced men and women, with nothing but kindness and pleasant curiosity in every face. The author began slowly to understand the import of this assemblage and was much affected by it, saying "It seemed as if I had not only touched the English shore, but felt the English heart."

Two miles out of town was "The Dingle," the beautiful

home of their unseen friends. Here they were met with the generous hospitality for which England has always been celebrated, in this case intensified by the enthusiastic interest and unusually demonstrative feeling which had been aroused for the author of "Uncle Tom's Cabin."

But this, Mrs. Stowe did not fairly comprehend and, as always, unconscious of herself, attributed all the amenities to the natural kindness of the good people and sat down in her pleasant apartment, before an open fire, with a sense of perfect comfort and rest, which was a realization of home.

With her passion for trees and flowers, she felt a very rapture over the ivies, and climbing vines, which were so green and full at the early season, and looking at the hedges, and the holly trees with their glossy leaves, the American woman said to herself "Ah! Really this is England!" She made rapid acquaintance with a real English "robin redbreast" which is not half as large and debonair as our bird of the same name, but he was the identical "cock robin" renowned in song and story, one who was undoubtedly a lineal descendant of the poor fellow whose death and burial are so vivid a memory of our childish hours.

While the Stowes were at dinner with the Cropper family, who in consideration of their fatigue had arranged a quiet meal with them, a sister-in-law from next door, another Mrs. Cropper, came to invite Professor and Mrs. Stowe to a breakfast at her house the next day. After a night's rest they dressed, remembering the invitation to breakfast, but without the slightest idea of anything but a quiet family party, when to their astonishment, they found assembled a company of forty guests, the ladies sitting with their bonnets on, as for a call. With her innate grace and

true culture it was impossible for Mrs. Stowe to feel more
than a momentary embarrassment, at customs which were
strange to her. The Stowes could take themselves for
granted, and with the ease, begotten of quiet self respect and
consciousness of a knowledge of the great essentials in
social intercourse, they never failed to impress people as
being well bred, and grounded in courtesy.

Mrs. Stowe took her seat at the table, by the side of one
of the most distinguished divines of the established church in
Liverpool. The Rev. Dr. McNeile, at the request of the
hostess, who begged him to express to Mrs. Stowe the hearty
congratulations of the first meeting of friends in England, in a few cordial and sincere words, felicitated her and
the company upon the advent of the wonderful book she had
written, and earnestly welcomed her to the ranks of their
workers for the cause of freedom.

Mrs. Stowe was much surprised and moved, and with the
friendly and admiring eyes of the company upon her, could
only bow and make a sign to her husband to answer for
her, which he did, giving a brief history of the writing of
the book and a statement of the condition of affairs and
public opinion in the United States. He answered various
questions put by Dr. McNeile for the edification of the
company, and the event proved a most interesting and profitable exchange of ideas and sentiments.

In rare simplicity and the unconsciousness of self personality, which is only possible to great souls, Professor
Stowe and his wife sustained their part in the conversation
to the admiration and respect of the company and received the
honors of the occasion with a quiet dignity well befitting

an eminent professor of theology and a woman who had written the greatest book of the day.

When the breakfast was over Mrs. Stowe went to the door to find an array of bright eyed, rosy checked, neatly dressed children, who belonged to what was called the "Ragged School" of Mrs. E. Cropper, who under the direction of their teacher, broke out into a cheery song, and after some interesting exercises evinced great eagerness to speak to Mrs. Stowe. She said in a letter, "All the little rogues were quite familiar with Topsy and Eva, and *au fait* in the fortunes of Uncle Tom; so that being introduced as the maternal relative of these characters, I seemed to find favor in their eyes."

There were speeches by some of the guests, and the children dispersed with enthusiastic cheers.

After the children had gone there came a succession of calls, which lasted until dinner time. They were some from very aged people, veterans in the anti-slavery cause, and from every one, came fervent expressions of hope for abolition in America. It was not until after dinner that Mrs. Stowe was able to take a quiet stroll in the grounds of "The Dingle," which she gladly prolonged into the long twilight. Two little boys joined her, offering to act as squires and in her conversation with them she learned that one, was Joseph Babington Macaulay, and that Uncle Tom Macaulay was a prime favorite with the young people. Again the wild flowers claimed the loving attention of the daughter of the Litchfield hills, and she noted the English daisy, not like our own with " Its wide plaited ruff and yellow centre" but "The wee, modest, crimson tipped flower" which Burns loved, and was there called by various names, among them, the mountain daisy. Then there was in the dingley dells, the primrose of the poets, that of Wordsworth and Motley and Shakespeare and all the rest; such a flower, Mrs. Stowe once said " as Mozart and Raphael would have loved." The blue bell and the gorse or furze, and many another modest plant caught her observant eye, and was welcomed to her heart which throbbed so warmly for every creature, and increased in fervor as the object was modest, or by others undervalued.

The following day the Stowes were driven out to Speke Hall and saw for the first time a really ancient pile with its environs full of historical interest. In visiting its gloomy, armor-hung rooms, in passing through its haunted chambers, peering through the latticed windows and looking into its cavernous fireplaces, stone court yards, and dried wells, Mrs. Stowe exclaimed " If our Hawthorne could conjure up such a thing as the "Seven Gables" in one of our prosaic country towns, what would he have done if he had lived here!"

They entered a congenial atmosphere in the society of Liverpool, for the anti-slavery question had been from the very first, in England, a deeply religious movement. She found it difficult to make the good people, who considered it a matter of Christian principle, understand how conscientious Americans could allow political considerations to overrule their feeling of right and justice. The attitude of Christian ministers at the South, was to English divines utterly inconceivable. How much more inconsistent, seemed the stand taken by the people of the North, and especially New England!

The author of "Uncle Tom's Cabin" explained that the

most plausible view, and that which seemed to have the most force with good men, was one which represented slavery as a sort of wardship, by which an inferior race was brought under the watch and care of those who might lead them into Christianity. But when Dr. McNeile inquired if religious instruction was customary through the South and on the plantations, she was forced to confess that although systematic religious instruction was enjoined upon the masters by different denominations, the poor creatures, naturally of a religious temperament, were often left to work out their own salvation, while the advanced and cultured people escaped the twinges of conscience by shutting their eyes to the abuses and restrictions of the system.

Liverpool had originally been to the anti-slavery cause, what New York was, at the time of Mrs. Stowe's visit. Its commercial interests had been as largely implicated in the slave trade, and the virulence of its opposition to the leaders of the abolition movement was as bitter and uncompromising. But slavery in England had been abolished, and Mrs. Stowe found herself immeasurably cheered and encouraged by the social upholding of her prayerfully pondered convictions.

Professor and Mrs. Stowe went by invitation into Liverpool to attend a meeting of anti-slavery sympathisers. It was the Liverpool Ladies Anti-Slavery Association and presumably a modest affair, but to their surprise they found a great hall, packed with people, who greeted them with prolonged applause and the Chairman, A. Hodgson, Esq., opened the proceedings with an address to Mrs. Stowe, which ended with a very remarkable presentation. He told how Lord Shaftsbury had proposed and carried through a plan for a testimonial to the author of " Uncle Tom's Cabin " and stated that the December previous, a few ladies met to consider the best plan to obtain signatures in Liverpool to an address to the women of America on the subject of negro slavery. The expression of feeling had been very general, contributions from one penny upwards having been received. There were twenty-one thousand, nine hundred and fifty-three signatures. Of these, twenty thousand and more, had been obtained in Liverpool and the others were sent from London by friends who preferred their form of address. The speaker said it was given as an expression of their grateful appreciation of Mrs. Stowe's valuable services in the cause of the negro, as a token of admiration for the genius, and of high esteem for the philanthropy and Christian feeling which animated her great work, " Uncle Tom's Cabin."

Again Professor Stowe arose to return thanks for his wife. He spoke eloquently and with magnetic force, being often interrupted by applause. His address gave abundant testimony of his thorough culture and clear discernment of the signs of the times. His account of the feeling in America was heard with intense interest, and his entire speech so befitted the occasion and charmed the hearers that he no longer remained, even in their eyes, in the shadow of his wife's greatness, but stood forth a commanding figure upon the arena of the world's advancement. He was dignified in his personal appearance, his voice was pleasant and his language well chosen. He was fifty years of age, being some nine years the senior of his wife. He was of medium height, with a well proportioned and erect figure. The massive dome of his head rose high from the ears and overhung his kindly, piercing eyes with heavy, slightly grizzled brows, while his hair which was thinning on the crown, fell in soft waves upon his neck. He was a grand looking man, appearing every inch the eminent scholar and professor of Theological Literature that he was.

More speeches were made by the Rev. C. M. Birrell, Sir George Stephen, and others, all replete with enthusiastic admiration and respect for the American author, and the joy that comes from interchange of intellectual gifts and kind feeling, with worthy confreres.

Another invitation called them to Liverpool, to a meeting in a large residence of Anti-Slavery advocates, and there Professor Stowe being called upon, made some significant remarks on the general subject, and suggested that the free part of the world could if they would, withhold their support to slavery by refusing to buy the cotton which was the product of slave labor. His ideas were seriously considered by a number of guests who were prominent in the Cotton Exchange. When the party was dispersing the lady of the house told Mrs. Stowe that the servants had asked to see her, and accordingly she held a brief reception, which was equally gratifying to them and to her. They had all read "Uncle Tom's Cabin" and were full of sympathy, and she found them a good looking, intelligent class, quite superior to those employed in similar service in the United States. Here the housekeeper begged for her autograph, which was cordially given. She especially remarked and commended their manners adding, "Everybody's manners are more defferential in England than in America," a product of the monarchical system and its culture, which she found a pleasing contrast to the independence of republican manners, which so often amounts to rudeness.

The day before leaving Liverpool the Stowes were invited to meet the ladies of the Negro's Friend Society, and when they left the city a large party of ladies and gentlemen accompanied them to the station, whither flowers and other remembrances were sent, by numerous admiring friends. From Liverpool to Glasgow they went by train, and as they approached the Scottish soil, Mrs. Stowe began to feel all the affectionate desire to tread the sturdy earth of Caledonia which had for years been an ever recurring and enthusiastic wish to her. There came in the very air, and in the look of the north country.side, the vivid remembrance of the book of "Views of Scotland," which lay upon her mother's table, and over which she spent so many happy, dreamy hours, when a child. The Scotch ballads began to tune afresh in her a mind, the songs of Burns which had been a household treasure since her impressionable youth, and the enchantments of Scott, which were joyfully felt in early years but more fully realized with the enlarged powers of maturity, bore in upon her, inciting an ecstatic anticipation which she half feared was not to be realized.

They left Liverpool with hearts a little tremulous with feeling, surcharged with the sympathy and precious friendships they had formed; but the party of six, which just filled the compartment, was a merry and an intelligent one, and regrets were forgotten in present and anticipated pleasures.

Mrs. Stowe remarked that the sight of English scenery gave a new understanding of the spirit and phraseology of

English poetry and quoted those beautiful lines from Milton's L'Allegro, beginning—

> "Straight mine eye hath caught new pleasures
>   While the landscape round it measures;
>   Russet lawns and fallows gray,
>   Where the nibbling flocks do stray."

as an instance out of many passages in literature which once on English ground, start into new significance.

Mrs. Stowe, fatigued from the sight seeing and fêting of the past week, ensconsed herself in a corner of the compartment to sleep, but was wakened near Lancaster to see the castle built by John of Gaunt in the reign of Edward III., and soon Carlisle, (that of Scott's ballad, in the song for Albert Graeme in the Lay of the Last Minstrel) was seen. Historical reminiscences came thick to her mind, or were discussed by the party, and accounts of the conversation, in which merry making, humorous observations, and earnest reflections were interspersed, give one the impression of an ideal traveling party.

Gretna Green, the Mecca of English runaway lovers, the scene of many romantic marriages, sympathetic Gretna Green, which has winked at the escapades of many distinguished wedding parties, was passed, and they were on Scottish soil. This, and a glimpse of Solway Frith naturally suggested young Lochinvar, and the travelers wondered how many authors it would take to enchant our country from Maine to New Orleans as every foot of ground is enchanted there in Scotland. The sun went down and night drew on, but they were in Scotland and Scotch ballads, Scotch tunes, and Scotch literature held sway. They sang "Auld Lang Syne," "Scots who ha' wi' Wallace Bled," and "Bonnie Doon" and then changing the metre came out strong upon "Dundee," "Elgin," and "Martyrs." They gave full range to the enthusiasm of coming to Scotland for the first time, and Mrs. Stowe, always his ardent admirer, sighed, "Ah, how I wish Walter Scott were alive."

At Lockerby, where the real "Old Mortality," that is, the person who stood for the character, is buried, the train stopped and in the darkness outside, they became aware of a throng of people and broad Scotch tongues inquired for Mrs. Stowe. She went to the window. There were men, women, and children, and hand after hand was extended to her, while hearty words of welcome came from their honest hearts. This reception, which was peculiarly grateful to her who had so warm a heart for this country, affected Mrs. Stowe deeply and she says she shall never forget the thrill of their words, "Ye're welcome to Scotland," and the "Gude nights," as they rolled away from the station. By some mysterious divination, people at other stopping places had been advised of their coming, and the responsive woman shook hands, thanked the people, waved a towel instead of her handkerchief, more than once in her excitement, and sat down, wiping tears from her glad eyes, amid the irrepressible exclamations and gratified wonderment of her companions. Many times through the night were they thus pleasantly aroused, and came into Glasgow in the early morning with the flames from the great chimneys of the numerous iron works lighting the sky with a lurid glare. Sleepily recalling the picturesque times when the country was so lighted by the fires which the marauding Highlanders had set on various hills of the Lowlands, and the song of Rhoderick Dhu—

"Proudly our pibroch has thrilled in Glen Fruin,
And Banmachor's groans to our slogan replied;
Glen Luss and Ross Dhu. they are smoking in ruins,
And the best of Loch Lomond lies dead on her side."

They were driven to the hospitable mansion of Mr. Baillie Paton, and speedily fell asleep in much needed rest. They awoke stiff and weary, but enjoyed the viands set forth at a Scotch breakfast. They were indeed in "the land of cakes."

There was porridge, and herring and bannock, and besides, many other good things, but these were quite too well known to be considered by the guests, who were saturated with a Scotch humor. Their host was a member of the city council and the one whose speech at a public meeting had led to their invitation from the Mayor to visit the city. After breakfast, callers began to arrive.

Among the first, a friend of the family with her three beautiful children, the youngest of whom was the proud bearer of a handsome album containing a pressed collection of the sea mosses of the Scottish coast. Knowing Mrs. Stowe's passionate fondness for natural beauties, from hillside, or meadow, sandy shingle or rock-bound shore, could anything have been more delicate and acceptable? Callers came and went, books and flowers and fruit were sent in. Deputations arrived of prominent citizens from Paisley, Greenock, Dundee, Aberdeen, Edinburgh, and Belfast,— every man full of deep enthusiasm which yet was subdued by the dignity of his position and the importance of the occasion,—honest whole-souled, sturdy men they were, who pressed her small hand within their great palms, and went away moved with her simple manners, and the fact that they had spoken face to face with the author of "Uncle Tom's Cabin."

When the street door was not swinging with coming or departing visitors, the postman's ring opened it, and letters, so many that it took Professor Stowe from nine o'clock in the morning until two in the afternoon to read and answer them in the briefest manner, drifted upon them. They were from all classes, high and low, rich and poor, the cultured and illiterate, in every style of writing, composition and stationery; some mere outbursts of feeling, many of advice, requests for locks of hair, autographs, or written sentiments, and many, many invitations to go everywhere, stay any length of time, and see everything, in Scotland. Mrs. Stowe has said this day seemed like a dizzy, confused dream. The tax upon her feelings and nervous system was even greater than upon her physical strength. She was overwhelmed, and quite unnerved. The depth and intensity of her emotions all of pleasure, gratitude, responsive sympathy and inexpressible surprise, amounted to an unutterable sadness, just as joy, when inexpressible, finds vent in tears.

She afterwards said that she knew that she, as the individual who had called forth such an outburst was altogether inadequate and disproportionate to it, and realized that it was the great heart of universal brotherhood, surging forward in a huge sympathetic wave. That she received it, was the accident of the age.

How few great minds have so modest an estimate of the importance of their relation to worldly affairs!

In the afternoon Mrs. Stowe rode out with the Lord Provost, who is an officer of the same grade as our mayor or more strictly speaking, to the lords mayors in England, where the office is more dignified. On the way the streets

were blocked up by a crowd of people who had come out
to see her, but she was so worn out she could only bow
occasionally and hardly could walk through the cathedral.
This was the edifice where a part of the scene of Rob Roy
is laid and she aroused to its imposing aspect and observed
the statue of John Knox on the opposite eminence "with
its arm uplifted, as if shaking his fist at the old cathedral
which in life he vainly endeavored to battle down."

In consequence of her over exertions Mrs. Stowe was
the next day so ill as to need the attendance of a physician,
and remained in bed all day, uninformed of the stream of
callers and squall of letters which came, but she arose and
dressed at night for she "had engaged to drink tea with
two thousand people."

Among their distinguished new found friends, were Rev.
Dr. and Mrs. Wardlaw, who called for Mrs. Stowe and took
her with them in their carriage to the great hall where the
meeting was to take place.

This occasion, so unique and so very Scotch in many of
its features, is worthy of a description. A great crowd surrounded the building, through which they with some difficulty made their way, as every one pressed and jostled and
bore down another's shoulders and craned his neck to get a
glimpse of the little lady who was the object of so many
honors. Yet we may well believe that idle curiosity was
not their chief impelling motive. It was the author of
"Uncle Tom's Cabin" which they had all read, the mother of
gentle "Eva" and "St. Clare and "Miss Ophelia" and
"Topsy" poor "Uncle Tom," whom they would see, even if
they had to step on a fellow's toes to do it. For that offense
could be righted later, and the chance to see Mrs. Stowe

10

might never occur again, and Jock and Sandie and Tullie and Robin were as good naturedly rude as it was in their kind natures to be. Could one be much offended with them? Surely the woman whom they detained, had no impatience in her heart, at this most flattering annoyance. Once inside the hall Mrs. Stowe found herself in a dressing-room with Mrs. Wardlaw, shaking hands with a great many ladies who pressed into the apartment. They then passed into a gallery fronting the audience which arose with cheers as the party took their seats.

Many narrow tables were stretched the whole length of the spacious hall, which were set with cups and saucers, biscuit, and tea cakes, and at the proper time, attendants passed the fragrant decoction, so that without the least confusion they all literally took tea together. Mrs. Stowe's table, at which were Mrs. Wardlaw, ministers of the different churches and ladies and gentlemen of the Glasgow Anti-Slavery Society, under whose auspices the "tea" was given, was stretched across the gallery and they drank tea there "in sight of all the people."

Mrs. Stowe was much pleased and amused by the unusual character of the entertainment, and has since said, "It seemed to me such an odd idea, I could not help wondering what sort of a tea-pot that must be, in which all this tea for two thousand people was made. Truly, as Hadji Baba says, I think they must have had the 'father of all tea-kettles' to boil it in. I could not help wondering if old mother Scotland had put two thousand teaspoonfuls of tea for the company, and one for the tea-pot, as is our good Yankee custom."

After tea, the whole assemblage sang together some

verses of the seventy-second Psalm in the old Scotch version. Then the speeches began, the Rev. Dr. Wardlaw leading in a stirring, and witty address, in all respects appropriate to the occasion and the theme of nearest interest to every one, the cause, the woman, and the book.

When Professor Stowe rose to reply, the hall shook with vociferous applause. He thanked them for Mrs. Stowe, and when, in reference to the book which had so wonderfully taken hold of the people, he said he could not imagine how any written work could have elicited such expressions of attachment, that he was inclined to think it had not been written at all—he "spected it grew," the tremendous cheers from the two thousand throats and the waving of hundreds of handkerchiefs testified, as no assurances could have done, to the familiarity of the crowd with the book, and their irrepressible delight in the character of Topsy, whom for the moment he quoted.

Dr. Stowe's speech most pleasantly touched the various sensibilities of the audience, and his periods were always closed with cheers, laughter, or earnest cries of "Hear, Hear." More speeches followed, and a second service of fruit, grapes, oranges and sweet cakes, was served, as the tea had been.

It is easy to see what a strain this unexpected and overflowing mead of praise, this constant reception of good will and enthusiastic friendliness, this spirited discussion of the heart-breaking issues she had been dwelling upon intently for more than two years, must have been to Mrs. Stowe, who went abroad for rest and recuperation for an already over-taxed constitution. She was so nearly prostrated that she withdrew from the meeting before it closed, but happily was somewhat resuscitated by a long night's rest.

The next day they rode to Bothwell Castle, once the residence of the black Douglas, and afterwards to the famous Bothwell Bridge which Scott has immortalized. Then to the elegant mansion which in former days belonged to Lockhart, the son-in-law of Sir Walter Scott. In this house "Old Mortality" was written. After their return from the morning excursion, the party were entertained at luncheon and the splendor of the hot house flowers which adorned the table, elicited Mrs. Stowe's special admiration.

In the evening there was another soiree, proposed by the working classes, to give admission to many who had not been able to purchase tickets to the "tea" of the evening before. The arrangements and entertainments were the same as those of the previous evening, but this was, if possible the more interesting occasion to Mrs. Stowe, as it brought together just the class she was anxious to meet. As she sat in the gallery and looked over the audience, she saw what appeared very like a similar gathering in America and remarked what has so often since been noted, the resemblance of the Scotch middle classes to the average New Englander. There was the same quiet good taste in dress, the same air of self respect and honesty, the same plain and a little hard featured though earnest expression, of countenance. It is only in the middle classes that peculiarities, and national differences or resemblances can be traced, for culture and the highest civilization deprive the highest class of mind of nationality, and what it gains in cosmopolitan air and expression, it loses in characteristic individuality.

She also found with some surprise, that Walter Scott was not the popular favorite they had supposed. Allusions to "Bannockburn," and "Drumclog," never failed to bring down the house, but mention of the great Sir Walter met with but cool response. The Stowe party discussed this matter afterwards and wondered at it, but came to the conclusion that it was because he belonged to a past age and not to a coming one, and that hope which springs eternal in the human breast, looking ever and always to the future, spontaneously answered to the voice which pointed forward. Scott's writings partook largely of the spirit of the times in which they were written. He was inclined, by the leading strings of family and ancestral greatness, to retrospection. He represented one pole, that of aristocracy, while Burns was at the apex of the other, or represented democracy, which meant humanity. Burns was instinctively for the people, as Tolstoi is intellectually and religiously persuaded of their needs and rights. "Uncle Tom's Cabin" combined and grandly embodied, this living sympathy with all men, and marvelously touched the universal heart.

CHAPTER VII.

MRS. STOWE IN SCOTLAND. SAIL DOWN THE CLYDE. ENTHU-
SIASTIC RECEPTION FROM THE COMMON PEOPLE. RECEP-
TION AT EDINBURGH BY THE LORD PROVOST, MAGISTRACY
OF THE CITY, AND COMMITTEES OF ANTI-SLAVERY SOCIE-
TIES. RECOGNIZED BY RIOTOUSLY EXPRESSIVE STREET
BOYS. THE GREAT EDINBURGH MEETING, AND SCOTCH
PENNY OFFERING IN BEHALF OF THE AMERICAN SLAVES.
INSCRIPTION UPON THE MASSIVE SALVER WHICH BORE A
THOUSAND GOLDEN SOVEREIGNS. HOSPITALITIES AT ABER-
DEEN. GREAT PUBLIC MEETING AND PRESENTATION TO
THE AUTHOR OF UNCLE TOM'S CABIN. DUNDEE OVATION,
AND PRESENTATION OF WORKS OF LOCAL AUTHORS. AN-
OTHER SOIREE AT EDINBURGH, GIVEN BY WORKING MEN.
VISIT TO ABBOTSFORD, DRYBURGH AND MELROSE ABBEYS.
THE CAUSE OF FREEDOM AND TEMPERANCE ONE IN SCOT-
LAND. GREAT TEMPERANCE MEETINGS. ARRIVAL AT
LONDON. THE LORD MAYOR'S DINNER. DISTINGUISHED
GUESTS WHO UNITED IN HONORS TO MRS. STOWE. DINNER
WITH THE EARL OF CARLISLE. LONDON GIN PALACES.

On the 17th of April the Stowe party, with a large company of friends which quite filled the small steamer, went
for a sail down the Clyde. Dunbarton Castle with the romantic shades of the great Wallace, made classic by the
pen of Miss Porter; the Leven—the identical "Leven
water" of song and story—the old seat of the Earls of

150

Glencairn which recalled Burn's most eloquent "Lament for James, Earl of Glencairn," and then old Cardross Castle, where it is said Robert Bruce breathed his last, made the excursion one of exquisite delight and excitement, for every name suggested a poem, and every scene recalled a history in prose or verse. Mrs. Stowe, who had a most remarkable verbal memory, needed only a suggestion to recall entire poems, which she recited with excellent effect. They dreamed of David Deans and Jeanie and Effie, and half expected to see them, hereabout. They were not to be seen, but at one of the landings there presented himself, a broad-shouldered Scotch farmer who stood some six feet two inches in height, who told Mrs. Stowe he had read her book and had walked six miles to see her, and declared he "would do it any day." So massive and ponderous did he seem, that he represented not illy a bit of the rugged landscape, as if the very rocks and burns had come to greet her. She said—"When I put my hand into his great prairie of a palm, I was as a grasshopper in my own eyes." He was one of the Duke of Argyle's farmers and, she thought, were all his henchmen of this pattern he might be able to speak to the enemy in the gates, to some purpose.

They landed at Gare Loch, which is but a bay made by a widening of the river Clyde, and went through the little village of Row. As they walked along, a carriage which came after them, stopped and a bunch of primroses fell at Mrs. Stowe's feet. She picked it up, and turning saw two ladies, who asked if she were the author of "Uncle Tom's Cabin!" Being answered in the affirmative, they begged her so earnestly and gracefully to come under their roof and take refreshment, that leaving the rest of the party, Professor and

Mrs. Stowe entered the carriage and were driven to a charming villa which, surrounded by flower gardens and pleasure grounds, stood at the head of the lake. Their hostesses told her that being much confined to the house by illness and one by lameness, they never expected to see her, but considered this encounter nothing less than Providential kindness to them. Seeing that she needed rest, they made her retire to a cozy bedroom, where in absolute quiet, so grateful to her tired senses, she slept for a time.

Leaving Row, it was decided that they would ride back to Glasgow through the places which line the river side, and Dr. Robson and Lady Anderson were their carriage companions. Mrs. Stowe has humorously narrated how awkwardly she acquired the custom of addressing people by their titles, and says she usually said "Mr." or "Mrs." and then begged pardon, and corrected it to "Lord" or "Lady," making a general hitch in the conversation. Lady Anderson, who was a hearty, genial Scotch woman, appreciated her difficulty and quite enjoyed the mistakes, entering mirthfully into the spirit of the hour, which was all of pleasantness and good feeling. News of their coming preceded them along the way, and people appeared at their doors, bowing, smiling, waving their handkerchiefs, and many times was the carriage stopped by burly men, and blushing women, who would shake hands; and young girls and children, who literally heaped the carriage with flowers.

Was there ever anything like it? Had any beautiful queen a more triumphal passage through a country, than this plain American woman, in her happy journey through Scotland? It was a queenship by Divine right, indeed! A spontaneous crowning of one who stood upon a throne made of the hearts of the people, which were so willingly cast at her feet at the touch of love and sympathy for all men, which breathed throughout her wonderful work !

At every village, and at wayside inns, they found people waiting to see them pass, and food and drink enough for the most giantesque gourmand, were offered and pressed upon them at scores of hospitable houses, whose inmates came into the road to speak to them. Mrs. Stowe has said of this welcome: "What pleased me was, that it was not mainly from the rich, nor the great, but the plain common people. The butcher came out of his stall, and the baker from his shop, the miller dusty with his flour, and the blooming comely young mother with her baby in her arms, all smiling and bowing with that hearty intelligent friendly look, as if they knew we would be glad to see them."

Was it strange? Had they not abundant assurance of that, in the spirit and tone of her written characters? Had it not been felt in these organ tones of deep feeling, which set vibrating the delicate sympathetic strings, which are common to all classes? Sunday was a day of rest, mostly spent in bed by Mrs. Stowe, though at evening she strolled out with her husband along the river Kelvin, quite to its junction with the Clyde. They looked over to the south and imagined, far out of sight, the cottage of Burns on the bonny banks of Ayr.

The Stowes left Glasgow and reached Edinburgh after a two hours ride. At the station was a great crowd of people, among whom, like white flecks upon a summer cloud, appeared white bonnets and the drab dresses of many Friends. The lord provost or mayor met them at the door of the car and presented them to the magistracy of the city, and the committees of the Anti-Slavery societies. They entered the carriage with the lord provost and their hostess Mrs. Wigham, and drove away, with the crowd following with shouts and cheers. They drove to the Castle, to Holyrood, to the University, to the hospitals, and through many of the principal streets, and met everywhere loud and enthusiastic greetings from the people, while some boys, with the pertinacious and enterprising spirit of our own modern street urchins, for a long time strove to keep up with the carriage. " Heck !" cried one of them breathlessly to his earnest companions, " That's her ; see the curls."

It appeared that the artists and engravers who had met the public demand for her pictures, had depended principally on that feature as a striking characteristic, and the boys rightly thought there could be no mistake here. The boys ran riot that day, and vastly enjoyed themselves in giving utterance, to what must have equalled the suppressed vociferation of the whole city. How quick are they to sense the public feeling ! how nice are their instinctive perceptions of false pretenses or real worth ! how embarrassingly free are their expressions of opinion upon the most personal matters ! But boys, take them as they run, have their hearts in the right place and they sprang up joyfully to greet the author of " Uncle Tom's Cabin."

Mrs. Wigham, with whom Mrs. Stowe was staying, was most thoughtful of her health and nursed her and ministered to her slightest wish with tender care. The family were Friends, who without ostentation, enjoyed all that wealth and culture could bring to home enjoyment. The amount of letters found waiting for them in Edinburgh was, if anything, more appalling than that in Glasgow. Among them was one from the beautiful Duchess of Sutherland, and another from the Earl of Carlisle, both desiring to make appointments to meet them when they came to London. There was a very interesting note from the Rev. Charles Kingsley and his wife, and from many other distinguished people and divines, and scores more, which were chiefly interesting as indicative of the public mind upon the themes which most concerned the author of "Uncle Tom's Cabin."

One was from a shoemaker's wife with some very fair verses, many contained gifts, others accompanied flowers, which they had learned were among the most precious gifts to be offered Mrs. Stowe.

On the evening of April 20th transpired the great Edinburgh meeting, accounts of which filled the Scottish and English papers for some days after. It was in some respects a repetition of what had passed in Glasgow; the hall was surrounded by a dense crowd who blocked the entrance and testified the same respectful curiosity to see Harriet Beecher Stowe. The dressing-room was filled with people who wished to meet her, the hall was packed with a great crowd of people from whom arose such a thunderous peal of applause when Mrs. Stowe entered, that for a few moments she was stunned and almost overcome, but recovering from the strange sensation, she saw that every one looked so heartily pleased, and felt so sensibly the all-pervading atmosphere of geniality and sympathy which rushed as a mighty wind to meet her, that she became calm, and took her seat with a new happiness and feeling of home welcome. Note the rare simplicity of a woman so fêted, so honored, so worshiped by the whole people of a foreign country, who wrote to her friends and *believed what she said*—"After all I consider that these cheers and applause, are Scotland's voice to America, a recognition of the brotherhood of the countries."

The Lord Provost opened the meeting by reading letters from a number of distinguished people who were unable to attend, among them Professor Blackie, the Earl of Buchan, Dr. Candish, and Sir W. Gibson Craig, all of whom were earnest sympathizers and regretted their enforced absence. There was a note from Lord Cockburn, so full of genuine good feeling to the cause, and the person they delighted to honor, that the meeting broke into applause. The Lord Provost then proceeded with his address of welcome, which was constantly applauded by the audience ; spoke of the address with signatures which was to be presented later in the evening, and also of what they had chosen to term a penny offering, in order that none might be deterred from contributing the smallest amount, which they desired to have used, through her instrumentality, as a means of miti- gating the horrors of slavery as they came under her per- sonal observation. The national penny offering which had been poured out in a stream of small sums, had amounted to a noble tribute, and was embodied in a thousand golden sov- ereigns on a magnificent silver salver which rested upon a stand, in full view of the audience. The salver, which was a massive vessel of sterling silver, with a wide border on which in an exquisite design were twined the shamrock, the rose and the thistle, as typical of the sympathy and co-operations of the people of Great Britain in the cause of Anti-Slavery, bore upon its surface, underneath the pile of shining coins, this inscription—

Presented to

Harriet Beecher Stowe,

in testimony of the high appreciation in which they

hold her as a woman,

as a Christian and the friend of

Humanity,

and in Memorial of her visit to this city and of

the presentation in gold of

The Scotch National

Penny Offering,

now placed upon it amounting to £1000 Sterling.

To be appropriated by Mrs. Stowe for

The Cause of the Slave.

Numbers, Chap. VI., Ver. 24, 25, 26.

Edinburgh, Apr. 20, 1853.

The Rev. Mr. Ballantyne, who presented it, gave the history of its collection, telling how the people of all grades and classes had contributed to it, many of the thousands of gifts coming from the homes of direst poverty, even the blind and sick bringing their penny.

The salver with its golden burden was received by Professor Stowe amid tremendous applause, and his speech that followed was a marvelous exposition of conditions in far away America, and the principles which should, and he doubted not would, in the future, however distant, overrule the sordid love of gain or mistaken political honor of the people.   Mrs. Stowe left long before the meeting was over, and from excess of emotion and deadly fatigue, did not sleep at all that night.

It may be said here, that this and other similar "offerings," which might have indeed proved an embarrassment of riches to a traveling party, were given to the care of friends to be shipped to America.   The money was judiciously and conscientiously employed to educate several former slaves, and the vessels of massive silver, remain precious souvenirs of these occasions.

One of the following beautiful days the Stowe party drove out to Craigmiller Castle, formerly one of the royal residences.   It was here that Mary Queen of Scots retreated after the murder of Rizzio, and the chroniclers say was heard day after day weeping, and wishing her unfortunate life ended.   Here Mrs. Stowe found some small daisies which a young friend told her were the "gowans" of Scotch poetry. There was a view of "Auld Reekie," Arthur's Seat, Salisbury Crags, and far down the Frith of

Forth, in the dim distance was seen Bass Rook, the cele-brated prison where the Covenanters were immured.

Bidding Edinburgh farewell, they took a train for Aber-deen. The application of old, poetic and historical names to railway stations, made the travelers smile and Mrs. Stowe recalled the humorous lines of whimsical Tom Hood, on a possible railroad through the Holy Land, an idea, by the way, which is not so new and strange to us of the present day, as it was forty or more years gone by. It was quite incongruous to ride swiftly up to a neat little station and hear "Bannockburn" called out by the guard, who unlocked doors, bustled about on the platform and signalled the engineer to get away, as unconcernedly as if just here were not the Marathon of Scotland, the place hallowed to warlike memories, and the air redolent of superhuman bravery and the death sighs of the warrior slain.

There was little but the hills and rocky glens to speak of this to modern travelers, but at Stirling still stood the castle, magnificently seated on a towering rock, looking worthy to have been the gathering place, as it was for many years, of Scotland's brilliant court. Here are laid the scenes, described with the minuteness and local color only possible to a Scottish poet and that poet Walter Scott, with his full, vivid freshness of diction, and pictures from the "Lady of the Lake" treasured in Mrs. Stowe's mind, were realized in fact, and seen as something long familiar and dear.

Still farther on, and appropriately surrounded by dark and solemn woods, stood Glamis Castle, the scene of the tragedy of Macbeth. Only glimpses could be seen from the

road, but those stimulated the imagination enough to temporarily transport them back through the ages to the rude
Saxon period, "When Knights were bold and Barons held
their sway," when witches held the fate of clans in their
warning voices and castles were stormed and taken by
sheer force of arms and personal brawn.

It was a long leap, but they came back to the 19th century, the Dee was soon crossed, and the city of Aberdeen
was reached late in the afternoon. The Lord Provost of
Aberdeen, met them (and, by the way, how very kind, and
gallant, and gifted in speaking, were all those Lords Provosts of the cities of Scotland,) and as they drove to the
house of good Mr. Cruikshank, a genial Friend, who was
to entertain them, he pointed out the places of interest, and
proved Aberdeen was not less gracefully represented by its
public officer than other cities of the land. An excellent,
simple supper was on the table awaiting them, and some
haste was needed, for a public meeting, another great demonstration, was awaiting them at the city hall. They, for
some reason, enjoyed this occasion with peculiar zest.

Mrs. Stowe was surrounded on the stage by a company of charming young ladies, one of whom presented
her with a beautiful bouquet, some of the flowers which
made a part of it, being pressed in an album and
treasured even to this day. There was some very
animated speaking, all ingeniously contriving, Mrs.
Stowe humorously remarked, "to blend enthusiastic
love and admiration for America, with detestation of slavery." The coast had reminded Mrs. Stowe of the rugged
rock-bound shore of the state of Maine, and the people
whom she saw at the Aberdeen meeting, seemed like the

plain, strong, warm-hearted folk of that New England community. Their physical make-up, no less than their moral convictions and sympathy with Americans who had stood up for right against oppression, made her exclaim that the children of the Covenanters and the children of the Puritans, were indeed of one blood.

They presented to Mrs. Stowe at this meeting a handsome offering, in behalf of the slaves, of gold coin in a beautifully embroidered purse.

The Americans were shown the town the next day. The Cathedral, the Bridge of Balgounie, built in the time of Robert Bruce which has a weird prophecy connected with it and was written of by Byron, and Kings College, were visited, and Mrs. Stowe made a study of the industrial school system which was carried on by philanthropic people of the city. She wrote letters home, explaining minutely the operation and benefits of the institution, and suggested that it held many valuable ideas for American communities.

They bade farewell to Aberdeen with real regret, and on the way to Dundee, at every station where the train stopped, were crowds of people who pressed about the author of "Uncle Tom's Cabin" with friendly greetings, with thanks in the name of humanity, with blessings upon her. Old Dundee was "all alive with welcome," and they went with the Lord Provost Mr. Thoms, to his residence, where a large party had been awaiting them for some time.

Apparently of "meetings" there was no end, and one densely crowded, full of enthusiasm and conducted as the others had been, was held that evening in the largest church of the city. When they came to the closing hymn Mrs.

Stowe hoped they would sing Dundee, but whether from modesty or because the old national and characteristic melodies had given way to modern ones, she was disappointed. They made a large contribution to the Scottish offering for the succor of American slaves; and presented Mrs. Stowe with a handsome collection of the works of the authors in Dundee.

The next morning there was a breakfast party, composed mostly of ministers and their wives. After breakfast the ladies of the Dundee Anti-Slavery Society called, and later the Lord Provost took the American guests out in his own carriage, to see the city. From Scottish and foreign papers which reported the proceedings wherever Professor and Mrs. Stowe appeared, are gleaned testimonials of the favorable impression every where produced by the personality of this American woman. Her sincerity, straightforward plain speaking and kind, affectionate spirit, took strong hold on the British heart, and the exhilaration of feeling which is often sadly lowered by sight of and contact with an idealized personality, was deepened and intensified in the true hearts, who saw in this woman one worthy of their love and admiration, in all respects eminently satisfying to every instinct as to how the author of such a book as "Uncle Tom's Cabin" should look and speak and feel.

They returned to Edinburgh, and attended another *soiree* of the workingmen of that city. It need not be dwelt upon, as it was quite of the nature of the one in Glasgow and served to show most gratifyingly, that the class who were coming into decided power in the future were beginning to understand themselves. Letters were received, urging Mrs.

Stowe to return to Dundee and Glasgow to attend meetings
in those cities, but the lack of time, and the limitations of
physical strength, obliged her to decline.

Professor Stowe and Chas. Beecher had agreed to go back
to Glasgow to speak at a Temperance Meeting given by the
students of Glasgow University. Professor Stowe remarked
that the address tendered them there was "particularly gratifying on account of its recognition of the use of intoxicating
drinks as an evil analagous to slave holding, and to be eradi-
cated by similar means." The rest of the party remained for
the purpose of seeing Abbotsford, and Dryburgh and Melrose
Abbeys. Finding herself in the region of the Ettrick, the
Yarrow and the Tweed, Mrs. Stowe instinctively turned to
her "Lay of the Last Minstrel," and while dreaming over
Scott's lines—

> "Call it not vain; they do not er.
> Who say that when the poet dies,
> Mute nature mourns her worshiper,
> And celebrates his obsequies."

the guard called out "Melrose" and they found it rained.
They moved with some haste, for they were to "do" the
three places in one day and as she wittily said, "There was
no time for sentiment; it was a business affair that must be
looked in the face promptly if we meant to get through.
Ejaculations of poetry could of course be thrown in, as William of Deloraine pattered his prayers while riding." Her
account of the visit as seen in a letter, is a delightful combination of the practical, reminiscent and appreciative, of
the poetic and picturesque, which is quite unrivalled in
modern travel letters, and might still serve as the pleasant-
est guide possible, to those interesting localities.

Walking back from Dryburgh through the village, they

saw a knot of respectable looking laboring men who conferred together, and cast curious glances towards them.
One at last approached and asked respectfully if that were
Mrs. Stowe. When she answered they all exclaimed heartily, "Madam, ye're right welcome to Scotland," and stood
with hats in hand, while the chief speaker begged them to
do him the favor to step into his cottage hard by, for a little
rest and refreshment after their ramble. To this they assented with alacrity, and entering the neat stone house, took
the comely wife by surprise. She bustled about to serve a
cup of tea, meanwhile lamenting that she could not have
had the best room open. They stayed long enough to talk
pleasantly with the husband and wife, to see their children
who came rushing in, rosy cheeked, from school, and hear
that they all know Topsy and Eva, the book having been
read aloud to the family by the "Gude Mon."

"Ah" said he, "such a time as we had, when we were
reading the book; whiles they were greeting, and whiles in
a rage."

Could the simple Scotchman have more perfectly described the condition of thousands who had read, and still
read, the book?

The day after they returned from Melrose they spent
riding about and had two engagements for the evening, one
at a party at the home of Mr. Douglas of Cavers and
another at a public Temperance *soiree*. The Laird who
entertained them was a man of good family, a large landed
proprietor, a zealous reformer and a devout Christian. At
his house the servants assembled in the main hall to meet
Mrs. Stowe and the Temperance meeting was large and conducted by distinguished people. All the clergymen of

Edinburgh were there, and Lady Carstairs, Sir Henry and Lady Moncrief, Dr. Guthrie, and Dr. John Brown, were among those presented to her.

In Scotland the cause of freedom and temperance seemed to be one; quite in contrast to the ideas of modern apostles of moral as well as physical free agency, who hotly claim that any restraint upon a man's right to make a beast of himself through alcoholic intemperance, directly controverts the sacred privileges of humanity. The principle of conservative non-interference in the wrongs of mankind "constitutional" or self inflicted, seemed not to have obtained in the British Islands. They saw not the reverse side of a national liberty which in America insisted upon (as it still insists) perfect liberty in soul-suicide, while then hesitating to object to the enslavement of a whole race. They looked with clear eyes through the quibbles which often envelop a vital question, straight to the principle of the greatest good to the greatest number, which is God's principle in the mighty laws of the universe.

The next day, Professor and Mrs. Stowe called upon many people, among them, Lord and Lady Gainsborough, who was one of the queen's household then staying at Edinburgh. They called upon Sir William Hamilton and his wife, and he and Professor Stowe were soon deep in discussions on German, English, Scotch and American metaphysics in which Dr. Stowe had a remarkable insight and was particularly well versed. Mrs. Stowe says that everywhere in good society, the conversation turned upon the condition of the laboring classes, and ideas and plans for their education and moral betterment were fashionable themes.

In spite of the rain which fell fitfully and hung in the air as a mist, Mrs. Stowe walked about the estate, and ran and scrambled to sightly points, seeing Roslin Castle in the distance and finding the ground in certain dells, spotted with yellow primroses. Then for the first time she saw the heather spreading over rocks and clinging about the gnarled roots of ancient trees. It was not in flower, as it blooms in July and August, and her Scotch friends were at a loss to understand her joy over its unobtrusive greenness.

After that, they went to see George Combe, the eminent physiologist, and then by special invitation to "Classic Hawthornden," whither Lady Drummond's carriage conveyed them.

So utterly worn out with sight-seeing and the excitement of the honors heaped upon them since their arrival at Liverpool were the Stowe party, that they resolved on leaving Edinburgh to seek some quiet retreat and, keeping their identity a secret, get somewhere "away from the madding crowd."

In a letter written to her brother Henry, Mrs. Stowe said, "remembering your Sunday at Stratford, I proposed that we should go there."

Their friend Mr. Joseph Sturge of Birmingham had cordially invited them to visit him. So, as Stratford was away from the line of the railroad they decided to stay with him, advising him of that intention in a note which enjoined the strictest secrecy as to their whereabouts. By Preston Pans, where was fought the celebrated battle by Dunbar, where Cromwell told his army to "trust in God and keep their powder dry;" through Berwick-on-Tweed and Newcastle-on-Tyne; by the old gates and towers of York, and in view of Durham Cathedral in the distance, they pursued their journey. At Newcastle and several other places, they were approached by friendly strangers who waited at the stations, many bringing bouquets of choice flowers.

As they had never seen Mr. Sturge it became an interesting question how they were to know him at the station at Birmingham, but Charles Beecher insisted that instinct would tell them, and in a few moments he pitched upon a cheerful middle-aged gentleman, with a decided though unobtrusive broad brim to his hat, and they were soon trotting away to his place at Edgbaston, feeling very snug and well content that they had so successfully eluded the pleasantly curious crowds, which everywhere else had greeted them in England and Scotland. Mr. Sturge was a zealous advocate of the anti-slavery cause, an ardent disciple of the principles of peace, and a warm friend of Elihu Burritt, the Connecticut man, known as the "learned blacksmith," who was then in Great Britain, preaching his doctrines of universal brotherhood.

The visit to Stratford was a most enjoyable one, filled with thoughts of the old days of tradition, and full of topics of present interest, all clustering about the home of the bard of Avon. On the way thither Mr. Sturge told Mrs. Stowe that there was a friend who wished very earnestly to see her and, willing as she always was to meet people who had a sincere interest in her and the great cause for which she was laboring, she stopped at a comfortable house which stood in pleasant grounds, and made a call upon an invalid woman who received her with deep emotion, even tears, and spoke of the sacredness and solemnity of the cause, which from its first conception in the times of Wilberforce and Clarkson had lain so near her heart. It was a memorable interview and Mrs. Stowe came away pleased and yet sorrowful, thinking how far from the universal feeling exhibited here, was the temper of the public mind in her own country.

The pleasure felt in traveling, in viewing nature, in meeting distinguished people, in seeing works of art, in musing over by-gone glories, is gauged and tempered by the capacity of the mind to receive impressions, to understand causes and effects, to reason out deductions based upon facts. How full of deep enthusiasm and appreciation was this visit of the Stowes, Charles Beecher, Mrs. George Beecher, her son and Mr. Buckingham to the home and burial place of Shakespeare, can only be realized with a knowledge of their rounded culture, and innate comprehension of the truly great in earthly things. Mrs. Stowe wrote most intelligently and eloquently of this visit, and, apropos of the recent agitation upon the authenticity of the plays attributed to Shakespeare, it may be noted that she said,— "I have often wondered at that inscription, that a mind so sensitive, that had thought so much, and expressed thought with such startling power on all the mysteries of death, the grave, and the future world, should have found nothing else to inscribe on his grave but this :—

'Good Friend for Jesus sake forbear,
To dig ye dust enclosed here.
Blest be the man that spares these stones,
And curst be he that moves my bones.'"

From Stratford they drove to Warwick, familiar to modern travelers, and then to Kenilworth, so full of associations of Elizabeth and Leicester, poor Amy Robsart and the rest. Then on to Coventry, with its cathedral and its precious tradition of Lady Godiva. This excursion through what is acknowledged to be the most picturesque part of England, quite fulfilled Mrs. Stowe's idea of the "old country." But in the evening they were again drinking tea in Mr. Sturge's cosy parlor in Birmingham, and Elihu Burritt came in. Mrs. Stowe described him at that time as in middle life, with fair complexion, blue eyes, and air of delicacy, and refinement of manners of great gentleness. Her conception of "the learned blacksmith" had, by natural association of ideas, been something altogether more ponderous and peremptory, but she listened with deep interest to the exposition of his plan of operations which tended towards universal good feeling, and peace and good will among nations and races, as between individual souls. His ideas, which seemed Utopian to many hard headed people, Mrs. Stowe testified had been of great effect in smoothing over international disagreements, in more than one instance, preventing ill considered war between England and France. Charles Beecher had been with Mr. Sturge during the previous day to a meeting of Friends, and the evening was passed in lively discussion of various correlative themes.

The fact that the author of "Uncle Tom's Cabin" was in Birmingham, could not long be suppressed, and the morning before she left, she met a circle of Friends who composed the Abolition society of the town, a guild which was of long standing, dating back to Wilberforce and Clarkson. A throng of friends accompanied them to the station, and greatly to their pleasure Elihu Burritt went with them on the train to London. Mrs. George Beecher and her son, who had gone on before them and taken lodgings near Rose Cottage in Walworth, where the Stowes were to be entertained, met them with the announcement that they were all invited to the Lord Mayor's dinner that night. "What," said Mrs. Stowe, "the Lord Mayor of London that I used to read about in Whittington and his Cat?" So strong and well adjusted was her mental ballast of child-lore, home associations and unexaggerated self-respect, that instead of feeling elated at the honor doubtless about to be offered her, she listened only to the echo in her ears of the old chime of youthful story, wherein all the bells of London rang so merrily, saying—

"Turn again Whittington,
Thrice lord mayor of London."

It was the annual dinner given to the judges of England by the lord mayor, and there were the whole English bar and hosts of distinguished people besides. The Stowes were accompanied by their hosts, Rev. and Mrs. Binney, and soon entered the Mansion House and a large illuminated hall supported by pillars. Chandeliers were glittering, servants with powdered heads and gold laced coats hurried to and fro, a throng of ladies and gentlemen in evening dress moved about within, in conversation which came to their ears through several rooms, in a polite din. Titled guests arrived and were announced, and the lord Chief Justice and the other eminent barristers, came in their black small clothes with swords by their sides, silk stockings and their three-cornered hats under their arms, many of them with their hair tied behind in small silk bags. Mrs. Stowe heard her name passed along from one lackey to the next until it came to the lord mayor's ears and they entered, being very gracefully received by him and the lady mayoress. Mrs. Stowe was recognized by many of the company and was instantly surrounded by eminent persons seeking an introduction. Among others Lord Chief Baron Pollock, a very dignified gentleman, dressed in black velvet, with frills of priceless, (and aristocratically dirty,) point lace at his bosom and wristbands, sat down by her, telling her he had been reading the legal part of the "Key to Uncle Tom's Cabin," remarking several decisions as having made a deep impression upon his mind. He said that nothing had ever given him so clear an idea of the essential nature of slavery. Soon the room was a perfect jam of legal and literary notabilities and there was scarce room to speak to the scores who were presented to the American party.

About ten o'clock dinner was announced, and they were conducted into a splendid hall where the tables were laid. The lord mayor and his wife, had on their right hand the judges and on their left the American Minister Mr. Ingersoll, while high "above the salt," and directly opposite to Charles Dickens, whom she then saw for the first time and was surprised to find so young, sat Mrs. Stowe. The business of toast drinking, which was reduced to the nicest possible system, began. After the usual loyal toasts, the health of the American Minister was proposed, to which Mr. Ingersoll responded handsomely, and the American legal profession received a very handsome compliment from Lord Chief Baron Pollock, who spoke particularly of Judge Story, making Mrs. Stowe's heart warm with responsive feeling.

Then Justice Talfourd proposed the *literati* of the two countries under the head of Anglo-Saxon Literature. He made a handsome allusion to "Uncle Tom's Cabin," and to Mr. Dickens' works, to which that gentleman replied in a graceful and humorous strain, giving Mrs. Stowe a full measure of appreciation and thanks.

They arose from the table about midnight, and the ladies withdrew to the drawing-room, where Mrs. Stowe, among other distinguished ladies, met Mrs. Dickens. Mrs. Stowe saw in Mrs. Dickens a good specimen of the genuine English woman; tall, large and well developed, with a fine healthy color and an air of cheerfulness and reliability. A friend whispered that she was as observing and fond of humor, as her husband. Plainly the shadow of the trouble that later separated her from him had not come upon her. It at least was not perceptible to the eyes of one who always looked for the bright and good things in life, where they could possibly be found. When the gentlemen joined them Mrs. Stowe had a pleasant conversation with Mr. Dickens and always retained a most favorable impression of him.

The Lord Mayor left the Mansion House to go to the House of Commons, and enthusiastic brother Charles Beecher proposed to "make a night of it" and follow him, but Mrs. Stowe found it necessary to get rest in sleep. They were not used to the London fashion of turning night into day, but she has since said that if she could but have had a relay of bodies to change as one puts on a fresh suit of clothes when one is used up, she would have been quite willing to go on sight-seeing forever.

The following morning Mrs. Follen, whom with her husband Dr. Follen, Mrs. Stowe had known in Boston as ardent abolitionists, who then lived at West End, called upon her and they had a long talk together. That evening the Stowes dined with the Earl of Carlisle. He had been in America and was one of the first and few English travelers who have viewed and written of this country with appreciation. Leaving such important matters as the breaking of a breakfast egg at the wrong end, to the Trollopes and a host of large minded visitors who have since discussed the manners and culture of Americans, Lord Carlisle discerned and interpreted the characteristic strength and possibilities of this growing country. He had not disguised his convictions on the anti-slavery question while in the United States, and wrote an introduction to an English edition of "Uncle Tom's Cabin." They drove to Lord Carlisle's in the usual drizzling London rain, crossing Waterloo Bridge, and began to realize something of the vast extent of the city. Altogether the most striking objects passed in this evening ride were the gin-shops, flaming and flaring in the most conspicuous positions, with plate glass windows and glaring lights, thronged with men, women and children drinking destruction. The number and size of these liquor saloons was apalling to the Americans, who saw in them an institution which was of greater detriment to the nation than that of slavery lately abolished; an institution, which under the banner of personal liberty permitted a voluntary enslavement of body and soul, more crushing and complete than any enforced servitude could ever possibly be; an institution beside which the institution of negro slavery it were as child's play to abolish, for while in one case the majority of mankind and the victims were joined against it, in this, the victims were its willing and persistent defenders and had with them the appetites and tendencies of all the lower moral nature of mankind.

CHAPTER VIII.

It was to be a family party at Lord Carlisle's, but it embraced such a noble company of titled men and women as is seldom seen, even in the best families of the English peerage. There was the beautiful Duchess of Sutherland and her sisters, Lady Dover, Lady Lascelles, and Lady Labouchere, the Earl of Burlington and the Duke of Devonshire, all near relatives of the host. The only person present not of the family, was Mrs. Stowe's discriminating reviewer and correspondent, Mr. Arthur Helps. She expected to see in him a venerable sage who contemplated life from the door of his hermit cell, but instead here was a genial young gentleman of not more than twenty-five,

174

who looked as if he might enjoy a joke as well as any man living, and it transpired that he did. Mrs. Stowe had the place of honor next to Lord Carlisle. Mr. Helps came next, and proved himself a very agreeable and amusing neighbor.

When the servant passed wine, it was observed that all of the Stowe party left their glasses untouched. The temperance question was raised, and the company showed much interest in the Maine law, then in force in that State. Later, in the drawing-room, Mrs. Stowe was presented to the aged Countess of Carlisle, the Earl's mother, a lady of great distinction and loveliness of character. The house was everywhere adorned with works of art by the best masters, and Mrs. Stowe often recalled to mind a Rembrandt which hung over the fireplace, and one or two Cuyps, which she thought might have been painted in America, so perfectly did they show the hazy atmosphere of our October days.

After the gentlemen rejoined them, there came the Duke and Duchess of Argyle and Lord and Lady Blantyre to pay their respects. These ladies were both the daughters of the Duchess of Sutherland. The Duke of Argyle, whose place had been seen in Scotland, was then a member of the British cabinet, though at a very early age, and had already distinguished himself as a writer of various works bearing upon political economy, as well as ecclesiastical history.

They formed an intelligent company, and the conversation fell upon American men of letters. Particularly were Emerson, Longfellow, and Hawthorne admired, and Prescott seemed to be a special favorite. Mrs. Stowe afterwards said—"I felt at the moment that we never value our

literary men so much as when placed in a circle of intelligent foreigners; it is particularly so with Americans, because we have nothing but our men and women to glory
in—no court, no nobles, no castles, no cathedrals; except
we produce distinguished specimens of humanity, we are
nothing."

Did not her own presence worthily demonstrate that
besides these then named, America had much to be proud
of?

The quietness, grace and culture of this evening circle,
the air of refined and generous hospitality, and the evident
sincerity of character shown in every person, made it a
most delightful occasion. Mrs. Stowe afterwards declared
that she never felt herself more at home, even among the
Quakers. Nobility of character, and grace of hospitality,
are fortunately not the exclusive possession of aristocracy,
though they certainly reflect beauty upon high social position.

The next morning, although very tired, Mrs. Stowe
attended the meeting of the Bible Society. It was anni-
versary week, and a confluence of all the religious societies
of London met at Exeter Hall, with Lord Shaftesbury,
whom Mrs. Stowe then saw for the first time, in the chair.
Mrs. Stowe has related with great enjoyment, the mild surprise with which the English people read certain American newspapers of that period, which, now that they became aware of Lord Shaftesbury's sympathy with anti-
slavery, exhorted him to confine his attention to English
affairs, to look into the factory system of his own country
and explore the collieries where human beings were worked
as slaves, *as if he had been doing anything else for more*

than twenty years. She attributed their ignorance as possibly due to the facility with which titled Englishmen change their names, the Earl of Shaftesbury having been in the House of Commons as Lord Ashley, and upon the death of his father entered the House of Lords under his hereditary title of Lord Shaftesbury. However, she could not wonder that the contrast which a certain very staid religious paper in the United States, drew between Lord Ashley and Lord Shaftesbury—not at all to the credit of the latter—did not strike the people over there, as particularly apposite!

Another day or two filled with sightseeing, visiting picture galleries, and meeting celebrated people, among them Martin Farquhar Tupper, and sweet Mary Howitt, and Mrs. Stowe was so utterly worn out that, in her own words "There was scarcely a chip of her left."

But on Saturday, the eighth day of May, came the great meeting at Stafford House, which stood on the borders of St. James Park opposite to Buckingham Place, overlooking the Park and beautiful gardens on the other side.

The Stowe party was received by two stately Highlanders, in full costume, who stood at the door. A multitude of servants in livery, with powdered hair, and all the grandeur of official importance, bowed and waved them through the entrance rooms, passing their names along in sonorous tones with great dignity of manner. At last the dining room was reached, and as no person was present, they had ample time to look about and compose themselves. The Duchess of Sutherland soon appeared. She was tall, with a stately bearing, a fullness of outline, and a noble air. Her fair complexion, blond hair and full lips,

12

spoke of Saxon blood. In her youth she might have been a Rowena, with however, much warmth and expressiveness added to that rather luke-warm character. She was dressed in white muslin, with a drab velvet bodice slashed with satin of the same color. Her luxuriant hair was confined by a gold and diamond net, on the back part of her head. She looked even handsomer by daylight than she had the evening before, and received them with the grace and cordiality which were preëminently her own.

Thomas Carlisle said, "Show me the man you honor, I know by that better than by any other, what kind of a man you yourself are." Mrs. Stowe's character is in no way so clearly exhibited, as by her description of the people and the events which most moved her. While mere pomp, imposing social honors, offered by mere celebrity seekers, or compliments from royalty itself, separated from true worth and sincerity, would have utterly failed to touch a responsive chord, these distinguished members of the highest nobility were tested by her standard of worth, and then accorded a full appreciative, enthusiastic admiration and love—a love in no way different, nor tinged with one deeper shade of pleasure, than what she felt, in response to the beating hearts of the honest Scotch people, or returned to truly noble hearts and minds wherever met.

The Duke, who was the head of one of the Highland clans, was seen to be a tall, slender man of delicate health with a chronic deafness which, while preventing him from entering much into general society, did not preclude his tender interest in the cause of humanity, nor hinder his devising and executing schemes for the benefit of his numerous dependents.

Here may be noted a little episode, entirely feminine in its character which, while we smile, affords a feeling of nearness and sympathy with these two women. They represented the highest peerage of England, and the intellectual queenship of America, yet consulted as earnestly, in sweet privacy and confidence, upon a matter of dress and social etiquette as the simplest and most womanly creatures of us all. Mrs. Stowe modestly attired, sought a private conversation with the Duchess in her boudoir and frankly confessed a little anxiety respecting the arrangements for the day. Having lived all her life in such a sequestered manner, she naturally felt some apprehension as to the things expected of her upon such an occasion.

With her characteristic, straightforward action, she said as much, and asked for direction. The Duchess, who was notably unconventional in her manners, pressed her hand and begged her to be entirely easy, as if among her own friends, which they would be. She told her she had invited a few guests to luncheon, and that afterwards others would call; that later there would be a short address from the ladies of England, read by Lord Shaftesbury, which would require no answer. She adjusted a ribbon on Mrs. Stowe's bonnet, fastened an escaping curl in place, as a sister might do, and they returned to the drawing room, where friends had already begun to assemble. The announcement at the door of the names of the guests, obviated any necessity for introductions; English society fully understanding the rule that "the roof" was sufficient guarantee to all its guests, of the desirability of knowing each other.

The Duke and Duchess of Argyle, Lord and Lady Blan-

tyre, the Marquis and Marchioness of Stafford, and Lord
and Lady Campbell arrived first. Then followed Lord
Shaftesbury with his charming Lady, and her father and
mother, Lord and Lady Palmerston. Lord Palmerston was
of middle height, with a keen black eye and black hair
streaked with gray. Mrs. Stowe found him quite what she
had expected from his public actions, and in talking with
him, remembered vividly how often she had heard her
father, Dr. Lyman Beecher, and Professor Stowe, exulting
over his foreign dispatches, by their home fireside. The
Marquis of Lansdowne, formerly known as Lord Henry
Pettes, who, with Wilberforce and Clarkson had taken so
prominent a part in the abolition of the English slave
trade came, and also Lord John Russell, Lord Grenville
and Mr. Gladstone, who was two or three years her senior.

When luncheon was announced the Duke of Sutherland
gave his arm to Mrs. Stowe, and her neighbor on the other
hand, was Lord Lansdowne, who conversed very intelligently with her, about men and things in America.

Mrs. Stowe's description of a luncheon at the finest palace
in England thirty-five years ago is a notable one, and of
especial interest to American society people, who of late
are coming to place such a high value upon manners and
social usages. Her Grace's *chef*, bore the reputation of being the first artist of his class in England. The preparation
and serving of the viands was Parisian in taste and fertility
of ideas, and Mrs. Stowe pertinently remarked that, "the
profession thus sublimated, bears the same proportion to
the old substantial English cookery, that Mozart's music
does to Handel's, or Midsummer Night's Dream, to Paradise Lost."

The luncheon was then as now, a social occasion which was less elaborate and ceremonious, than dinner. The ladies sat down without removing their bonnets, everything was placed upon the table at once and the children were admitted to the table, even in the presence of guests. The servants moved noiselessly to and fro, taking up the dishes and offering them to each guest. One of the dainties served at this luncheon was a plover's nest, precisely as the plover made it, with five tiny, speckled, blue eggs in it. It was then a "fad" in table fashions, to thus set the delicate eggs before a guest, but it had such a sylvan picturesqueness and realism about it, that it brought up to at least one of the company, memories of robins' nests in the old sunny orchard at home, and she could not profane the image by eating one of the eggs.

It was remarkable how the personal aspect of the men and women who graced this occasion, differed from those of equally great persons in America—how far less they bore the marks of age, than men in America who had similarly been engaged in affairs of state or intellectual progress. They wore an air of freshness and youthful alertness, which was a marvel to the visitors, used to the marks of anxiety and care, which deeply lined the faces of American statesmen and men of letters. They hardly knew whether to attribute it to the less exhausting climate, or the solidity of political institutions and ideas which rest firm, where ours are constantly shifting and drifting, like the sand. The tone of this highest social life, was delightfully simple and unaffected. It was friendly, natural, and sincere. They gave no evidence of anxiety as to deportment, either in eating or in conversation. They talked like people who thought more of what they were saying than how they said it, and in this simplicity and kindness, which will alone induce a natural perfection of manners, they found the Americans, whom they honored, similarly gifted.

After luncheon the whole party ascended the grand staircase—then acknowledged the most magnificent in Europe—to the picture gallery. This room, which is a hundred feet long by forty wide—was surmounted by a dome richly finished with golden palm trees and elaborate carving. The hall was lighted in the evening by a row of lights placed outside the ground glass of the dome, which was thrown down in brilliant radiance by reflectors, without the usual oppressive heat of gas light. The gallery was peculiarly rich in paintings of the Spanish school, among them two superb Murillos taken from convents by Marshal Soult during the time of his career in Spain, of whom it may be said, as of his chief, Napoleon, that if he was no better than a magnificent robber, he at least stole with taste.

There was a painting by Paul de la Roche of the Earl of Stafford led forth to execution, the original of the prints so well known at that time in America, and one by a Flemish artist representing Christ under examination by Caiphas. It was a candle light scene, with only two faces, the calm and resolute, though downcast and foreseeing face of Christ, and the vehement upturned countenance of the questioning high priest. Mrs. Stowe often referred to this wonderful picture and said that its presence there in the midst of that scene, was deeply affecting to her.

The immense apartment began to fill with guests. Many

presentations were made, among them: Archbishop Whateley with his wife and daughter, Macauley with two of his sisters, Milman the poet and historian, the Bishop of Oxford, Chevalier Bunsen and the Baroness, and many more.

Among other celebrities Mrs. Stowe met the historian Sir Archibald Allison, whom she described as a tall, fine looking man, of very commanding presence.

Shortly after the Duke of Sutherland presented Mrs. Stowe to the distinguished company, composed of lords and ladies, peers of the realm and great commoners, men of high standing in church and state, and women of beauty and intellectual endowments, the greatest in all England.

Our Harriet Beecher Stowe bowed simply, but her eyes shone with pleasure and heartfelt gratitude that, as she has since expressed it, the most magnificent of England's palaces had that day opened its doors to the slave. Always thinking of herself as the instrument in the hands of Providence, merely as the one to whom a great message had been entrusted, she forgot her own personality and gratefully received this overwhelming ovation as a greeting particularly directed to American bondmen.

She sat quietly in a chair which had been conveniently placed for her, closely attended by the Duchess of Sutherland and a group of distinguished ladies, while the imposing company, of the most eminent and intelligent men and women in England, sat and stood, filling the grand gallery. In a few words, speaking for the Duchess of Sutherland and the ladies of the two committees appointed to conduct "The Address of the Women of England to the Women of America on the Subject of Slavery,"

the Duke gave her welcome, and called upon Lord Shaftesbury to make the presentation of the great testimonial
which had had its first inception with him.

Lord Shaftesbury arose, and reading the short preliminary address, presented, to Mrs. Stowe what is probably the
most remarkable testimonial ever tendered to any person.

The address was upon vellum, handsomely inscribed in
illuminated text in these words.

"THE AFFECTIONATE AND CHRISTIAN ADDRESS OF MANY
THOUSANDS OF WOMEN OF GREAT BRITAIN AND IRELAND TO
THEIR SISTERS, THE WOMEN OF THE UNITED STATES OF
AMERICA.

"A COMMON ORIGIN, A COMMON FAITH, AND, WE SINCERELY
BELIEVE, A COMMON CAUSE, URGE US AT THE PRESENT MO-
MENT TO ADDRESS YOU ON THE SUBJECT OF THAT SYSTEM OF
NEGRO SLAVERY WHICH STILL PREVAILS SO EXTENSIVELY,
AND EVEN UNDER KINDLY DISPOSED MASTERS, WITH SUCH
FRIGHTFUL RESULTS, IN MANY OF THE VAST REGIONS OF THE
WESTERN WORLD. WE WILL NOT DWELL ON THE ORDINARY
TOPICS—ON THE PROGRESS OF CIVILIZATION; ON THE
ADVANCE OF FREEDOM EVERYWHERE; ON THE RIGHTS AND
REQUIREMENTS OF THE NINETEENTH CENTURY; BUT WE
APPEAL TO YOU VERY SERIOUSLY TO REFLECT, AND TO ASK
COUNSEL OF GOD, HOW FAR SUCH A STATE OF THINGS IS IN
ACCORDANCE WITH HIS HOLY WORD, THE INALIENABLE RIGHTS
OF IMMORTAL SOULS, AND THE PURE AND MERCIFUL SPIRIT
OF THE CHRISTIAN RELIGION.

WE DO NOT SHUT OUR EYES TO THE DIFFICULTIES, NAY,
THE DANGERS THAT MIGHT BESET THE IMMEDIATE ABOLITION
OF THAT LONG ESTABLISHED SYSTEM; WE SEE AND ADMIT

THE NECESSITY OF PREPARATION FOR SO GREAT AN EVENT; BUT IN SPEAKING OF THE INDISPENSABLE PRELIMINARIES, WE CANNOT BE SILENT ON THOSE LAWS OF YOUR COUNTRY WHICH, IN DIRECT CONTRAVENTION OF GOD'S OWN LAW, INSTITUTED IN THE TIME OF MAN'S INNOCENCY, DENY IN EFFECT, TO THE SLAVE THE SANCTITY OF MARRIAGE WITH ALL ITS JOYS, RIGHTS AND OBLIGATIONS; WHICH SEPARATE, AT THE WILL OF THE MASTER, THE WIFE FROM THE HUSBAND AND THE CHILDREN FROM THE PARENTS. NOR CAN WE BE SILENT ON THAT AWFUL SYSTEM WHICH EITHER BY STATUTE OR CUSTOM, INTERDICTS TO ANY RACE OF MEN, OR ANY PORTION OF THE HUMAN FAMILY, EDUCATION IN THE TRUTHS OF THE GOSPEL, AND THE ORDINANCES OF CHRISTIANITY.

A REMEDY APPLIED TO THESE TWO EVILS ALONE WOULD COMMENCE THE AMÉLIORATION OF THEIR SAD CONDITION. WE APPEAL TO YOU THEN AS SISTERS, AS WIVES, AND AS MOTHERS, TO RAISE YOUR VOICES TO YOUR FELLOW CITIZENS, AND YOUR PRAYERS TO GOD, FOR THE REMOVAL OF THIS AFFLICTION FROM THE CHRISTIAN WORLD. WE DO NOT SAY THESE THINGS IN A SPIRIT OF SELF COMPLACENCE, AS THOUGH OUR NATION WERE FREE FROM THE GUILT IT PERCEIVES IN OTHERS. WE ACKNOWLEDGE WITH GRIEF AND SHAME OUR HEAVY SHARE IN THIS GREAT SIN. WE ACKNOWLEDGE THAT OUR FORE-FATHERS INTRODUCED, NAY, COMPELLED THE ADOPTION OF SLAVERY IN THOSE MIGHTY COLONIES. WE HUMBLY CONFESS IT BEFORE ALMIGHTY GOD; AND IT IS BECAUSE WE SO DEEPLY FEEL, AND SO UNFEIGNEDLY AVOW, OUR OWN COMPLICITY, THAT WE NOW VENTURE TO IMPLORE YOUR AID TO WIPE AWAY OUR COMMON CRIME, AND OUR COMMON DIS-HONOR."

The Testimonial, consisting of twenty-four large, bound

volumes, containing the names of nearly six hundred thousand British women, beginning with the nobility, of which there were many hundred, continuing with the names of wives of prominent commoners, and finishing with thousands of conscientious English speaking women whose hearts were full of the cause, was formally presented to Mrs. Stowe by Lord Shaftesbury. Then the Duchess of Sutherland arose and in a few graceful words made her own gift, which was of a bracelet made of massive links of fine gold, typical of the slave's fetters. As she took the chain from her own fair round wrist and clasped it upon the small arm of Harriet Beecher Stowe she said, "We trust it is the memorial of a chain that is soon to be broken."

These words were inscribed upon one of the large links. Upon another was engraved the date of the abolition of the English slave trade, and on another, the date of the abolition of slavery in the last of the English territories. The beautiful Duchess begged Mrs. Stowe to keep it, until she should be able to place upon its remaining links, the date of the emancipation of the slaves in America.

Mrs. Stowe acknowledged that she never expected to live to see that day. But the mills of God were grinding faster than she knew.

The accounts of this memorable occasion having been published in the English papers, sundry American journals intimated very plainly that it was a political movement; but that accusation was strongly denied by Mrs. Stowe, who declared that it had its origin in the deep religious feeling of Lord Shaftesbury, a man whose whole life was devoted to the abolition of white-labor slavery of Great Britain; who explored the darkness of the collieries, and counted the weary steps of the cotton spinners; who penetrated the dens where the insane were tortured in darkness with cold and stripes, and the loathsome alleys of squalid London haunted with fever and filth, with cholera, and moral plagues not less to be dreaded. It is well known that when in the Parliament of England, he was pleading for women in the collieries, who were harnessed like beasts of burden, and made to draw heavy loads through miry and dark passages and for children, who often at three years of age were taken to labor where the sun never shines, he was met with furious opposition, and accused of being a disorganizer, and of wishing to restore the dark ages.

Very similar accusations and injustices were done him during the seventeen years campaign which at last resulted in the triumphant passage of the celebrated "factory bill." He was therefore not surprised that misconstruction should have been put upon his espousal of the anti-slavery cause, and the welcome prepared through his means by the women of Great Britain for the author of "Uncle Tom's Cabin." Neither did the Duchess of Sutherland allow herself to be disturbed by the ridiculous stories and scandals, which found their way into American prints, immediately following the event just described, recognizing as the animus of them, the bitterness and impotent rage which filled the hearts of the unknown writers, because of the glorious support given in England to a woman who appeared as the most eloquent exponent of a cause which, thus far, had received little support from society in the United States.

As among the minor, though extremely gratifying attentions, shown Mrs. Stowe at the Duchess of Sutherland's, it may be mentioned that a pretty Quakeress, of mature years, made a little speech to the author of "Uncle Tom's Cabin," and hung upon her arm an embroidered reticule in which some of the first English anti-slavery tracts had been carried for distribution.

An artist named Burnand, a young man who had attained some celebrity, presented her with a fine cameo head of the great abolitionist Wilberforce, cut from a statue in Westminster Abbey. He also begged leave to make a bust of Mrs. Stowe, and though she declared that, considering the melancholy results of former attempts, it made her laugh to think of sitting for a new likeness, she was so entreated by her friends that she finally consented. Her host gladly allowed his study to be turned into a studio, and the work began.

Then came another sculptor on the heels of the first, who told her he had a bust of her begun, which was to be finished in Parian and published, whether she sat for it or not, though, he added ingenuously, of course he much preferred to have an occasional look at her. So her host told him he might come too, and for some days she was perched upon a stool, dividing her glances and her conversation between the two enthusiastic artists, one of whom was taking one side of her face and one the other.

Mrs. Stowe went with a party, in which was Lord John Russell, to visit a model school for children of the poorer classes, and with Mrs. Cropper and Lady Hatherton, to visit the poet Rogers in his home, which was a perfect cabinet of rare and costly works of art, and adorned with choice books. Rogers was then old and quite feeble, but he welcomed her most cordially, and apparently took great pleasure in her admiration of the rare pictures, marbles, vases, gems and statuary, that constituted his wonderful collection. He presented her with his poems, beautifully illustrated by Turner, with his autograph upon the fly leaf.

With the Duke and Duchess of Sutherland, the Stowe party visited many rare collections of paintings. They spent an evening at Lord John Russell's, and became so thoroughly wearied with a succession of pleasures, that even Professor Stowe succumbed and ingloriously went to bed, remaining there several days to recover from the strain upon body and mind which this memorable visit had induced.

Mrs. Stowe was invited to breakfast with Sir Charles and Lady Trevelyan at Welbourne Terrace, and in a letter to her daughter, described some of the eminent literary people whom she met, saying, "In your evening reading circles, Macauley, Sidney Smith, and Milman, have long been such familiar names, that you will be glad to go with me over the scenes."

Lady Trevelyan was the sister of Thomas Babington Macauley, whom Mrs. Stowe described as peculiarly English in physique, short, stout, and firmly knit, hearty in his manner, with a full, round, deep chest voice, who talked just as he wrote. He was about fifty, a bachelor, but with as unmistakable a social domestic nature as that so charmingly displayed, under similar circumstances, by our own Washington Irving.

The conversation having turned upon Shakespeare, several guests were comparing ideas and some one asked Mrs. Stowe which was her favorite play. Before she could reply Macauley quickly answered, " Oh, Mrs. Stowe prefers Othello, of course."

" Why do you think so, my lord" said that lady.

" Because it is the only drama in which a black man runs away with the affections of a white lady," said the essayist, his eyes sparkling with mischievous enjoyment of his joke at the expense of the author of " Uncle Tom's Cabin," who with all other abolitionists, had been reviled as an amalgamationist.

Mrs. Stowe was seated at table between Macauley and Milman, whom she described as of striking appearance, tall, stooping, with a keen black eye, and perfectly white hair, a singular and poetic contrast. Having been for many years dean of Westminster, he talked most entertainingly of its antiquities, and with both men talking almost incessantly upon delightful and instructive topics, Mrs. Stowe was sadly tried in her effort to listen with both ears and keep the conversations clear and separate.

The historian, Hallam, was also present, a quiet retiring man, with a tinge of sadness in his face, which suggested the shadow of the loss of his son Arthur, the one to whom Tennyson wrote " In Memoriam." In conversation about this breakfast Mrs. Stowe afterwards said, " there were doubtless other celebrities there whom I did not know. I was always through my visit finding out that I had been with somebody very remarkable whom I did not suspect at the time."

Professor and Mrs. Stowe lunched the same day, in the early part of May, a time so beautiful in England, at Surrey parsonage. This chapel and parsonage had been the church and residence of the celebrated Rowland Hill, and the then present incumbent, Rev. Mr. Sherman, proved a model host. Among the very agreeable company were Martin Farquhar Tupper, and the artist Cruikshank, who had illustrated several of the English editions of " Uncle Tom's Cabin." He asked many questions about the appearance of the slaves and the topography of the country in Kentucky, as well as the style of the houses, dress of the planters' families, and other details.

It was destined to be their most dissipated day in London, for they were engaged to dine at Sir Edward Buxton's, and by the time she had arrived there Mrs. Stowe was was quite exhausted. But she met a number of people whom she was exceedingly interested to see, Mr. Samuel Gurney, the father of Lady Buxton, who was a brother of Elizabeth Fry, with his wife and daughters, all of whom had the air of benevolent friendliness, which is characteristic of the Quakers; Dr. Lushington, the venerable associate in Parliament of Wilberforce, some fifty years before; Dr. Cunningham; and a master of Harrow School, with whom she had a long conversation upon educational literature, Greek, and Latin.

The next evening they dined at Lord Shaftesbury's, meeting such guests as Dr. McCall, Hebrew professor in King's College, Lord Wriothsley Russell, one of the private Chaplains of the Queen, the Archbishop of Canterbury, the Bishop of Tuam, Lord Chief Justice Campbell, Lady Stratheden, Lord and Lady Palmerston and others.

On the 13th of May the Stowe party all went out to Stoke-Newington to visit Mr. Alexander, a genial Quaker who was a particular friend of Dr. Lyman Beecher, who passed many pleasant hours there when in England. With him

they attended the Congregational Union, which was then
in session, occupying seats upon the platform, where they
were the cynosure of hundreds of interested eyes. After a
resolution introduced by Mr. Binney, expressive of love and
good fellowship with their American brethren, the Rev.
John Angell made an address glowing with enthusiasm and
constantly interrupted by applause, which gave welcome to
the author of "Uncle Tom's Cabin" and paid a ringing
tribute to the work and the good cause for which it had
been written.

Professor Stowe replied, making brief mention of the
connection of his English ancestors with the Congregational churches of London, and amid great cheering, stated
his belief that as a body the Congregationalists of the
United States were free from the sin of slavery, that he did
not think there was a Congregational church in the United
States in which a member could hold slaves without subject-
ing himself to discipline. This remark, which the Professor
afterward modified, was received with vociferous acclamation, and his whole address, which gave a resumé of the
religious and political situation in America, was heard with
intense interest.

At Stoke-Newington was the grave of Dr. Watts, which
was visited, and the place held further interest as the home
of Daniel Defoe, whom, with Shakespeare, and Bunyan,
Mrs. Stowe considered a model in the English language.
That evening, Mrs. Stowe overpowered by fatigue, was
obliged to forego a dinner at the Highland School, and one
at Charles Dickens'.

On the evening of the sixteenth of May was the great
Anti-Slavery meeting at Exeter Hall. The event was ac-

cepted at that time as a public representation of the strong
democratic, religious element of England. Lord Shaftesbury
was in the chair, the Duchess of Sutherland was cheered as
she came in and took a seat in the gallery, and when Mrs.
Stowe entered taking her place by the side of her grace, the
excitement was so demonstrative that even after her experience in Scotland, its vehemence and volcanic power
made her tremble. She thought she saw plainly enough
where Concord, Lexington and Bunker Hill came from, for
it seemed that there was enough of this element of indignation at wrong and resistance to tyranny, to found half a
dozen republics as strong as the United States. A woman
fainted in a distant part of the house and a policeman attempted to force a way with her through the densely packed
crowd. The services were stayed for a few moments, and
the dark mass of human beings surged like a mighty sea
sending up hoarse murmurings, showing only too plainly to
those above what a terrible scene might ensue should any
panic occur or sudden excitement break up the order of the
meeting.

The speeches, with the exception of Lord Shaftesbury's, were denunciatory and painful to the national feel
ing of the Americans. It was the swinging of the old
Saxon battle axe, without fear or favor; but when Professor
Stowe spoke in response, dwelling on the fact that the cotton trade of England was the principal support to slavery,
and read extracts from Charleston papers, which boldly declared that they did not care for any amount of moral indignation wasted upon them, by nations who after all must
buy the cotton they raised and sold, the great gathering
seemed to be agitated with a new idea of the situation.

13

The meeting was a very long one, and Mrs. Stowe was quite worn out with excitement and fatigue when it was over.

The next day the Stowes were invited to a luncheon party which numbered Mr. and Mrs. Binney, Rev. Mr. Sherman, Lady Hatherton and Lady Byron, whom Mrs. Stowe had not met. But she preferred a quiet day with her family and went to Windsor, the place which embodies the English idea of royalty, and which has been immortalized by Shakespeare's "Merry Wives," and had still standing in its park the Herne Oak, where the mischievous fairies played their pranks upon old Falstaff. Here also was the fishing ground of Izaak Walton, and the gentlemen of the American party were very joyous and filled with anticipations.

CHAPTER IX.

A FAMILY PARTY AT WINDSOR. MISPLACED SENTIMENTAL-
ISM. PORTRAIT OF MRS. STOWE BY RICHMOND. A BROWN
SILK DRESS FOR THE AUTHOR OF UNCLE TOM'S CABIN, THE
OCCASION OF AGITATION ALL OVER ENGLAND. MRS. STOWE
DINING WITH THE DUKE OF ARGYLE. A SECOND MEETING
WITH MR. GLADSTONE. MRS. STOWE'S RECOLLECTIONS OF
HIM. A RECENT LETTER FROM HIM TESTIFYING TO THE
FAVORABLE IMPRESSIONS OF THE AUTHOR OF UNCLE TOM'S
CABIN RETAINED BY THE GRAND OLD MAN. BREAKFAST
AT RICHARD COBDEN'S. CONCERT AT STAFFORDHOUSE.
THE BLACK SWAN. FIRST MEETING WITH LADY BYRON
PRESENTATION OF A MASSIVE SILVER INKSTAND AND GOLD
PEN TO MRS. STOWE. WITH MARIA WESTON CHAPMAN
IN PARIS. SOME ART CRITICISMS. THROUGH SWITZER-
LAND. MRS. STOWE ARRAIGNED FOR CRUELTY TO AN
ANIMAL.

IT was a merry, alert and critical party which went
through the state apartments at Windsor, and Mrs. Stowe
and her irrepressible brother Charles, had many a disputa-
tion on art, in which the little woman was not usually
worsted, and the grave Professor listened with amusement
and not a little pride at the clash of friendly arms. Mrs.
Stowe was beginning to realize her possibilities as an art
critic and, in her discussions and conclusions, evinced a
penetrating appreciation of the essentials that was most

gratifying to her husband, who had been over this ground
before and thought out many of the ideas to which she,
with rare insight, jumped at a bound. A fragment of her
experience gives an instance of her freedom from conventional influences, which was eminently characteristic
and is particularly delicious in these days when common
sense seems to have almost nothing to do with "high art."
They had seen a certain group of statuary, nothing less than
the monument to the Princess Charlotte in St. George's
Chapel. They were enchanted with the pathos of it, and
the technical working of all the effects. Furthermore, it
made them all cry, a fact of which, Mrs. Stowe always maintained, she was not ashamed.

Next day she was expressing her admiration of it to an
artist, one of the authorities, when he professed it a shocking thing, in bad taste, and as a final condemnation, pronounced it terribly melodramatic. Mrs. Stowe felt for an
instant inclined to reconsider her tears, *for this critic knew
everything that should be admired,* but her own sense
came to her support, and very pithily she afterwards
wrote: "A thing may be melodramatic or any other *atic*
that a man pleases; so that it be strongly suggestive,
poetic, pathetic, it has its own peculiar place in the world
of art. If artists had their way in the creation of this
world, there would have been only two or three kinds of
things in it; the first three or four things that God created
would have been enacted into fixed rules for making all
the rest." This with much more, equally apart from artistic canons, and free from binding rules, was elicited by the
word of the artist, which was intended to be final with her,
as his verdict was known to be, with English society

The Stowe party dined at the White Hart, that day in Windsor, and under the influence of the rollicking traditions which group around the place, and the fact that husband and wife, brother, sister-in-law and nephew had not been for so long a time alone together, they had an overflowing, merry time of it.

They rode to Eton and saw the boys playing cricket. They leaned pensively upon the wall and recited Gray's Elegy over a churchyard, which, however, was not quite satisfactorily defined as the one thought of by the poet.

After getting separated from the youngest member of the party, and losing an opportunity to visit Labouchere Park in consequence, they returned to London to find that their "dispositions to melancholies" had been indulged over a spurious churchyard—that the one they looked for was at Stoke. There was nothing to console them except the thought that the emotion at least was admirable, if misplaced.

They were staying with the rector of Mary-le-Bone parish, one of the largest districts in London, who was also one of the court chaplains. Professor and Mrs. Stowe met many eminent divines there, and with him they went to the studio of Richmond, the celebrated artist, to whom Mrs. Stowe was to sit for a portrait, which was to be presented to Professor Stowe by several of his friends.

This was done in crayon, and was forwarded to the United States in an appropriate frame, at the foot of which was a tablet with this inscription—

THIS PORTRAIT OF

HARRIET BEECHER STOWE,

FROM THE SAME HAND WHICH DREW TO THE LIFE

WILBERFORCE, BUXTON AND ELIZABETH FRY,

IS PRESENTED TO

HER HUSBAND AND FAMILY

BY

SOME ENGLISH FRIENDS.

A. D. 1853.

It is doubtless a rather idealized likeness of Mrs. Stowe in the early forties, and is at present in possession of her youngest daughter, Georgianna, wife of the Rev. Chas. F. Allen, rector of the Church of the Messiah in Boston. The accompanying plate was engraved from a copy of the picture, which was courteously loaned to the writer by the Rev. Charles E. Stowe, of Hartford, Conn.

Professor and Mrs. Stowe went to call upon Kossuth who since his liberation and return from his visit to America had been living in obscure lodgings in London. The Revolutionist held a firm faith in the triumph of his cause, one which incited him a little later, upon the outbreak of the Italian war against Austria, to lead nearly all of the Hungarian refuges to Italy.

The Stowes dined with Lord John Russell and met several distinguished people. They were entertained at Lambeth Palace by the Archbishop of Canterbury, and visited at Palyford Hall, the oldest of the fortified houses in England, and the only one which, according to the feudal custom, kept water in its moat. It had been for some years

the residence of Thomas Clarkson, and was then occupied
by his widow and family. What reminiscences of the old
time were talked over that day! Of the by-gone age when
good, pious people imported cargoes of slaves as they did
sugar, molasses and rum. When these articles of mer-
chandise were supposed of necessity to come together to the
English shores. Of the experiences of the reformer, who so
early dared to condemn the trade, and the signs of the coming crisis in American affairs.

And what strength and hope were gathered in, considering how the victory over wrong was won, and might be
won again!

About this time arose an agitation in London at which,
seeing the insignificance of its immediate origin, one feels
tempted to smile but realizing that its source was in the new
unrest and change of ideas upon various questions of public
good, it assumes an importance quite disproportionate to
its local cause. It was nothing of more consequence
than the making of a dress for the author of "Uncle Tom's
Cabin," which set society seething and provoked the vehement denunciations of the great London journals, from which
echoes were heard across the sea.

When Mrs. Stowe was preparing to go abroad, she was
so utterly worn out, and upon several occasions really ill,
that her modest arrangements were somewhat delayed.
There was a brown Chinese silk which remained to be
fitted when Mrs. Stowe was too much exhausted to come
under the hands of the dress-maker, and it was therefore
folded and put into the trunk, to be made in England in
case it was needed

Finding that constant travel was considerably dimming the
freshness of her wardrobe, Mrs. Stowe now decided to have

the brown silk made.   A kind friend volunteered to man
age the business, and in due time a respectable person
waited upon Mrs. Stowe, offering to make the dress for a
specified sum.   Peacefully anticipating the return of the
completed garment, Mrs. Stowe was astounded one morning to read in the *Times* a thundering leader, which stated
the important fact that Mrs. Stowe had contracted for the
making of a new gown, and asked if she knew in what kind of
a place the dress was made.   The editorial was accompanied
by a letter from a dress-maker's apprentice, stating that it
was done piecemeal, in some of the most shocking and distressed dens in London, by poor, miserable white slaves,
who were worse treated than the African slaves in America.   Immediately upon the publication of this, came letters from all parts of England, earnestly begging Mrs.
Stowe to interfere, deprecating the possibility that she was
patronizing the holders of the white slaves of England, and
urging that she would employ her talents against oppression in every form.

Mrs. Stowe sent for the woman who took the dress,
thereby assuming unconsciously the burden of the celebrated
author's public patronage, who appeared in a very tragical
state, protested her ignorance of any dens, and insisted that
she held no slaves.   The *Times* implied that Mrs. Stowe
ought to take up the matter at once, array herself against
the system presumably by refusing to accept the work
and not profit by means of its starvation labor.   The
whimsicality of the affair did not appear to strike the
literal British mind, and instantly the public was awake,
even alert, with sympathy with the poor needlewomen, who
doubtless needed it badly enough, but who it may be
assumed were not especially ground down by the making

of Mrs. Stowe's plain dress. As a result of the agitation, Lord Shaftesbury brought forward documents issued by him within the previous seven years, several of which were directed particularly towards the relief of overworked and poorly paid, milliners and dressmakers. It appeared that Societies had been formed some years before for the amelioration of the condition of needlewomen and had a large membership among the great and influential ladies, not only in London, but in Manchester and other cities. It therefore was seen that this *to do* was but the revival of past agitations, and while doubtless of benefit in keeping alive the sympathy for that class of workers, in calling renewed attention to their ill-paid labor, it was a decidedly unpleasant episode for the American woman who, quite unaware, became a prominent object to which to fasten a manifesto.

Professor and Mrs. Stowe dined with the Duke of Argyle meeting again Lord Carlisle, the Duchess of Sutherland and their daughter Lady Blantyre, with Lord Blantyre, Lady Caroline Campbell, the Duke's sister, the scientist, Sir David Brewster, Lord Mahon, the historian, and his wife, and Mr. Gladstone, then one of the ablest and best men in the kingdom. Mrs. Stowe looked at him with much interest and thought that for one who had already attained such celebrity both in theology, and politics, he looked remarkably young. He was tall, with dark hair and eyes. He had a thoughtful face and was very agreeable and easy in his manners.

A letter recently received from the hand of the great English statesman, testifies that the favorable impression was mutual, for after thirty-five years he writes "the fact has not escaped my memory that I had the honor of meeting her (Mrs. Stowe) at dinner."

The last week in May, when England was in the height of its fresh summer beauty, they went to breakfast at Richard Cobden's. The eminent and very popular "apostle of Free Trade," was a slender man, rather under medium height with a lithe, springy body and a frank and most fascinating smile. His appearance seemed to be sufficient reason for his popularity, for his very presence seemed to bring with it an atmoshere of life and exhilaration. Their conversation turned naturally upon politics, and the comparative condition of England and America, and the vexed question of the cultivation of cotton by free labor, was thoroughly ventilated.

Professor Stowe's speeches on the subject of cotton made no little agitation in the British mind. The London papers were full of them and the question, declaring for or against the trade with considerable earnestness. These practical Americans had some ideas which proved strongly disturbing to the English heart, just then very complacent and somewhat superior, on account of their precedence in the abolition of slavery. It was disagreeable to be told in effect, that self-righteous congratulations over the emancipation of their own slaves, were hardly consistent with the support of slave holders in the United States, who were able, by means of slave labor, to furnish cotton to English markets.

After dining at Surrey parsonage, they went the same evening, to a concert at Stafford House, which was of more than ordinary interest to them, being in the great hall before described, presided over by Sir George Smart, attended by the cream of the nobility, in handsome demi-toilets, while the singer was an American negress, Miss Greenfield, assisted by the best glee club in London. The phenomenal voice of the singer called "The Black Swan," Mrs. Stowe describes as so keen, vibrant and penetrating, that it cut its way to the heart like a Damascus blade. With its double timbre, the songstress made most startling effects, for instance singing "Old Folks at Home," one verse in a pure tenor, and the next in a thrilling bird-like soprano. Two of the Duke's Highland pipers made their appearance after the concert was over, playing their bagpipes as they promenaded the Halls. Their wild barbaric playing and brilliant costume, recalling the picturesque garb of the ideal American Indians, had a peculiar effect, and proved again the artistic skill with which the Duchess contrived to enhance her famous entertainments. The Rev. R. S. Ward, a full blooded African, was a notable figure in the scene.

Later in the evening, brother Charles Beecher persuaded Mrs. Stowe to accept with him an invitation to hear the oratorio of "The Creation," at Exeter Hall, as performed by the London Sacred Harmonic Society. There was a gallery reserved for them, and Mr. Surman, the founder and conductor of the society presented Mrs. Stowe with a beautifully bound copy of the score.

About this time while taking luncheon with a friend at Oxford Terrace, Mrs. Stowe met Lady Byron, with whom she had a few moments conversation. In that brief time the hearts of the two women met, and that friendship which afterwards led Harriet Beecher Stowe into a painful position, but which to the last had not released a tithe of its affectionate tenacity, was formed. Mrs. Stowe described Lady Byron at that period as slight, delicately formed, with face, form, dress and air uniting to impress one with her singularly dignified, pure and gentle, yet strong character.

A few words dropped by her upon the religious aspect of England—remarks of such quality as are seldom heard—made their way to the inner soul of the strong earnest American woman, and nothing ever occurred to make her swerve from her firm loyalty, to the much discussed and vilified wife of the erratic poet. Mrs. Stowe found that Lady Byron's course had been made beautiful by consistent, active benevolence, and her feelings went out to her spontaneously as the patroness of the American outcasts, William and Ellen Crafts, those names memorable in Annals of Boston Abolitionism. She observed the frailty of Lady Byron's health with concern, and in subsequent interviews they held those conversations, which in later years made the subject of one of Mrs. Stowe's most earnest and conscientious strokes for what she believed to be justice.

Upon the soirees attended, the interesting and distinguished people met, the schools examined, the tenement-house visitations, which were quite different in spirit and manner from the modern " slumming," and the model lodging houses exhibited under the enthusiastic leading of Lord Shaftesbury, it is impossible to enlarge.

It is the history of one of the most wonderfully honored and distinguished visits ever made by an American to the old country. There are chapters in every day's experience and thoughts sufficient to fill volumes.

Professor Stowe, having quite used up his leave of absence, bade good bye to his wife, and sailed for New York on the first of June, to resume his duties at Andover. Mrs. Stowe, her sister-in-law, her young nephew and William Buckingham crossed to the Continent, under convoy of Charles Beecher.

Not however, until Mrs. Stowe had been invited to
an entertainment made in her honor at Surrey Chapel,
where Lord Shaftesbury occupied the chair; the Duchess
of Argyle and Marchioness of Stafford attended; Miss
Greenfield sang several songs; Rev. Mr. Binney threw
back to the nobility through Lord Shaftesbury, the
compliments showered by that gentleman upon the people. Both said obliging things about and to Mrs.
Stowe, and the ladies ended by presenting her with a solid
silver inkstand, and a band of children added a gold pen.

The inkstand, which for years was a familiar object
upon Mrs. Stowe's desk in her library at Hartford, and is
still undimmed in its sterling lustre by the lapse of time
and conditions of atmosphere, is eighteen inches long with
a group of silver figures upon it, representing Religion
with a Bible in her hand giving Liberty to the Slave.

The figures, particularly that of the Slave, are masterly.
He stands with hands clasped for joy, while a white man
knocks the fetters from his feet. It bears this inscription:

Presented to

Mrs. Harriet Beecher Stowe,

by the Ladies of Surrey Chapel, London,

as a memento of their estimation

of the genius, piety and zeal manifested in her efforts

for the emancipation of the American slaves.

May 26, 1853.

Mrs. Stowe was much moved by the testimonial, but the only speech she made, was to the children, who bore the gold pen. She gathered them around her and talked a few minutes.

On the fourth of June, the party started for Paris, having a smooth passage across the dreaded Channel and escaping the custom officers with little annoyance. They found a home with friends who were anticipating their arrival with enthusiasm, and soon began to enjoy Paris. Charles Beecher found where all the best music was to be heard, and, accompanied by her friend, no less a person than Maria Weston Chapman, the noted abolitionist, an American lady whom years of residence there had converted into a veritable *Parisienne*, Mrs. Stowe visited the shops and reveled in the fascinations which were dear to her woman's heart, and the tastes which were natural, and never to be perverted by any possible hardening or decolorizing influences.

The brother and sister visited the Louvre, and took in their fill of art, and, much to Charles Beecher's exultation, his sister was obliged to recant some of what he called her heresies, in regard to the masters.

Mrs. Stowe acknowledged that for the first time in her life she was filled, permeated, deliciously saturated and unexpressibly satisfied with her feast of pictures. Having lived for days in the enchanting atmosphere of Paris, having visited the boulevards, the Bois, the Luxembourg, the Tuileries, and Versailles, they drove some three miles out of town to the villa of Monsieur Belloc, the Director of the Imperial School of Design, whose wife it was who had first translated "Uncle Tom's Cabin" into French, with whom there had been a delightful correspondence for some months.

This time in Paris was a delicious rest and refreshment to Mrs. Stowe, who had for years been wrestling with the stern necessities of life, putting forth and enforcing ideas and principles bearing upon the needs of the human race, meeting the friction of strong minds, with the firm, keen surface of her own intellectuality. She wrote to a friend: "At last I have come into dreamland; into the lotos eater's paradise; into the land where it is always afternoon. I am released from care, I am unknown and unknowing; I live in a house whose arrangements seem to be strange, old and dreamy. My time is all my own."

She was free to enjoy to the full, the light airiness of local existence, to fill her soul with beautiful forms and ideas in art, to wander aimlessly in the gardens, hearing the bands of music, watching the children play, viewing with no responsibility, the gay fleck and foam of the irredescent life of Paris.

All the joyousness, all the humor, all the love of the beautiful, which in her was a cultivated inheritance from her sweet mother, all the artistic feeling, which was sometimes smothered under the cares and restrictions of New England life, burst forth and blossomed into exquisite flowers of fancy and graceful expression. In reading the letters sent from Paris to her husband and friends, one obtains a new comprehension of the softer, the æsthetic side, of her nature, which indeed appears occasionally in her writings, but was known only in its fullest beauty to the intimate friends, who saw it called forth day by day by a flower, a fine painting, a view of a lovely landscape, a handsome building, a pretty child, a picturesque person, a patient animal, or a dainty bird.

She was peculiarly susceptible to the simplicity of nature, and equally responsive to the niceties of art and civilized existence. Her great, broad nature enjoyed as well, the upthrusting of a blade of grass, or the formulation of a grand idea for the benefit of the whole human race. When in one personality is so combined strength, morality, religious feeling, taste, humor and kindness, there is seen a notable character. This one has left its impress upon the universal mind and serves as an adored example of human possibility to every one who was fortunate enough to have known her.

The naturalness and unsullied truth of her art criticisms, are a marvel to those who have to learn how to feel, about pictures and statuary. She carried into the galleries the balance with which she examined everything in life, and her opinions were strangely true to art in its best sense. Pages of pertinent paragraphs could be quoted for the benefit of those who may sometime see the pictures, without the discriminating taste which was her own, but only one or two can be given.

"There were Raphaels there, which still disappointed me, because from Raphael I asked and expected more. I wished to feel his hand on my soul with firmer grasp; these were too passionless in their serenity and almost effeminate in their tenderness."

"But Rubens, the great joyous, full-souled, all-powerful Rubens!—there he was, full as ever of triumphant abounding life; disgusting and pleasing; making me laugh and making me angry; defying me to like him; dragging me at his chariot wheels; in despite of my protest, forcing me to confess that there was no other but he."

Remember, reader, that this was written thirty-five years ago, before Europe, art, and the old masters, had been discussed by every one, fit and unfit. If you fail to see originality in these criticisms remember that many a flowery *critique* may have been founded upon them. If you do not perceive their truth, realize that perhaps conventionalties have deprived us of the freshness and penetrating appreciation which were hers, inherent and so thoroughly characteristic that nothing served to dim the clearness of her vision, which always looked straight through the film of various and accruing thought, to the essentials in whatever she regarded.

"One of my favorites was Rembrandt. I always did admire the gorgeous and solemn mysteries of his coloring. Rembrandt is like Hawthorne. He chooses simple and every day objects and so arranges his light and shadow as to give them a sombre richness and a mysterious gloom. The House of Seven Gables is a succession of Rembrandt pictures done in words instead of oils."

Mrs. Stowe did not forget, as many picture lovers do, that art is not confined to brush and pigments.

She was one of the first to express, what we all may have felt, of the relation of all branches of art to each other. She compared Milton to grand organ tones in music; she saw the Shakespearean flavor in the variety and vital force of Rubens' artistic power. Paul de la Roche suggested the picturesqueness of Walter Scott. She saw in the French galleries a dramatic effect which was unworthy as it must weary upon close acquaintance.

14

She felt the poetry in the architecture of one cathedral, and
heard an anthem in the solemn harmony of another grand
composition of stone. In French painting she perceived
the minor artistics, the exquisite trivialities which pertain
to and characterize French life. She said she would as
soon trust Tom Moore to write her a prayer book, as Cor-
regio to paint religious ideas.

While in Paris Mrs. Stowe made the acquaintance of
Ary Schoeffer and his pretty English wife. She saw his
celebrated picture of Francisca de Rimini and was much
affected, feeling its agony of love and despair as a libel
upon her Father in Heaven. She exclaimed " No, it is not
God, who eternally pursues undying, patient love, with
storms of vindictive wrath."

In writing of Schoeffer and his works, which so pleased
and wrought upon her best feelings, Mrs. Stowe said,—
"The knowing ones are much divided about Schoeffer.
Some say he is no painter. Nothing seems to me so utterly
without rule or compass as this world of art. Divided into
little cliques, each with his shibboleth, artists excommuni-
cate each other as heartily as theologians, and a neophyte
who should attempt to make up a judgment by their help
would be obliged to shift opinions with every circle."

Mrs. Stowe predicted a success for Ary Schoeffer and
said, with her uniform faith in the judgment of unconventional taste, " His best reward is in the judgments of the
unsophisticated heart. A painter who does not burn incense to his palette and worship his brushes, who rever-
ences ideas above mechanism, will have all manner of evil
spoken against him by artists, but the human heart will
always accept him." This axiom can doubtless be applied

to all kinds of art and fits none more perfectly than literary presentations.

Charles Beecher tells in his diary, of how they attended a *musicale* with the Princess Czartoryski at the piano, and Frankomm of the Conservatoire to play his Stradivarius of great age and fabulous price; when he acted as interpreter between the violinist and his sister, who talked much with the *virtuoso* about music, and found quite unexpectedly that he had read "Uncle Tom's Cabin," and that he protested when he read it, "This is genuine Christianity." Charles Beecher speaks in the same place with pride, of the easy and dignified demeanor of his beloved and distinguished sister, and tells of the consideration everywhere accorded her.

At a dinner party they met La Rochejacquelin and Peter Parley, at one time consul to Paris. While the others were chatting, Weston Chapman and Charles Beecher slipped out and went to the Jardin Mabille, of which he gave his sister, next morning, a very ingenuous and vastly entertaining description.

On the 22nd of June the party left Paris for Chalons, thence by steamer, (in a boat so diminutive that Charles Beecher said he thought Ichabod Crane might have sat astride of it and dipped his feet in the water,) down the Saone to the Rhone and Lyons.

From Lyons to Geneva by diligence, and they had their first view of Mount Blanc. At the Swiss towns, people began to discover by some method of thought transferrence never to be understood, who the little lady with the bright gray eyes and the brown curls was, and as Charles Beecher said it was "Scotland all over again." Everybody had read " Uncle Tom," and the honest, secluded mountaineers, pressed about her, more than one urging her to write another book for they said, " Remember, our winter nights here are very long."

One polished gentleman came to her and said with emotion that he " had lost an Eva " and thanked her with tears, for her beautiful picture of that sweet young life. At Chamouni they made another halt. It is quite characteristic of Mrs. Stowe that she said in speaking of the mountains—" I rejoiced every hour while among those scenes, in my familiarity with the language of the Bible. In it alone, could I find vocabulary and images to express my feelings of wonder and awe."

The party [Mrs. Stowe, Mrs. Beecher, young George, William Buckingham and Charles Beecher,] took mules and ascended the mountains, to La Flegére from which was then to be had the best view of the whole range to the Mer de Glace, and points of interest in all directions. Charles Beecher let out the exuberance of spirits which was natural to all the big boys of that illustrious family, and rolled rocks down the precipices, threw poles down the ice gorges into the clear pools below, and played with his nephew in the most rollicking and undignified fashion. From Chamouni they went to Martigny, and in the villages perched upon the precipices, there came to Mrs. Stowe the question which she asked of her guide, why all the little children did not fall over the cliffs and get killed. One has had the same idea about Venice, and the lagoons which lay under each window, waiting to drown luckless babes.

From Martigny they ascended the St. Bernard pass and found a hundred people at the hospice.

Back to the Martigny, and the next day by carriage to Lake Leman, where at Hotel Byron they found themselves overlooking the Lake, with Castle Chillon mirrored in the still waters. They drove to Thun, to Inerlachen and Lauterbrunnen. Pursuing their journey they crossed the Wengern Alps and rested at Grindelwald. From Grindelwald they went to Meyringen and to the Rigi Kulm.

People in general seemed to accept Mrs. Stowe as a champion of the rights of all creatures, human or brute. An incident which furnishes an amusing instance of this feeling, occurred at Chamouni. The party had taken donkeys and under the convoy of guides had ascended various mountain paths, spending several days in these to them, novel and most delightful, excursions. After their return, while resting one evening in the parlor of the hotel, Mrs. Stowe was accosted by a stern female, whose righteousness was visibly tinged with the verjuice of envy and ready fault finding. Asking if it were Mrs. Stowe and being politely answered, she said that she felt it her duty to remonstrate against the cruelty of which she heard she had been guilty that day, and to ask her, if she considered beating an inoffensive animal, consistent with her influence as a woman who professed to feel for the helpless!

Mrs. Stowe was considerably astonished, and replied that she professed nothing which she could not carry out, in at least her private actions, and asked for an explanation. "I refer," said the stern female, "to the abuse of your donkey to-day, upon Montanvert. I am told you whipped the poor animal unmercifully. I am surprised at your glaring inconsistency, Mrs. Stowe."

She looked as if she were rather glad of it. Mrs. Stowe

dismissed her with a few words.   Charles Beecher declared his sister should have told the impertinent female, that they might have been more careful of the donkey's feelings had they expected to thus encounter another member of the family!

The truth of the matter was, that Charles Beecher found himself astride of a particularly obstinate animal, who ingeniously selected the most precarious places in which to balk and kick, much to the annoyance and danger of his rider.   Mr. Beecher was provided only with a stick, which he had cut from a bush by the way, and although he soon broke it over the animal's shaggy head, it was evident that the donkey was scarcely aware that his rider objected to his performances, for it was only when the guides took hold of the bit and belabored him from behind, that he consented to break the several blockades which he caused the train.

Leaving Heidelberg with regret about the first of August, the party went to Frankfort, putting up at the Hotel Russie.   Among the attractions of the place they saw of course Dannecker's Ariadne, the beautiful female riding upon a panther, which is in a pavilion in a garden.   It is interesting to note that Mrs. Stowe perceived in this work a lack of religious feeling, which left it "cold as Greek mythology."

The house where Goethe was born, and the library where they looked for Luther's Bible and saw instead, only his shoes, and the picture gallery, were objective points and thoroughly enjoyed.

His sister humorously wrote that Charles had espoused himself to an "Amati" at Geneva and like most young bridegrooms was oblivious to all else.   So absorbed was he drawing from it sweet melodies of Mozart, and Beethoven adagios, that when they found the picture gallery closed he exclaimed, " What a mercy ! "   Down the Rhine to Cologne they went with the expected sensations at Bingen, Coblentz, Ehrenbreitstein, Bonn, Drachenfels and all the rest, reading Childe Harold by the way.

At Cologne, after feasting in the sublimities of the cathedral, they went to St. Ursula's church, where the various ghastly relics, of very doubtful nature, were shown them by the priest.   In Mrs. Stowe's description of this scene, the remarkable statements of the exhibitor, the solemn chaffing of Charles Beecher, the shocked indignation of sister-in-law Sarah, and the irrepressible laughter of herself, one sees a farce very similar and quite as amusing and irresistably provocative of sympathetic smiles, as the well known skit of Mark Twain in " Innocents Abroad," ending with, " Is he dead ? " written twenty-five years or so, later.

They went from Cologne to Dusseldorf and Leipsic, where they were entertained by Tauchnitz, the celebrated publisher, who had an interest in the German editions of " Uncle Tom's Cabin."   At Dresden, Mrs. Stowe sent her card to Jennie Lind Goldschmidt, but that lady, having a young babe, was unable to see her whom she admired and loved so sincerely.   They went to Berlin, to Wittenburg ; saw the house and burial place of Luther and the monument in the public square to him, and then on to Erfurt and Eisenach.   Mrs. Stowe's art criticisms upon the Dresden galleries as reproduced in "Sunny Memories of Foreign Lands " are so instrinsically valuable, just and correct that they should be considered by every person of taste.   In speaking of the culinary paintings in which cabbages, brass kettles, onions and potatoes are reproduced with remarkable industry and painstaking, she gives expression to an idea that might well engage the attention of certain of the modern school of novelists. She felt that the thing so carefully painted was not in itself worthy of so much modish art. She says, " For my part I have but little more pleasure in a turnip, onion or potato in a picture than out, and always wish that the industry and richness of color had been bestowed upon things, in themselves, beautiful."

CHAPTER X.

By August 20th the Stowe party were back to Paris,
having made a brief visit in Antwerp, with its various
quaint and charming effects, its beautiful bells, and churches,
and galleries, where Rubens was the saint to which the
city erected its shrine.

Again at the hospitable home of Monsieur and Madame de
Bellock, with more art, and more sight seeing, a little final
shopping, and thoughts now turning eagerly to home and

217

native land across the sea.   Mrs. Stowe met Beranger the
poet, then an old man, a very charming person full of benevolent kindness and universally popular with the responsive common people.   Mrs. Stowe's representation of the
virtues, and admirable qualities of the French people is
very pleasant to contemplate, leaving the heart warm and
sympathetic with the kindly conventionalism which per-
vades their social customs and governs their manners.

Mrs. Stowe was superior to the mistrust which Anglo-Sax-
ons generally evince for the sincerity of a nation which
habitually deals in conversational elegancies and compliments.   Every French heart should love Mrs. Stowe for the
appreciative things she has said about them, and said with
the perfect sincerity which is inseparable from her character.
One wishes for the sake of the French people known and
loved, to make selections from her estimate of their life, character and qualities.   It may be found among the last letters
published in the volume before referred to, and should be read
by those who have no opportunity to make personal observations upon the peculiarities and attributes, of the several
nations which Mrs. Stowe had studied.

There is, in her discussion of these matters, of men and
things, of persons and political history, to be seen, one of
the best bits of writing emanating from her powerful pen.
Her grasp of situations, and insight into causation there
appears, not dependent upon local experience or intuitive
overwrought feeling, but as the abstract intellectual force
and judgement, the mental power, the perfectly disciplined
intelligence, which is capable of taking a correct view of
any problem, or situation which is presented to it.

When Mrs. Stowe was in Paris she was repeatedly visited by an aged French gentleman, a Count, who in youth had spent some years as a student at the Law School in Litchfield when she was a child, and declared the society of the place was at that time "the most charming in the world."

During her sojourn in Paris Mrs. Stowe received many visits from the members of the Old French Abolition Society which existed there for many years. A Catholic lady wrote to ask her why she had not included in her "Key" as among the friends of emancipation, the Romish clergy of the United States, as it had been the boast of their church in France. Mrs. Stowe was forced to reply that the Roman Catholic clergy had not identified themselves with the anti-slavery cause, but allowed their influence to go with the multitude.

A gentleman, who was among the guests of one evening earnestly discussing the powers and capabilities of the African race and referring to their taste for music and the fine arts, asked why, with cultivation, they might not be trained to exhibit characteristic pantomimes and dances. Whereupon Mrs. Chapman, whose experiences in Boston had sharpened into keen dislike of American inconsistency, spoke up quickly to the mingled amusement and chagrin of Mrs. Stowe quoting to him the action of one of the Old School Presbyterian churches in America, which was agitated to its very foundations by the question as to whether a man might legally marry his deceased wife's sister, yet in the same meeting declined to condemn slavery, which denied legal marriage to all slaves, and denounced dancing, with a vehemence commensurate to its place as one of the atrocities of a world lying in wickedness. The poor

man was lost in amazement, and probably never was able
to realize how principles were valued in this country.

The party now homeward bound, crossed from Boulogne
to Folkstone and thence to York and Leeds, having been
intercepted by Lady Carlisle and taken home with her at
York. At Leeds they were received into the home of
Mr. Baines, whose father was an earnest and progressive
parliamentarian. The next day the house was filled with
company and the "Leeds Offering" was made by a deputation of citizens. It was a massive and very elegant silver
basket, piled high with gold pieces and bore this inscription :—

The Lord grant them according to their own heart
and fulfil all thy course.
Presented by a few ladies to
Harriet Beecher Stowe,
the friend of the slave.
"Pro Rege et Lege."
The readers of Uncle Tom's Cabin place £100
in this basket as an offering of gratitude.
Leeds.

Sept. 3rd, 1853.

A telegram was received from the Mayor of Liverpool
asking them to stop at that city, but Mrs. Stowe, on ac-

count of fatigue was obliged to decline. Before starting
for home they made another brief visit to their friends, the
Croppers at the Dingle, their first and last resting place on
British soil. Here there were letters from home, some sad
ones, telling of the death of friends.

A deputation from Ireland called upon the author of
"Uncle Tom's Cabin" there, with an address, and a present
of a beautiful Bog Oak Casket lined with gold and carved
with shamrock leaves and the national emblems, the harp,
and a hound attached to it by a tiny gold collar and chain.
This was filled with sovereigns and upon the inside of the
gold lined cover was the inscription,

Presented to

Harriet Beecher Stowe

by some of her Irish friends in grateful appreciation

of the services rendered

To the Cause of the Slave

by her publication of

Uncle Tom's Cabin

Dublin, 1853.

The mayor of Liverpool and the Rev. Dr. Raffles break-
fasted with the party on the morning of their departure
from British soil, and after the latter had made an earnest
prayer to God for their safe voyage home, attended them

to the wharf, where a large party were waiting to bid them good-bye. "And thus almost sadly as a child might leave its home," says Mrs. Stowe, "I left the shores of kind old England—the mother of us all."

When Mrs. Stowe parted from her friends, with whom for some months she had sojourned so pleasantly upon foreign shores, and returned to her home at Andover, to be welcomed by her husband and children and take up again the threads of domestic life and work, her thoughts very naturally reverted to the remarkable tour, and in looking over the letters sent home from many places, filling in the interims with facts brought to recollection by notes in her own, and her brother's diaries, the journey was enjoyed in retrospect, as it often is more vividly realized, when the mind travels over the scenes, unincumbered by the infirmities which pertain to the body.

The family friends wanted the story of the journey put into permanent form; and, moreover, as the political situation grew more violent, and the tide of hostile feeling ran high against all who had dared to lift a voice against the "institution" of slavery, there were desperate misrepresentations, malicious falsehoods, told in the newspapers and among people, concerning the facts of Mrs. Stowe's reception abroad; against the distinguished and godly people who welcomed her; and in denunciation of the speeches ringing with no uncertain sound, which were made by Professor Stowe on various occasions. It was therefore decided to publish these facts and impressions of the trip.

"Sunny Memories of Foreign Lands" was prefaced by an introduction by Professor Stowe. He copied the press accounts of the public meetings held in honor of the author of "Uncle Tom's Cabin" in many cities and towns, and threw a parting hot shot at "the reckless faithlessness and impudent falsehood of our national pro-slavery legislation" which, goaded to madness by the rising indignation of the best thought of the age, was then becoming boldly aggressive, thus surely preparing the way to its own downfall.

The book was issued from the press of Phillips, Sampson and Co., of Boston, and appeared simultaneously in England, under the sanction of the author, from the house of Sampson and Low. Mrs. Stowe took this occasion to thank publicly, those publishers in England, France and Germany, who had shown a liberality beyond the requirements of obligation. The royalties which they voluntarily rendered to the author of "Uncle Tom's Cabin" and the "Key," which was also in great demand, were debts of honor, and received by her with appreciation. If there had been an international copyright law, or all publishers as honorable as these, Harriet Beecher Stowe would have speedily become the wealthiest author living.

"Sunny Memories of Foreign Lands" was published in the spring of 1854 and had a large sale. On account of some technicality as to the copyright, it has been for some years out of print in the United States. It is, however, one of the best guide books which is extant, to the salient thought points, and the intellectual scenery of the journey through the British Islands and the Continental tour described, and will doubtless be re-issued. Messrs. Sampson, Low, Marston, Searle and Rivington, the London publishers, have sold up to the present time, nearly forty thousand copies.

Shortly after her return, in answer to an urgent demand, Mrs. Stowe published a small book for children, entitled, "A Peep into Uncle Tom's Cabin." It was a simple outline of the story, and sold freely.

In 1855 Mrs. Stowe prepared a dramatization of "Uncle Tom's Cabin," which was called "The Christian Slave." About this time Phillips, Sampson and Co., of Boston, published a new and enlarged edition of "The Mayflower." The copy in the possession of the present writer is from the twenty-fourth edition—proof that it was eagerly welcomed by a public who were ignorant of its earlier appearance.

Upon the fly-leaf of this volume, which is so precious a testimonial of the genius of young Harriet Beecher, is inscribed in the infirm hand of the aged woman who had become so venerated and loved as to incite this work of affection now in hand,—"Accept this memorial of your friend, H. B. Stowe, Oct. 29, 1887."

Once more free to devote herself to the education of her children, Mrs. Stowe led them through studies and reading, and in leisure hours busied herself in preparing a "Geography for My Children," which was published and proved very useful to other mothers in their loving labors with their little ones. Master Charles now no longer a baby, and Georgiana, his sister, but little older, were out of arms, and though home cares were pressing and might have crushed a less vigorous spirit, Mrs. Stowe began the writing of another anti-slavery book. It embodied some of her experience and ideas, which could not be promulgated in "Uncle Tom's Cabin."

It was called "Dred, or Nina Gordon." Held in compari-

Accept this memorial of
Your Friend

H B Stowe

Oct 29. 1887

son with her first great book, aflame as that was with indig-nation and deep feeling, "Dred" has been justly criticized as lacking in the strength and literary power which so won-derfully distinguish "Uncle Tom's Cabin." "Dred" is less a novel and more an argument. It is less artistic and more historical. It often turns aside from the story into moraliz-ings, and the disenchantments of explanation and vindica-tion of the grounds taken. That she put her first accumu-lated force and best thoughts into "Uncle Tom's Cabin," there is no doubt, but none the less is "Dred" worth reading and thinking over. It is a strong supplement to the first book, and fills in and rounds out, the reader's idea of so-ciety, languishing and diseased under the weight of slavery.

It effectually shows that the author saw no reason to retract or modify her views as previously expressed. Any sequel seems an anti-climax, from not only being considered in comparison with the first effort, but because of a waning enthusiasm, and a sort of knowing superiority in the reader which is superinduced by the possession of foregoing facts and causes. So "Dred" will be viewed, but one may base upon the fact of its undeniable superiority to the ma-jority of American novels, an idea of the greatness of the work which dwarfs and throws it into a pale light, as a lesser luminary before the sun.

Possibly had Mrs. Stowe anticipated the retrospective verdict of the literary art critics, she might not have affixed this after thought to "Uncle Tom's Cabin," but having in mind only a noble purpose and the pressing home to the American people the question of their moral responsibility on the subject of slavery, she wrote "Dred." Who shall say that it was an ethical mistake even though it lacked

the grand unity and movement of the first, and was interrupted in its artistic progression by sundry droppings into
argument and an array of proofs, which it was evident the
author had not considered called for, in her first book.

The issues between Liberty and Slavery had every year
grown more important, and the most momentous crisis of
our national career was imminent.

The United States stood forth upon a conspicuous stage,
to decide before the nations of the earth, whether political
precedent and commercial expediency should obtain against
right, and justice to a race of down trodden people

The American people were about to answer the question
whether slavery should be extended into free soil and
across lines which had hitherto held it in check.

It is safe to say that Mrs Stowe recked not of the
literary value of a work which followed " Uncle Tom's
Cabin," upon the same theme. She wrote " Dred" as she
has always written and spoken, because she had something
to say. It was a true heart, speaking to fellow beings upon a
subject that thoroughly absorbed and possessed it. This
was the secret of Mrs. Stowe's great success. From this
motive emanated " Pilgrims Progress," and all the great
books, ancient and modern, which hold a vital tenacity upon
the human mind, which quite baffles the critics, but clearly
demonstrates one of Mrs. Stowe's own utterances when she
said, " People always like simplicity and truth, better than
finish."

The strength of " Uncle Tom's Cabin " had been devoted
to a vivid description of the pitiable condition of the bond-
men under existing institutions. Little more could be
said to strengthen that impression. But there was another

side to the question which had been but faintly touched upon. In "Dred" Mrs. Stowe showed the reflex effects of the system, upon the aristocratic owners. She did what John C. Calhoun declared in Congress, that the Abolitionists were doing everywhere. Ridiculing the notion that they proposed to liberate the slaves by force of arms, he said, "The war which they wage against us is of a very different character, and far more effective,—it is waged not against our lives, but against our characters."

Mrs. Stowe demonstrated that a man cannot hold another in slavery, without being in some sense, himself enslaved.

In the pictures of spoiled little Nina Gordon, her debauched brother Tom and her selfish Aunt Nesbit, we see the direct results of the pernicious system, upon the class counted the favored one. In the knotty questions, and unpleasant dilemmas which confronted the polished and cultured Judge Clayton and his noble daughter, and in the crushing weight of comprehended responsibility which sobered the life of Edward Clayton, there is cleverly portrayed the seamy side of the upper social fabric, so often thrown into high lights and artificial colorings by zealous defenders of the "institution."

Again, where could be found a more pathetic presentation than that of the mental and physical condition of the Cripps family, whose father was one of the worthless individuals so graphically termed by the colored men, "poor white trash"? This was a type of a class which could only exist under the cloud of ignorance and moral degradation, made possible by a system which neglected public schools, and all provision for the good of the commonwealth. This cloud negro slavery entailed no less upon the so-called free men of all grades, than upon the African chattels.

Upon the part of the brave woman who had set the fires of liberty burning upon every hill-top of the North, this was a new warfare. And, though one, which we gladly believe failed to touch the universal heart, like a call for sympathy with the oppressed, it may be supposed to have appealed quite as forcibly to the selfish feelings of those, who, inured to the system, were not susceptible to the pathos of "Uncle Tom's Cabin." The aristocratic nature of society at the South so completely segregated people of certain position from any knowledge of what was going on in the human life below them, that facts pertaining only to the sufferings of the negroes, had no appeal to them, being unnoticed or ignored with as much ease as the people of wealth and culture of our great cities, dismiss all concern with the squalid wretchedness in their slums. Their own disadvantages made, therefore, the only vulnerable point of attack upon the aristocracy who held in a free country, the anomalous position of feudal lords. This Mrs. Stowe perceived, and promptly acted upon.

Opening the book with the impression of the strength and depth of Harriet Beecher Stowe's first great book upon one's mind, the description of the frivolous mistress of Canema is almost a shock. If, however, one has seen, through her bright and sparkling mental experiences in "Sunny Memories" the new lightness and relief from the earnest, even stern trend of her New England manner of thought, one can better understand this strain, which is new and almost foreign to Mrs. Stowe.

The story opens, with Nina Gordon just returning from

boarding school, engaged to marry three men. She is declared by the author—and one of her lovers, Edward Clayton—to be pretty, bewitching, full of native shrewdness and vitality, with an instinctive preference for kindness and justice, which it must be confessed, is not yet quite apparent to the reader. She is engaged in overhauling her trunks, abstracting therefrom various articles of millinery and ornament, which quite fill her mind, and she exhibits perfect indifference to the consequences of her triple betrothment, and the fact that her financial affairs are unpleasantly involved. The business manager and guardian, who tries in vain to impress the last fact upon her mind, is Harry, the quadroon son of her father, Colonel Gordon; her unknown half-brother, whose tinge of dark blood, hardly to be seen in his countenance, holds him in bondage.

The trust of the property, Harry holds by will of the late Colonel Gordon, for his sister and mistress, Nina, to the partial exclusion from his natural rights, of Tom Gordon, a white son, who had become so wild and degraded before his father's death, that he saw the necessity of protecting Nina, and his slave family, from the violence and cruelties of the expectant heir.

The state of feeling which possessed Tom Gordon regarding his sister, and the man Harry, is effectively displayed and the melancholy virtue and acrid religious principle of Aunt Nesbit, Nina's female relative and would-be guide, show how utterly hard and unlovely, a woman who yet supposed herself a Christian, could be. In the character of Tomtit we have a masculine Topsy, with new oddities and a course of exasperatingly comical conduct, which would prove irresistible were we not in a position to say,

"Oh, yes, we have seen this character before and it hardly compares with the other," without realizing that familiarity has dulled the keen edge of our first enjoyment of the small deviltries of Topsy.   The picture of the home life of Harry and Lizette, his pretty French quadroon wife, another humming-bird, another gay, unthinking vain creature, who may have conduced to Harry's ennui and mental dyspepsia —for bon-bons are not good as a steady diet—is an idealized view of a theatrical character, and though very pretty reading, does not sweep the chords which thrilled so deeply to the more earnest and sober existence of George and Eliza. A sense of their misfortunes, even as threatened in the lust of Tom Gordon for Harry's dainty, sprightly wife, does not reach us, because it lacks the reality which we have felt in other cases.

Must we allow that this story seems forced, that it lacks the spontaneity and intensity of " Uncle Tom's Cabin," and that our feeling of loss is not wholly to be accounted for by the fact of some acquaintance with the phase of life here shown?   Were it not so, it might well cause a blush that our sensibilities were so soon blunted.   The conclusion is again that this book was written, more as any other author might have written, and that it is somewhat disappointing, after the story which would not be repressed, which told itself, with all the forceful feeling accumulated in years.

The character of Old Hundred, the deliberate mass of obstinacy and good nature who stood for the Gordon's coachman, and his calm tyranny over his young mistress, a salient point in the subjugation of the slave owners, is very amusingly depicted.   Neither does the situation lack for entertaining developments when the several affianced lovers of Nina Gordon appear at the same time, to make a visit upon their volatile little betrothed. Edward Clayton, the favored one among the three young men to whom Miss Gordon was contemporaneously engaged, appears an earnest, cultured person, weighed down with the responsibilities and burdens, which the pernicious system of slavery imposed upon all masters, while few were, like him, conscious of it. In the author's analysis of this character, we feel more of the power of Mrs. Stowe, and we like to believe that families, like the one which consisted of the refined and cultivated Judge, Edward Clayton and his noble sister, were not rare in the South under the old regime, or not rarer than they are elsewhere upon the earth.

The Cripps family, living in squalor and poverty, which is only relieved by the faithful ministrations of their sole retainer, old Tiff, have little to do with the story, except to call forth the latent kindness and sweet benevolence of Nina Gordon. But this group, in this gathering of literary fragments, serves to bring forth one of the best characters ever depicted by the author. There is a pathetic devotion, a hound-like fidelity and untiring effort in old Tiff, a despairing persistence on his part to keep up the respectability of the family for the sake of what they were on their mother's side, and a patient determination to see the best of all situations, which makes him an African Mark Tapley and notable among the wonderful character portraits drawn by Mrs. Stowe. During the period following the death of the mother of this family, Nina Gordon begins to get experience in the sadder things of life and under the influence of Edward Clayton, who accompanies her upon her errands of mercy and respect to the neglected dead, she finds her love for him, which is to be her life's best influence.

As has been said, the key-note to the second story written by Harriet Beecher Stowe, on the subject of slavery, is the effect of the system upon the mental and moral characters of the aristocracy, and beyond what might be casually considered the direct reflex influence, and inevitable effect of this foul evil upon the sensibilities of the privileged class. When the hero of the story appears, there is shown another of the most paralyzing effects of the institution. It was the abject fear among the slave owners, of an insurrection, always present to the mind, always menacing them with the horrors once experienced in the uprising of the blacks at Southampton, when Nat Turner, with six men ran amuck, going from plantation to plantation in Louisiana, killing more than fifty persons, men, women and children, in less than forty-eight hours.

The terrible deeds, the hunting down of the offenders, and the execution and punishment of nearly sixty of the fanatical blacks, who believed themselves avengers, were familiar to every planter's family, to every scion of the class which lived upon the labor of the negro. While the law makers soon resumed their old lines of thought, quickly recovering from the alarm which this and several threatened insurrections had occasioned, the people were haunted with this fear. This was an undercurrent of dread, but nevertheless an ever-present possibility, and Mrs. Stowe made it a strong weapon. The character of " Dred " (note the ominous sound of the name) was founded upon that of the renegade Turner, and she, in representing his view of the situation, and giving an intelligent negro's idea of the system which bore so heavily upon his race, threw out a warning which she knew would be but too startling to the people who had never forgotten the panic of 1831. Every reader is bound to respect the rebellion of "Dred," and there is no human heart but that must throb in sympathy with his wrongs.

Here—when the author comes to intense work—we find the best writing in the book. Her descriptions of the weird scenery of the Great Dismal Swamp; the strange, night effects, the wild grief and indignation which deepen in the heart of the black man, who is hiding from the light of day, into a barbaric desire for retribution; his stealthy excursions into the open country and night visits to his old haunts, his vehement words and exhortations and warnings which rise into awful majesty at times, his deep sonorous chanting and defiant, exultant songs as he retreats far away into the fastnesses of the swamps, suffice to fill the heart with the awesome fear, which then shadowed the hearthstones of the most supercilious gentry of the South.

The camp meeting, served as a rendezvous for the various classes represented by the families of the Gordons and their friends, the Cripps, the brutal father and the woman who, an appropriate mate for him, was to become a poor mother to her children; old Tiff and the children whom he watched over with tender solicitude; the principal slaves who are introduced to the reader, and the clerical leaders of several denominations of religious bodies which were prominent in the South.

The picturesqueness of the meeting is undeniable and the episodes are suggestive and comprehensive. Here also

come in conversations between brother ministers, clerical
jokes and grave discussions, the last of which embody the
existing views and state of religious opinion which prevailed in the Southern ecclesiastical societies at that period.

The scene in the grove at the evening session, is one
of the most highly dramatic passages, in all the author's
writings. Clouds obscure the sky and flaring torches give a
fitful light, which now irradiates, now leaves, in shadow, the
sea of faces turned toward the speaker's stand. The tide of
feeling runs high, and hymns, prayers, and excited exhortations follow in quick succession—spurred on by the voice
of the minister, who welcomes and applauds every soul
who declares itself a convert—groans, exclamations and
shouts, come from all parts of the ground. Suddenly, a
voice speaking in clarion tones, rings through the trees!
Words of warning and vengeance in lofty language burning
with awful force, full of savage imagery, eloquent with natural grace, send terror to every heart. The throng is
startled into stillness! They listen breathlessly. We see the
superstitious terror of the people, feel with them the awful
portent of this strange manifestation, almost believe with
them, that this is a supernatural message. It is no wonder
the meeting breaks up in awe, that groups talk fearfully
of the judgment day, that slave traders feel their hair rise
at recollection of it, that drivers suffer temporary remorse
over recent cruelties and try to justify their course by citing the religious tolerance of an usage, which makes abuses
inevitable !

In depicting the visit of Nina Gordon to the home of the
Claytons, the author very cleverly shows, in her introduction of a fête in Nina's honor, planned and carried out by

the slaves of the plantation, the capabilities of the African race in the way of singing, dancing, and spectacular and histrionic art. She also represents in the school taught by Miss Anne Clayton the opportunities, too generally neglected, which were open to the conscientious slave holder or his wife or daughters.

In the account of the case in court, undertaken by Edward Clayton, which was in prosecution of a man who had shamefully maltreated, even to shooting, the slave woman Molly, whom he had hired from the Gordon family, Mrs. Stowe gives the results of her study of the legal aspect of the rights of a slave, and a full digest of the laws, which resulted in the decision of Judge Clayton against his son. It is unnecessary to say that this decision is not an imaginary one, but founded upon a fact in the history of Southern jurisdiction. This decision, which is doubtless familiar to many readers, declared it the imperative duty of the judges to recognize *the full dominion of the owner over the slave*, and that *this dominion was essential to the value of slaves* as property, to the *security of the master* and the public tranquillity, greatly dependent upon their subordination. The scene in court, the earnest feeling of Edward Clayton, who assumed the case upon conscientious grounds; the clear, dispassionate words of the Judge, who is obliged to declare against his sense of justice and his affection for his son; the attitude of pretty Nina Gordon, who dilates with indignation at the outrage of her faithful nurse, and pride at her lover's stand, the comments of the listeners and Edward Clayton's dignified, public withdrawal from the bar, which imposed such conditions upon the exponents of the law, forms a highly interesting and instructive chapter. The after conversation of Judge Clayton and his son, gives a fair idea of the pros and cons of the system which made society what it was, in the South.

Then follows the intense description of the coming of the dark pestilence which had been threatened in that section. We see the horrors of cholera, as it raged in the United States at several periods, written from Mrs. Stowe's observation as an eye-witness, and a victim who narrowly escaped death. She gives a vivid portrayal of the scourge which devastates plantations, sweeps away whole families, leaving homes desolate, and culminates, so far as the reader's interest is concerned, in the death of Nina Gordon, then just coming into the beauty and developed grace and goodness of her womanhood. No one can read without emotion of her brave devotion to her people, her fearless and spontaneous kindness to the stricken and dying on every hand, and at last, of her own sinking before the hand of the destroyer and passing away, when the hopes of all are centered in her.

The death of Nina, relegates her people to the ownership of the wretched Tom Gordon, who begins full soon to wreak his vengence upon his hated half brother, and to give free rein to his lust for Lizette, Harry's pretty quadroon wife, whom Nina had bought, to rescue from him. Harry Gordon escapes with his wife upon horseback to the wild fastnesses of the Dismal Swamp, where Dred, and other hunted beings make their refuge, and old Tiff, with the Cripps children, who were suffering abuse under the hands of a depraved and brutal father, soon follows them to their retreat. In the chapters called "A

Clerical Conference" and "The Result," the author sets forth without passion, the state of the "Old School" of Presbyterians who were largely slave holders, and their differences with their brethren of the "New School" among whom were many ardent abolitionists. A careful study of the facts, here collected and put into form, will clear away some of the mistaken impressions, which have caused many good people to make sweeping denunciations of the whole of that branch of the evangelical church, in the United States.

Mrs. Stowe appears in this, as in all other questions which she has undertaken to discuss, not as a violent partisan but as a faithful exponent of the truth. Being the woman she was, she could not have done otherwise.

The chapter headed " Jegar Sahadutha " contains some terrible scenes. They are nevertheless all founded upon facts in judicial record, of the most fiend-like cruelty, terminating in the death of the victim, the perpetrators of which, though judiciously examined, escaping death and often any punishment as penalty for the crime. In her Appendix,— for Mrs. Stowe had seen the necessity of citing her authorities,—there are several cases which prove that her representation was not overdrawn. The bright and very matter-of-fact conversations of Frank Russell, a young lawyer friend of Edward Clayton, now make a vastly entertaining chapter, wherein may be seen the average appreciation and respect for " the powers that be," whose authorities could not be denied except by pointing as did Edward Clayton, to a force, which, by the pro-slavery advocates, seemed entirely left out of the question—God.

The lynching of good Father Dickson, by rash Tom

Gordon and his desperate followers, affords a view of a state of society now hardly possible in any corner of our land, not even in the most remote regions of the mountainous mining camps of the far west, there being men of culture, men of right feeling and justice under the rough exterior of those pioneers, who prevail. A state which could only have been possible in the United States, except under just the system so graphically described in this work, which had been defended very earnestly, as " a Christianizing Institution." ! ! !

The hunting out of the slaves, who had intrenched themselves in the swamps, the killing of Dred and others; the escape of Harry Gordon, his wife, Aunt Milly and other negroes to the north, the working of " lynch law," which this time threatened Edward Clayton, who was only saved by the perspicacity of his friend Frank Russell, who tolled the ruffians down to Muggins groggery and assisted them to get drunk, with further discussions of the political situation by the polished lawyers and influential gentlemen who visited Judge Clayton,—brings the story to an end. Does it not offer a strange fabric to the eye of the reader? This is woven of the threads of human existence, but it is not the coarse cloth of the slave garb. True it has rough threads, coarse fiber and rude excrescences, but it is unmistakably woven of the material found in the lives of the Southern aristocracy. There are lines of fine silk, occasional hues which are rich and pleasant to look upon, but the whole fabric is rotten, filthy and loathsome to the senses.

Mrs. Stowe had launched her broadside at the " system " which so cruelly oppressed black men. She now held up

to its advocates, a mirror in which they must view themselves, as they had become, under its influence.

The unities of the story are not well preserved. The
progress of the theme is halting, and it is plainly evident
that this is a mere framework set up by the author upon
which to hang her facts and deductions, concerning the
state of social life under slavery. But there are constantly
introduced in conversation, dissertations and ideas upon
this theme, which, while they doubtless mar the artistic
value of "Dred" as a novel, make it a valuable supplement
to "Uncle Tom's Cabin." After reading these anti-slavery books, no vulnerable point seems left untouched, no
argument in favor of slavery remains unanswered.

Anything emanating from the pen of the author of
"Uncle Tom's Cabin" was now sure of a large sale and
"Dred" was widely circulated, adding materially to
the income of its hard-working writer. One hundred and
fifty thousand copies were sold in the United States in a
twelvemonth, and it has been in constant demand for thirty-
five years. On account of the numerous changes made in
the publishing firm which issued this book, it is not
feasible to estimate how many editions have been sold in
the United States. The London publishers, now merged
into the firm of Sampson, Low, Marston, Searle & Rivington, courteously report a sale up to the present time of one
hundred and sixty-five thousand copies, upon which they
have paid a handsome royalty. Allowing at the lowest
estimate, an equal number, for the United States, and pro-
portionately smaller sales in France, Germany and all other
countries it will be seen that "Dred" has had a sale, second
only to "Uncle Tom's Cabin."

CHAPTER XI.

MRS. STOWE'S SECOND TRIP TO EUROPE. THE AUTHOR OF
"UNCLE TOM'S CABIN" IN HER HOME AT ANDOVER.
SOME DOGS WHO HAVE APPEARED AS CHARACTERS, IN
MRS. STOWE'S WRITINGS. THE DEATH OF HENRY STOWE
AT DARMOUTH. THE INFLUENCE OF THE SAD EVENT UPON
MRS. STOWE'S THEOLOGICAL VIEWS. JAMES RUSSELL LOWELL
AND FRANCIS H. UNDERWOOD VISIT MRS. STOWE AT ANDOVER
IN BEHALF OF THE ATLANTIC MONTHLY. ACCOUNT OF
THE BEGINNINGS OF THAT MAGAZINE. MRS. STOWE'S
ATTITUDE TOWARDS THE MONTHLY. "THE MINISTER'S
WOOING." A WONDERFUL PIECE OF THEOLOGICAL CRIT-
ICISM. AS WARMLY WELCOMED AND BITTERLY ASSAILED,
AS HER ANTI-SLAVERY STORY. THE INDIVIDUALS WHO
STOOD FOR SOME OF THE PROMINENT CHARACTERS.

When, in the spring of 1856, the story of "Dred" was
ready for the press the Stowes again began to plan for a
trip to Europe. Mrs. Stowe went for the purpose of bringing it out in London and Paris, simultaneously with its publication in Boston, to thus secure for it a copyright in those
countries. Professor Stowe, accompanied his wife, and
a party consisting of Mrs. Stowe's sister Mrs. Perkins, her
twin daughters now nearly twenty years of age, and her
oldest son, Henry, joined them in this journey. When
the necessary business had been attended to, the party was
broken up by the return to America of Professor Stowe

240

and his son, who was a student at Dartmouth College. The daughters were placed at Madame Beaurieau's *pension*, where they remained for the ensuing year, studying the French language and literature, and going out under the chaperonage of the excellent Madame. Mrs. Stowe and Mrs. Perkins then went to Italy, spending some time at Florence and Rome, enjoying much in art, and collecting materials for the Italian tale which later appeared.

Mrs. Stowe returned home rested and strengthened. She was now the famous American woman, and received at her home in Andover, distinguished visitors from all parts of the United States and from foreign countries. Those who had had the slightest acquaintance with her or her family, hastened to renew their friendship, and paid her many attentions, most of which were deeply gratifying. Did any savor of toadyism or cant, she still received them with quiet courtesy, for was it not a tribute which indicated the growing sympathy of the world in the cause nearest to her heart?

She singularly failed to realize the curiosity which centers about a celebrated person, and frequently said to visitors, in her simple directness of manner.

"Certainly I am glad to see you. Glad to know you have read 'Uncle Tom.' I don't see why you should care to come so far to see me, for I am not much to look at, and my home is very plain, but I thank you for your kind words."

Would it were possible to convey an idea of the indubitable sincerity which shone in the clear gray-blue eyes and the homely kindness which was felt in the voice and the firm clasp of her small hand! It had a charm so peculiar and impressive, as to instantly convert enemies into friends, changing indifference or mere curiosity into an enthusiastic feeling of loyalty and love.

From a gentleman distinguished in American literature and public affairs, we receive a glimpse of the home at Andover:

"I visited Mr. and Mrs. Stowe in Andover. They lived in a large, comfortable stone house and enjoyed the well-earned leisure. Their circumstances had not been very brilliant before the success of the great novel. When fortune turned Mrs. Stowe was besieged on all hands by needy people, even by strangers, and, as she was generous, a large part of her income was given away in charity. The children were nearly all handsome, and in every way attractive. They were full of animal life, too, and were dancing about with eager laughter and beaming eyes. I said something to Professor Stowe about their lively ways and ready speech, and he, with a look of deep pride, exclaimed, "Yes, Beechers, every one of them!" This was said quite naturally as if there could be no question which side of the house their brilliant qualities came from. The self-abnegation rather touched me. I did not find it at all comic."

There was furthermore an element in the domestic life of the Stowe family, which cannot be unmentioned without leaving out one of the most lovable characteristics of the family, and one which frequently appears impersonated in Mrs. Stowe's writings. It was the fondness for pets, and especially dogs and cats, in which the children were fully supported by the scholarly professor of theology and the warm hearted mother, now grown famous through her literary work.

At Cincinnati there had been a noble mastiff, "poor old Carlo," as they fondly referred to him, who had been the devoted slave and loving protector of little " Prince Charley "who died. He was as big as a calf, of a tawny, yellow color with great, clear, honest eyes. He fell in love with the Stowe children, and ran away from his less attractive home to be with appreciative friends. He was particularly fond of the Professor and would pat quietly into the study, where he was engaged with his Greek and Latin books, and wait for a word, until the busy student was fain to stop and give him the caress he asked, when he would retire, content.

When Prince Charley's merry voice was heard no more, and his little feet trotted no more through the halls, Carlo's mournful search for his lost little master, and low cries over the empty baby carriage, were the most heart-breaking things in those days of grief. Much to the sorrow of the family Carlo was left at Cincinnati when they wended their way to the new home upon the piney coast of Maine.

Once settled there, a neighbor having a litter of Newfoundland puppies, and knowing how happy any dog might be who found a welcome in the home of the Stowes, presented the children with a brisk, funny puppy, whom they welcomed with acclamation, and christened Rover. It was not a misnomer, for he became their constant companion in the tramps of the four elder ones, by the seashore, fishing, clamming, or sailing ships, hunting flowers and birds nests in the woods, or dashing and splashing among the cattails and sweet flags as familiarly as so many muskrats. In the words of his illustrious mistress, upon whom he often dashed with the most friendly confidence,—" a jollier, livelier, more loving creature never wore dog skin," and his pranks and knowing performances were often recounted by her.

When the Stowes left Brunswick for Andover, Rover went with them, and Charley the Second, the youngest child, born a few months before Mrs. Stowe's immortal "Uncle Tom's Cabin" was commenced, regarded the dog with the deepest affection and respect. The attempts of the toddling boy, who made disastrous attempts to scratch his ear with his foot as Rover did, and once came home dripping from a neighboring swamp, where he had been lying down in the water with his canine friend, are traditions which still cause much merriment in the family.

Rover formed a part of every domestic scene. At family prayers he laid beside his master, looking up reflectively with his great soft eyes, which held all the sweet seriousness of the hour. When singing or frolicking or games were going on, Rover was in the thickest of the mêlée, barking and frisking in insane glee. At night he stretched his furry length by the bedside of his master and mistress and slept with one ear open for strange noises.

Later, when the older boys were away at school and the young ladies thinking of going to Paris for "finishing," the youngest son prevailed upon his father, who had declared no dog should ever take Rover's place, to admit a little, jolly, low-bred cur to the house for his playmate. When Master Charles' friends reviled him as a dog of no degree, he sturdily informed them his papa said, "he was a pure mongrel," which no one cared to dispute. This small black individual was named "Stromion" from a German fairy tale, which the Professor was fond of reading in the family circle.

Then Henry, who was in the Academy, led home an enormous, old black Newfoundland which had fallen to his ten-

der mercies, and Eliza, seeing that the edict against dogs
had been withdrawn, having cast her eyes longingly upon a
charming Italian greyhound at a Boston fancier's, returned
one day with him in her arms. He was a fairy-like creature, white as snow with the exception of one mouse-colored
ear. He was named Giglio and fully embodied all the
beauty, grace, and coquettish action of a young prince from
elfland.

Professor Stowe was somewhat indignant, when he learned
that a third dog had been brought into the house, but his
righteous impatience lost force, when, two mornings after
his Highness' arrival, the Professor was seen carrying him
down stairs, petting him in the most natural and approved
small talk.

So the stone house at Andover became a veritable Cunop-
olis, in which the family were always more or less under
the paw of these four-footed tyrants, who often went beyond
their privileges, and overrun the house and its most staid
visitors. Mrs. Stowe related with many a smile, how
the most reverend theological dignitaries, were reduced to
unbending and even grave familiarities, by the impudence
of doughty Stromion, who would seat himself attentively
before them, and place a stumpy paw upon the broadcloth-
covered knee, going so far as to bark imperatively, if recognition were delayed.

"Old Prince" was passionately fond of music and would
push and elbow his way into the parlor with dogged determination, when there was playing or singing.

When the young ladies went to Paris to enter Madame
Beaurieau's *pension*, Giglio the beautiful, was smuggled on
board the Fulton, and during the very stormy and cold

March passage he lay rolled up in his blanket like a sea-sick gentleman.

Once in Paris, Giglio, who was evidently spoiled by the attentions he had received upon the voyage ran away leaving his mistress desolate.   Months afterwards, they saw him in the Champs Elysées tenderly cared for by a liveried servant, and left the fair inconstant to his brilliant destiny.

When Mrs. Stowe and her sister, arrived at Florence, they made the acquaintance of a lady who presented her with a beautiful King Charles spaniel, of the special breed called "Demidoffs," as they were raised at the kennels of a Russian prince of that name, who had a villa in the suburbs.   She was a pretty, beseeching little pet, looking as if she had just jumped out of some of the splendid old Italian pictures and was of the rare type which Ruskin calls "fringy paws."   She was christened Florence after her native city.   She was taken to Rome, went with the party to visit ruins and palaces, and rode out of town to the Campagna and the Pamfilia Doria.   One day going to St. Peter's, Florence jumped out of the carriage and wandered for some hours about the strange streets, but at last found her way to the lodgings of her overjoyed mistresses who had mourned her as lost.   She even ascended Vesuvius and was nearly choked in the sulphurous fumes, but soon recovered her spirits, and day after day barked her greeting to the blue-coated, red-legged soldiers, and once "yapped" impudently in the very face of His Holiness, the Pope, who walked near the carriage.   He smiled and put out his hand in sign of blessing and so the little dog brought a benediction on them all.

Florence came through France where dogs were interdicted

on the railways, and more than once made her presence known by whines and complaining barks, but the officials, recognizing her mistress, feigned neither to see nor hear, and she came unmolested to Paris.

When Mrs. Stowe returned to England, while visiting in Kent she was presented with another pet, a skye terrier of the most disheveled and devoted kind, but withal a frantic ratter, who often roused the house in his excited hunt after predatory rodents. After the return to Andover, Florence had two puppies who were named Beethoven and Milton, but whether from the weight of their titular responsibility or too much petting, they died young. Wix, the Scotch terrier who suffered bravely and persistently in battle with Miss Jenny's great cat, and was so mischievous, and lacking in moral responsibility that he had to be sent to Boston when the family removed to Hartford, ends the catalogue of canine pets as described by herself, until Mrs. Stowe's later residence in that city, when in time, came new pets with which the writer had a personal acquaintance and warm friendship. They may be introduced, for surely to the sympathetic reader, in every affectionate family,

"The cat will mew and dog will have his day."

In the autumn after Mrs. Stowe had returned home from her second European trip, occurred one of the great sorrows of her life. It was the accidental death of her son Henry, just coming into noble manhood and full of promise of an honorable future in this life. The young ladies being in Paris and this son at college, Mrs Stowe had felt her burdens somewhat lightened and found time for rest and recreation. She was at this time visiting her brother

Henry Ward Beecher in Brooklyn. Professor Stowe was
at home with his youngest daughter, when Professor Park,
of the Theological Seminary, to whom the sad intelligence
had been sent, came to tell him of the drowning of his son.

Henry Stowe had been bathing with a party of students
and although a good swimmer, had been seized with cramps
and drowned before aid could be given him. The story
which good people are fond of repeating, to the effect that
Professor Stowe met Dr. Park upon the threshold saying,
" Brother Park, you need not tell me, my son Henry is
dead, I saw him drowning," is not verified by the facts.
It would most interestingly accord with a so-called clairvoyant faculty which Professor Stowe possessed, but
Dr. Park states that no such conversation occurred. Professor Stowe was totally unprepared for the sad announcement. How Mrs. Stowe received the crushing announcement and came home to weep over the body of her dead
boy it is not the purpose of this history to describe,
though it was an event which saddened her life and gave
rise to new and wondering thoughts, upon the ordering of
the universe and the baffling incongruities of human existence.

Having written three anti-slavery books, Mrs. Stowe
had the comforting consciousness that while she worked
or rested, whether she was sleeping or waking, holding the
subject in mind or releasing herself temporarily from its
thrall, they were speaking for her, the world around—speaking movingly and with convincing argument to millions of
eager readers. Mrs. Stowe lived on quietly her home life
at Andover. She put forth at this time a small volume
entitled " Our Charlie," which, in treating of the methods

employed in the education of her own youngest born, extended a helping hand to all mothers of irrepressible youths of six or seven years. But with her daily routine of house keeping, sewing teaching and writing, went always the thought of her dead boy, and her eyes were often blinded with sorrow, though she strove with all the strength of her great nature to be reconciled to his untimely taking off.

Her thoughts were turned in upon herself, upon the painful mysteries of this life and the future existence, with many questionings of her theological beliefs which this heart rending event, was putting to a severe test. To her anguish of mind, endured under the fear that this son was "unregenerate" at the time of his death, and her intense rebellion of feeling against the awful idea of his condemnation through all eternity on that account, has been attributed Mrs. Stowe's repudiation of the sterner theological beliefs of her early life and her acceptance of the more comforting ideas of Divine Mercy. Her own description of the experience of a similar afflicted mother will be seen in the character of Mrs. Marvyn in a story written soon after. It was a work which was destined to add materially to her great fame, and arouse nearly as much discussion in American homes as had her first work. It was "The Minister's Wooing," the second of her three great books.

"Uncle Tom's Cabin" had been the irrepressible outburst of highly charged feeling and genius. "The Minister's Wooing" was a literary achievement of the highest order. It was an intellectual effort, with a maturer purity of style, and all the ideal strength and logic of her first great work. It was replete with delicate discrimination and judicial calmness, luminous with deep feeling, brightened with humorous perceptions, all of which overlaid a phenomenal grasp of the theological aspects of old New England thought. It was so admirably constructed and unified, that where the reading world had before wept and raged, carried out of themselves upon the strong current of her emotional thought, they now marvelled, and admired this new evidence of the author's intellectual possibilities. It was founded upon early New England life and, as inseparable from it, dealt most powerfully with the severities of the old theology, as held by the Calvinistic church of that period.

Not wishing to discuss anything more stern and painful, Mrs. Stowe represented the Hopkins school, which was only one of the multiform phases of New England theology during the eigtheenth century. The Rev. Samuel Hopkins of Newport whom she took for her hero, was not only a pupil of the elder Edwards, with whom he resided as a studen of theology—but also his literary executor and biographer.

Mrs. Stowe's work which aside from the charm of its delineations is a subtle and masterly criticism of the New England theology, was one of the first results inevitable upon the extreme doctrines of these great divines. At a later date Mrs. Stowe said of Jonathan Edwards.

"He sawed the great dam and let out the waters of discussion all over New England and that free discussion led to all the shades of opinion of our later days. Little as he thought it, yet Waldo Emerson and Theodore Parker were the last results of the current set in motion by Jonathan Edwards."

It was at the stern cruelty of the exaggerated form of New England theology, as it was known in many of the utterly atrocious and revolting ideas of the past age, that she shuddered, and was moved to delineate for posterity this picture which, is now generally admitted to be marvellously true to the mental and moral condition of the time. In a letter written from England during her first memorable visit, Mrs. Stowe speaks of the preaching of the Rev. Dr. Mc-Neile of Liverpool, one of the leading men of the established church, and a strong millenarian.

" It was a sermon after the style of Tholock and other German sermonizers, who seem to hold that the purpose of preaching is not to rouse the soul by an antagonistic struggle with sin through the reason, but to soothe the passions, quiet the will and bring the mind into a frame in which it shall incline to follow its own convictions of duty. They take it for granted that the reason why men sin is not because they are ignorant but because they are distracted and tempted by passion; that they do not need so much to be told what is their duty, as persuaded to do it. To me, brought up on the very battle field of controversial theology, accustomed to hear every religious idea guarded by definitions and thoroughly hammered on a logical anvil, before the preacher thought of making use of it for heart or conscious, though I enjoyed the discourse extremely, I could not help wondering what an American theological professor would make of such a sermon. To preach on faith, hope and charity all in one discourse ! Why, we should have six sermons on the nature of faith, to begin with ; on speculative faith ; practical faith and the faith of miracles ; then we should have the laws of faith, and the connection of faith with evidence, and the nature of evidence, and the different kinds of evidence and so on. For my part, I have had a suspicion since I have been here, that a touch of this kind of thing might improve English preaching ; as, also, I do think that sermons of the kind I have described would be useful by way of alterative among us. If I could have but one of the two manners, I should prefer our own, because I think that this habit of preaching is one of the strongest educational forces that form the mind of our country."

It will be observed that Mrs. Stowe had a high respect for the intellectual discipline which was found in the theological methods with which she was most familiar, but as will be seen, pure logic was found sadly wanting in seasons of affliction when feeling rose higher than thought, and would not be curbed by formulas or creeds.

"The Minister's Wooing" began as a serial in the Atlantic Monthly at the end of the first year of its brilliant existence, under the editorship of James Russell Lowell. The story began in the December number of 1858 and ran quite through the following year, being contemporary with Oliver Wendell Holmes' second series of essays. "At the Breakfast Table," under the character of "The Professor."

It is probable that few of the literary critics who had acknowledged her power as a writer upon the great subject which found marvellous expression in "Uncle Tom's Cabin," were prepared for so strong a literary work as "The Minister's Wooing." It made one of the striking successes of the young "Atlantic Monthly," largely increasing the subscription of that magazine, helping to bear it upward in its creditable career.

Just here, it may be said that Mrs. Stowe's first great work had been one of the direct causes of the establishment of this magazine. Francis H. Underwood, LL. D., now the United States Consul to Glasgow, who was the projector, and for some years managing editor of the "Atlantic," was an earnest Abolitionist. He was then a young writer, but has since become known to the best

literary circles, as the accomplished biographer of James
Russell Lowell, of John Greenleaf Whittier, of H. W.
Longfellow, and the author of various text books of high
value.

"Harper's" and "Putnam's" were the chief month-
lies in existence at that time but neither of them
ventured to discuss themes of living interest. Publishers and editors were nervously susceptible to any
article that might offend slaveholders, and their northern apologists and allies. Mr. Underwood saw, however, that the leading authors of the north were nearly all
on the side of freedom. Mrs. Stowe's "Uncle Tom's Cabin"
was meeting the most unparalleled success, and he believed
that if poets like Longfellow and Whittier, essayists like
Holmes, wits with a purpose like Lowell, and novelists like
Mrs. Stowe, were to unite their force, a profound impression
might be made. Mr. John P. Jewett, the publisher who
was making a fortune out of "Uncle Tom's Cabin," agreed
to publish such a magazine, but at the last moment he faltered, and Phillips, Sampson & Co., after three years of
persuasion, promised to undertake it. They had already
succeeded in securing the publication of "Uncle Tom's
Cabin," "Sunny Memories" and "Dred," and were carrying also Emerson's and Prescott's works. When the plan
was taking form in 1857, Mr. Underwood and Mr. Lowell
went out to Andover and spent a day with Professor and
Mrs. Stowe, and her promise to be an early contributor was
secured. Mrs. Stowe wrote a short story called "The
Mourning Veil," for the first number of the Atlantic, but it
attracted little attention, being like all the other articles,
unsigned, and, while containing good writing, inculcated

the lesson of profit in bereavements, in the somewhat lack-
idaisical vein of Washington Irving's earlier, sentimental
tales. In February 1858, Mrs. Stowe contributed a sketch
of " New England Ministers," which was a spicy and entertaining article, containing analysis of character and reminiscences of noted divines such as the daughter of Lyman
Beecher was well qualified to write.

Correspondence with Francis H. Underwood has elicited
a letter in which he writes:

I entered the employment of Messrs. Phillips, Sampson & Co.
with the hope of persuading them to establish a magazine of high
literary excellence with anti-slavery principles. I had come to
Boston with that idea in my head. It took a number of years of
effort to bring together the forces. The larger part of my early
correspondence is upon that subject. Mrs. Stowe was one of the
strong friends of the project, and never let an opportunity pass of
impressing her views upon Mr. Phillips. The project was also
favored by Mr. Lee, one of the partners.

After long preparations the magazine was started, and its name,
" The Atlantic Monthly," was suggested by Dr. Holmes. It is
not necessary to add any details of the beginning; but I wish to
say that without the aid of Mrs. Stowe I doubt if it would have
been published.

It was hoped that Mrs. Stowe would write a serial novel for it.
The earliest fiction we were able to secure was not remarkable;
but *The Autocrat* saved the venture and made it a brilliant success.

"The Minister's Wooing" occasioned wide discussions
and many heart burnings, which indeed revive at the present day whenever its subject matter is mentioned to some
devoted theologians of the "old school." Rev. E. P. Parker,
D. D., of Hartford, writes of it in a sketch of the author,

as a "wonderful piece of theological criticism." He proceeds to say: "As such it was no less warmly welcomed than bitterly assailed. But whatever may be thought of its soundness and merit, there can be no doubt of its great influence. Few books that have been published within the last twenty years have done more to confirm the popular suspicion that the most perfectly compacted dogmatic systems of theology, are of all things the most imperfect, inadequate and unsatisfactory, and to strengthen what may be called the liberal, evangelical party of New England."

It was the first of the religious novels, those lay sermons, which have come to be a prodigious power in intellectual progress, and by no means the least important among the influences which have followed to lead modern thought ' away from traditionalism towards the scriptures, away from a scholastic towards a vital theology."

In these works, which are sometimes condemned, Dr. Lyman Abbott, with a genial optimism, which in itself is a cheering testimony to the generous attributes possible to the rest of the human race, sees a spirit of original investigation which is not skepticism, but a new and vital interest in religion; not merely a revolt against dogmatism either, but, if he is correctly understood, a defence of the holy certitudes of life, which were in danger of being unrealized, so encumbered as they have been by human creeds and doctrines. Dr. Oliver Wendell Holmes recently wrote in an open letter, "There was a time in which I, among the rest, felt bound to protest in the name of humanity and of common sense against certain doctrines I had heard preached in my tender years. I had to suffer for it. In fact I had to undergo martyrdom in newspaper paragraphs. What a change in religious sentiment and temper since 30 years ago. If one who has thought out for himself a creed differing from that of his father had thought it necessary in those days to defend himself, he might have suggested that a child commonly has a mother as well as a father, and that the harshest doctrines passed through the moral constitution of a woman, and especially of a mother, come out as different from what they were when they went in as the vaccine vesicle is from confluent smallpox. Remember the part which women like Mrs. Stowe and Miss Phelps, and Mrs. Ward and Mrs. Deland, have taken in the work of startling the heathenized churches out of their hideous dreams."

Mrs. Stowe did not essay to pierce the boundaries of Heaven or to form a new theology. She contented herself with illustrating the influence of the Calvanistic creed upon different human minds. She did not ignore the mental keenness and moral strength attained by natures which survived the intense friction of those beliefs, but she most tenderly and sympathetically portrayed the effect of certain logical conclusions upon more impressionable hearts. The spontaneous answer of the reading public, demonstrated how full of power was her delineation.

The scene is laid in Newport, in the latter half of the 18th century, when the small seaport was all unconscious of its present fame as a fashionable resort. "The Widow Scudder," who was in the first sentence introduced to the reader, is a type of one of those efficient women to whom nothing, in the way of womanly achievements is impossible, one who by force of her own "faculty," which the author defines as "Yankee for *savoir faire,* and the opposite virtue to shiftlessness," reigned supreme in every circle she entered, quick of speech, ready of wit, comely in person, finely bred, and with the first glance demonstrating her right to be. She has from a girl been able to harness or ride any horse she required, to row a boat, to do fine embroidery, paint in water colors, wash, bake, brew, make wine and jelly that always was sure to "jell," and at the opening of the story, appears as the widow of a young Christian sea captain, who, from discouragement at want of worldly success, and lack of power to cope with the adversities of life, succumbed to yellow fever in a southern port, leaving his ship to come home without him. Of George Scudder and his wife, the author writes:

" He had been one of the first to attach himself to the unpopular and unworldly ministry of the celebrated Dr. Hopkins, and to appreciate the sublime ideality and unselfishness of those teachings which then were awakening new sensations in the theological mind of New England. Katy Scudder, too, had become "a professor" with her husband in the same church, and his death deepened her religious impressions. She became absorbed in religion after the fashion of New England, where devotion is doctrinal, not ritual. As she grew older her energy of character, her vigor and good judgment, caused her to be regarded as a mother in Israel; the minister boarded at her house, and it was she who was first to be consulted on all matters relating to the well being of the church. No woman could more manfully breast a long sermon or bring a more determined faith to the reception of a difficult doctrine." Then follows this delicious touch so characteristic of the gentle philosophy of the author:

"To say the truth, there lay at the bottom of her doctrinal
17

system this stable corner-stone—'Mr. Scudder used to believe it
—I will.' And after all that is said about independent thought,
isn't the fact, that a just and good soul has thus or thus believed,
a more respectable argument than many that are often adduced?
If it be not, more's the pity,—since two-thirds of the faith in the
world is built on no better foundation."

The event which was known as Mrs. Scudder's "having
company to tea," is inimitably described and the view which
is soon presented, of the state of society when "the majority of the people lived with the wholesome, thrifty simplicity of the olden time, when labor and intelligence went hand
in hand in perhaps a greater harmony than the world has
ever seen," hold a marvelous fidelity to truth, in its comprehension of the moving springs of thought and conduct,
affecting New England social life.   To this is superadded
the bright picture of beautiful Mary Scudder, the heroine
of the story, the only daughter of "Widow Scudder," which
shows the hand of a master, and at once commanded a
hearing with all the great *clientele*, who had been brought
by her first work, to respect the words of Harriet Beecher
Stowe.   It is a precious thing that so vivid and enduring a
picture of a New England maiden of the highest type has
thus been preserved for posterity which already begins to
speak slightingly of the woman of that period, sometimes
from the standpoint of masculine detraction of their intellectual force, and again from the ground of the advanced
woman of to-day, who is inclined to disparage the conventional boundaries within which the maidens of that period
are supposed to have been cramped.   Take this summing
up of Mary's accomplishments :

"She could both read and write fluently in her mother tongue. She could spin both on the little and the great wheel; and there were numberless towels, napkins, sheets, and pillow cases in the household store that could attest the skill of her pretty fingers. She had worked several samplers of such rare merit that they hung framed in different rooms of the house, exhibiting every variety and style of possible letter in the best marking stitch. She was skillful in all sewing and embroidery, in all shaping and cutting, with a quiet and deft handiness that constantly surprised her energetic mother, who could not conceive that so much could be done with so little noise. In fact in all household lore she was a veritable good fairy; her knowledge seemed unerring and intuitive; and whether she washed or ironed, or moulded biscuits or conserved plums, her gentle beauty seemed to turn to poetry all the prose of her life."

It was a refreshing and salutary picture for the young woman of thirty years of ago, it is no less an interesting and suggestive portrait to the "society girls" of to-day. See this exposition of her religious faith and feeling.

"From her father she had inherited a deep and thoughtful nature, predisposed to moral and religious exaltation. Had she been born in Italy, under the dissolving influences of that sunny, dreamy, clime, beneath the shadow of cathedrals, where pictured saints and angels smiled from every altar, she might, like fair Catherine of Sienna, have seen beatific visions in the sunset skies, and a silver dove descending upon her as she prayed; but, unfolding in the clear, keen cold New England clime, and nurtured in its abstract and positive theologies her religious faculties took other forms instead of lying entranced in mysterious raptures at the foot of altars, she read and pondered treatises on the Will, and listened in wrapt attention, while her spiritual guide, the venerated Dr. Hopkins, unfolded to her the theories of the great Edwards on the nature of true virtue. Womanlike she felt the subtle poetry of these sublime abstractions which dealt with such infinite and unknown quantities—which spoke of the universe, of its great Architect, of man, of angels as matters of intimate and daily contemplation; and her teacher, a grand minded and simple hearted man as ever lived, was often amazed at the tread with which this fair young child walked through these regions of abstract thought,—often comprehending through an etherial clearness of nature what he had laboriously and heavily reasoned out. The elixir of the spirit that sparkled in her was of that quality of which the souls of poets and artists are made; but the keen New England air crystalizes emotions into ideas, and restricts many a poetic soul to the necessity of expressing itself in only practical living. The rigid theological discipline of New England is fitted to produce rather strength and purity than enjoyment. It is not fitted to make a sensitive and thoughtful nature happy, however it might ennoble and exalt."

One need not apologize for extending excerpts where every paragraph holds a truth and a depth of philosophy second to that of no writer of the modern age. In fact, nothing can so refute and disprove the charges sometimes made as to Mrs. Stowe's unfairness to New England theology as her own words. She says:

"It is not in our line to imply the truth or the falsehood of those systems of philosophic theology which seemed for many years to have been the principal outlet for the proclivities of the New England mind, but as psychological developments they have an intense interest. He who does not see a grand side to these strivings of the soul, cannot understand one of the noblest capabilities of humanity. No real artist or philosopher ever lived who has not at some hours risen to the height of utter self-abnegation for the glory of the invisible. There have been painters who would have been crucified to demonstrate the action of a muscle,—chemists who would gladly have melted themselves and all humanity in their crucible if so a new discovery might arise out of its fumes. Even persons of mere artistic sensibility are at times raised by music, painting or poetry to a momentary trance of self-oblivion, in which they would offer their whole being before the shrine of invisible loveliness. These hard old New England divines were the poets of metaphysical philosophy, who built systems in an artistic fervor, and felt self-exhale from beneath them as they rose into the higher regions of thought. But where theorists and philosophers tread with sublime assurance, woman often follows with bleeding footsteps ;—women are always turning from the abstract to the individual, and feeling, where the philosopher only thinks, it was easy enough for Mary to believe in self renunciation for she was one with a born vocation for martyrdom and so, when the idea was put to her of suffering eternal pains for the glory of God and the good of being in general, she responded to it with a sort of sublime thrill, such as it is given to some natures to feel in view of uttermost sacrifice. But when she looked around on the warm, living faces of friends, acquaintances and neighbors, viewing them as possible candidates for dooms so fearfully different, she sometimes felt the walls of her faith closing around her as an iron shroud,—she wondered that the sun could shine so brightly, that flowers could flaunt such dazzling colors, that sweet airs could breath and little children play, and youth, love and hope, and a thousand intoxicating influences combine to cheat the victims from the thought that their next step might be into an abyss of horrors without end."

The author of " The Minister's Wooing " thus gives in a few paragraphs in her second chapter, the intellectual and spiritual effects of the severe theology of the time, upon a nature limpid with truth and purity which, willing to sacrifice itself, could yet but feel a strong repulsion at the carrying out of the doctrine upon her fellow beings.   This is the key note to much that follows in the struggles and developments of several characters.   Mary Scudder, young, beautiful, and full of natural sweetness and light, though so held and martyred in spirit by her religious convictions, yet felt the breath of warm impulse and natural feeling, and had become attached to a young man, a distant cousin, whose family connection had given him free access to the house at all times and seasons.   James Marvyn was a sailor, a frank, joyous, thoughtless lad, with merry dark eyes and a head of curling black hair, and a tall lithe figure, which was full of reckless manly grace, most fascinating to all.

He was the idol of his old colored nurse, black Candace, the hope and pride of his mother, as far as her painfully distressed mind allowed her hope and pleasure in anything, and from nature and grace, became a favorite with the old and young, the poor, the wealthy, the merry and wise; the reckless companions who devotedly followed him, and the good people who out of respect to their religious professions, felt bound to sigh over his careless happiness and animal spirits.

Mary Scudder was somehow specially concerned about his spiritual welfare, and from the clear depths of her pure heart, gave him anxious counsel and entreaties to consider his future condition.   The present was bright and joyous enough for young James Marvyn, and though he listened with great tenderness to Mary because he loved her, it was

surely the maiden, and not the Word that touched his
heart. In the description and analysis of the mixed feelings which Mary felt for James, we have one of the keenest
perceptions, one of the largest ideals and tenderest appreci-
ations of the heart of a typical New England maiden of the
last century, which has ever seen the light. To those who
have grown up in the lore and the lingering light of some
of those lives of the girls of a hundred years ago, it appears
delightfully true and pleasant to look upon. There is the
reincarnation of our idyllic grandmothers, in Mary's sweet
young womanhood. Those may well feel loss who cannot
so regard it.

The character of Dr. Hopkins stands out as an artistic
representation of first, a gentleman, and secondarily a theologian, while yet the philosophy which has permeated his
very soul does not absorb or quite overcome the human
naturalness of his heart. His majestic and manly person,
his courtly grace, his merciful kindness to the lower classes,
his noble aims and maintenance of right against his own
temporal interests, his depth of thought and eloquence of
utterance are presented with the pen of a sincere admirer.

Particularly does the writer testify to Dr. Hopkins' earnest
action against the holding of negroes as slaves, a custom
which obtained in his time in New England, though the
condition of things, climatic influences which set every
man to work, made the owners depend comparatively little
upon the labor of the slaves, who were held as a class of
privileged family retainers. Of such the character of Old
Candace is a type. The description of her peculiarities of
person and mind is one of the inimitable things in the language.

In the character of Mr. Zebedee Marvyn we have perpetuated, a type which was common to the New England fathers. He was a strict, conscientious man, an ardent Federalist, with an energy of thought and clearness of mentality which marked the New England character of that time; a well read and careful theologian, a man occupied with public trusts; deacon of the church; chairman of the school committee; following up his knowledge of the law and his sense of right with unflinching conclusions, which he enforced equally upon indifferent persons, his own family or himself.

Mrs. Marvyn, it may be interesting to note, was drawn from the character of the mother of young Professor Fisher, whose death at sea made an unmarried widow of Catherine Beecher. He is referred to in the story as the eldest son, who was a mathematical professor in one of the leading colleges of New England. Mrs. Marvyn was a tall, sad-eyed, gentle mannered woman of a thoughtful nature, which, under the pressure of prevalent theological thought had grown into a morbid conscientiousness and insane fear of God, which darkened her life.

She had an artistic soul, was full of beautiful instincts, was by nature drawn to the delights of existence. She longed for grand music, for soul stirring pictures, for poetry, and grace and culture. She starved upon the forbidding look of the old meeting house, and the wrenching fugue tunes of the uncultivated choir, upon the worsted angels, and needle work grave yard scenes upon the walls of the homes she visited. She pined for noble themes, for lofty imaginations upon the beauties of the world, upon the sweet affections and tendernesses of humanity.

What she received was stony doctrines, cruel threatenings, metaphysical discussions upon intangible horrors, word paintings of the imminent terrors of the world to come, and constant conversations and despairing wrestlings with the awful, irreconcilable questions of Forcordination and Free Will. For relief, to get away from the lines where madness lay, she occupied herself for days with mathematical problems, for instance, once pursuing a certain imperfect treatise upon Optics until she found a mistake in the diagrams, corrected it and made the demonstration complete. Utterly unable to feel, as she was commanded by theologians to believe, she regarded herself as a child of wrath, one of the non-elect, an heir to perdition, waiting fearfully for the interposition of a God who appeared to come not near to her. In speaking of the effects of the system of theology that induced such a state of feeling the author says,—

"These systems, so admirable in relation to the energy, earnestness and accuteness of their authors, when received as absolute truth, and as a basis of actual life, had, on the minds of a certain class, the effect of a slow poison, producing life habits of morbid action very different from any which ever followed the simple reading of the Bible."

Harriet Beecher Stowe seemed possessed of the "Realometer" desired by Thoreau with which to pierce the sludge and alluvium of human opinion and custom, and strike the enduring facts of existence. By it, she was enabled to distinguish the seeming from the being, to discriminate between the thought structures of men and the eternal word of God. Her perceptions had been cleared through earnest thought and suffering. Only one who had endured similar spiritual agony could so speak from the inner consciousness, from the secret chambers of the heart; one who had escaped from the horror within, out into the sunshine of a gentler, natural faith, in the love and mercy of God.

Those who have so suffered, or been intimate witnesses of the torments of friends can judge of the truth of this representation. That it is almost universally received, as truth especially among modern New Englanders whose hearts still echo like tolling bells to the familiar memories of the old thought, is sufficient proof that the writer had presented no warped perspective or unreal picture, but instead had again held the mirror up to facts, struck the chord of experience and feeling, in the souls of a million readers.

No sporadic arguments can disprove the testimony of the universal heart. Indeed one may safely presume that the general reader has so spontaneously accepted this picture as a reflection of the truth, that any defense seems a work of supererogation. There are, however, questions of literary and historical observance of material events, which will be noted, further on.

Mary Scudder who had parted from her lover, giving him her little Bible with its marginal notes, next appears in the pleasure of a new experience, the event of a brilliant party given in honor of the marriage of the daughter of one of the greatest Newport families, bringing several influential associations into her serene existence. She was attired most exquisitely under the fingers of Miss Prissy, the little spinster dress maker who went from house to house through the town, creating out of stuffs useful and tasteful

garments, a character which has become classic for its clear
cut outlines and peculiar fidelity to a class now passing
away under the changed conditions of social life. Under
the chaperonage of her mother and escorted by Dr. Hopkins in all the dignity of his personal appearance and
divine office, Mary Scudder went to the splendid fête.
Aaron Burr who at the period of which the author writes,
held a name associated with most brilliant success, is here
introduced as one of the personages of the story. Quite
familiar by hearsay and historical knowledge of the apt,
subtle, dazzling and peculiarly engaging grandson of the
great divine, Jonathan Edwards, who had figured conspicuously in the society of Litchfield, Mrs. Stowe saw in his
brilliant personality an admirable figure for her tale. He
therefore steps upon the stage at the Wilcox's party, a
startling, distinct, keenly delicate, fascinating and unscru-
pulous character, a most effective foil to the hero, quite the
antipodes of Mary's rustic admirers in general and in sharp
contrast to young, frank James Marvyn, in particular.
That the practiced, high bred man of the world made a
strong impression upon women whenever he met them, is
well known.

Mary Scudder is attracted to him, but not all his artful
tact and wary shrewdness in compliment, disarm her calm
self-poise or win more than a friendly glance. Indeed the delicious coolness with which she responds to his most ardent
advances, is thoroughly enjoyable. Burr became interested
in this New England maiden, whose pure unimpassioned
beauty seemed to have a stellar remoteness from him, and
began to experiment upon her, to his own rare discomfiture.

The entrance of Madame de Frontignac, the volatile,

scintillating, but true hearted French woman, who for the time is held in the thrall of Aaron Burr's Satanic fascination, brought to American readers a character which remains one of the most bewitching depictions of our literature. Beautiful, generous, impulsive, with all the graces of mind and character which the author had learned to love in the French people, Virginie de Frontignac appears as the wife of a Colonel upon LaFayette's staff, a grave and dignified man who was some twenty-seven years her elder.

Married after the French custom which consigns its maidens most willingly to respectability and station, regardless of such a thing as love before the event; consenting gleefully in order that she might emerge from the convent, that she might wear velvet, lace and diamonds, that she might go out without surveillance; regarded by her husband as a beautiful though very absurd little pet; it was not until Virginie met Aaron Burr, that she knew what it was to love, then alas, with only mortification as its result, and the risk to her happiness doubly great, from the dishonorable character of the man.

Her meeting with Mary is the event upon which turns her destiny, for contact with another pure woman's soul, one scarcely vulnerable to the temptation which threatens hers, saves her from her giddy self, and transforms her into her higher possibility as a noble wife and devoted mother, but not immediately, for Colonel Burr is yet to be understood by Mary Scudder; the bewitching little Madame is yet to be won and softened and changed by the atmosphere of the homes of the Scudders and Marvyns, into which she enters as a friend.

Madame de Frontignac soon proposes to give French les-

sons to Mary and Mrs. Marvyn. The latter was drawn to
the charming French woman as to a beautiful poem. She
had for some time been studying the language to fit
herself to master an astronomical treatise, which she had
found written in that tongue. Virginie gives the lessons,
simultaneously improving her lisping English, and making
a picture at the spinning wheel with her dainty ways and
pretty costumes, her rings sparkling in odd contrast to
the severe plainness of the wooden chair and whirring
wheel. She soon penetrates Mary's sweet secret concerning the black-eyed lad at sea, and chatters on most
entertainingly with a mingling of storytelling, airy philosophy and matter of fact observation, which bewitches
her hearers.

CHAPTER XII.

THE MINISTER'S WOOING, CONTINUED. DOCTOR HOPKINS AS
A LOVER. THE LOSS OF JAMES MARVYN'S SHIP. A
MOTHER'S INCONSOLABLE GRIEF FOR HER UNREGENERATE
SON. "VIEWS OF DIVINE GOVERNMENT." THE RELIGION OF
OLD BLACK CANDACE. COLONEL AARON BURR. MADAME DE
FRONTIGNAC. RETURN OF JAMES MARVYN. MISS PRIS-
SY'S INTERVENTION. THE EFFECT OF THE STORY UPON
EMINENT THEOLOGIANS. PROFESSOR PARK'S CONVERSA-
TIONS WITH THE AUTHOR. A RECENT TESTIMONIAL OF
HIS ADMIRATION AND ESTEEM FOR MRS. STOWE. THE
MINISTER'S WOOING NOT A HISTORICAL NOVEL EXCEPT IN
ITS REPRESENTATIONS OF THE METAPHYSICAL EVENTS
BROUGHT ABOUT BY THE INFLUENCE OF THE THEOLOGY
OF THE PERIOD. VARIOUS HISTORICAL ANACHRONISMS.
ARCHBISHOP WHATELY'S ESTIMATE OF THE LITERARY
VALUE OF THE WORK. A LETTER FROM GLADSTONE.

The summer passes. Madame de Frontignac has returned to Philadelphia with her husband, from whence she
sends very polyglot letters to Mary.

The good Doctor has gone on with his work, waging
war upon the Newport slaveholders, who are also his
wealthiest supporters, and winning afresh golden opinions
of his women friends at the Scudder cottage, who fully
appreciate his self-abnegation in what he considers a just
cause. Nothing is heard of James Marvyn, and Mary

270

is so steadily silent about him that Mrs. Scudder's heart lightens with the hope that her affections may be turning to the (in her opinion) more worthy object nearer by, for it is the hope of her devoted heart that Mary shall marry Dr. Hopkins, who she is assured entertains a deep love for her child. It is Miss Prissy who comes one day to tell dreadful news to Mrs. Scudder, and her words, descriptive of Mrs. Marvyn's agony at the news from her son's ship, that fall upon Mary's stricken ears. The scene that ensues is alive with feeling. Mary's crushed heart, the futile sympathies of her friends and the prayer of the good Doctor raised to Heaven over her quivering but almost senseless frame, recall that sorrow which befell the Beecher family in the years long gone by when sister Catherine thus suffered, while all stood by, helpless, except in prayer.

To Mary only, the agonized mother expressed her grief, she instinctively turns to her young arms and Mary remains some days at the Marvyn's home, the two stricken women weeping, conversing and imploring help in the privacy of their sacred seclusion. In the 23rd Chapter entitled " Views of Divine Government," is the heart of the book. It is an incomparable discussion and presentation of the whole religion of feeling, in contrast with the metaphysical theology which then prevailed.

See the effect of such doctrines upon a grief-stricken soul!

"Mary," she said, "I can't help it,—don't mind what I say, but I must speak or die!—it is all hard, unjust, cruel!—to all eternity I will say so! To me there is no goodness, no justice, no mercy in anything! Life seems to me the most tremendous doom that can be inflicted on a helpless being! *What have we done,* that it should be sent upon us? Why were we made to love so, to hope so,—our hearts so full of feeling, and all the laws of Nature marching over us,—never stopping for our agony? Why, we can suffer so in this life that we had better never have been born!

"But, Mary, think for a moment, what life is! think of those awful ages of eternity! and then think of all God's power and knowledge used on the lost to make them suffer! think that all but the merest fragment of mankind have gone into this,—are in it now! The number of the elect is so small we can scarce count them for anything! Think what noble minds, what warm, generous hearts, what splendid natures are wrecked and thrown away by thousands and ten thousands! how we love each other! how our hearts weave into each other! how more than glad we should be to die for each other! And all this ends . . . . O God, how must it end?—Mary! it isn't *my* sorrow only! What right have I to mourn? Is *my* son any better than any other mother's son? Thousands of thousands, whose mothers loved them as I love mine, are gone there!—Oh, my wedding day! Why did they rejoice? Brides should wear mourning,—the bells should toll for every wedding; every new family is built over this awful pit of despair, and only one in a thousand escapes!"

Mrs. Marvyn's grief at last amounts to frenzy and Mary failing to find strength in her bruised heart to console James' mother, appeals to Mr. Marvyn who sits determinedly reading his Bible; but old Candace, takes her in her arms like a weary child and rocking her back and forth upon her broad shoulder talks to her, not of theology, nor systems, but of her heavenly Father, of His love and pity, of His tenderness and love to his suffering creatures.—

"Honey, darlin', ye a'n't right,—dar's a drefful mistake somewhar," she said. "Why, de Lord a'n't like what ye tink,—He *loves* ye, honey! Why, jes' feel how *I* loves ye,—poor ole black Candace, an' I a'n't better'n Him as made me! Who was it wore de crown o' thorns, lamb?—who was it sweat great drops o' blood? —Who was it said, 'Father, forgive dem?' Say, honey!—wasn't it de Lord dat made ye?—Dar, Dar, now ye'r, cryin'!—cry away and ease yer poor little heart! He died for Mass'r Jim,— loved him and *died* for him,—jes' give up his sweet precious body and soul for him on de cross! Laws, jes' *leave* him in Jesus' hands! Why, honey, dar's de very print o' de nails in his hands now!"

The flood gates are rent; and healing sobs and tears shake the frail form, as a crushed flower shakes under the soft rains of summer. All in the room weep together.

"Now honey," said Candace, after a pause of some minutes, "I knows our Doctor's a mighty good man, an' learned,—an' in fair weather I ha'nt no 'bjection to yer hearin' all about dese yer great an' mighty tings he's got to say. But, honey, dey won't do for you now; sick folks mus'n't hab strong meat; an' dat ar's *Jesus*. Jes' come right down to whar poor ole black Candace has to stay allers,—it's a good place darlin'! *Look right at Jesus*. Tell ye, honey, ye can't live no other way now. Don't ye 'member how He looked on His mother, when she stood faintin' an' tremblin' under de cross jes' like you? He knows all about mothers' hearts; He won't break yours. It was jes' 'cause He know'd we'd come into straits like dis yer, dat he went through all dese tings,—Him de Lord of Glory! Is dis Him you was a-talkin' about?—Him you can't love? Look at Him, an' see ef you can't. Look an' see what He is!—don't ask no questions, and don't go to no reasonin's,—jes' look at *Him*, hangin' dar, so sweet and patient, on de cross! All dey could do couldn't stop his lovin' em; he prayed for 'em wid all de breath he had. Dar's a God you can love, ain't dar? Candace loves Him,—poor, ole, foolish, black, wicked Can-

18

dace,—and she knows He loves her,"—and here Candace broke down into torrents of weeping.

They laid the mother, faint and weary, on her bed, and beneath the shadow of that awful suffering, came down a healing sleep on those weary eylids. It was true, natural, religion this homely exhortation of the unlettered colored woman, and the bleeding heart was softened and healed by the burst of tears which relieved the tension of the dis-traught nerves and made life and reason possible.

Certain critics question Mrs. Stowe's theology, but no one can fail to be moved and benefitted by her religion, if never shown but in this scene.

Mary remains many days at the white house, for during the illness that follows, no one can smooth the throbbing temples, no one stroke the nervous hands, no one speak to the sore heart, as she. Mary keeps silence upon her own feelings and when once more resuming the routine of her home life, maintains the calm execution of her duties with a gentle sweetness, scarcely different from her old manner.

Madame de Frontignac comes back to Newport with the shadow of a sorrow upon her too, and at last gives Mary the history of her life with the confession of her love for Aaron Burr, which happily but how wrenchingly, had been broken, by the finding of a letter written to him by a friend, in which the stranger spoke of her so lightly, that she knew Burr was false to her, as he had been to honor, in approaching her. It had been in time, and her dream is over, though the memory of it is bitter. The interview of the two women affords a striking picture. The frail wife, the staunch maiden; the deceived one, and the bereaved sufferer; the one France, the other New England ; the one looking for strength and guidance to the priest of the Roman church which held its wings over her, the other striving with Puritan theology to understand and be reconciled to a system, which seemed to shut her away from the God whom she yet instinctively sought, and believed to be a loving Father.

It is a powerful piece of work, an intellectual canvas which presents the mingled threads of life, conforming most marvelously with the quaint fashion of the last century, but revealing the best qualities and the enduring traits of the human heart.

With her flowered satins, her ribbons, laces and plumes, her diamonds and rouge, Virginie leaves behind her at Philadelphia, the old frivolous heart, and comes back to Newport, with her simple costumes, her innocent tastes and her sunny lovableness, a blessing to them all in the Scudder home.

The year has gone around and Mary has conquered the sharpness of her grief, though the deep sadness of it remains in her heart, hidden from view. Then comes the proposal of Doctor Hopkins for her hand in marriage, made to Mrs. Scudder in true courtly style. Mary's reception of it is touching in the extreme, and her consent, unselfishly given in the hope of making some one happy, is the thing to be expected from her.

The reader comes nearer to loving the Doctor, in the scene when he is told of Mary's acceptance, than at any time in the previous chapters. The impression of the grand, self-contained nature, so strongly going out to this young girl, yet so bravely waiting a possible refusal and so gratefully, with all humility, accepting the blessing, almost

makes one forget the natural objection to fate, which has
given to him the happiness, which should have belonged to
the young and now lost lover. The betrothal is made,
and to casual eyes, even to her own desiring heart, Mary
seems to be happy.

Madame de Frontignac, warned by her own experience
regards her with attention. Not altogether understanding
the hearts of New England maidens, she yet holds a faith
that girls are much alike the world over, and she can
not believe that this marriage is to be a good thing, but
she keeps her own counsel. The excitement in the parish
when the prospective marriage is formally announced, the
presentation of numerous gifts, various and widely differing
in value, the energetic preparations of the good wives who
speedily find vent for their enthusiasm in "a quilting"
for the minister's new housekeeping, are brought before the
eye in the natural procession of events. Then comes Colonel Aaron Burr back to Newport and makes an attempt to
renew his power over Madame de Frontignac, who has dismissed him some time before. He calls at the Scudders
only to meet Mary, and receive such a rebuff and admoni-
tion as it is probable he had never before encountered. One
should read the chapter describing it, to see what can be
said by a pure woman, who is defending her friend from a
libertine. It is strong and salutatory and will so remain
while society stands. While Burr remains in Newport,
Mary stands between her friend and him, pleading, cooling,
admonishing and saving.

Much to the astonishment of modest Doctor Hopkins,
who never imagined that his marriage to Mary Scudder, in
whose family he had for some years resided, and where he

intended to remain at least for a time, would make such a social earthquake, the preparations and arrangements for his wedding appear to be convulsing the whole parish.

As the interest approaches the focal point, which is at the Scudder cottage, it has served to dismantle the house, to uproot and tear apart the contiguity of the household goods and throw all into a preliminary chaos, for the house is to be cleaned, an operation which always precedes any public social occasion, and after that sewing is to be done, and baking, brewing and conserving are to immediately precede the great event. When the heavier work is done, Miss Prissy comes to make the wedding dress, and the family is absorbed in the operation.

Madame de Fontignac ably seconds Miss Prissy's efforts, and adds sundry delicate touches and suggestions which make the bridal robe and appurtenances, a dream of beauty. Indeed, so fully does the spirit and sympathy of the occasion permeate the pages of the story at this point, that no woman can read it without a thrill of interest in every slightest detail.

Sweet Mary Scudder walks by the shore one evening, only three days before her expected marriage, filled with calm anticipations of the duties of her new life, when from the air behind her comes a voice which stops her heart, "Mary!" and the tall figure of James Marvyn bends over her, his dark eyes looks into her own, his black curls shut out the blue sky, his strong arms clasp her to his beating heart.

For an hour she forgets all but him. Knows only that he lives, is there, and that he loves her. But suddenly

comes the recollection of all the rest, and Mary goes home.
It is true to her character that she does not for an instant
think of breaking her word to the Doctor. It has come to
her as one of the inevitable things in life, and she considers herself as firmly bound by her word, as if the ceremony
of marriage had been performed.

On the ship with James came his letter from Canton,
telling of his safety and full of his spiritual experiences and
and an account of the misfortunes which had overtaken
his ship. Her Bible has been an anchor to him, or rather
a pole star, by which to guide his course more steadily
than in the days when he had not found it. James Marvyn has come home somewhat sobered, more serious in
thought, more worthy of Mary. He has become the man
she always hoped and prayed he would be, but she is promised to another, and that one, a man whom she reveres and
loves with a peculiar respect and trustfulness; whom she
regards as the best man she ever knew.

But—here is James, alive, and more than ever master
of her girl's heart, and all light seems to go out of the future. The description of Mary's sad resignation to her
strange fate; the anxious fears of her mother which are stilled
by Mary's view of her duty; the remonstrances of Madame
de Fontignac privately offered to Mary's sympathetic heart;
the innocent complacency of the Doctor who, dwelling high
up in the realms of lofty thought, has no inkling of the danger that menaces his domestic happiness; the artful intervention of Madame de Fontignac in upsetting a stand and
breaking a water pitcher, which takes Mrs. Scudder up
stairs, so that James has a moment to speak one last loving entreaty to Mary; and at last, the fearful determination

of little Miss Prissy to sacrifice herself, brave ignominy, death, if necessary, rather than that Mary should be sacrificed to a promise which under the present circumstances never could have been made; the irruption of Miss Prissy, desperate with conflicting emotions, into the Doctor's study, where she manages to quiet her beating heart long enough to tell the good man the true state of affairs, is a passage which is a masterpiece of realistic writing. It is one which remains a pleasant memory, as of an actual event, in the mind of each reader.

Dear little Miss Prissy, whom happy wives and romantic maidens will never cease to bless for having broken the truth to the Doctor, knows nothing can set things back as they were. With this bitter knowledge of the youthful loves of Mary and James, the good man cannot require his bride, and with a noble self abnegation, only possible to such disciplined natures, he resigns her to the dashing sailor lad, whom she loves with a feeling so different from her affection for him. The scene in which he received the blasting tidings and the one following, wherein he, most dignified, courtly and graceful in manner, though with a breaking heart, gives his bride to James Marvyn, is doubtless one of the most artistic and moving passages in the book. With it, is completed "The Minister's Wooing."

Miss Prissy's letter, which gives a delightfully detailed and feminine account of the wedding and the prosperity which came to James from an acquaintance formed in China, and the brief chapter giving a last glimpse at the De Frontignac's, now happy and blest with sons, and the mention of the erection by unknown hands, of a monument upon Burr's lonely grave, close the work. Any sketch is necessarily a mere outline. It so utterly fails to give a hint of the strength, and artistic effect of the story, that the writer is tempted to cut it all out, only entreating those to whom it is unfamiliar to read and carefully digest "The Minister's Wooing," which so far transcends anything that can be said in its praise.

The effect of the story upon the theologians of the School at Andover was very marked and productive of some un-pleasantness. Prof. Park, the President of the Seminary, called upon Mrs. Stowe several times before the story was completed, and also previous to its issue in book form, urg-ing strenuously that she should modify some of its features. This she quietly but firmly refused to do. It was not the habit of Harriet Beecher Stowe to put forth an ill-consid-ered work, and having decided upon the truth of a thing she did not lack the courage of her opinions. She reminded the theologian that no one but herself would be responsible for "The Minister's Wooing." That it appeared to her to be a truthful representation of religious thought and feel-ing in the past century, and that it must stand. Having studied and thought out its conclusions from historical facts and the personal impressions of many people whom she relied upon as impartial witnesses, Mrs. Stowe felt no obli-gation to modify her statements or disguise her views to suit the forms of differing opinion. She desired it to go forth as her own. She did not swerve from its support when it met reprisal. However, the impression which has sometimes been given that the President of the Theological Seminary was thereby prejudiced against Mrs. Stowe, is shown to be a false one by the sub-joined paragraph from a letter lately received from Dr. Park, in answer to inquir-

ies upon the subject, which contains nothing but expressions of sincere friendship and admiration.

"As I loaned Mrs. Stowe some copies of my Memoir of Dr.
Samuel Hopkins, I was led to converse with her from time to time
in regard to her representations of him. I regarded these representations as incompatible with the character of Dr. Hopkins. I
thought that all his wooing was conducted in a more logical and
theological style than that which was portrayed in her novel. I
thought that his friends would regard her description of him as
incompatible with fact. There were some historical and geo-
graphical inaccuracies which I thought might be easily rectified.
After the volume was published some resident of Rhode Island
wrote an article for some Rhode Island newspaper criticising Mrs.
Stowe's volume in a humorous way. The article purported to be
a letter written by Dr. Hopkins from his heavenly abode. It was
a very exact imitation of the style in which he wrote when living
here below. He was pleased to receive Madam Stowe's information regarding Newport, the place of his former residence. He
was rather surprised, however, to learn that the sun had changed
its place of rising and of setting. He did not exactly comprehend
the reason for the sun's rising and setting in such unwonted
places.

"After I had mentioned to Mrs. Stowe some of the criticisms
which would be made upon her volume, she wrote me a very
beautiful letter, which I loaned to a friend, who loaned it to a
neighbor, who loaned it to a collector of autographs; and, of
course, I have never been able to recover it. In her letter she
stated that she had planted her seed, that it had germinated and
was growing rapidly; she did not think it safe to cut off the branch
that was too long, nor to lengthen the branch that was too short,
nor to interfere with the natural growth of the plant. She thought
that facts were very useful in their place, but nature should

not conform to them, they were so stubborn. Her letter was a rare specimen of genius. I regret that I was so much pleased with it as to lend it.

"So many years have elapsed since the publication of Mrs. Stowe's volume that I have forgotten the particulars in which, as I thought, she misrepresented the theological system of Dr. Hopkins. Of course, she did not intend to leave any wrong impression in regard to his speculations or his character. I shall be very happy to see your Memoir, which will be read, I presume, by thousands of her admirers.

Very respectfully, dear Madam, I am,

Your friend and servant,

EDWARDS A. PARK."

It will be seen that their difference was not serious and that to the end of her life she retained the esteem and admiration of the eminent theologian.

It appears, however, that there were points upon which just criticism might be made, an opportunity which her detractors did not neglect.

While it should be remembered that the author was dealing more especially with a history of theological thought, rather than public actions, she perhaps rather daringly ignored the literary Chadbands who stood ready to dissect her work, and with some temerity, adapted historical events to her wants for a novel.

Though appearing as such, "The Minister's Wooing" can not be taken as a historical novel, except in its representation of the metaphysical events brought about by the influence of the theology of the period. There are anachronisms in the sequence of historical events which are easily discernible to anyone who chooses to regard the story from a "Dry-as-Dust" point of view. It is indeed a question how far the novelist's license may go in introducing well-known personages, and how much may be forgiven to an author's liberty in transferring actual events to meet the demands of his construction and putting them into different relation to other real or imaginary occurrences. This license Mrs. Stowe took with the utmost freedom, without perhaps sufficient consideration of the fact, that having borrowed so generously from history she owed it careful handling in return. She deferred the love disappointment of an eminent divine, which actually occurred in youth, to an age when he was happily married and the father of a family with several grand-children; not only transferring his love affair from Berkshire to Newport, but from the age of the early 20's (Dr. Hopkins being married at 26) to his declining years, thereby imputing to him the eccentricity (a thing very rare with New England divines) of having lived to middle age, a bachelor.

This had been of trifling account had not the dates which the advent of Aaron Burr forces us to assume 1791 —1797, also deferred some twenty-five years, his outspoken objection to slavery. This, though certainly unintentional, appears to some people, an actual injustice. His argument with Dr. Bellamy, which resulted in the instant emancipation of his colored retainer, so admirably reproduced in the scene with Zebedee Marvyn, must have occurred at least as early as 1784, as will soon appear.

Friends of Dr. Stiles also felt that injustice had been done that worthy and philanthropic divine, in representing him, as endeavoring to vindicate slavery as "a dispensation for giving the light of the Gospel to the Africans," for at a date prior to Hopkins' manifesto, he had made a vigorous protest against the slave trade. Moreover at the date when the story must have been laid, Dr. Stiles had for twenty-five years ceased to be a resident of Newport.

So it will appear, that by the bringing of so many events forward to include Aaron Burr, the author had much belated other occurrences, which have to the literal readers a far greater significance. For instance with the erroneous impressions received above, the careless reader is open to the belief that Rhode Island was still importing slaves as late as 1795. It had abolished slavery in the same year with Connecticut, viz: 1784.

The uncomplimentary fact, that the average reader does not pause to make these reflections, or perceive the anachronisms, does not absolve an author from responsibility. Much discussion would have been saved if Mrs. Stowe had received a clearer view of the essential bearings of her tale, and, preferring to displace events which from childish reminiscence were specially familiar to her, brought Aaron Burr to life a quarter of a century earlier. Fewer critics would have been interested to disprove his date. Her desire to introduce this brilliant villain as a foil to good Dr. Hopkins and handsome James Marvyn, while evincing the novelist's dramatic instinct, seems indeed to have led her into a coil with many distinguished critics.

The introduction of Aaron Burr was a daring thing, but how vividly interesting, the memories of readers who then for the first time realized his personality, will prove. It has been deprecated that Mrs. Stowe did not sufficiently hold him up to detestation, and it has been charged that she was not capable of understanding the true import of a love affair between him and the young wife of a French fellow-officer. Her belief in the good impulses which yet remained to the grandson of the great divine, Edwards, and her faith in womanhood, even when petted and unsupported by stern principles, are surely not to be regretted by any who desire to think well of human nature.

The interest of "The Minister's Wooing," to a thoughtful reader lies not so much in the external events of the story, as in the wonderful delineation of character and the metaphysical history; the mental and spiritual growth under the existing theological system, strangely distorted in several instances, but yet holding a form which commands respect while it moves to pity.

This was a far more difficult task than writing of life under negro slavery. In "Uncle Tom's Cabin" she had only to go from one section of the United States to another; only to eliminate distance. In "The Minister's Wooing" she had to take her readers backward three quarters of a century, to roll back the years and see and show what had been. In the first, it was only necessary to examine and investigate an existing institution, to prove the truth of her words. Writings upon a past age had to be proven by historical leavings, and those moreover, which pertained to so evanescent and shifting a thing, as thought. But mental and spiritual impressions remain and become hereditary possessions, when political and social events are forgotten, and "The Minister's Wooing" was generally accepted, as conforming in all essential points with the actual conditions of

religious thought in New England one hundred years ago.
"The Minister's Wooing" was published in London in
parts, simultaneously with its appearance in the Atlantic
Monthly. It was issued by Phillips, Sampson & Co., in
book form in October, 1859, two months previous to its
completion in the magazine. It was also published by
Sampson, Low & Co., in London at the same date and up
to March, 1869, a little more than ten years, had sold fifty
thousand copies. It was re-published by Tauchnitz in
Leipsic, having a very large sale in the German.

James Russell Lowell in introducing it to the public said,
"Already there have been scenes in ' The Minister's Wooing' that in their lowness of tone and quiet truth, contrast
as charmingly with the timid vagueness of the modern school
of novel writers as 'The Vicar of Wakefield' itself; and we
are greatly mistaken if it do not prove to be the most characteristic of Mrs. Stowe's works and that on which her fame
will chiefly rest with posterity."

Archbishop Whately wrote to the author in terms of the
highest praise, not only pronouncing it her greatest literary
achievement, but classing it among the most powerful
works of fiction in the English language.

As late as May, in 1884, Right Hon. W. E. Gladstone,
then Prime Minister of England, wrote to Mrs. Stowe concerning "The Minister's Wooing":

"Indisposition rather more prolonged than usual with
me, gave me an opportunity some month or two ago, of
recovering a few of my literary arrears. It was only then
that I acquired a personal acquaintance with the beautiful
and noble picture of Puritan life, which in that work you
have exhibited upon a pattern felicitous beyond example,

so far as my knowledge goes. I really know not among four or five of the characters (though I suppose Mary ought to be preferred as nearest to the image of our Saviour) to which to give the crown."

CHAPTER XIII.

In 1859 Mrs. Stowe became a contributor to *The Inde-pendent*, which was under the editorship of her brother, the Rev. Henry Ward Beecher. To this weekly, now the most popular and influential religious journal in the United States, Mrs. Stowe contributed articles—more strictly speak-ing—sermons, upon "The Higher Christian Life," which were eloquent and full of vital force, evincing a mental power which showed a near kinship with that of her illus-trious brother.

During the summer, Mrs. Stowe's youngest daughter was married to Rev. Charles F. Allen, of Boston, a young clergyman of strong ritualistic tendencies, at present rector of the Church of the Messiah, in that city. Dr. Lyman Beecher, then nearly eighty-four years of age, attended the wedding. He was hale and cheerful, and denied losing his memory, saying that "like his son Henry, he never had any." At that period the venerable divine used occasionally to preach a sermon, proving the truth of Lord Brougham's favorite quotation, "In the ashes live their wonted fires."

Mrs. Stowe went to Europe later in the season, and during the next eight months sent a series of foreign letters, which appeared at frequent intervals in "The Independent." These it is needless to say were read with great interest by the large number of subscribers, as they presented an intelligent discussion of affairs abroad, and especially in Italy. She wrote from Milan in October, full of Italian enthusiasm. She devoted much space to descriptions of churches, and discussed with vigor the political question then agitating Europe, upon the arrangement of the Italian states, and the balance of ecclesiastical power. It was at this time that Mrs. Browning, who ten years before had viewed the struggle of the Tuscans for liberty from "Casa Guidi Windows," was writing her last noble and generous themes, many of which were upon Italian liberty; and the two remarkable, English speaking women, sympathized in their view of the situation.

Mrs. Stowe, always in favor of the emancipation of men, wrote:

"There is nothing develops a man like a vote. It changes him from an animal to a reasonable creature, and this voting busi-

19

ness in Italy has done the work of years in awakening dormant minds and making *men* out of clods."

Mrs. Stowe and her sister and daughters visited Herculaneum and Pompeii, and spent some months in Rome, where she heartily enjoyed small housekeeping. They were the recipients of much attention from prominent persons, and Mrs. Stowe met many painters, sculptors, and literary people of note. She was found to be no less interesting in conversation than in writing, and various narrations and descriptions which she gave to small companies, of the peculiarities of negro life, or New England character, made a very delightful sensation, and Mrs. Stowe was more than ever besieged with invitations and honors.

Soon after her return in the summer of 1860, Mrs. Stowe contributed to "The Independent" an article on the recent visit to the United States of the Prince of Wales. It was full of her kind feeling towards England, as will be seen from an extract.

"It is not merely the generous and kindly boy in the kindliest and most interesting period of opening life ; but it is an embodiment, in boy's form of a glorious, related nation, of whose near kindred America has every reason to be proud. England herself, with all her old historic honors, with garment woven in memorial threads from the looms of Milton, Spenser, Bacon, Shakespeare,—comes modestly walking by our doors in the form of a boy just in the fresh morning of his days,—modest, simple, kindly, the good son of a good wife and mother, and it is something to make the tear start to see how quickly the American heart felt the pulsation of relationship, and the veneration for the dear old kindred blood of fatherland, and the proud remembrance of centuries of united Anglo Saxon history, when as yet the tiny American Oak lay a hidden germ in the leafy bosom of the grand old English mother."

In 1860, when the political situation of the United States had become alarming, Mrs. Stowe wrote for "The Independent" several articles upon the crisis. One on "The Church and the Slave Trade," which was full of fire. In November, after the election of Lincoln, a prophetic pæon called, "What God hath Wrought," and later a discussion of "The President's Message," which held Buchanan up to public view in no enviable light. The files of "The Independent" also show various poems and minor sketches signed by the author of "Uncle Tom's Cabin," of which "The Deacon's Dilemma, or the Use of the Beautiful," is an example.

With the beginning of Volume Four of "The Atlantic Monthly," there appeared the first chapters of a new novel by Mrs. Stowe. "Agnes of Sorrento" was planned and largely thought out during Mrs. Stowe's second visit to Italy.

This romance which has sometimes been hastily dismissed by the critics as lacking in the freedom and grace which characterize those stories of Harriet Beecher Stowe which are laid in her native land, is doubtless one of the sweetest exotics ever transplanted from foreign soil and selected from past ages. It was written in the enchanted atmosphere of the blue Mediterranean, amid associations rich with historical reminiscence, and scenes replete with visions of the past. The story is laid in Italy at the interesting and picturesque period known as the renaissance.

It was an age of awakening intelligence and artistic glories; when the greatest possible enthusiasm was manifested for the revived literature and sculptured marble of Greece and Rome; when Columbus was seeking a western passage to India; when Cardinal Bembo was writing Latin essays; when Ficino was teaching the philosophy of Plato; when music had become a written language and gentlemen sang and played upon the violin, the harp and the flute. The intelligence and culture of the upper classes so far surpassed that of western Europe, that it was obscured as under a cloud. Government roads traversed the mountain ranges with thoroughfares as level and hard as a granite floor.

Lorenzo de Medici was the patron of scholars and artists, and Florence, next to the city upon the banks of the Tiber, whose wonders and glories have never been exhausted, was the most attractive place in all Europe. It was at the very noon-tide of glory in Italian art.

Donatello, he of the sweet and cheerful temper, had shone the brightest light of Italian sculpture and gone out, leaving his eminently masculine creations in marble and bronze, the St. George, the Hercules, and the David, as models of Christian heroism sustained by faith.

Ghiberti had worked out his exquisite sense of beauty in matchless bas-reliefs.

Leonardo da Vinci, the poet, painter, architect, and statesman, a man gloriously rounded in his sphere of faculties, and Lorenzo, and Perugino, had lived and wrought, and Verocchio, made grand accomplishment and passed away.

The Della Robbias had bequeathed to the world the unearthly beauty of their Madonnas and the symmetrical forms of their pottery. Agostino had discovered æsthetic possibilities in terra cotta from which he improvised a new charm, and the hosts of unknown artists who sought expression of feeling in pictured forms, had left their hand work everywhere. Their ideals, transformed into marble were drawn upon walls, painted upon simple shrines, running in countless friezes, looking from the frescoes of innumerable cupolas and domes, breathing upon a world of canvas and living upon wood or stone; even upon so homely a surface as a barrel head, where Raphael in his eager haste, fastened one of his inspired visions.

Michael Angelo, a young man, was moulding the "Battle of Hercules with the Centaurs;" and Bramante was making plans for a new St. Peters. The shadows of the Middle Ages were fast dispersing, great enterprises had been commenced and manners and tastes were marked with a refinement which permeated even the lowest stratas of the common people.

But dry rot had begun in high places. The age had begun to be hideous for its debaucheries, its murders and its disgraceful levities, cruel tyrants reigned in cities and rapacious priests fattened upon the credulity of the people. Several wicked popes, the worst of which was, doubtless, Alexander the Sixth, who held the pontificate when this story opens, had so corrupted the religion of the times, that monks peddled indulgences all over Europe.

Many monasteries, which at an earlier period had been peopled with sublime enthusiasts, were filled with gluttons and sensualists, boys were elevated to episcopal thrones and the sons of popes made cardinals and princes. So abhorrent had the sins and crimes of the papal and municipal government become to conscientious Christians, that families abjured the church, and lived apart, in peril of their lives, after their estate and fortunes had been confiscated. An apathy to holy things had come over the nobility and a profound superstition, which we, considering the circumstances, cannot quite agree with some historians in pronouncing degrading, held the common people. It appears to have been their only stay and comfort, when such unbridled license and unblushing wickedness reigned over their unconscious heads.

It was then that Savonarola, the incarnation of a fervid, living, piety, the fearless and untiring denunciator of the personal venialties which defamed the church through its dignitaries, the stern gloomy ascetic, emaciated with fasting and prayers, preached religion, morality, purification; refusing absolution to the dying Lorenzo de Medici, who would not restore the liberties which he and his family had taken away, leaving him to die without comfort. Savonarola was a patriot, as well as preacher, who persisted against ex-communication, and passed through mortal dangers, until he died the death of a martyr. As Mrs. Browning beautifully recounts in "Casa Guidi Windows," the people still strew with violets the pavement where his ashes fell,—and says—

> "I, too, should desire,
> When men make record, with the flowers they strew
>
> *   *   *   *   *   *   *   *   *   *   *
>
> To cast my violets with as reverent care,
> And prove that all the winters which have snowed
> Cannot snow out the scent from stones and air,
> Of a sincere man's virtues."

When Agnes of Sorrento is first brought before the reader, Alexander the Sixth, with his children, Cæsar and

Lucrezia Borgia, whose very name stands for execration all over the civilized world to-day, controlled church and state at Rome, and while the lovely child lived on her innocent life amid the groves of Sorrento, untroubled and unimagining of the sins of the world, the church and the nation were approaching a state of corruption, which for a time threatened to destroy their very existence, and would have done so, but for the stratum of right feeling which lay beneath in the hearts and consciences of the people. This saving element is admirably set forth by Mrs. Stowe who never failed to recognize the virtues of true religion, in purifying and sweetening the lives of Christians, however hampered or limited it may have been by canonical forms, official corruption or theological bigotry.

"Agnes of Sorrento" is begun with a sunset scene near the city gateway, over which presides the stone figure of St. Antonio, about the year 1490. Beneath the arch, where the little birds flutter and chirp and take all manner of small liberties with the old brown stone saint, sits Agnes, selling golden oranges. A child of fifteen, with a beautiful saintly face, yet mature in womanly beauty, as at this age are the daughters of the warm south lands, she is telling her beads, while the Ave Maria is tolling from the Cathedral tower. Her grandmother, a woman of stern aspect, and strong will and purpose, whose thoughts are more upon the practical affairs of the day's trade, than upon the religious plane upon which the child so devoutly dwells, looks up from her mechanical prayers to see a handsome cavalier regarding her child with undisguised admiration.

When the wave of prayer, which has bowed every head as a breeze bends the nodding grain, has passed down the

street, and, with the ceasing of the bell, the world has resumed its business, the cavalier speaks to Agnes, asking for oranges. He impulsively kisses the wondering
maiden upon her forehead and nothing daunted by the
fierce denunciations of the old woman, gives the pretty devotee, a diamond ring from his finger, asks her to pray for
him, and walks slowly away.

He is Agostino Sarelli a scion of a noble family who has
been robbed of fortune, family, hope and all that life holds
dear, by the treacherous cruelty of Cæsar Borgia, whom the
insane affection of his father, Pope Alexander Sixth, has
made a cardinal, and placed absolute ruler over Rome.

Sarelli with a hundred men, not one of whom but has
lost houses, lands or friends through the fiendish rapacity
of Cæsar Borgia, has taken refuge in the fastnesses of the
mountains, and they are called robbers, because they have
gone out from the assembly of robbers, that they may
lead honest and cleanly lives   There are those among
them, whose wives and sisters have been forced into the
Borgia's harem, there are those, whose children have been
tortured before their eyes, there are those, who have seen
their fairest and dearest, slaughtered by the men who sit in
the seat of the Lord, and all know by experience, of the
private life of the men who make the Pontificate infamous
by acts that revolt the conscience of even that licentious
period, and make a sentiment of hatred which grows into
universal execration before Alexander's death.

They know of him as a man of outrageous sensuality, of
unbridled lust, of versatile diplomacy, of subtle priesthood,
who controls the councils of kings, who chants the sacra-
mental service on a Roman Easter day, in a manner which

moves the listening world. They know that he is inces-
tuous, a murderer many times repeated, a buyer of the
holiest offices of the church.   Is there not a current
epigram; "Alexander sells the keys, the altars, Christ.
Well, he bought them; so he has a right to sell them?"
He is "more evil and more lucky than ever for many ages,
peradventure had been any pope before."

Naturally the respect of Sarelli's followers for the edicts
of the church, as issuing from such a vessel, is small.   Ex-
communication has no terrors for them.   They glory in
rebellion against the men whom they know are emissaries
not of the Lord, but of the devil.

But the beauty of the town of Sorrento upon its elevated
plateau, running even to the sunny waters of the Mediterranean, the perfumed air blowing coolly through the orange
groves which nestle in the valley within sight of the mountains, a land where flowers and perfume, and out of door
life, and sunshine and physical beauty are the rule and not
the exception!   Where also dwells a native grace and courtesy, and an easy expression of sentiment which has blossomed forth in art, in music, in melodious speech, in gentleness of manners!   A sharp contrast indeed is it to the
ragged New England coast and inclement weather of the
northeastern climate, to the stern and angular aspect of
the inhabitants, to the inflexible principles which in the
author's native atmosphere governed every slightest act,
even every hidden thought.

Mrs. Stowe has so felt the languid loveliness of Italy, so
warmed and expanded in feeling under its climatic and
æsthetic influences that the reader receives a sense of what
she has seen, and is permeated with the atmosphere,

receiving through her art, full and pleasurable understanding of the situation.

Dame Elsie who loves her grandchild with a fierce devotion, fears the approach of any change which may take her child from her, and of late has become seriously troubled to know how to guide her existence. The maiden, in her saintly innocence and naturally religious character inclines toward a conventual life. Dame Elsie would fain keep her for herself, a living pleasure for her old age, but sees that a good marriage is perhaps the best and safest thing for so lovely and artless a nature. Agnes is the child of Dame Elsie's only daughter, who, pretty and intelligent, had been the maid of a noble mistress, who was seized with a caprice to educate her, to give her fine accomplishments and bring her into contact with people far above her social station. As a natural result, the son of the patrician, loved his mother's companion, and, sincere in his love as few young men of the period under such circumstances would have been, he secretly married her. The birth of a child sent the unfortunate young wife home to sorrowing Dame Elsie, in disgrace, and the impetuous young husband, into at least temporary, banishment.

So Elsie has reared the girl with fear, and sees with anguish how beautiful she grows, and that her native refinement and dainty ways are almost sure to attract some vulture in human form. She, therefore, keeps an eagle eye upon the maiden, protecting her day and night with her presence, or upon occasions, sending her to the convent where she is much beloved by the Sisters. The education of Agnes has rendered her peculiarly sensitive to all religious impressions and she lives in an unseen world, peopled with saints and fairies, tricky fauns, dryads and elves, dreaming in a devout ecstacy of Heaven, knowing literally nothing of human nature, and this world.

When, therefore at evening, after meeting the cavalier at her stand in the city, she hears a strange weirdly sweet, and passionate voice singing below in the gorge one of the most charming love songs, which float in the ken of the people, rising clear and unearthly in cadence, to the cottage upon the hillside where she sits, Agnes is thrilled with a strange emotion, and thoughts of the stories she has heard the nuns tell, of wandering spirits who sing mortals away to destruction. But Dame Elsie recognizes the voice of cavalier, and with her eyes gleaming dagger blades, down into the gorge, vigorously sprinkles the parapet with holy water and leads her child to bed.

Dame Elsie being considerably perturbed by the serenade of the previous evening, resolves to go to confession on her way to town and tell Father Francesco of the matter. In the description of the monastery, lately under the pastoral care of a jolly, pleasure loving friar, who took a long rope at the waist, and the recent very trying changes which the ascetic Father Francesco had inaugurated, there is a *genre* picture, which leaves as vivid an impression, as though each rotund monk with shaven poll and sandalled feet stood upon a canvas before one. The brighter side of conventual life is by no means ignored. It is shown to be a needed shelter for woman's helplessness, during age of political uncertainty and revolution, and the congenial retreat of the artist the poet, and the student. The man devoted to ideas, here found leisure undisturbed, to develop them under the consecrating influences of religion. But the author also humor-

ously depicts a conventual life of far less elevating and refined order.

"The convent of which we speak had been for some years under
the lenient rule of the jolly Brother Girolamo,—an easy, wide-
spread, loosely organized body, whose views of the purpose of
human existence were decidedly Anacreontic.   Fasts he abomi-
nated,—night-prayers he found unfavorable to his constitution ;
but he was a judge of olives and good wine, and often threw out
valuable hints in his pastoral visits on the cooking of maccaroni,
for which he had himself elaborated a savory recipe ; and the cel-
lar and larder of the convent, during his pastorate, presented so
many urgent solicitations to conventual repose, as to threaten an
inconvenient increase in the number of brothers.   The monk in
his time lounged in all the sunny places of the convent like so
many loose sacks of meal, enjoying to the full the *dolce far niente*
which seems to be the universal rule of Southern climates.   They
ate and drank and slept and snored ; they made pastoral visits
through the surrounding community which were far from edifying ;
they gambled, and tippled, and sang most unspiritual songs; and
keeping all the while their own private pass-key to Paradise
tucked under their girdles, were about as jolly a set of sailors to
Eternity as the world had to show.   In fact, the climate of Southern Italy and its gorgeous scenery are more favorable to voluptuous
ecstasy than to the severe and grave warfare of the true Christian
soldier.   The sunny plains of Capua demoralized the soldiers of
Hannibal, and it was not without a reason that ancient poets made
those lovely regions the abode of Sirens whose song maddened by
its sweetness, and of a Circe who made men drunk with her sens-
ual fascinations, till they became sunk to the form of brutes.

"Here, if anywhere, is the lotos-eater's paradise,—the purple
skies, the enchanted shores, the soothing gales, the dreamy mists,
which all conspire to melt the energy of the will, and to make ex-

istence either a half doze of dreamy apathy or an awaking of mad delirium.

"It was not from dreamy, voluptuous Southern Italy that the religious progress of the Italian race received any vigorous impulses. These came from more northern and more mountainous regions, from the severe, clear heights of Florence, Perugia, and Assisi, where the intellectual and the moral both had somewhat of the old Etruscan earnestness and gloom.

"One may easily imagine the stupid alarm and helpless confusion of these easy-going monks, when their new Superior came down among them hissing with a white heat from the very hottest furnace-fires of a new religious experience, burning and quivering with the errors of the world to come—pale, thin, eager, tremulous, and yet with all the martial vigor of the former warrior, and all the habits of command of a former princely station. His reforms gave no quarter to right or left; sleepy monks were dragged out to midnight prayers, and their devotions enlivened with vivid pictures of hell-fire and ingenuities of eternal torment enough to stir the blood of the most torpid. There was to be no more gormandizing, no more wine-bibbing; the choice old wines were placed under lock and key for the use of the sick and poor in the vicinity; and every fast of the Church, and every obsolete rule of the order, were revived with unsparing rigor. It is true, they hated their new Superior with all the energy which laziness and good living had left them, but they every soul of them shook in their sandals before him; for there is a true and established order of mastery among human beings, and when a man of enkindled energy and intense will comes among a flock of irresolute commonplace individuals, he subjects them to himself by a sort of moral paralysis similar to what a great, vigorous gymnotus distributes among a fry of inferior fishes. The bolder ones, who made motions of rebellion, were so energetically swooped upon, and consigned to the discipline of dungeon and bread-and-water, that less

courageous natures made a merit of siding with the more powerful
party, mentally resolving to carry by fraud the points which they
despaired of accomplishing by force."

It is an example delicious in its realism, of a condition
which the license of the period permitted, with the unpopular reforms and pious inflictions brought about by a sternly
conscientious Prior. The character of Il Padre Francesco
however, is one to be remembered with respect and pity.
The wave of a great religious impulse—which in these
times would be called a revival, had swept him, with many
others within the fold of the church.

It was the fervid preaching of Jerome Savanorola which
had broken his heart, with the multitudes of those who had
wept, beaten their breasts and trembled under his awful
denunciations. The analysis of his change from the gay
dissolute young Lorenzo Sforza who, in rites of awful solemnity died to carnal life, and arose spiritualized from the
coffin in which he had laid ; the mental and spiritual experiences of the reconstructed man, in whom however in spite
of all, the old Lorenzo would occasionally revive, is a masterpiece of expression. The daughter of the New England
divine had need to think and feel much, to come out from
her own conditions and enter into those of olden times and
a foreign country, before she could set forth such a life.
After dwelling at some length upon the inner life of Father
Francesco, the author thus describes the influence of Agnes'
pure sweet spirit upon the haggard soul of the ascetic, who
thought he had foresworn women, as unworthy companions.

"The cloud of hopeless melancholy which had brooded over the
mind of Father Francesco lifted and sailed away, he know not

why, he knew not when. A secret joyfulness and alacrity possessed his spirits; his prayers became more fervent and his praises more frequent. Until now, his meditations had been most frequently those of fear and wrath,—the awful majesty of God, the terrible punishment of sinners, which he conceived with all that haggard, dreadful sincerity of vigor which characterized the modern Etruscan phrase of religion of which the " Inferno " of Dante was the exponent and the out-come. His preachings and his exhortations had dwelt on that lurid world seen by the severe Florentine, at whose threshold hope forever departs, and around whose eternal circles of living torture the shivering spirit wanders dismayed and blasted by terror.

" He had been shocked and discouraged to find how utterly vain had been his most intense efforts to stem the course of sin by presenting these images of terror : how hard natures had listened to them with only a course and cruel appetite, which seemed to increase their hardness and brutality; and how timid ones had been withered by them, like flowers scorched by the blast of a furnace; how, in fact, as in the case of those cruel executions and bloody tortures then universal in the juris-prudence of Europe, these pictures of eternal torture seemed to exert a morbid demoralizing influence which hurried on the growth of iniquity.

" But since his acquaintance with Agnes, without his knowing exactly why, thoughts of the Divine Love had floated into his soul, filling it with a golden cloud like that of old rested over the mercy-seat in that sacred inner temple where the priests was admitted alone. He became more affable and tender, more tolerant to the erring, more fond of little children ; would stop sometimes to lay his hand on the head of a child, or to raise up one who lay overthrown in the street. The song of little birds and voices of animal life became to him full of tenderness; and his prayers by the sick and dying seemed to have a melting power, such as he had never known before. It was spring in his soul,—soft, Italian spring,—such as brings out the musky breath of the cyclamen, and the faint, tender perfume of the primrose, in every moist dell of the Apennines."

In the confession of Dame Elsie he receives a shock, which throws his whole being into a passionate agitation, which astonishes and dismays him. He finds, alas how shameful! that Elsie's plans for marrying Agnes to a young peasant are scarcely less revolting to him than the thought of her exposure to the addresses of a licentious cavalier, as these people had hastily decided Sarelli to be. Not yet fully understanding his frail heart, he believes that he ought to use his influence to bring Agnes into the convent, where as member of the pure sisterhood of nuns he could be the guardian and director of her soul, the one to whom she should be implicitly obedient and submissive.

CHAPTER XIV.

AGNES AT THE CONVENT. A SELECTION WHICH SHOWS THE
AUTHOR'S FEELING AGAINST THE SENTENCE OF UNMITI-
GATED DOOM WHICH ACCOMPANIED THE GLAD TIDINGS OF
SALVATION. HER APPRECIATION OF SOME OF THE BEAU-
TIFUL SENTIMENTS OF THE EARLY ROMAN CATHOLIC RELI-
GION. FATHER ANTONIO, THE ARTIST MONK. SAN MAR-
CO. SAVANOROLA'S CONVICTION THAT THE SONGS OF A
PEOPLE HAVE MORE PERSUASIVE POWER THAN ITS LAWS.
AGNES AND OLD ELSIE MAKE A PILGRIMAGE TO ROME.
SARELLI'S MOUNTAIN REFUGE. RECEIVED BY A PRINCESS.
FALLING INTO THE JAWS OF THE PAPAL MONSTER. RES-
CUED BY SARELLI. ROMANTIC CONCLUSION.

Agnes' day at the convent, the morning walk in the dew
bespangled path upon the mountain side, her affectionate
reception by the nuns, the moonlight delicacy of person
and temperament which characterize Mother Theresa and
the blunt commonplaceness of Sister Jocunda, with whom
Agnes spends much of the day, hearing tales in which religious and heathenish characters figure indiscriminately, give
a view of the inner side of conventual existence which presents its practical realities most entertainingly. The terrible things upon which old Jocunda gloats with a grim satisfaction, are agonizing to the sensitive soul of little Agnes,
and the author proceeds to discuss the severities of the
Catholic religion of the fifteenth century as painful in the
extreme. As painful, were the metaphysical hair split-

ting refinements of Calvinistic torture, as digested and exaggerated by skilful and morbid theologians of three hundred years later, to the spirits of such persons as Mrs. Marvyn in "The Minister's Wooing." The following selection gives abundant example of the feeling that Mrs. Stowe entertained towards the sentence of unmitigated doom which accompanied the glad tidings of salvation.

" Ages before, beneath those very skies that smiled so sweetly over her,—amid the bloom of lemon and citron, and the perfume of Jasmine and rose, the gentlest of old Italian souls had dreamed and wondered what might be the unknown future of the dead, and, learning his lesson from the glorious skies and gorgeous shores which witnessed how magnificent a Being had given existence to man, had recorded his hopes of man's future in the words—*Aut beatus, aut nihil;* but, singular to tell, the religion which brought, with it all human tenderness and pities,—the hospital for the sick, the refuge for the orphan, the enfranchisement of the slave,—this religion brought also the news of the eternal, hopeless, living torture of the great majority of mankind past and present. Tender spirits, like those of Dante, carried this awful mystery as a secret and unexplained anguish ; saints wrestled with God and wept over it ; but still the awful fact remained, spite of Church and sacrament, that the gospel was in effect, to the majority of the human race, not the glad tidings of salvation, but the sentence of unmitigable doom.

" The present traveler in Italy sees with disgust the dim and faded frescoes in which this doom is portrayed in all its varied refinements of torture ; and the vivid Italian mind ran riot in these lurid fields, and every monk who wanted to move his audience was in his small way a Dante. The poet and the artist gave only the highest form of the ideas of their day, and he who cannot read the " Inferno" with firm nerves may ask what the same representations were likely to have been in the grasp of coarse and common minds.

"The first teachers of Christianity in Italy read the Gospels by the light of those 'fiendish fires which consumed their fellows. Daily made familiar with the scorching, the searing, the racking, the develish ingenuities of torture, they transferred them to the future hell of the torturers. The sentiment within us which asserts eternal justice and retribution was stimulated to a kind of madness by that first baptism of fire and blood, and expanded the simple and grave warnings of the gospel into a lurid poetry of physical torture. Hence, while Christianity brought multiplied forms of mercy into the world, it failed for many centuries to humanize the savage forms of justice; and rack and wheel, fire and fagot were the modes by which human justice was supposed to extend through eternity."

Yet in the next selection is demonstrated what was Harriet Beecher Stowe's comprehension and appreciation of some of the beautiful sentiments of the early Roman Catholic religion. It is certain that she never underrated its benificent influence upon those who embraced it in its purity, and acted it in their lives.

"To the mind of the really spiritual Christian of those ages the air of this lower world was not as it is to us, in spite of our nominal faith in the Bible, a blank, empty space from which all spiritual sympathy and life have fled, but, like the atmosphere with which Raphael has surrounded the Sistine Madonna, it was full of sympathizing faces, a great "cloud of witnesses." The holy dead were not gone from earth; the Church visible and invisible were in close, loving, and constant sympathy,—still loving, praying, and watching together, though with a veil between.

" It was at first with no idolatrous intention that the prayers of

the holy dead were invoked in acts of worship.   Their prayers
were asked simply because they were felt to be as really present
with their former friends and as truly sympathetic as if no veil of
silence had fallen between.   In time this simple belief had its
intemperate and idolatrous exaggerations,—the Italian soil always
seeming to have a fiery and volcanic forcing power, by which
religious ideas overblossomed themselves, and grew wild and ragged with too much enthusiasm ; and, as often happens with friends
on earth, these too much loved and revered invisible friends became
eclipsing screens instead of transmitting mediums of God's light
to the soul.

" Yet we can see in the hymns of Savonarola, who perfectly
represented the attitude of the highest Christian of those times,
how perfect might be the love and veneration for departed saints
without lapsing into idolatry, and with what an atmosphere of
warmth and glory the true belief of the unity of the Church, visible
and invisible, could inspire an elevated soul amid the discourage-
ments of an unbelieving and gainsaying world."

The advent of Father Antonio, the brother of old Elsie,
who is an artist-monk from the convent of San Marco in
Florence, where religion was devout, poetic, and elevating
under the ministrations of Savonarola, whom all his followers
adored ; a visitor from the retreat which was recognized as
an ideal community where religion, beauty and utility were
wonderfully blended, is an epoch to the reader, as well as
to Elsie, who is troubled about her child's future, and to
Agnes, who welcomed with her uncle, pleasant hours of
social converse, and a sight of rare pictures.   For he made
his drawings by the way, and finished them in the garden
by her side, replacing the voluptuous and unworthy sketches
which defaced many a shrine, with visions of saintly purity
and grace.

He was called into counsel concerning Agnes, and made her confidant when Elsie had gone into town with her oranges, leaving them two with a long glorious day together.

Agnes had found in her path, a locket set with precious stones, which contained upon a bit of crumpled parchment a sonnet, breathing pure love for her, and became more and more agitated by the strange urgency of her desire to pray for and save the gallant cavalier from perdition, whence she was assured that he was swiftly sliding, having been banished from the church and made an outlaw by his own volition. While Father Antonio sits in the groves and singing Latin hymns and painting exquisite flowers and chubby cherubim, old Elsie raises the large basket of oranges to her head and turns her stately figure towards the scene of her daily labors.

Dear uncle Antonio opens his portfolio and seats himself upon the garden wall to retouch some of his sketches and Agnes places herself cosily by his side for a long chat. But the good man is called away, to minister at the bedside of a dying man, and Agnes betakes herself to prayers for the passing soul. When she raises her head from her devotions she sees the cavalier, waiting patiently near the shrine, and the long sought interview is accorded him. He is received by the devout maiden as one who not strangely craves her intercessions with the saints, for his spiritual welfare. When Father Antonio returns Agnes is still on her knees, and old Elsie, arriving home an hour later, observes with satisfaction that she has effectually convinced the cavalier that he is not wanted about her orange stand, that he has not been seen in the vicinity that day!

The following paragraph presents the author's thought about the simple faith of the young girl in a manner which draws the sympathy of the universal heart to her.

" Brought up from infancy to feel herself in a constant circle of invisible spiritual agencies, Agnes received this wave of intense feeling as an impulse inspired and breathed into her by some celestial spirit, that thus she should be made an interceding medium for a soul in some unknown strait or peril. For her faith taught her to believe in an infinite struggle of intercession, in which all the Church, visible and invisible, were together engaged, and which bound them in living bonds of sympathy to an interceding Redeemer, so that there was no want or woe of human life that had not somewhere its sympathetic heart, and its never-ceasing prayer before the throne of Eternal love. Whatever may be thought of the actual truth of this belief, it certainly was far more consoling than that intense individualism of modern philosophy which places every soul alone in its life-battle,—scarce even giving it a God to lean upon."

In discussing the religion which had its birth in the life of Christ, but was shaped in outward expression in this atmosphere of an almost tropical fervor, Mrs. Stowe finds the reason for the form of the Roman Catholic faith. She perceives that soil and climate no less than principles, make religions. That the same precious truths which blossom into luxuriant colors and fantastic forms in the soil of Italy, grow sparse and thin and full of knots and angles, in the land which the Puritans selected as their refuge. This is natural, physical effect. When mind rises above matter, and intellect and culture bring all countries and climes into æsthetic and intellectual harmony, then, perhaps will the spiritual manifestations of the same grand ideas, be similar in outward expression. Until then, the author of Agnes of Sorrento felt, that cause and effect should be realized, and good wherever found, greeted with pleasure.

Harriet Beecher Stowe had no capabilities for bigotry. She knew nothing of the limitations which, as has been remarked of the late Matthew Arnold, were "an essential part of his equipment for the work he performed." She needed not to shut out the light of day, to make microscopic examinations under artificially concentrated rays. It was not necessary to close her ears to the hum of the world to receive a whispered message from the gods, nor that her path towards a point, should be walled up on either side. She walked upon a broad plain, in view of the blue sky, with the sunshine upon her, hearing the singing of the birds, feeling a delicious kinship with mute nature, receiving the flutter of the leaves and sweetness of flowers as a personal caress, conscious of the great Whole, feeling its throb as an undercurrent or background of joy and holy certitude, while considering the manifestations of life, the higher ideals, and grosser failings of humanity.

When Agnes of Sorrento goes to her Father Confessor, it becomes apparent that men are often weaker than their conscience, and that the physical body does sadly limit the aspirations of the pure soul. Father Francesco learns that Sarelli is excommunicated from the church and welcomes with joy his power to turn Agnes from him. Even when he becomes aware of his own love for her, which from the nature of his vows is for him a sin, he desperately swears that he will love her, but later enters upon a conflict with his carnal nature, a harrowing experience which is set forth with marvellous strength and feeling. His struggle and self-imposed penance of three days and nights in the mouth of the crater of Vesuvius, a literal foretaste of hell in physical and mental suffering, has a lurid picturesqueness and intensity of feeling which is rare in modern writings.

Hard indeed might it have gone with the love of Sarelli and the little devotee, had not the cavalier made friends with good Father Antonio. He, an inmate of the monastery of San Marco, and a follower of Savonarola, understood of how little true value was the favor of the Pope, and how small consequence was the excommunication which was freely pronounced against any whom that potentate could not bend to his evil designs. But it was difficult to explain the condition of things to Agnes, without ruthlessly destroying her beautiful faith in the whole body and soul of the church, and he bade Sarelli be patient, promising to be his friend when occasion permitted. For Agnes had acknowledged her love for the gallant outlaw, and had promised to be his wife, should she ever marry any man, which she seemed little inclined to do. In the meantime Father Antonio interceded with old Elsie, that the child should be left free from agitation for a time, urging that the arrangements for the marriage of Agnes and the handsome, bovine, peasant lad, which she and old Meta had begun, should be allowed to rest.

Several of the hymns, which Savonarola desired should supplant the obscene and ribald songs which defiled the morals of the youth of the period, are reproduced in all the passionate tenderness of the Italian words, with excellent translations into English, upon the pages of this story. The great reformer well realized that the songs of a nation have more persuasive power than its laws, and in the quaintness and purity of sentiment shown in those he supplied, may be felt the animus of many of the grand hymns of the modern Protestant church.

Father Antonio returns to Florence, and with him, riding over the summit of one of the hills which overlooks the city, is the cavalier who has accompanied him to San Marco, to meet Savonarola. The view of Florence, lying like a gem in the shelter of the mountains, is a charming one and their subsequent arrival at the convent, and meeting with Savonarola, is full of intense interest which augments and reaches a dreadful climax, in the tale of the attack upon the Cathedral, and the death of several devoted monks who defend their master from the arrest, which closely preceded his death.

Elsie and Agnes have been advised to make a pilgrimage to Rome, and though the old woman is filled with a dread of seeing again, the city wherein occurred her daughter's misfortune, she is constrained to go with Agnes to the Holy City. She has an undefined fear of bringing Agnes within the walls of the city which had seen her mother's disgrace, but the commands of their superiors are not to be disobeyed, and they start on foot for their long and trying journey. It means days and weeks over rough mountain passes, in deep, solitary valleys, with such food as the householders by the way may give them, with possible, nay, very probable, dangers of every description.

They set forth, first receiving the benisons of the sisters at the convent, and take their way along the road from Sorrento to Naples. The scene with the shimmering sea upon the one hand and the luxuriant hillsides teeming with richness of color is picturesque with an almost unearthly charm. They are fanned by soft breezes which bear upon their wings the indescribable odors of thousands of flowers. The burnt sides of old Vesuvius rise high above them, streaked with changing color and flashing from shadow into brightness under the passing clouds. It is like an en chanted dream to Agnes who is filled with an overpower ing sense of its beauty and charm. Old Elsie grumbles not a little at having to leave home at a time when the oranges are most plentiful and sweet.

Having reached Naples, on they go through the Pontine Marshes where Elsie, recking not of the sealike expanse which, waving with lush grasses and dotted with flowers presents a new and delightful spectacle to her child, thinks only of malaria, and persuades a man with horses to carry them some miles on their way. This is deprecated by Ag nes who believes in making the pilgrimage in the most arduous manner, but the old woman fears illness and death, and wishes to fare on as rapidly as possible, to healthier places. To quote the words of the author, Elsie, even in the course of a religious pilgrimage, "in common with many other professing Christians, felt that going to Para dise was the dismalest of alternatives—a thing to be staved off as long as possible."

After many days they find themselves in a lonely dell at the going down of the sun, with the forbidding sides of a steep mountain rising before them. Agnes is very weary, and sinks upon the earth to repeat her evening prayer. Elsie also prays, but as she tells her beads she casts a cal culating eye at the village, so far up the mountain side, and is somewhat alarmed to see several horsemen approaching them. They draw near and accost the old woman, saying they have come to help them, and in spite of her emphatic refusals, imperatively raise Agnes to a place upon one of the saddles when Elsie is fain to follow. Thus they are carried seven miles up the crags to the mountain town.

Arriving at the settlement they stop at a large stone inclosure, and Agnes shown through many passages into an apartment furnished with the utmost comfort, and luxury beyond what she has ever dreamed. Soon a strangely familiar titter is heard, and Guiletta, the coquette of Sorrento, who has married one of Sarelli's men, enters the apartment. She informs Agnes that her grandmother is quite comfortable and enjoying her supper, and brings her food. Agnes soon finds that she is in the castle of the cavalier, who has heard of her journey, and wishes to give her a period of rest and refreshment, as well as to again present his claims to her favor as a lover.

Agnes sleeps long and well, and is waited upon the next morning by Guiletta who enters, fresh and blooming, bearing a tray, with breakfast. Soon after, Agostino Sarelli, who has ridden hard from Florence to meet her whom he knows within the walls of his fortress, appears to Agnes. He has come from the scenes at San Marco burning with indignation against the Pope and the whole hierarchy then ruling in Rome, his sense of personal wrong having been converted into a fixed principle of opposition. He feels that the time has come to show to Agnes the true character of the men she is " beholding through the mists of veneration arising entirely from the dewy freshness of ignorant innocence."

He pleads with her to renounce her pilgrimage and remain within his protection; to abandon her resolve to take the veil, and be his well loved wife. But the maiden remembering the anathemas of Father Francesco, who had threatened perdition not only to her, but also to Sarelli's soul, if she should listen or yield to his entreaties, refuses to hear, and bidding her lover, whom she loves, farewell, she pursues her way to Rome, she is carried down the mountain upon horseback, as is also her grandmother, who ere now has begun to think well of a gallant gentleman who can so nobly provide for the comfort of his guests. At last they came to Rome, and enter the Holy City with a kind of exaltation in which is mingled a great humility as they are received with ceremonials due to holy pilgrims, and a Princess takes them to her home.

The Princess bathes Agnes' feet and her servant attends them with kind office and wholesome food. Agnes immediately asks how she can gain audience with the Pope, as she has much upon her heart she wishes to lay before the man whom she believed to be Heaven's representative upon earth. The Princess is much troubled to know how to answer her, as she and her family had long been too near the seat of power, not to see the base intrigues by which that solemn and sacred position of Head of the Christian Church had been debauched and traded for, as a marketable commodity.

Elsie and Agnes go out in the morning to witness the most magnificent ceremonials that the world ever saw, when Alexander Sixth received the homage of the kings of many nations and carried through with unequalled grace and dignity, the pageantry and grandeur of ceremonies which commemorated the humble advent of Christ into Rome, centuries before. Agnes is marked by a gay young man who belongs to the Borgias' suite, and an hour or two later she is summoned to appear at court, whither she goes in a religious ecstacy, believing her prayers have thus been answered. Old Elsie is left in an agony of fear, hardly daring to imagine what may become of her innocent child. When the servant of the good Princess Paulina, who has come to invite Agnes and her grandmother again to her villa, is informed of her summons and departure, she evinces extreme distress and anxiety as to the fate of the lovely pilgrim, who has fallen into ruthless hands.

The Princess is aroused from her sleep that night, by the arrival of a horseman, and Agostino Sarelli whom she recognizes as the last of a fallen family of nobles, asks admission and brings the pale and almost lifeless body of Agnes within the hospitable portal and lays it upon a couch. He leads aside the lady whom he knows to be a daughter of the Colonnas, who were the companions of his family in misfortune, and hurriedly tells her how he has rescued Agnes of Sorrento from the very jaws of the monster.

The Princess Paulina has that day learned that Agnes is her near kinswoman, a Capuchin monk having made a dying confession to her, that he had united her brother in marriage to the daughter of old Elsie, years before. She had sent for Agnes only to find her gone, and welcomes with inexpressible joy, her rescuer and his train. Agnes recovers from the deadly shock which the terrible experience has given her, and as soon as preparations can be made, the Princess with her retainers join Sarelli's band and together they seek safety in his mountain retreat. The death of Savonarola takes place about this time, and shortly after, Father Antonio joins his friends at the fortress of Agostino

Sarelli.   Princess Paulina acting for her family, quite ap-
proves of Sarelli's suit for Agnes, and Father Antonio
gives the maiden such excellent counsel that she accepts
the knight, and the good monk unites them in marriage.

" In the reign of Julius II., the banished families who had been
plundered by the Borgias were restored to their rights and honors
at Rome; and there was a princess of the house of Sarelli then at
Rome, whose sanctity of life and manners was held to go back to
the traditions of primitive Christianity, so that she was renowned
not less for goodness than for rank and beauty."

CHAPTER XV.

"THE PEARL OF ORR'S ISLAND." SCENE AT HARPSWELL, MAINE, AT THE BEGINNING OF THE PRESENT CENTURY. LIFE UPON THE RUGGED NEW ENGLAND COAST. FLOTSAM AND JETSAM. EFFECT OF JEFFERSON'S EMBARGO OF 1807. THE CHARACTER OF MR. SEWELL BASED UPON THE PERSONALITY OF JOHN P. BRACE. MRS. STOWE'S IMPROVEMENT IN LITERARY STYLE. MRS. STOWE'S "REPLY" TO THE AFFECTIONATE AND CHRISTIAN ADDRESS OF THE WOMEN OF ENGLAND TO THE WOMEN OF AMERICA. DEATH OF DR. LYMAN BEECHER. MRS. STOWE'S ACCOUNT OF HIS MENTAL CONDITION. DYING AS AN OLD TREE DIES AT THE TOP FIRST. "SOJOURNER TRUTH—THE LIBYAN SIBYL." STORY'S STATUE, MATERIALIZED FROM MRS. STOWE'S DESCRIPTION OF THE AFRICAN PRIESTESS. "HOUSE AND HOME PAPERS."

DURING the latter part of the year 1860, Mrs. Stowe was engaged in writing a story which appeared in "The Independent." It was another serial, called "The Pearl of Orr's Island." It ran through the greater part of the year, being published at the same time, in London, in "Cassell's Illustrated Family Paper." It was a story of singular pathos and beauty, representing life upon the rugged coast of Maine, ninety years ago, being located at Harpswell, about eighteen miles from the town of Brunswick, where Professor Stowe was settled when the first great book was written.

So vividly does this tale picture the sad, yet attractive scenery of the eastern shore, with its descriptions of the rocks and sands and pine forests, then growing almost to the water's edge, that one can smell the salt in the invigorating breeze, can feel the heat of summer as it rises from the gleaming dunes and hear the lapping of waves upon the beach and the roll of the surf against the castellated rocks which bound the indented coast.

Not alone do her pictures of sea and land transport the reader, but her delineations of the old time, purely characteristic, limited New England life, send a thrill of satisfaction and pleasure through the consciousness of the native reader, which amounts to ecstacy. This phase of American life, with the influx of summer visitors and the encroachments of travelers, is fast becoming merged into greater scope and culture, and losing its relation to the soil. Now that the good old fashion of New England life seems to have become a thing of the past, it is a frequent matter of regret that its records are so few. One of the greatest bequests to posterity left by Harriet Beecher Stowe is her reproduction and preservation of the outward and spiritual life of the descendants of the Puritans. What was real of the Puritans, their staunch principles, their honesty, homely kindness and practical reason endures, and will endure as long as the history of the locality is preserved, and hereditary tendencies influence American character. Their mistakes and severities drop unregretted into forgetfulness. Only loyal pride and the gratitude of those to whom these appear as sacred memories, are felt for the life and its delineator.

By the magic of her graphic power, the reader finds himself in the wagon which goes slowly along the sandy road below the town of Bath, towards "Orr's Island"

and the Kennebec, which winds in view of the flashing
water upon the coast of the State of Maine. He becomes
instantly acquainted with the old man who holds the reins
over the sedate horse, and admires the pure beauty of
Naomi, who rides with her father, as they look out to sea,
now roughened and angry after a day's storm, for the
expected vessel which brings her husband home.

He sees with them the incoming ship, the fatal mistake of
the Captain who takes the narrow channel, and the terrible
dashing of the vessel upon the cruel rocks, where it soon
splits to pieces and goes down before their eyes !

This story of the homeward-bound ship going down in
sight of home, with the sailors dressed in their holiday
clothes in anticipation of soon greeting their sweethearts
and wives, is founded upon fact, and is still told upon the
coast, in many fishermen's homes. The narration of the
washing ashore of the dead sailor lad who had been Naomi's
husband, bedight in his best attire ; the view of the body
in its dripping clothes in the darkened parlor of the plain
old house, of the ghastly sound of the salt water, which
drops from his dark hair upon the carpet; the premature
birth of the young widow's child; the death of Naomi;
the grief of the stricken parents, the ceremonies of the
funeral ; presents a singularly sad but fascinating example of the inexorable cruelty and hardness of the sea, and
the ungraceful lines in local personality and character, which
seem as harsh, and unlovely.

Zephaniah Pennel, " a chip of old Maine—thrifty, careful,
shrewd, honest, God-fearing and carrying an instinctive
knowledge of men and things under a face of rustic simplicity ;" his timid, affectionate wife ; Aunt Roxy and Aunt

21

Ruey, the seamstresses and general factotums who received new-born infants into their capable arms, and presided over the last rites of the dead ; Captain Kittredge, dry and bent and full of imaginative sea stories and sly humor ; his stern disciplinarian, in the person of his black-eyed, fault-finding wife ; the dignified and scholarly minister, Mr. Sewell, and his inquisitive, chatty sister, are all native New England types, formed of the dry soil, bearing fruits of usefulness, but having no flowers of thought, no blossoms of culture, no hint of luxuriance in their growth.

They are all as salutary, as invigorating, as the salt in the air, as weather beaten as the dark rocks, as ungraceful as the rough-barked trees, and the scrubby savin which grows upon the arid earth.   And yet there is in this glimpse of life, a pleasure and a sort of pride which indeed may not obtain with children of warmer zones, or the rich Western country, but which braces and suits one who claims New England blood, as does the inhospitable brine of its waters, and the sad sighing of the wind through its strong pines.

The child, who was named Mara according to the wish of the dying mother with whom the Almighty had dealt so bitterly, lived and grew into a winsome child, a delicate, fairy-like creature, who seemed so pure a thing in contrast from the rough, practical lives and aspects of the place, that they called her the Pearl of Orr's Island.

When she was three years of age, there came another cruel wreck upon the immovable rocks of the iron-bound shore, and the body of a beautiful woman, with a living child, a handsome Spanish boy, clasped close in her rigid arms, was washed ashore. He was taken home by the Pennels and became the companion of little Mara, and the dashing, head-

strong, erratic and manly hero of the story. The story of
Mara's devotion to her adopted brother who was four years
her elder, his boyish, easy acceptance of it, his selfish schemes
and unknowing harshness to the little heart that so loved
him, is a pathetic reproduction of what the author may
have experienced with her bright, masterful brothers. It
finds corroboration in the experience of many loving little
women and an interesting literary counterpart in George
Eliot's "Mill on the Floss," in the brave self-effacement of
Maggie for love of her brother.

The unrevealed romance which is indicated in the emotion of good Mr. Sewell, who recognizes in the body of the
beautiful woman which floats ashore, one who has been
much to him, and his subsequent care over her boy, affords
an element of interest above his position as the tutor of
young Moses and little Mara. An interest, foreign indeed
to the artistic construction of the novel, but nevertheless
existing, lies in the fact that this character is based upon
the personality of John P. Brace, under whose wise and
stimulating tuition, Harriet Beecher and her brothers studied
together. Again the author lays herself open to the objection of a champion (quite unneeded) of New England divines, by making Mr. Sewell a bachelor, but the novelist's
license permits her making exceptions to the general rule
which was, especially among ministers, of an early marriage.

A pleasing element is introduced in the matter of fact
and very refreshing person of Sally Kittredge, who was
a childish companion of Mara and in later years exhibited some delicious coquetry with Master Moses
Pennel. A salient point of the story is reached when
Mara is about thirteen and her brother, then seventeen,

falls into pernicious associations and is sadly misled and tempted, by certain bad men who are engaged in smuggling.

This locates the story at the time of Jefferson's embargo of 1807, which stopped at once the whole coast trade of New England, condemned her thousands of ships to rot at the wharves and ruined thousands of families. As an inevitable result of weak and unworthy legislation and the prevalent feeling that Congress had usurped authority, in annihilating commerce, which it was only empowered to regulate, there was induced a contempt of law which had a strong influence, even in a community noted for its rigid morality and respect for the edicts of the government. Vessels were constantly fitted out which, in defiance of the law, ran to the West Indies and other ports and though the practice was punishable as smuggling, it found many sympathizers among citizens usually submissive to political authority.

The practices which arose from this condition of things were of course, in the last degree demoralizing to the community, and fatal to the integrity of a large class of bold, enterprising young men, who naturally turned to adventure and felt a reckless pride in a life which combined excitement with a partial justification, in the mind of the community.

Moses Pennel, with his hot, dark Spanish blood, at an age when the restraints of home began to be irksome and the manly sense of right and honor had not quite asserted itself, was an easy prey to the man Atkinson and his accomplices, with whom the lad indulged in many an orgie at night, by a lurid fire in the recesses of the rocks, eating and drinking, taking terrible oaths and planning dangerous projects. One night, Mara followed her brother and his disreputable acquaintances to their rendezvous, and crouching in the brush, heard things that froze her pure soul with horror and led her to confide her trouble to good Captain Kittredge who, while secretly sympathizing with the smugglers, and profiting pecuniarily by their trading in foreign ports, *drew the line* at their leading away the adopted son of his friend. He induced Zephaniah Pennel to send Moses to China upon a long voyage.

The author had boys of her own, the elder of whom was giving her deep anxiety, and in this description of the handsome, black haired boy with the restless temper and rebellion to the salutary restraints of his parents, one may read between the lines and feel the ache in the heart of the mother who penned them.

The return of Moses, grown in three years into a handsome man, his animated flirtation with lively Sally Kittredge, who was the bosom friend of Mara, are most naturally depicted. The realistic conversations and vivid trivialities of homely existence are drawn with a delicate touch which reminds one of the modern school of novelists who unfortunately do not always choose so worthy characters about which to group these details.

Moses and Mara at last find their love for each other and are betrothed, but the marriage never takes place, for the "Pearl of Orr's Island" is too frail for life upon the harsh Eastern coast, and fades away into another sphere, just when life seems brightest and fullest of promise. Moses goes away to sea again, but after some years' absence comes back, and finding Sally Kittredge, softened and grown into an attractive, capable womanhood, marries her.

The plot is slight but smoothly finished and the hand of the trained writer is visible in its construction. The beauty and pathos of the story cannot be shown in an outline, but rather rest in the fine descriptions, character drawing and perceptions of the moving springs of the restricted lives, ninety years ago, upon the northeastern coast line of New England. It may be pertinent to notice here that while much of the early fervor and burning force of Mrs. Stowe's first writing had cooled, she had improved in no inconsiderable degree, in literary form. This in spite of the fact, that like her brother, Henry Ward Beecher, she was impatient of the slow methods of literary success. She was unwilling to remodel or polish her work, did not receive the suggestions of proof-readers or editors with gratitude, and is even accused of having shown resentment towards some of her most friendly and conscientious precautionary critics. There can be no doubt however, that the high standard of literary excellence demanded by her publishers, had a potent influence upon her style and method.

Her slip-shod manner in writing was a sore trial to those who had the supervision of its publication, and to quote one who has seen many of her original manuscripts, "she was one of the most careless and inaccurate writers existing. Her faults were deep, structural, going to the foundations of grammar, and she seldom punctuated except by dashes which might signify anything or nothing."

The critic's task was no sinecure, for the rush of her thoughts precluded studied effects, and a certain disregard for artistic method, which has been shown in various instances, prevented the revision and re-touching which is necessary to finished work. But she was "born under epistolary stars," and though perhaps not in literary style, the "Pellucido" whom good Dr. Watts so finely describes, her thoughts were positive, and easily understood. They were put with a homely force which obtained an instant hearing and lodged them in the readers' minds. It is significant that one always seizes upon the *thought* first, and it is only afterwards, if he be of a critical spirit, that he deprecates some faults in style. She was acknowledged to be one of the three greatest women novelists—being classed with Charlotte Bronte and George Eliot—and America's greatest literary woman. Greatest as a creator of dramatic scenes, greatest in value of literary work done, and incomparably so in results achieved. But one must admit that personal characteristics, such as impetuosity, disregard of modifying causes, and careful and mature revision of her work, while giving us something of greater worth than mere artistic finish, prevented her from being the *best writer*. She was a great genius, which is quite a different thing. Correctness of style would not have made "Uncle Tom's Cabin," would not have created the animus of "The Minister's Wooing." But how marvellous a figure in literary history would Harriet Beecher Stowe have been, could she also have been cited as a model of writing, like Thackeray, Irving, or Lydia Maria Child!

The "Pearl of Orr's Island" was published in book form in 1862 by Ticknor & Fields, who had succeeded to Phillips, Sampson & Company. They published about the same time, June, 1862, "Agnes of Sorrento," which had been running in the Atlantic from May, 1861, to April, 1865.

When the war had been raging more than a year and a half, and Americans began to realize that the issue was serious beyond anything that had at first appeared to the conflicting parties, when there came calls for more men, when the three months' volunteers and the nine months' men had returned or re-enlisted for "three years or the war," when our country was seen by the interested and sympathetic circle of foreign nations to be in mortal danger, then the women of the United States came to the front. They put away their tears and trembling, they wrote brave letters to the "boys" at the seat of war, they crushed down their agony at sight of their dear dead, and sent husbands and brothers out to battle, with their blessing.

They became a great moral support, as well as the ministering angels at hospital beds. Their tongues and pens urged the buying of American products that our crippled industries should be supported; the wearing of American goods that our spindles might be kept whirring even while the pangs of intestine war threatened to cramp every trade. True, the women of America came slowly up to the level of the time. It was not strange. They had little of the excitement, the enthusiasm which comes from action. They could only think with terrible fear of the loss of their brave supporters. They had still to learn the trying lesson that "They also serve, who only stand and wait."

But in the cutting and making of coats and garments, in the knitting of stockings and mittens, in the shredding of lint and the tearing and rolling of bandages, they came through their first paralyzing timidity, into heroism, into a fire of clear, steady burning patriotism which went forth

in inspiriting currents from every home, from every farm
house and mansion and tenement room, in all the land
where there was a good woman. They could not finish
the war with their needles, nor nurse back into peace the
burning enmity of fighting brothers; but they could and
did exert an intellectual and spiritual influence which was
a powerful factor in events.

With many other Northerners who had rejoiced in the
sympathy and support of the English people in the anti-
slavery movement, Mrs. Stowe saw with almost overpow-
ering surprise, that the sympathy and support of England
was now, in the most trying hour, given to the slave-holders, to the South who had fired the first gun, and maintained its fusilade with the fierce determination to perpet-
uate and extend slavery and—raise cotton. It was indeed
difficult to believe that commercial interests could in England, act as they had for so many years in this country, and
rise above and stifle right and justice !

Harriet Beecher Stowe read and re-read the "Affectionate and Christian Address of Many Thousands of Women
of Great Britain and Ireland to their Sisters, the Women
of the United States of America," saw their preamble,
which contained glad confession of a common origin, a
common faith and a common cause, read their urgent
appeal to American women to exert their influence for the
speedy abolition of slavery, their reference to "God's own
law," their confession of complicity in the introduction of
slavery into American shores, and their entreaty to American women to wipe away "our common crime and our
common dishonor."

She thought of the great meeting at Stafford House, not

ten years before, and held in her hand the bracelet of links
of massive gold, which the most beautiful Duchess in England had clasped upon her wrist, with the fervent wish that
the American author of "Uncle Tom's Cabin" might soon
be able to inscribe upon its remaining links the date of
American abolition. She turned over the leaves of the great
testimonial, holding nearly six hundred thousand names,
a most curious collection, commencing at the very steps of
the throne, numbering thousands of titled names in every
style of autograph, and running way through the ranks of
the intelligent people wherever Britain ruled, and also from
Paris to Jerusalem, covering an area vaster than any over
which any similar document had ever spread. She felt
irresistibly moved to make a counter appeal to them, in
the hour of America's need—in the hour when it became
apparent that *slavery* was the issue of the war, and the republic could only be maintained by making every man
free.

Her "Reply," which was dated Nov. 27th, 1862, at
Washington, D. C., whither she had gone to attend the
solemn religious festival which took place there on Thanksgiving Day, and was celebrated by more than a thousand
slaves, recently emancipated by Lincoln's proclamation,
was addressed to a score or more of the distinguished
women who had signed the great English testimonial. They
were Anna Maria Bedford (Duchess of Bedford); Olivia
Cecilia Cowley (Countess Cowley); Constance Grosvenor
(Countess Grosvenor); Harriet Sutherland (Duchess of
Sutherland); Elizabeth Argyle (Duchess of Argyle);
Elizabeth Fortesque (Countess Fortesque); Emily Shaftesbury, (Countess of Shaftesbury); Mary Ruthvan, (Baron-

ess Ruthvan); M. A. Milman (Wife of Dean of St. Paul's); R Buxton (Daughter of Sir Thomas Fowell Buxton); Cároline Amelia Owen (Wife of Professor Owen); Mrs. Charles Windham, C. A. Hatherton (Baroness Hatherton); Elizabeth Ducie (Countess Dowager of Ducie); Cecilia Parke (Wife of Baron Parke); Mary Ann Challis (Wife of the Lord Mayor of London); E. Gordon (Duchess Dowager of Gordon); Anna M. L. Melville (Daughter of Earl of Leven and Melville); Georgiana Ebrington (Lady Ebrington); A. Hill (Viscountess Hill); Mrs. Cobat (Wife of Bishop Cobat of Jerusalem); E. Palmerston (Viscountess Palmerston), and others.

Our great woman began her "Reply" by quoting to the women of Great Britain their "Affectionate and Christian Address" of nine years before. Every sentence of which was an intense reflection upon the position of England, towards the people who were then giving their heart's blood to free the slave.

Mrs. Stowe replied that it had been impossible to send an answer at all like in kind to the "Address," as the people who welcomed it were scattered over vast territories, and, possessed of the spirit which led to the efficient action then going on, had no time for it. All their time and energies were already absorbed in direct efforts to remove the great evil, and their answer, had been the silent continuance of those efforts. The South, had received the address with frantic irritation, and unsparing abuse of an act which brought the united weight of the British aristocracy and commonalty, upon the most diseased and sensitive part of our national life. Mrs. Stowe continued—

"The time has come however, when such an astonishing page has been turned in the anti-slavery history in America, that the women of our country, feeling that the great anti-slavery work to which their English sisters exhorted them is almost done, may properly and naturally feel moved to reply to their appeal, and lay before them the history of what has occurred since the receipt of their affectionate and Christian Address."

Then follows a succinct, and in many ways remarkable history of the United States, from the repeal of the Missouri Compromise to the date of her writing. It states clearly with an eye single to the vital points, the situation of the North and South in the war, with the political and moral issues at stake. Then comes a moving appeal to her friends in England, the women who by thousands welcomed her, as the author of "Uncle Tom's Cabin"—as the representative of a feeling, which was now the active principle of the North.

"And now, Sisters of England, in this solemn, expectant hour let us speak to you of one thing which fills our hearts with pain and solicitude. It is an unaccountable fact, and one which we entreat you seriously to ponder, that the party which has brought the cause of Freedom thus far on its way, during the past eventful year has found little or no support in England. Sadder than this, the party which makes Slavery the chief corner-stone of its edifice finds in England its strongest defenders."

The rest of this remarkable document cannot here be reproduced. It is a masterly grasp of the complicated situation, and an arraignment of the English people, which might well have made them blush for their inconsistency.

Thus does Mrs. Stowe close one of the most remarkable manifestoes in history:

"And now, Sisters of England, think it not strange if we bring back the words of your letter, not in bitterness, but in deepest sadness and lay them at your door. We say to you—Sisters, you have spoken well; we have heard you; we have heeded; we have striven in the cause even unto death. We have sealed our devotion by desolate hearths and darkened homesteads: by the blood of sons, husbands and brothers. In many of our dwellings the very light of our lives has gone out; and yet we accept the life-long darkness as our own part in this great and awful expiation, by which the bonds of wickedness shall be loosed and abiding peace established on the foundation of righteousness. Sisters, what have you done, and what do you mean to do?

In view of the decline of the noble anti-slavery fire in England; in view of all facts and admissions recited from your own papers, we beg leave in solemn sadness to return to you your own words —'A common origin, a common faith, and, we believe, a common cause, urge us at the present moment, to address you on the subject of that fearful encouragement and support which is being afforded by England to a slave-holding Confederacy.

We will not dwell on the ordinary topics—on the progress of civilization, on the advance of freedom everywhere, and the rights and requirements of the nineteenth century; but we appeal to you very seriously, to reflect and to ask counsel of God how far such a state of things is in accordance with his Holy Word, the inalienable rights of immortal souls and the pure and merciful spirit of the Christian religion.

We appeal to you as sisters, as wives and mothers, to raise your voices to your fellow citizens and your prayers to God for the removal of this affliction and disgrace from the Christian world. In behalf of many thousands of American women,

HARRIET BEECHER STOWE."

This was indeed a prompt and pointed " retort court-
eous " though given with the solemn earnestness and spirit
of forbearing kindness which always actuated the great
woman. It was not only a "reply," it was an appeal for
aid, freighted with the accumulated suffering and fears of
the whole woman heart of America. Harriet Beecher
Stowe never spoke nor wrote for mere verbal effect, she
was the one who could voice the deepest feelings of the
nation, the grief and surprise, with which the whole people
saw that the mother country was false to her faith, appearing, after all, to be a mercenary old dame, who in spite of
her better impulses, kept always an eye to her own advantage. This article appearing January, 1863, naturally made
a profound impression upon its readers, stimulating and encouraging Mrs. Stowe's compatriots, and wringing the withers
of the English sympathizers with the "independence " of
American Southerners, in a most uncomfortable fashion.
To the active, enthusiastic, successful and regenerated
people of "The New South " her prediction may now be
repeated with cordial congratulation.

" Mark our works! If we succeed, the children of these very
men who are now fighting us, will rise up and call us blessed. Just
as surely as there is a God who governs in the world, so surely all
the laws of national prosperity follow in the train of equity ; and if
we succeed, we shall have delivered the children's children of our
misguided brethren from the wages of sin, which is always and
everywhere, death."

" The reply " was published in the Atlantic Monthly and
in Macmillan's (London) Magazine, afterwards in book form
by Sampson, Low & Co., who sold some six thousand
copies.

On the 10th day of January, 1863, Dr. Lyman Beecher passed out of this existence, in his 88th year. The last four years of his life had been shadowed as by a veil which was continually drawn closer about his mental faculties. His memory, particularly the retention of dates and names, even those of his most cherished friends, utterly failed and the last year of his life all the organs of communication and expression with the outer world seemed to fail. From the last pages of his autobiography we select a paragraph written by Mrs Stowe, who spent as much time as possible assisting her step-mother to care for him,—

" His utterances were, much of the time, unintelligible sounds, with only short snatches and phrases from which could be gathered that the internal current still flowed. Still his eye remained luminous and the expression of his face, when calm, was marked both by strength and sweetness. Occasionally a flash of his old quick humor would light up his face, and a quick reply would break out in the most unexpected manner. One day, as he lay on the sofa, his daughter, Mrs. Stowe, stood by him brushing his long white hair; his eyes were fixed on the window, and the whole expression of his face was peculiarly serene and humorous. 'Do you know,' she said, stroking his hair, 'that you are a very handsome old gentleman?' Instantly his eyes twinkled with a roguish light, and he answered quickly, 'Tell me something new.' "

The description of his mental condition is peculiarly significant in view of the similar affliction which overtook his illustrious daughter in ' declining days. It seemed to be ordained that several of his family should die as he did, as did Emerson and Alcott, showing decay, as do old trees, at the top first.

In April, 1863 Mrs. Stowe published an article in the Atlantic Monthly entitled "Sojourner Truth, The Libyan Sibyl." It was a description of the strange and very interesting person, a powerful and wildly eloquent African woman who had been known in the early years of Abolitionism as a frequent and impressive speaker at anti-slavery meetings in the northern states, from one to another of which she traveled as a self-appointed agency. She was a full blooded African, possessed of that silent and subtle power which is called personal presence, tall and strong, even majestic in her carriage, and strikingly terse and pointed in her speech.

She called upon Mrs. Stowe at a time when her house at Andover was occupied by several visiting clergyman of distinction, among whom was Dr. Edward Beecher and Professor Allen, and the account of her appearance and conversation furnishes a strong picture of a peculiar character; a striking example of the notable outgrowths of a down-trodden race; a personage whose barbaric eloquence might have proved, with the same culture, as immortal as the words of St. Augustine or Tertullian. So impressed was Mrs. Stowe with the history and personality of the woman, that during a breakfast in her honor given by Story the American sculptor, at Rome, she gave a vivid representation of Sojourner. The sculptor whose mind had begun to turn upon Egypt, in search of a type of art which should represent a larger and more vigorous development of nature than the cold elegance of the Greek lines was strongly impressed with the subject, and conceived the idea of a statue which should be called "The Libyan Sibyl." He was, however, then dwelling on the "Cleopatra," bringing into mental form the broadly developed nature, the slumbering passion, with which that statue is surcharged. But two years later, in another interview with Mrs. Stowe, he told her that his conception of "The Libyan Sibyl" had never left him, and a day or two later showed her his plaster model. The inspiration which came to him taking shape in the glorious form of the Sibyl, was received from the graphic language of the author of "Uncle Tom's Cabin."

It was made and formed one of the loftiest and most original works of modern art, and became one of the most impressive figures at the World's Exhibition in London. This work should not be confounded with the fresco decoration of the Sistine Chapel in Rome upon which Michael Angelo's Sibyls are the worthy companions of the Biblical Prophets. These are, the aged Pythoness of Cumae, and her of Persia who reads so earnestly, and the *Sibyl of Lybia*, who holds up an immense volume whose pages rise and wave in the air like wings. The figure of Michael Angelo's Sibyl bears a marked resemblance to a piece of statuary, the painter having been, up to the time when he undertook the Sistine decoration, an artist in sculpture only.

Story, the modern artist, who narrowly escaped being a poet, doubtless received a suggestion from this, for his original and striking work. Story's attitude is equally strong and original. The legs of his Sibyl are crossed, chin resting upon hand, elbow on knee, looking across the desert into a weird, unimaginable future. It is a fitting monument of the graphic power of Mrs. Stowe, who saw her mental impression materialized in marble through the hand of another.

22

Professor Stowe having resigned his chair at Andover Theological Seminary in 1864, the family moved to Hartford, Connecticut. Mrs. Stowe built a commodious, and attractive house, in the western suburbs of that city, which is still to be seen, considerably neglected and run down, in what has become an unfashionable quarter upon the edge of Glenwood.

In 1864 Mrs. Stowe commenced in the Atlantic a series of papers, beginning with "The Ravages of a Carpet," which continued for twelve months. They were afterwards collected under the title of "House and Home Papers," their authorship being thinly disguised under the *nom de plume* "Christopher Crowfield." Mrs. Stowe's object in taking this synonym was, obviously, that she might write from the standpoint of the masculine head of a family, being thereby enabled to introduce many observations, which could not so pertinently emanate from a woman's pen. These essays were in a vein quite new to the famous author, and attracted close attention from thousands of readers to whom their topics were of vital and present interest. They touched upon the dearest sanctities of home, and brought the best thoughts of life to centre about the fireplace and reading table of every household. There was in them, the literary flavor of the "Autocrat" who had chatted so delightfully at the "Breakfast Table," the rare grace and fine humor of the writer of the "Back Log Studies," who followed somewhat later, and above and illuminating all, the sweetness of domestic love and home enjoyment.

How much they did to centralize and intensify the sometimes lax devotion of indifferent and stern New Englanders about the hearthstone, can not be estimated. Every reader

House Built by Harriet Beecher Stowe, Hartford, Conn., in 1864.

must feel a heart glow, and pure pleasure and desire quicken within him, at their perusal, and even now when the public mind has turned more upon the " house beautiful " and the amenities of family living, they lose nothing of their inherent charm.

" *The Ravages of a Carpet* " is an amusing and " o'er true tale," of how a new carpet, which was incongruous in style and richness with the household furniture, succeeded in setting all things at heads and points, in the Crowfield home and, in the temporary aberration which permitted the women of the family to seek more after fashion than comfort, almost alienated the domestic fairies of simplicity, good cheer and serene content. It is written from the real masculine standpoint, and while holding much of truth, is cleverly held open to the feminine objections of the wife and daughters, which are promptly introduced by those characters.

" *House-Keeping vs. Home-Making* " illustrates Benjamin Franklin's proverb, " Silks and satins put out the kitchen fire," showing how the prim luxuries of housekeeping and a vain-glorious regard for the circumstance of daily living, have often extinguished the infinitely more sacred flame of domestic love—a lesson by the way, still to be learned, by many a modern housekeeper of more thrift than culture.

" *What is a Home and How to Keep it* " sets forth the evident fact that a dwelling owned or rented by a man, in which his own wife keeps house, is not always, or of course, a home. In this essay which is replete in every paragraph with valuable suggestions, Christopher Crowfield deprecates purchasing things too fine for use, too choice for comfort and liberty. He advises against articles which must be shrouded from light and dust, or used with fear and trembling because their cost is above the general level of one's means, and they cannot easily be replaced. He humorously, and with a pathos which will be felt by hundreds of readers who have passed through a similar, trying childish experience, describes the anguish of his boyhood, when houses, furniture, scrubbed floors, white curtains and bright tins and brasses were made to seem the permanent facts of existence, and men and women, and particularly boys, meddlesome intruders upon divine order. How many little human beings have at some time experienced the same reversal of the essentials of life, through the distorted judgment and limited view of sundry human authorities who represented the powers that be.

"*The Economy of the Beautiful*" is a delightful discussion of the true utility of beautiful things in the domestic environment. The author advocates most satisfactorily the advantage of sparing expense upon so called "decorations," by which wall papers, window draperies, carpets and upholstery have come to be designated, and becoming possessed of them in their richest form, of statues, pictures and vases, even though they be no more than correct models or good copies, of celebrated works. She pertinently says,—

"No child is ever stimulated to draw or to read by an Axminster carpet or a carved centre table, but a room surrounded by photographs and pictures and fine casts, suggests a thousand inquiries. The child is found with a pencil drawing, or he asks for a book on Venice, or wants to hear the history of the Roman Forum.

This essay is well worth the careful consideration of every family who are making a home.

"*Raking up the Fire*," brings to the imagination a vivid picture of comfort, affectionate confidence and intelligent pre-somnolent chit-chat, which warms the heart and makes the group around the dying embers, real people to us all. It is a rare season, with genial Christopher Crowfield in the middle of the half circle, his wife busy with her work basket at a table near by, and Jennie and Marianne and Bob Stephens the prospective son-in-law, gathered about the faintly glowing embers. They talk of many things, æsthetic, theological and scientific, always bringing the themes home, making them personal and dear, never talking or thinking at other people, but only of what concerns them all, and us, and every one. House furnishing, flower raising, book shelves and china, come into the rambling talk which is characteristic of the hour, making one of the most charming of the many delightful papers in the series.

"*The Lady who does her own Work*" is an essay which carries with it a flavor which is purely American, a suggestion of conditions only possible to the life of the mass of intelligent people of the United States, and a form which is so distinctly indigenous to the soil of New England, that a foreigner who would laugh at the title, might well be considerably confused at the matter of the piece. It is a pleasant and respectful handling of a theme upon which the writer evidently dwells with pride. That one can do her own work and be a lady; that American women can successfully perform the duties of household work, saving their hands by the use of their brains, by their good judgment and mental acumen turning drudgery into honorable labor, which is so deftly performed as to be graceful and in every way dignified, is a fact which Christopher Crowfield declares with a glow of personal gratification. It is possible that this sketch will not now be so generally appreciated as in the earlier days when many, even most, American women were capable of directing their servants and if necessary, performing the duties of cook or housemaid with dignity and self respect.

While these papers were appearing, the echoes of the bitter and bloody war now long drawn out and raging more fiercely than ever, came to the hearthstones of every home, and Christopher Crowfield who watched the times with deep anxiety, saw an opportunity to again write upon a topic of political interest.

"*What can be got in America*," is a patriotic appeal to American women who could labor so effectively in Sanitary Fairs, and minister so tenderly to the wounded soldiers in hundreds of army hospitals, to be as thoughtful and consistent, in all things affecting the prosperity of our stricken country, and to strengthen its industries by buying, eating, and wearing, American productions.

It may be mentioned as it is a custom, now for obvious reasons unpermissible, that this, as well as other of these papers, contains various easy and undisguised references to mercantile houses in Boston, which evoke a certain mercenary wonder, even excite a momentary suspicion in the mind of the practical reader. This, however unworthy, may be excused as it is born of the adroit advertising of the present decade, and the machinations of writers who "get pay at both ends of an article." Perhaps it will be remembered how Mr. Howells astonished the more suspicious readers of the country, by his graceful unconsciousness of unwritten literary rules which forbid such localizing of purchases made, and set many drawing-rooms buzzing with discussions as to whether certain Boston firms, to whom he pointed by name when his heroines wanted dinner dresses and small accessories, *had* subsidized him; how he came to do it if they had not done so; and whether his editors would "stand it."

These questionings were, of course, outside of the athenic atmosphere where even authors seem to love the very names of the local business houses. It is superfluous to say that Mrs. Stowe's article, upon which many modern mercenary efforts have apparently been formed, was as purely honest and disinterested as were all her utterances, written or spoken. She had created her own prerogative to plain speaking, and saw no reason to repress her approval, even though it might pecuniarily benefit certain tradesmen. Was not the country dependant upon individuals, and never in so dire need of the welfare and success of the mass of the people?

"*Economy*" is a clear and forcible presentation of the essentials of life, a sensible valuation of the things worth having and the duty of every one to live according to the best use of his income, be it great or small. The ideas are more than usually broad and comprehensive, and the essay of permanent value, especially to Americans, who, on account of their feeling of unlimited possibilities in station, in culture, and style, are prone to outlays which, quite permissible in a millionaire, are so often the ruin of a poor clerk.

The paper upon "*Servants*," is an article which should be digested by every American housekeeper. It unites in a rare degree, a sense of justice to both parties, those who are too often opposed in our domestic economy; an underderstanding of the limitations which our political system impose upon any arbitrary power on the part of employers; and a Christian feeling towards, and a generous appreciation of, the good qualities of servants, which is unfortunately uncommon even to this day. In this, as in all other subjects she has treated, Mrs. Stowe seems to have absorbed and assimilated all the good ideas in existence, and to have them set forth with lucidity and great power. Those who in this generation have given some thought to the ethics of "servant-girlism" and perhaps written what they believed to be fresh matter, are surprised to find that Mrs. Stowe had thought and said it all, and much more, years ago.

Christopher Crowfield, who maintains very successfully his masculine attitude toward the order of things in a home, begins his paper on "*Cookery*" with apologies and acknowledgments to Mrs. Crowfield which are quite proper, as it soon becomes apparent that the intelligent and discriminating disquisition on the preparation and serving of bread, butter, meat, vegetables and tea which are considered as the essentials of a healthful regimen, could have emanated from none but a practical housekeeper's mind.

"Still the wonder grows" upon the modern reader who takes up a volume of these "House and Home Papers" and reads the thoughts of Christopher Crowfield upon "*Our House.*" They are full of rich suggestions for beauty, comfort and health. The author's ideas upon ventilation, heating and bathing conveniences, all of which combine utility and æsthetic charm, are set forth with wonderful taste and perspicacity. Christopher Crowfield, recommended light and air, when they were not so fashionable as today. He advocated the use of native woods, left in their natural beauty of grain and coloring, at an epoch when all interiors were adorned with white paint. He dared to speak for conservatories, and open windows, and clear lawns, when all New England was grown up with shrubbery even to the front door steps; when flies dominated good taste and enjoyment of nature, being the tiny black beasts who stood in the way of light, airy apartments, and sunlight and picturesque outlooks. People at large have been almost a quarter of a century educating up to the author of "House and Home Papers" in these things.

The last of the articles, is upon the tender and vital themes grouped under the head of "*Home Religion.*" Probably no better statement of Harriet Beecher's Stowe's religious habit could be given than Christopher Crowfield describes in his wife when he says,

"My wife is a steady, Bible-reading, Sabbath-keeping woman, cherishing the memory of her fathers and loving to do as they did —believing for the most part, that the paths beaten by righteous feet are best and safest, even though much walking therein has worn away the grass and flowers. Nevertheless, she has an indulgent ear for all that gives promise of bettering anybody or anything, and therefore is not severe on any new methods that may arise in our progressive days of accomplishing all such objects."

The wide awake son-in-law Bob Stephens, whom Mrs. Crowfield calls *Robert*, on Sunday evenings, is the advocate for the innovations which have crept in, making the modern Sabbath entirely different from the over-strictness and wearisome restraints which caused the Puritan Sabbath to be a day of suffering to many good people. The question being reasonably raised, is well answered by Mr. Crowfield and his wife, to whom, not strangely perhaps, the author imputes much excellent sense and tactful right feeling. Sabbath keeping in all its vexed phases is thoroughly discussed, and in this conversation may be found the only answer to the discussions of the desirability of throwing off the good old ways, for the looseness of European Sunday life. To treat home religion and Sabbath keeping with fair mindedness and an unbiased desire for the best results, has indeed seemed as impossible, as to conduct arguments upon the political welfare of the nation with calmness and brotherly love; but those who need truth well presented, for support to their unexpressible convictions, will find most admirable and considerate arguments in this article. It appears that there can be no other answer to the questions so often raised. And so upon this Sunday night, after the singing of good old hymns and the talking over the autumn fire, upon topics so good to dwell upon, we part with the Crowfields, not, however, without a strong desire to know them better.

CHAPTER XVI.

IN 1864 there appeared in the Atlantic Monthly, a series
of essays by Mrs. Stowe, written under the now transparent
pseudonym of Christopher Crowfield, called "Little Foxes."
They were seven papers upon the insignificant little habits
which mar domestic happiness. The author selects "Fault-
finding, Irritability, Repression, Persistence, Intolerance,
Discourtesy and Exactingness, of a verity, a company of
seemingly small sins, which in family and social life often
become furies more dangerous to peace than the daughters
of Hecate, with their many heads and serpentine hair. Of

347

Faultfinding let us quote a paragraph from the midst of the essay:

" Saddest of all sad things, is it to see two once very dear friends, employing all that peculiar knowledge of each other which love had given them only to harass and provoke,—thrusting and piercing with a certainty of aim that only past habits of confidence and affection could have put in their power, wounding their own hearts with every deadly thrust they make at one another, and all for such inexpressibly miserable trifles as usually form the openings of fault-finding dramas.

" For the contentions that loosen the very foundations of love, that crumble away all its fine traceries and carved work, about what miserable, worthless things do they commonly begin !—a dinner underdone, too much oil consumed, a newspaper torn, a waste of coal or soap, a dish broken !—and for this miserable sort of trash, very good, very generous, very religious people will some-times waste and throw away by double-handfuls the very thing for which houses are built and coal burned, and all the parapher-nalia of a home established,—*their happiness.* Better cold coffee, smoky tea, burnt meat, better any inconvenience, any loss, than a loss of *love*; and nothing so surely burns away love as constant fault-finding."

" There is *fretfulness*, a mizzling, drizzling rain of discomforting remark ; there is *grumbling*, a northeast storm that never clears ; there is *scolding*, the thunder storm with lightning and hail.   All these are worse than useless; they are positive *sins*, by whomso-ever indulged,—sins as great and real as many that are shuddered at in polite society."

Genial Christopher Crowfield after a most amusing des-cription of one of his own bad half hours, says of *Irritability:*

" Irritability is, more than most unlovely states, a sin of the flesh.   It is not, like envy, malice, spite, revenge, a vice which we may suppose to belong equally to an embodied or a disembodied spirit. In fact, it comes nearer to being physical depravity than anything I know of. There are some bodily states, some conditions of the nerves such that we could not conceive of even an angelic spirit confined in a body thus disordered as being able to do any more than simply endure. It is a state of nervous torture; and the attacks which the wretched victim makes on others are as much a result of disease as the snapping and biting of a patient convulsed with hydrophobia."

And again offers valuable advice for the control of the moody state of mind :

"There is a temperament called the HYPOCHONDRIAC, to which many persons, some of them the brightest, the most interesting, the most gifted, are born heirs,—a want of balance of the nervous powers, which tends constantly to periods of high excitement and of consequent depression,—an unfortunate inheritance for the possessor, though accompanied often with the greatest talents. Sometimes, too, it is the unfortunate lot of those who have not talents, who bear its burdens and its anguish without its rewards.

" People of this temperament are subject to fits of gloom and despondency, of nervous irritability and suffering, which darken the aspect of the whole world to them, which present lying reports of their friends, of themselves, of the circumstances of their life, and of all with which they have to do.

" Now the highest philosophy for persons thus afflicted is to *understand themselves* and their tendencies, to know that these fits of gloom and depression are just as much a form of disease as a fever or a toothache, to know that it is the peculiarity of the disease to fill the mind with wretched illusions, to make them seem miserable and unlovely to themselves, to make their nearest friends seem unjust and unkind, to make all events to appear to be going wrong and tending to destruction and ruin.

" The evils and burdens of such a temperament are half removed when a man once knows that he has it and recognizes it for a disease, and when he does not trust himself to speak and act in these bitter hours as if there were any truth in what he thinks and feels and sees. He who has not attained to this wisdom overwhelms his friends and his family with the waters of bitterness; he stings with unjust accusations, and makes his fireside dreadful with fancies which are real to him, but false as the ravings of fever.

" A sensible person, thus diseased, who has found out what ails him, will shut his mouth resolutely, not to give utterance to the dark thoughts that infest his soul."

After telling a story which characterized the social life of the last generation, and still obtains in many of the natures which have the inherent shyness with regard to amenities, which they are far from exhibiting when unpleasant truth is concerned, Christopher Crowfield says:

" And now for the moral,—and that is, that life consists of two parts, *Expression and Repression*,—each of which has its solemn duties. To love, joy, hope, faith, pity, belongs the duty of *expression:* to anger, envy, malice, revenge, and all uncharitableness, belongs the duty of *repression*.

" Some very religious and moral people err by applying *repression* to both classes alike. They repress equally the expression of love and of hatred, of pity and of anger. Such forget one great law, as true in the moral world as in the physical,—that repression lessens and deadens. Twice or thrice mowing will kill off the sturdiest crop of weeds; the roots die for want of expression. A compress on a limb will stop its growing; the surgeon knows this, and puts a tight bandage around a tumor, but what if we put a tight bandage about the heart and lungs, as some young ladies of my acquaintance do,—or bandage the feet, as they do in

China? And what if we bandage a nobler inner faculty, and warp *love* in grave-clothes?"

Of *Persistence* which is another name for self-will in speech as well as in action, Christopher Crowfield says:

"This love of the last word has made more bitterness in families and spoiled more Christians than it is worth. A thousand little differences of this kind would drop to the ground, if either party would let them drop. Suppose John is mistaken in saying breakfast is late,—suppose that fifty of the little criticisms which we make on one another are well or ill-founded, are they worth a discussion? Are they worth ill-tempered words, such as are almost sure to grow out of a discussion? Are they worth throwing away peace and love for? Are they worth the destruction of the only fair ideal left on earth,—a quiet, happy home? Better let the most unjust statements pass in silence than risk one's temper in a discussion upon them.

"Discussions, assuming the form of warm arguments, are never pleasant ingredients of domestic life, never safe recreations between near friends. They are, generally speaking, mere unsuspected vents for self-will, and the cases are few where they do anything more than to make both parties more positive in their own way than they were before."

The paper upon *Intolerance*, opens with a shot which scattering just enough to hit the whole covey, hits all of us between the eyes and demands attention.

"People are apt to talk as if all the intolerance in life were got up and expended in the religious world; whereas religious intolerance is only a small branch of the radical, strong, all-prevading intolerance of human nature.

"Physicians are quite as intolerant as theologians. They never have had the power of burning at the stake for medical opinions,

but they certainly have shown the will. Politicians are intolerant. Philosophers are intolerant, especially those who pique
themselves on liberal opinions. Painters and sculptors are intolerant. And housekeepers are intolerant, virulently denunciatory
concerning any departures from their particular domestic creed."

This is the prelude to one of the best of the strong and
pertinent series. It will be apt and pointed as long as
human nature exists in its present form.

One or two selections from the essay upon *Discourtesy*
are the key-note to the whole, which teems with advice
and suggestions which alas, are still needed, more than a
score of years after their writing.

"My second head is, that there should be in family life the
same delicacy in the avoidance of disagreeable topics that characterizes the intercourse of refined society among strangers.

"I do not think that it makes family-life more sincere, or any
more honest, to have the members of a domestic circle feel a
freedom to blurt out in each other's faces, without thought or care,
all the disagreeable things that may occur to them : for example
'How horridly you look this morning! What's the matter with
you?'—'Is there a pimple coming on your nose? or what is that
spot?'—'What made you buy such a dreadfully unbecoming
dress?'—Observations of this kind between husbands and
wives, brothers and sisters, or intimate friends, do not indicate
sincerity, but obtuseness; and the person who remarks on the
pimple on your nose is in many cases just as apt to deceive you as
the most accomplished Frenchwoman who avoids disagreeable
topics in your presence.

"Many families seem to think that it is a proof of family union
and good-nature that they can pick each other to pieces, joke on
each other's feelings and infirmities, and treat each other with a

general tally-ho-ing rudeness without any offense or ill-feeling. If there is a limping sister, there is a never-failing supply of jokes on ' Dot-and-go-one ! ' and so with other defects and peculiarities of mind or manners. Now the perfect good-nature and mutual confidence which allow all this liberty are certainly admirable ; but the liberty itself is far from making home-life interesting or agreeable.

" Jokes upon personal or mental infirmities, and a general habit of saying things in jest which would be the height of rudeness if said in earnest, are all habits which take from the delicacy of family affection.

" In all rough playing with edge-tools many are hit and hurt who are ashamed or afraid to complain. And after all, what possible good or benefit comes from it? Courage to say disagreeable things, when it is necessary to say them for the highest good of the person addressed, is a sublime quality ; but a careless habit of saying them, in the mere freedom of family intercourse, is certainly as great a spoiler of the domestic vines as any fox running."

Exactingness, which is shown to be Ideality grown impatient, is deprecated and the effects of the habit of over demand upon one's self and friends was never more cleverly shown than in the comparison of the Mores and the Daytons which is subjoined :

" The poor woman in the midst of possessions and attainments which excite the envy of her neighbors, is utterly restless and wretched, and feels herself always baffled and unsuccessful. Her exacting nature makes her dissatisfied with herself in everything that she undertakes, and equally dissatisfied with others. In the whole family there is little of that pleasure which comes from the consciousness of mutual admiration and esteem, because each one is pitched to so exquisite a tone that each is afraid to touch another

for fear of making discord.   They are afraid of each other everywhere.   They cannot sing to each other, play to each other, write
to each other ; they cannot even converse together with any freedom, because each knows that the others are so dismally well
informed and critically instructed.

"Though all agree in a secret contempt for their neighbors
over the way, as living in a most heathenish state of ignorant contentment, yet it is a fact that the elegant brother John will often,
on the sly, slip into the Daytons' to spend an evening and join
them in singing glees and catches to their old rattling piano, and
have a jolly time of it, which he remembers in contrast with the
dull, silent hours at home.   Kate Dayton has an uncultivated
voice, which often falls from pitch; but she has a perfectly infec-
tious gayety of good nature, and when she is once at the piano,
and all join in some merry troll, he begins to think that there
may be something better even than good singing ; and then they
have dances and charades and games, all in such contented, jolly,
impromptu ignorance of the unities of time, place, and circumstance, that he sometimes doubts, where ignorance is such bliss,
whether it isn't in truth folly to be wise.

"Jane and Maria laugh at John for his partiality to the Daytons', and yet they themselves feel the same attraction.   At the
Daytons' they somehow find themselves heroines ; their drawings
are so admired, their singing is so charming to these simple ears,
that they are often beguiled into giving pleasure with their own
despised acquirements ; and Jane, somehow, is very tolerant of the
devoted attention of Will Dayton, a joyous, honest-hearted fellow,
whom, in her heart of hearts, she likes none the worse for being
unexacting and simple enough to think her a wonder of taste and
accomplishments.   Will, of course, is the farthest possible from
the Admirable Crichtons and exquisite Sir Philip Sidneys whom
Mrs. More and the young ladies talk up at their leisure, and adorn
with feathers from every royal and celestial bird, when they are

discussing theoretic possible husbands. He is not in any way distinguished, except for a kind heart, strong, native good sense, and a manly energy that has carried him straight into the heart of many a citadel of life, before which the superior and more refined Mr. John had set himself down to deliberate upon the best and most elegant way of taking it. Will's plain, homely intelligence has often in five minutes disentangled some ethereal snarl in which these exquisite Mores had spun themselves up, and brought them to his own way of thinking by that sort of disenchanting process which honest, practical sense sometimes exerts over ideality.

"The fact is however, that in each of these families there is a natural defect which requires something from the other for completeness. Taking happiness as the standard, the Daytons have it as against the Mores. Taking attainment as the standard, the Mores have it as against the Daytons. A portion of the discontented ideality of the Mores would stimulate the Daytons to refine and perfect many things which might easily be made better, did they care enough to have them so; and a portion of the Daytons' self-satisfied contentment would make the attainments and refinements of the Mores of some practical use in advancing their own happiness.

These excerpts are doubtless better than any commentary of the writer. Indeed it is one of the difficulties of a devoted interpreter, to repress and condense to outline, and in so doing run the imminent danger of devitalizing and paling the ideas of a great author, while feeling always, that nothing can so well testify to their beauty and power as the writings which are under discussion, no word of which can really be spared.

Painting the lily and gilding refined gold is indeed a humiliating attempt, and nothing half so sincere and convincing as to the strength and ethical value of these essays of Christopher Crowfield can be offered, as an entreaty to read them for one's self.

During the year 1864 Mrs. Stowe contributed monthly articles to the Atlantic, which from the appearance of her story in the first number, had been her principal mouthpiece during the successive changes which ensued in its publishers and editorship. From the time of Phillips & Sampson whose deaths closely following had dissolved the firm, to Ticknor & Fields; Fields, Osgood & Co.; J. R. Osgood, and up to 1874, when the magazine passed into the hands of its present proprietors, Houghton, Mifflin & Co., its publishers have brought out Mrs. Stowe's books in America, its editors been her friends and gratified receivers.

They were upon a variety of topics, all holding interest to American readers and are to be found in a collection called "The Chimney Corner."

"WHAT WILL YOU DO WITH HER?" or "THE WOMAN QUESTION," deals with a dual problem, the opposing parts of which if adjusted as it would appear they might easily be, would each answer and satisfy the other's need. The author discusses the state of pride and prejudice which precluded, and still largely precludes, the assuming of the housework and care of another's family by competent and intelligent women, and the difficulties and trials of those who, lifted above want, find their accumulation of luxuries and privileges, only a new set of cares and troubles.

It is often asked in these later days, how Harriet Beecher Stowe regarded the struggle for Woman's Suffrage in which her sister, Isabella Beecher Hooker was so earnestly engaged. It has been declared that she was too lucid and fair-minded, too far-seeing and comprehensive to run away with the idea which brought such martyrdom upon its promulgators. As is well known the pioneers, in the dissent and impatience with which they were widely regarded, failed to secure the credit and gratitude of even women, who were doubtless indirectly benefited by their persistent efforts to bring them to the front, as a sex possessed of brains, mechanical ability and responsible capacity for important trusts. But see what Christopher Crowfield wrote in his paper upon " WOMAN'S SPHERE."

"As to the ' Woman's Rights Movement,' it is not peculiar to America, it is part of a great wave in the incoming tide of modern civilization; the swell is felt no less in Europe, but it comes over and breaks on our American shore, because our great, wide beach affords the best play for its waters; and as the ocean waves bring with them kelp, sea-weed, mud, sand, gravel, and even putrefying debris, which lie unsightly on the shore, and yet, on the whole, are healthful and refreshing,—so the Woman's Rights movement, with its conventions, its speech-makings, its crudities, and eccentricities, is nevertheless a part of a healthful and necessary movement of the human race towards progress."

As the conversation continues on we see—

" Then," said my wife, " you believe that women ought to vote ? "

" If the principle on which we founded our government is true, that taxation must not exist without representation, and if women hold property and are taxed, it follows that women should be represented in the state by their votes, or there is an illogical working of our government."

" But, my dear, don't you think that this will have a bad effect on the female character ? "

"Yes," said Bob, "it will make women caucus-holders, political candidates."

"It may make this of some women, just as of some men," said I. "But all men do not take any great interest in politics; it is very difficult to get some of the very best of them to do their duty in voting; and the same will be found true among women."

"But, after all," said Bob, "what do you gain? What will a woman's vote be but a duplicate of that of her husband or father, or whatever man happens to be her adviser?"

"That may be true on a variety of questions, but there are subjects on which the vote of women would, I think, be essentially different from that of men. On the subjects of temperance, public morals, and education, I have no doubt that the introduction of the female vote into legislation, in states, counties and cities, would produce results very different from that of men alone. There are thousands of women who would close grogshops, and stop the traffic in spirits, if they had the legislative power; and it would be well for society if they had. In fact, I think that a state can no more afford to dispense with the vote of women in its affairs than a family."

The whole article is a common-sense view of the many-sided and complex question, which in its legal issue is still unanswered, and the essay is wholesome reading for the too positive minds, who jump at conclusions, with all the more confidence because their knowledge of contingencies is slight. Without, however, harping upon the question of voting, Mrs. Stowe proceeds to mention the professions and vocations open to women. These *are* already generally occupied by them, amply fulfilling her prediction that women would excel in such capacities as authorship, literary work of all grades, painting, sculpture and the subordinate arts of photography, coloring and finishing, teaching, architecture and landscape gardening, agencies of various sorts, medicine and nursing.

"A FAMILY TALK ON RECONSTRUCTION" brings up an admirable view, in its discussion of the transition stage and uncertain condition of political and social affairs in this country, at the close of the war.

"IS WOMAN A WORKER" and "THE TRANSITION," treat further of the woman question in its different phases, and "BODILY RELIGION" is what was then a rather original idea of *the duty of good health*, which has of late been earnestly insisted upon by the small army of metaphysical professors, who are known as mind curers. No one can raise objection to Mrs. Stowe's position in the matter. She goes no farther than to urge a return to natural conditions and an acceptance of fresh air, plain food, sleep and cleanliness, and a natural impulse to love God and one's fellow beings. She merely sought a thought-current of good feeling, which many now believe may be received, if the mind is open to its beneficent influence.

"HOW SHALL WE ENTERTAIN OUR COMPANY?" "HOW SHALL WE BE AMUSED?" "DRESS" and "THE SOURCES OF BEAUTY IN DRESS," are treatises upon social and æsthetic topics of remarkable lucidity and directness. In the essay upon "THE CATHEDRAL" we find a loving tribute to a saint who was embodied in the aged Aunt Esther, (pronounced by them "Easter,") who was one of the potent influences mentioned in the formation of the character of the Beecher children, and who took up her abode with the Stowes after their return to the east, and lived honored and loved, with them until her death.

"The New Year" and "The Noble Army of Martyrs" are

beautiful and tender remembrances of the bleeding hearts everywhere scattered through the United States, for so through the victory of the Federal soldiers could they still be called, and a glowing tribute to the brave young men who had died during the terrible struggle for the settlement of the brotherly quarrel, which hinged upon the maintenance or abolition of slavery.

The grand fact of the emancipation of the American slaves which Mrs. Stowe never expected to live to see, had been suddenly accomplished. What no one had seen his way clear to do as a constitutional right, was in one-half hour effected, in the writing of a war order.

The final ending of a great wrong which had seemed so far distant, and only to be obtained through legislation, was done with a few scratches of a pen held in the gaunt fingers of that noble work of God, honest Abraham Lincoln, so soon to be one of the world's most illustrious and reverenced martyrs.

Then Harriet Beecher Stowe went to her cabinet, and took from its place, the bracelet of massive gold links which the English duchess had twelve years before clasped upon her small wrist at Stafford House, and had engraved upon its remaining links, the dates of Emancipation in the District of Columbia; that of Freedom Proclaimed in Missouri and Maryland, and the President's Proclamation, Abolishing Slavery in the rebel states!

The links were then all bearing an inscription which meant new life, intellectual advancement and spiritual freedom to millions of degraded and fettered bond-men, in the leading countries of the civilized world. The bracelet is in existence at the time of the present writing, and will be pre-

served as a memento of a life which was a great factor in
American civilization. At this period slavery, now a thing
of the past, was discussed with renewed interest, and the
sales of "Uncle Tom's Cabin" were tremendously increased. The thoughts of the opposed sections of the republic, were turned to the writer of the great book which
had been so important a factor in the moral preparation of
the world for this reform, and Mrs. Stowe was overwhelmed
by the hundreds of letters which drifted in upon her at the
home in Hartford. In the pleasant East room where the
greenery of the conservatory gave a glimpse of perennial
summer, and she pondered and passed through the alembic
of her mind, the subjects and causes of the hour, Mrs. Stowe
was called upon to receive many visitors.

Distinguished people made pilgrimages to Hartford to see
her, and congratulate and thank her. Scores of celebrity
hunters came to remark upon her personal appearance and
household environment, many representatives of the press
from the larger cities, intruded upon her with the varying
demonstrations and degrees of enterprising inquisitiveness,
which are many as the shades of their hair or the cut of their
clothes. All of these and many indiscribable forms of intru-
sion she met with politeness, many of them with real
pleasure which she showed in her cordial smile, and shining
soulful eyes, and it was indeed an aggressive and extraordi-
narily obnoxious person, whom she did not dismiss with
forbearance. Her manner was not conventional. No
words of trite commonplaceness came readily to her lips,
nor did any depreciation of her own works, seem to be
necessary to the woman who never employed the doubtful
assumption of false modesty which is easy to little natures.

While she seldom refused audience to visitors, at hours when she was not engaged upon her work, she always took the privilege of terminating the interview as soon as it ceased to be profitable and, rising, said "good bye" with a clasp of the hand and an honest look into the eyes, which disarmed the possible impatience of one who might have wished a longer conversation.

A neighbor, who once called at an inopportune season, found himself taken through an apartment where he thought he saw the figure of a woman lying upon a lounge. The servant presently returned, saying that Mrs. Stowe "was composing" and could not be seen. He rose to leave, and again passed through the room and close by the lounge upon which Mrs. Stowe rested, with closed eyes. He passed out in some confusion of mind, which it may be presumed was not in the least felt, by the great author, who, if she heard the conversation did not permit it, nor the fact of his presence, to come into her deep inner consciousness, where ideas were in process of evolution.

To preserve the liberty which is essential to any great life-work, one must deny the small ceremonies and ignore the petty conventionalities which guide less occupied lives. How little conception have the good people, who are aggrieved because they are sometimes prevented from intruding upon the attention of an author, of the imperative demands upon the time, and the drain upon the resources physical and mental, which are with difficulty supported, and will admit no fresh imposition, through the thoughtless selfishness of friends and lion hunters.

A lady from Cincinnati came to Hartford some years ago, and, naturally anxious to see the writer of the works she

HARRIET BEECHER STOWE AT WORK.

had found so enjoyable and profitable, called at Mrs. Stowe's house with considerable timidity, just to tell her how much she admired her and longed to touch her hand. Accosting a small woman in a shade hat, who was working among the flowers in the yard, she asked for Mrs. Stowe. The small figure arose, looked searchingly at her and said simply "I am Mrs. Stowe," and waited, half turned towards her flowers, for the visitor to speak again.

The caller stammered out a few words which half expressed her feelings, and Mrs. Stowe pulling off her glove, clasped her hand cordially, saying she was glad if she had been able to suggest anything to her. Then, cutting a few flowers she gave them to the visitor, and saying "good bye" in her simple manner, went into the house without another word or look, seeming in an instant to forget the presence of the lady who stood paralyzed with surprise. She came away, bringing the flowers and a remembrance of Harriet Beecher Stowe, which, when the confusing of the two minute's interview was over, at first deepened into chagrin at her prompt dismissal, but soon merged into pleasure and personal admiration, as she recalled the friendly clasp of her hand and the look of honest greeting which shone in the grey eyes, telling more than her lips, of the sincerity of her welcome.

Of her characteristic abstraction or absent-mindedness which was frequently a voluntary self-withdrawal, a power which she naturally possessed and had cultivated during years of mental labor, there are many stories. One which came from a lady who was the child witness to the episode, suggests the extreme of her peculiarity, which, in many instances, seemed to amount to neglect of social proprieties.

One summer the Stowe family spent several months at Bethel, Maine, enjoying the delightful air and beautiful scenery of that region. Soon after their advent, numerous residents and summer visitors asked that Mrs. Stowe would give them a reception. To this she acceded, showing, however, some wonderment that they should care to see her.

The afternoon designated came, and the proud landlady went to inform her famous guest, that many people were already in the parlor. To her surprise, Mrs. Stowe was not in her room, nor about the premises and did not appear until nightfall, when she unconcernedly walked in after all the guests tired of waiting had departed.

It then appeared, that quite forgetting the reception, she had taken the narrator of the story who was then a little girl, by the hand and gone for a long tramp up the hillside and into the woods where they had a delightful day, unmindful of the outraged and disappointed callers who waited in vain. It is also averred, that the great author only smiled in her far-away manner, when reproached by her friends. Neither did she appoint another day when she would be "at home" and was thereafter undisturbed in her rest, uninterrupted in her quiet pleasure.

In 1865 when the civil war was drawing to a close, Ticknor & Fields saw an opening for a magazine for boys and girls, and in January appeared the first number of "Our Young Folks," a magazine which continued in that form for nine years, and was eventually merged in that Prince of all youth's magazines, "St. Nicholas."

Among the contributors were Thomas Bailey Aldrich, T. W. Higginson, Dr. Dio Lewis, Mayne Reid, Rose Terry, Louisa M. Alcott, Oliver Optic, Mrs. A. M. Diaz, with an occasional poem by Whittier, Longfellow and R. H. Stoddard. The editors also supplied suggestive and entertaining articles, making it a collection of the most delectable intellectual viands, which up to that time had ever been set before favored youth. Mrs. Stowe wrote the leading article which was the first of a series in another new line, and one which proved particularly charming to her young friends, and will remain a most interesting epoch to those who knew her personally, as in these sketches about squirrels, and birds, hens, chickens and ducks, cats, dogs, mice, and insects she has put much of herself, her personal tenderness for all little folks in feathers and fur, and the solicitude and fondness for lesser creation, which is a characteristic of the greatest minds and noblest hearts.

What boy could read " Hum, the Son of Buz," and not be awakened to the infinite depth of protecting love with which this author regarded a poor humming bird, and vividly aware of many tiny graces and intelligent actions on the part of a being which he had before only attempted to catch in his net? " Aunt Esther's Rules and Stories," " Our Country Neighbors," " Sir Walter Scott," and the stories of " Our Dogs," which recount the personal appearance and characters of the canine pets which conferred happiness and varied amusement to the Stowe family during many years, are full of simple literary charm, and a graceful allusiveness which fitly ornaments the spontaneous feeling and loving tenderness, which appear in every paragraph. These sketches, which are collected under the captions of " Queer Little People " and " A Dog's Mission," were followed by the story of " Little Pussy Willow," " The Daisy's First Winter" and "The Minister's Watermelons," gathered an eager audience among the young readers of the delightful magazine which looked in upon so many American homes each month.

These collections were subsequently published in book form by Ticknor & Fields and their successors, and appeared simultaneously in England and Scotland, furnishing wholesome entertainment to the children of the admirers of " Uncle Tom's Cabin " and the subsequent books of Mrs. Stowe.

CHAPTER XVII

MRS. STOWE'S FIRST VISIT TO THE SOUTH IN 1865. PURCHASE
OF AN ESTATE UPON THE ST. JOHN'S RIVER. "MEN OF OUR
TIMES ; OR, LEADING PATRIOTS OF THE DAY." EIGHTEEN
BIOGRAPHICAL SKETCHES OF STATESMEN, GENERALS AND
ORATORS. " RELIGIOUS POEMS." MRS. STOWE APPEARS A
CO-EDITOR WITH DONALD G. MITCHELL (IK. MARVEL) OF
HEARTH AND HOME. MRS. STOWE'S THIRD GREAT WORK
APPEARS IN 1869. "OLD TOWN FOLKS," LAID IN THE
LAST CENTURY IN THE TOWN OF NATICK, MASSACHUSETTS.
SAM LAWSON AND OTHER CHARACTERS WHICH HAVE
BECOME CLASSIC. PROFESSOR STOWE FURNISHED MUCH
MATERIAL FOR THE WORK, AND IS DESCRIBED AS THE
HERO OF THE STORY. THE PECULIAR EXPERIENCES
OF "THE VISIONARY BOY." PROFESSOR STOWE'S OWN
PSYCHOLOGICAL PECULIARITY. CORRESPONDENCE WITH
GEORGE ELIOT UPON THE SUBJECT OF SPIRITUALISM. " SAM
LAWSON'S FIRESIDE STORIES."

In 1865, after the war was finished, Mrs. Stowe for the
first time in her life, went South. She spent some weeks in
Florida at Jacksonville, at a plantation upon the St. John's
river, and later, purchased an estate at Mandarin. Mrs.
Stowe made this purchase with a view to the comfort and
betterment of her oldest son Frederick, who had been from
his youth, afflicted with a delicate and nervous organiza-
tion, and a weak will, which could not restrain him from

indulgence in stimulants, which accentuated his misery, and made his unhappy life a deeper sorrow to his friends.

Under the supervision of a practical planter, the land was cleared, orange trees were set and a house built upon the banks of the St. John's river, under the shade of some immense live oak trees. This place became the much loved winter home which George Eliot in one of her letters to Mrs. Stowe refers to as "your Western Sorrento." Thither were annually transported the *lares* and *penates* of the family, animate as well as inanimate, for some pet dogs and cats made the trip several times, returning with the family, at the approach of warm weather, to their Hartford home.

Mrs. Stowe became deeply interested in the building of an Episcopal church at Mandarin, lending effective pecuniary assistance, as well as personal aid in collecting funds.

She humorously related to the writer how she once became an involuntary and successful speculator in real estate, —buying a small piece of land at $200, and selling it afterwards for $7,000, a fair profit, she thought upon the investment. The money was put to good use in the purchase of a parsonage for her youngest son, when he became pastor of the Windsor Avenue Congregational church in Hartford.

Professor Stowe who was now at liberty to employ his profound knowledge of ancient history, Eastern languages, ancient and modern, as well as his rich fund of Biblical lore, in giving to the world what had heretofore been locked in the ancient languages and specially studied by theological students, was deeply absorbed upon a work, which was pub-

lished two years later by the Hartford Publishing Company,—
"The Origin and History of the Books of the New Testament."

Of a very social nature, Professor Stowe naturally talked
of his work and his family were called upon to listen to
his conclusions. Mrs. Stowe as usual offered many suggestions of value, receiving in return practical assistance
from him in the literary work which pressed heavily upon
her.

During the year 1867 Mrs. Stowe prepared a set of biographical sketches which was published early in 1868, being
issued by the Hartford Publishing Company, "by subscription only." The collection made an octavo volume of some
five hundred and seventy-five pages, with eighteen fine steel
plate portraits. This house had made a success of Professor Stowe's book upon "The Origin and History of the
Books of the New Testament," selling some sixty thousand
copies. They sold about forty thousand of Mrs. Stowe's
"Men of our Times," paying her a handsome royalty, besides an extra thousand dollars for the sketch of her brother
Henry Ward Beecher, which she rather reluctantly supplied.

The volume, "Men of Our Times; or Leading Patriots
of the Day," comprised narratives of the lives and deeds of
American statesmen, generals and orators, including biographical sketches and anecdotes of Lincoln, Grant, Garrison, Sumner, Chase, Wilson, Greeley, Farragut, Andrew
Colfax, Stanton, Douglas, Buckingham, Sherman, Sheridan,
Howard, Phillips and Beecher.

It was appropriately dedicated to the young men of
America, and in the preface where the writer speaks of
herself as the editor, thus acknowledging her indebtedness

to various sources from which she collected her facts, she gives this terse and cheering paragraph.

"It will be found when the sum of all these biographies is added up, that the qualities which have won this great physical and moral victory have not been so much exceptional gifts of genius or culture, as those more attainable ones which belong to man's moral nature."

This line of literary work, which may perhaps without disparagement be called mechanical, as it certainly is not imaginative if the biographer be true to his high calling, is alas! frequently made to serve base uses, in which good will becomes the father to fair statement, or personal bias sees through a glass darkly, the doubtful incidents of a career. But Mrs. Stowe demonstrated, to the surprise of her friends, the possession of a faculty which is supposed to be quite apart from that of a graceful essayist, of a successful novel writer or the swift re-incarnation of painful realities into such a burning creation as that of "Uncle Tom's Cabin."

Mrs. Stowe's able handling of the complex political questions, and the sifting of the essential factors from a mass of materials bearing upon events in the history of the war which had lately closed, was natural to her logical mind and clear judgment, and enhanced by the intense interest with which she had for years, followed the succeeding events in our nation's history. Men were events, in those surcharged times, and Mrs. Stowe's sketches of reformers, politicians, generals and naval heroes are instinct with individual life and are rare memorials of men all of whom but one, Lincoln, were then living; more than two thirds of whom, have now with their illustrious biographer, passed into the "undiscovered country."

In the same year Mrs. Stowe published a small volume of Religious Poems. It comprised twenty-eight of her published contributions to *The Independent* and other periodicals. They are unassuming in style, but sweetly and tenderly religious in sentiment, with flavors of the woods and sky and youthful memories of music and poetry, pervading them all, as they did her prose writings.

In Dec., 1868, Mrs. Stowe, in answer to the solicitations of the projector appeared as co-editor, with Donald G. Mitchell (Ik. Marvel), of a weekly illustrated journal called "Hearth and Home." It was devoted to the interests of the "Farm, Garden and Fireside." Joseph B. Lyman and Mary M. Dodge, the present editor of St. Nicholas, were associate editors. Among the contributors were Oliver Wendell Holmes, William Cullen Bryant, J. T. Trowbridge, *Grace Greenwood*, Rose Terry and other well known writers of high literary merit. Mrs. Stowe, who followed Mr. Mitchell in the editorial columns in the first number, wrote a characteristic "Greeting," and furnished a long article descriptive of "How we kept Thanksgiving at Oldtown." The editor-in-chief appended a note announcing it as a foretaste of a new novel from Mrs. Stowe's pen, which was to appear the following season, and sure enough, here nearly all the personages which later appeared in "Old Town Folks," made their first bow. It was a draft from the salient points of her book then in preparation.

But Mrs. Stowe's precarious health forbade any engagement so exacting as that of editorship, and her connection with Hearth and Home continued but a few months.

As Mrs. Stowe became past middle life the fits of abstraction which were peculiar and natural to her, increased and deepened to so great a degree, that her personal appearance which had always been quite remarkable in various ways, became decidedly eccentric. A friend who was entertaining her in New York about this time, relates having invited a company of enthusiastic admirers, a number of whom were young ladies, to meet her at luncheon. As the time arrived, the hostess observed with considerable dismay that her distinguished guest was falling into a state of moodiness, which augered little for the entertainment of the expectant company.

When the ladies arrived and were presented, Mrs. Stowe greeted them with the far-away expression which was becoming habitual, and sat through the luncheon absorbed in thought, speaking only once of her own volition, when she requested some one to "Please pass the butter," and immediately relapsed into impenetrable mental solitude. It amusingly suggests those people so cleverly described in one of the essays of whimsical young Winthrop Macworth Praed, who in the midst of noisy crowds or the attacks of direct conversationalists, were still—alone. Mrs. Stowe afterwards declared that she was thinking out scenes for "Old Town Folks," which story she then had in hand.

Early in 1869, Fields, Osgood & Co. published this book, which must be counted as the third of Mrs. Stowe's great works and, though it is open to criticism on several points, judging as we must from the effect of a work, rather than by its conformation to certain canons laid out by literary law makers, it must be pronounced one of her most power-

HARRIET BEECHER STOWE AS THE AUTHOR OF OLD TOWN FOLKS.

ful and characteristic works. Its popular success, sufficiently attests to the intrinsic worth of its sentiments and
the picturesque power of its delineations.

Next in numbers to the people who universally respond
to a mention of "Uncle Tom's Cabin," are the vast army
of readers who know "Old Town Folks," and instantly express their enjoyment of it. Though announced and sometimes spoken of as a novel, it cannot, strictly speaking, be
characterized as such. It is rather, a series of vivid and
natural pictures of New England life, near the close of the
last century, loosely strung together upon the romance of
four young persons, a tale so uneventful in its course, and
mild in its denouments as to scarcely deserve the name of
plot.

In "Uncle Tom's Cabin" the author's strength was in
her burning earnestness of purpose in laying existing
facts before the Christian world. In "Minister's Wooing"
her power was in the practical grasp and forcible presentation of the results of certain theological doctrines.
In "Old Town Folks" she excels most rarely in the
admirable depictions of characters peculiar to the locality and time, in which the story is laid. The word characters is used advisedly, for Harriet Beecher Stowe
looked at the world from the outside, believing that
actions are materialized motives, and results, the
accumulation of intentions. She had no taste for the
analytical style which tends ever toward a dyspeptic
anxiety for the workings of internal springs, often disappointing expectation in resultant effects.

The story is laid in the town of Natick, Massachusetts,
at a period when New England was the seed-bed of Amer-

ican civilization. The author observed that New England had been to our republic what the Dorian Hive was to Greece; a capital place to emigrate from, whence were carried the ideas and principles which, disseminated over the vast area of our country, have grown into the tense and strong fibre of the American character. The author, who chose to write "Old Town Folks" under the pseudonym of "Horace Holyoke," acknowledges her studies for this object to have been pre-Raphælite, drawn from real characters, real scenes and real incidents. Some of her material was gleaned from early colonial history, but many of the characters were drawn from conversations with Professor Stowe, who had rare descriptive and mimetical powers, and suggested weaving some of his personal recollections and experiences into the work.

The portion laid in "Cloudland" plainly indicates reminiscences of her youth at Litchfield. The whole was connected by the genius of the writer, into the remarkable work so familiar to American readers, by whom it is fondly prized and believed in, as a rarely truthful and graphic description of the New England people, from whom sprung all the intellectual strength and firm principle which dwell in the American character.

The social history of Old Town, as it is known in these traditions, transpired during Professor Stowe's youth, and much of it is reproduced in this story, which is considered one of the most artistic of its gifted author. It appeared more easy, taking much of it from her husband's childish experiences, to write the book in the first person, and from a masculine standpoint. She must put herself into a boy's shoes to know Sam Lawson, who was an early friend of

Professor Stowe, as she has made us know him, the typical,
Yankee do-nothing and universal genius. Glimpses of
him we have seen embodied in various thriftless and
intolerable men, who yet had a vast and fascinating range
of homely lore, and that natural faculty to do interesting
things which is such a delight to youth. As well try to
describe Sam Lawson to the readers of this chapter, as to
tell them of Uncle Tom. He is as well known as George
Washington, and alas! perhaps dearer to the hearts of average republican humanity. He is perhaps the best instance
of character drawing, ever done by the artist who made such
portraiture her specialty.

Uncle "Fliakim," the dear Grandmother, Old Crab Smith
Miss Asphyxia, and Miss Mehitable Rossiter, are indisput-
ably real people. They still exist, possibly modified in
form by the friction of advancing civilization, which ever
tends to wear away individual peculiarities and reduce outward demeanor to a dead level of cultivated repression, but
we know them, or have known them at some time.

The stately Congregational minister in his white wig and
impressive silk gown with ruffles at his throat and wrists,
his awe-inspiring, brocaded "Lady," the colored retainers
who felt but lightly the fetters which bound them to their
Colonial owners, and the remnants of the tribes of Massachusetts Indians who are introduced as a sort of living
scenic effect, we do not know. But we can easily believe in
them, since all testimony goes to prove that they were
features of the time.

They all live and speak and possess distinct personality,
but the figures of Harry and Tina Percival do not strike us
as real young people. Tina, seems not half so charming as the

author would have us feel, in fact is a repetition of similar failures who appear up to this time in Mrs. Stowe's writing, whenever she essays to depict a pretty, frivolous darling, who beneath all her fascinating lightness and brilliant scintillations (which the reader cannot see) is said to have a fund of moral strength and right feeling. Harry, who is the poetical counterpart of the hero, is, in spite of the author's intentions, something of a prig. Neither does Horace Holyoke take on the rounded personality which we expect and desire in the scholarly, nervous, high strung and conscientious boy which he should appear. The inference is forced upon one, that she has not personally known such personalities and is not able to construct symmetrical characters, from stray bits of disjointed skeletons.

The interest and value of the work taken as a whole, would seem to raise it above criticism of these characters for it is no less art which employs models, when the portraiture is a perfect representation of life and the composition well balanced, and carefully managed as to tone and color, but they demonstrate the fact that imagination was not one of the special gifts of Harriet Beecher Stowe. She possessed rare descriptive power, a pure quality of humor, shrewdness, philosophy, and a certain happy selection of language which gave a graphic touch to the whole, but where purely creative genius was needed, she was not successful.

Indeed, her natural make-up, almost of necessity precluded this faculty, which is the concomitant of pure fiction. Its resultant action was remarkably absent in her life and social intercourse, as she never seemed to find a necessity for the polite prevarications or quick inventions which are sometimes employed to annoint the wheels of social life. Her inherent and instinctive honesty, her habitual concern for the higher certitudes of existence and for historical facts, were not related to the genius of fiction. She had rather, the talent for biography, having the memory for such work, and the perception of the logic of events, which has made her a historian, rather than a poet.

It is indeed a poverty of invention which necessitates or permits the chief characters in "Old Town Folks" to make their advent as waifs of foreign birth, and orphans who are thrown upon the charity of cross-grained relatives, who in various ways, short of absolute cruelty, make their young lives miserable; to re-incarnate her typical minister, Lyman Beecher, and schoolmaster, John P. Brace, under the thin disguise of new names; introducing again the woman of high education and deep feeling who suffers under the cruel logic of the theology of the period, who originated in Mrs. Fisher, lived in "Minister's Wooing" as Mrs. Marvyn, and again completes a short cycle and is born in "Old Town Folks" as Esther Avery; and showing forth the fascinations and villainies of a *cousin of Aaron Burr*, as the only possible conqueror of the well-read but inexperienced, country girls.

The reader loses faith in these persons who walk as cheerfully upon the stage as if they were a "new attraction," and wishes the artist could renew her selection of choice models. But these portraits taken from persons she had known, and the discussion of social and political questions always strongly flavored by theology, were Mrs. Stowe's natural, inherited stock in trade. This was her world, her line of thought, her idea of intellectual and physical existence. It was doubtless, taken all in all, the most remarkable literary endowment of the generation which rolled in a wave of talented American authors. In it we see reproduced her own spirit, tastes, preferences and beliefs. If for nothing else, "Old Town Folks" is valuable as a suggestion of her mental environment at mature life, for the conversations and tenor of life at Hartford, rested upon such topics and questions as these which underlay the story of "Old Town Folks," and formed a solid basis upon which to rest her opinions upon themes of recent occurrence, all over the world. It may be said that Mrs. Stowe had no literary life in its social sense. That while she met and talked with many of the gifted writers and thinkers of her day, she formed no intimacies, was not in the least diverted from her own individuality, or wrought upon by the gradual change, which was coming over the methods and manners of literature.

She remained first and always a Beecher, living in her recollections of New England people, contented, more, proud to dwell upon her family, past and present, and to let the less pronounced thinking world, go on its way, as she went on hers. In the second place, she was a Stowe, affectionately devoted to her husband, whom she fervently respected as a scholar of deep research, and acquirements which took hold upon the past, through ancient languages even to the word of God; who was furthermore possessed of versatile gifts, and some spiritual insights and perceptions, which were quite outside of common, human experience.

The fact that Mrs. Stowe wrote to George Eliot with whom she entered into an interesting correspondence at about this period, that Professor Stowe was the "visionary boy," whom she made the hero of "Old Town Folks," and that the experiences which she related, were phenomena of frequent occurrence with him, and had been so even from his earliest childhood, makes relevant a notice of some of the psychological conditions which were peculiar to the scholarly man, one who was by temperament and trend of mind as far as possible from the credulity or hallucination commonly attributed to believers in manifestations that appear to be supernatural. The descriptions of clairvoyant phenomena which in themselves scarcely give adequate excuse for their frequent introduction in the experiences of Horace Holyoke the hero of "Old Town Folks," take on new significance and interest, when it appears that they are unexaggerated instances of the spiritual visitations, if one chooses to so call them, which were a life long, and recurring fact, with Professor Stowe.

Certain it is that Professor Stowe came into the world possessed of an uncommon attribute, which may be adversely considered, either as a sixth sense revealing hidden things, or as peculiar hallucinations. The latter conclusion, and the more natural one perhaps, is hardly compatible with his clear mentality and the sound judgment, which he brought to bear upon this phenomena itself, no less than upon all other topics. Neither is the theory held by Professor Park of Andover that his sight of things which were not apparent to other people was due to a disease of the optic nerve, altogether reasonable in consideration of the nervous ebullition which preceded and accompanied his visions, as has been described in "Old Town Folks." The conclusion must be from the reader's point of view. Suffice to say that he was at times utterly unable to distinguish between tangible objects and the visions which passed before his mind's eye. In early childhood he was quite unaware that he held any power which was not common to humanity, supposing, naturally, that all people saw as he did, objects which were far out of reach of the eye.

As a near-sighted child sooner or later becomes aware that it is wanting in the far sight which is common, so Calvin E. Stowe early inferred that his friends could not see absent things, and departed souls as he did, and he became as a young man, somewhat in awe of his power, and loth to speak of it. When, however, in later years he recognized it as a peculiarity which he shared with a few other people, he came to regard it as an interesting fact, and conversed freely with intimate friends as to his sights and perceptions. In common with most other intelligent people, and especially so, because of his strange experiences, Professor and Mrs. Stowe became deeply interested in psychological manifestations. The matter was under frequent discussion and with friends they evoked surprising manifestations from " Planchette " and attended various so-called spiritualistic seances in New York. While in Rome, Mrs. Stowe in company with Elizabeth Barrett Browning and others, received some surprising evidences of things occult and strange.

Upon this theme much of the correspondence with George Eliot dwelt, and Mrs. Stowe most feelingly interpreted the wave of spiritualism then rushing over America, as a sort of Rachel-cry of bereavement, towards the invisible existence of the loved ones; but her mature judgment like that of her husband's, was against the value of mediumistic testimonies. So involved were they in trickeries, and so defiled by low adventurers, that it was impossible to regard the movement in its imperfect development (which has not materially changed in twenty years), as otherwise than repulsive.

Though filled with the yearning which draws human hearts so strongly towards the hidden future, Mrs. Stowe could not be satisfied that the veil had ever been rent for human eyes. Professor Stowe, never allied himself in any way with spiritualists, not deeming such revelations as had been given him, evidence which could be formulated into a creed, or depended upon as a religion. He joined his wife in the delightful correspondence with George Eliot and said, referring to the subject, "I have had no connection with any of the modern movements, except as father confessor."

He investigated his personal condition intelligently, and noted that the action of this sense depended greatly upon his physical condition, observing that when he was not in perfect health, his visions were of an unpleasant nature, though he did not perceive that an unhealthy state of the nerves or body, at all increased the frequency or clearness of his visions. This fact, of course, will in the mind of most readers, tend to relegate them to the realm of waking dreams, though it does not conclusively disprove the theory of the existence, either bodily or spiritually, of what he saw.

Those who desire to believe that Professor Stowe was a "medium" will receive as valuable testimony the fact that he not only saw, but believed he heard and conversed with these etherealized personalities. He was in the habit of conversing freely during the last ten years of his life with a dear friend, a young clergyman of Hartford, whom he found particularly vigorous in thought, and refreshing to his intellectual life.   He often spoke to him of talking with his son Henry who had died years before, and one morning told him that the devil, taking advantage of his illness, had been grievously tempting him, night after night. Coming in the guise of a horseman, with terribly dark, hostile and violent manner yelling that his son Charles was dead, and questioning his faith in various aggravating ways.

" But," said he smiling with satisfaction, "I was ready for him last night.   I had fortified myself with passages of Scripture.   I found some things in Ephesians which were just what I wanted, and when he came last night, I *hurled* them at him.   I tell you, it made him bark like a dog, and he took himself off.   He won't trouble me again."

Professor Stowe also recounted to a friend an interview which he declared he· had with Goethe, one day out under the trees.   He intensely enjoyed the discussion with the great mind of the German Shakespeare and reported a most interesting explanation which the author of Faust, gave of the celebrated closing lines of the second part of that great work—

> " All of mortality is but a symbol shown,
> Here to reality longings have grown;
> How superhumanly wondrous, 'tis done.
> The eternal, the womanly Love leads us on."

These experiences, which seem to so singularly combine scholarship and speculation, positive knowledge of the highest order and beliefs which by a literal minded generation, are generally deemed weakness, were not peculiar to his old age, but had continued with him all through his long, remarkably vigorous and logical, intellectual career.

While it must be allowed that Mrs. Stowe's representations of family life and its general trend of thought and conversation, are an inimitable reproduction of the thinking people of the old New England communities, and that this state of things was so general as to make families who were not so concerned and discursive, seem ignorant or set-apart as anomalies; dwelling so earnestly upon these themes in her books, not only proves her a true daughter and sister of her family, but by nature as naturally a minister of the gos-pel, a teacher of religion, a reformer and essayist, as Dr. Lyman Beecher himself, or the deepest thinker or most grace-ful speaker among his seven clerical sons. She had all of their impulse towards expression, all of their force and lucidity of thought, their grace, tenderness and humor, to which were added her feminine intuitions and sympathies.

George Eliot wrote to her—" I think your way of present-ing the religious convictions, which are not your own, ex-cept by indirect fellowship, is a triumph of insight and true tolerance." It made Harriet Beecher Stowe what she was, the most remarkable and influential woman of her time.

" Old Town Folks " was published in Boston in May 1869, and by the first of August twenty-five thousand copies had been sold. It appeared simultaneously through Sampson and Low, in London. It ran through three large editions there in the same time. By the first of June, five forthcoming translations were announced in Germany, and it still remains constant in demand in several languages. The name of Sam Lawson became a household word all over the land, and Mrs. Stowe humored the public wish for more of him and his entertaining conversations, by issuing through Jas. R. Osgood & Co., a collection of fifteen tales called "Sam Law-son's Oldtown Fireside Stories." It of course had a large sale and contains innocent amusement enough for many winter evenings.

CHAPTER XVIII.

THE LAST GREAT EVENT OF MRS. STOWE'S LITERARY CAREER.
"THE TRUE STORY OF LADY BYRON'S LIFE." AN ARTICLE
WHICH SHOCKED THE WHOLE READING WORLD. VOLUMI-
NOUS ABUSE OF MRS. STOWE BY THE DEFENDERS OF LORD
BYRON AND THE SERIOUS DEPRECATION OF MANY
FRIENDLY REVIEWERS IN THE UNITED STATES AS WELL
AS GREAT BRITAIN. MRS. STOWE'S CHILDISH IMPRES-
SION OF LORD BYRON. HER ACQUAINTANCE WITH LADY
BYRON BEGUN DURING HER FIRST VISIT TO ENGLAND.
LADY BYRON'S STORY CONFIDED TO HER IN 1856. LADY
BYRON'S CONSULTATION WITH MRS. STOWE. DECISION TO
REMAIN SILENT DURING LADY BYRON'S LIFE. RE-OPEN-
ING OF THE CONTROVERSY THIRTEEN YEARS AFTER, BY
BLACKWOOD'S MAGAZINE IN A REVIEW OF THE GUICCIOLI
BOOK OF MEMOIRS. THE REVIEWER'S ABUSE OF LADY
BYRON. THE SPIRIT OF THE ARTICLE ECHOED IN AMERICA
AND THE "MEMOIRS" OF BYRON'S MISTRESS, RE-PUBLISHED
IN THE UNITED STATES. MRS. STOWE'S EXPECTATION OF
A VINDICATION FROM LADY BYRON'S ENGLISH FRIENDS.
HER RELUCTANT ASSUMPTION OF THE DUTY. HER CON-
SCIENTIOUSNESS IN THE MATTER. HER REPULSIVE DIS-
CLOSURE WEIGHED IN THE BALANCE AGAINST LORD
BYRON'S SEDUCTIVE IMMORALITIES.

In September of the year 1869, when Harriet Beecher
Stowe was fifty-seven years of age; in the full strength of

her matured intellectuality; when the fires of youthful
passion and impetuous feeling had long since burnt themselves out, leaving only the clear, shining embers of well
considered purpose; in the zenith of her unparalleled
popularity and world-wide fame; standing high above all
women as a writer whose success in touching the popular
heart and conscience had transcended all those of her time;
she published in the Atlantic Monthly and simultaneously
in Macmillan's Magazine, an article of considerable length,
which bore with it a revelation so astounding, so monstrous
in its unimagined putridity, that the whole reading
world shrieked aloud, and turned upon the writer with
contumely, invective and personal reproaches which have
scarcely found a parallel in the history of literature. It
brought down upon her, not only the hatred and volumin-
ous abuse of the friends and defenders of the parties whom
it accused, but also the condemnation and rebuke of people,
who justly deprecate the dragging to light of filthy crimes
whose details have a pernicious effect upon society at large.

"The True Story of Lady Byron's Life" as told by Mrs.
Stowe, had sufficient airing. The reasons for its appearance, which the writer considered, fully justified her disclosure, were supplied by her and her friends, so that he
who would, might have been fully posted upon the unpleasant subject; but at the distance of twenty years, it may
be profitable to look over the ground again and realize why
it seemed to Mrs. Stowe right, to tell the "True Story of
Lady Byron's Life" which she firmly believed it to be.

It must not be supposed that she was wholly unprepared
for the storm that it aroused, though it is undeniable that
she was bitterly wounded by the sweeping censure with

25

which all parties, friends and foes alike, greeted her act. Her literary experience had not been all of pleasantness. She had not only suffered for the book which she had lately seen justified in the emancipation of the slaves, but she had met adverse, sometimes unkind, criticism upon her subsequent works. Though it cannot be said that these had had much effect upon her choice of subject, or manner of literary treatment, no one can believe that she found it agreeable or conducive to her peace of mind, to be thus held up as a target for the slings and arrows of an army of critics, which, if not always aimed with skill, or deserved by their victim, were dreadful and left their scars. But in all her acts, public and private, she chose what she deemed to be the right, and seeing beyond the brief alarms of this world and the objections of a less clear-minded and conscientious public, maintained it always. Why she felt called upon to do a thing which was so universally condemned, a brief consideration will show.

As early as the year 1821 when Harriet was a child of nine, the Beecher household at Litchfield, always accustomed to keep intelligently informed as to the happenings of the world, often discussed the subject of the separation of Lady Byron, from her talented and erratic husband.

It had taken place five years before, but was kept before the public mind by his poems, which referred to his domestic misfortunes under various fictitious heads. Byron's early poems had been favorites with the older members of the family, and his best efforts were read before the children, over whose innocent minds his unworthy sentiments and allusions passed without any effect. Harriet listened with anxious gravity while her father discussed the poet's career, with the ladies of his household, and declared that "he wanted to see Byron, give him his views of religious thought, and help him out of his troubles." With his misfortunes they all felt deep sympathy, in spite of his acknowledged idiosyncrasies. They, it appeared, were almost pardonable in so gifted a genius, and a man "who had the angel within him."

With the rest of the young women who were at susceptible age all over the English reading world, Harriet Beecher sang the heart breaking "Farewell Forever, and if Forever, then Forever Fare Thee Well," as set to music; and thrilled and wept in tenderness for the adorable man who could thus forgive and bless the severe, unforgiving precisian, whom he had taken for his wife, and so clearly described in his character of Donna Inez the mother of Don Juan, and again idealized in the exquisite description of Aurora Raby, in the same poem. Harriet Beecher had grown into womanhood, wifehood, maternity and famous authorship, if not in sympathy, at least in that toleration, for Byron, which has been accorded and doubtless, to the end of time will be accorded, to any handsome, talented, fascinating fellow who is in trouble, particularly if he happens to be a poet and a Lord.

As is well known, his wife, living in retirement in England, all her life maintained a silence upon the subject, which was universally felt to be severe, even atrocious, perhaps the more so, as women usually are depended upon to talk, upon all topics and occasions.

It was therefore, with some surprise that Mrs. Stowe next heard of Lady Byron as a philanthropist, and an ardent sympathizer in the anti-slavery movement. After the intimate acquaintance formed during her first and second visits, to England, Mrs. Stowe experienced a complete revulsion of feeling, from wonderment at her silence upon the subject of her reasons for deserting her husband, to astonishment at the Christian spirit which had enabled her to pass her blameless existence, calmly enduring such terrible wrongs.

When the author of " Uncle Tom's Cabin " visited England in 1853, in the first flush of the phenomenal success of her great work, she met Lady Byron at a luncheon party at the house of one of her friends.

Mrs. Stowe was struck with the gentle dignity of her personal appearance and thus describes her:

" The party had many notables, but among them all, my attention was fixed principally upon Lady Byron. She was at this time sixty-one years of age * but still had, to a remarkable degree, that personal attraction which is commonly considered to belong only to youth and beauty. Her form was slight, giving an impression of fragility; her motions were both graceful and decided; her eyes bright and full of interest and quick observation. Her silvery white hair seemed to lend a grace to the transparent purity of her complexion, and her small hands had a pearly whiteness. I recollect she wore a plain widow's cap of a transparent material; and was dressed in some delicate shade of lavender which harmonized well with her complexion. When I was introduced to her I felt in a moment the words of her husband:—

" There was awe in the homage that she drew ;
Her spirit seemed as seated on a throne."

* Twenty years older than our famous woman who afterwards became her champion.

Calm, self-poised and thoughtful, she seemed to me rather to resemble an interested spectator of the world's affairs, than an actor involved in its trials; yet the sweetness of her smile, and a certain very delicate sense of humor in her remarks, made the way of acquaintance easy. Her first remarks were a little playful; but in a few moments we were speaking on what every one in those days was talking about,—the slavery question in America. It need not be remarked that when any one subject especially occupies the public mind, those known to be interested in it are compelled to listen to many weary platitudes. Lady Bryon's remarks, however, caught my ear and arrested my attention by their peculiar, incisive quality, their originality and the evidence they gave that she was as well informed on all our matters as the best American statesman could be. I had no wearisome course to go over with her as to the difference between the general Government and State Governments, nor explanations of the United States Constitution; for she had the whole before her mind with perfect clearness. Her morality upon the slavery question, too, impressed me as something far higher and deeper than the common sentimentalism of the day. Many of her words surprised me greatly and gave me new material for thought. I found I was in company with a commanding mind and hastened to gain instruction from her on another point where my interest had been aroused. *

Their acquaintance during several interviews grew into tender friendship and when Mrs. Stowe went abroad three years later, in 1856, to secure a foreign copyright upon her

* Without doubt Mrs. Stowe invested Lady Byron with an ideal charm, for their characters seemed a natural compliment each to the other and Mrs. Hooker, relates how upon one occasion when "Sister Harriet" had been visiting Lady Byron, she came away in her absent-minded manner, leaving her gloves in Lady Byron's dressing rooms. "Never mind," said Lady Byron who had accompanied her to the station, "we wear the same size, take mine and I will keep yours." Mrs. Stowe took the gloves, which were of a delicate drab, but carried them in her hand—she never put them on—but years afterwards her sister saw them folded in tissue paper with rose leaves which dropped from a bud Lady Byron had worn at the same interview.

new book "Dred," among the brightest anticipations held
out by this journey, was the hope of once more seeing Lady
Byron. Though London was deserted Mrs. Stowe found
that Lady Byron was in town and called upon her, renew-
ing their congenial conversations and cementing the friendship which had sprung into being at their first interview.

Some days later, when Lady Bryon was able to leave her
room, a family party consisting of Professor and Mrs.
Stowe, their children and Mrs. Stowe's sister, Mrs. Perkins,
went to luncheon with her and passed a most enjoyable
day. Again, Mrs. Stowe, with her husband, and the son
Henry, who so soon after met a watery grave at Dartmouth,
spent an evening with the lady. Young Lord Ockham,
Lady Byron's grandson and Henry Stowe were made friends,
and talked of with pride by the mother and grandmother,
in their mutual confidences.

Some weeks later, Mrs. Stowe and Mrs. Perkins were
going from London to Eversley to visit the Reverend
Charles Kingsley. On their way, they stopped to take
luncheon with Lady Byron at her summer residence on
Ham Common, and by her request, returned there after
a few days, as Lady Byron had asked for a special interview with Mrs. Stowe to discuss an important matter.

It then transpired, that a cheap edition of Byron's works
was soon to be issued, accompanied with his biography,
in which was given the story of his domestic life, in the
version of his friends. It had been suggested to Lady
Byron, that she ought to break the silence which she had
maintained so long, and give to the public the vindication,
which she held, in the facts of her reasons for separating
from her husband. It was her desire to recount the whole

history to a person of another country, and one entirely out of the whole sphere of local and personal feelings, which must inevitably bias the judgment of one in the country, and station in life, in which the circumstances took place.

She felt a grave responsibility to society for the truth, and it had become a serious question, whether she could permit these writings to gain influence over the popular mind, by giving a silent consent, to what she knew to be utter false-hoods. Lady Byron was then enfeebled physically by the disease, pulmonary consumption, which four years later terminated her life, but the time was auspicious, for it appeared to be one of "her well days," and she was able to tell the story without difficulty.

Held by the bonds of womanly tenderness, sympathy and firm belief in the truth and perfect sanity of her friend, Mrs. Stowe "could not choose but hear" and she was much impressed and excited by the avowal and the responsibility which it had entailed upon her. She begged for two or three days in which to deliberate and form her opinion upon so distressing a question. Mrs. Stowe's decision was chiefly influenced by her reverence and affection for Lady Byron, who seemed so frail, who had suffered so much, and stood at such a height above the comprehension of the coarse and common world, that to ask her to come forth from the sanctuary of her silence and plead her cause before the public, would be like violating a shrine.

She could not advise the desecration of a reserve, which, under the circumstances, had become almost holy, in its self-abnegation and angelic sweetness.

After anxious consideration and conversation with her sister Mrs. Perkins, Mrs. Stowe at last wrote to Lady Byron, that while this act of justice did seem called for, and in some respects most desirable, it would involve so much that was painful to her (Lady Byron) that she considered that Lady Byron would be justifiable in leaving the facts to be published after her death. There was no special promise asked or given, that Mrs Stowe would do this, should it ever be necessary to defend the character of Lady Byron before the world, nor was her secrecy in the future, enjoined.

With this confidence, Mrs. Stowe felt she had received a responsibility which she afterwards could not disown or shirk. Some thirteen years later, nine years after the death of Lady Byron, and Lord Byron had found Lethe drinking in forgetfulness of earthly sin and sorrow and resting in the grave, one Madam Guiccioli, already notorious as the companion of Byron in his last stage of moral degredation, published a book of memoirs of him, which appeared to meet with great favor, and consisted of the story of the mistress *versus* the wife. This, Mrs. Stowe read with indignation which augmented and increased with further consideration, in the light of her own knowledge, of the wife and her story.

"Blackwood" the old classic magazine of Great Britain; the defender of conservatism, of aristocracy, the paper of Lockhart, Wilson, Hogg, Walter Scott and a host of departed grandeurs—was deputed to usher into the world this book, which was acknowledged by prominent reviewers to be a mere mass of twaddle over which they could scarcely maintain their gravity, its sole claim to notice admitted to be *its authorship*, the same long-established and influential magazine giving it introduction and recommendation *on that account.*

The reviewer proceeded to make it the occasion for re-opening the controversy of Lord Byron with his wife, attacking her character in a terrible manner, putting the facts together as a lawyer might array them in pleading the cause of a wronged man who had been ruined in name, shipwrecked in life, and driven to an early grave, by the arts of a bad woman, one all the more despicable and monstrous, that her malice was hidden under the cloak of religion!

The eloquent and cultured writer proceeded to say, "Lady Byron has been called 'The moral Clymtemnestra of her lord.' The moral Brinvilliers, would have been a truer designation."

He further claimed, that Lord Byron's unfortunate marriage might have changed, not only his own destiny, but that of all England. He suggested that but for this, Lord Byron instead of wearing out his life in vice, and corrupting society by impure poetry, might at that time have been leading the counsels of the state and helping the onward movement of the world. He charged Lady Byron with forsaking her husband in time of worldly misfortune, with fabricating a destructive accusation of crime against him, and confirming this accusation by years of persistent silence, more guilty than open assertion.*

The American woman who had been her trusted friend and ardent admirer, who felt that above all other women she was pure, self-abnegating, and terribly injured by her husband, read this language with amazement. It seemed to her brutal, and so unfair as to be unprecedented, to thus

---

*A glance at a file of Blackwood for July, 1869, will show all of this, and much more which was indeed terrible for the friends of Lady Byron, a few of whom knew her deepest wrongs, to endure.

publicly brand a virtuous lady of Christlike gentleness and purity of character with the name of the foulest of ancient, and most execrable of modern assassins, while Byron's *mistress*, a woman of no character and small mind, was taken by the hand by this important review. This attack seemed to call for the disclosure of the truth, however revolting. The facts could be no greater outrage to the sensibilities of the world than this accumulation of slander against an innocent woman; that, incited by Byron in self-defense, transmitted to his friends to be continued with increasing malignity after his death and culminating in the publication of the Guiccioli book and this re-opening of the bitter controversy. Mrs. Stowe looked confidently for a conclusive refutation of Lady Byron's cause.

No answer or announcement from any friend of Lady Byron appeared. The article was promptly reproduced in the United States, in Littell's Living Age, and the Guiccioli book was reprinted in America, by as prominent a publishing house as Harper Brothers.

It is denied that it attained any circulation worth considering, either in this country or abroad, and Mrs. Stowe perhaps over-estimated its influence, as well as the trend of sympathy towards the adulterous connection which it vaunted, and which Blackwood so plausibly condoned. Let us also hope the permanent effects of the Byronic poetry, which Shelley characterized as the foremost of the "Satanic School," were not so important as she feared, still she must infer from facts, how strong a sympathy was felt in high places with the life and writings of the "moral leper" whom it was the fashion of the hour, to pity and excuse.

Mrs. Stowe saw in a popular magazine, two long articles,

both of which represented Lady Byron as a cold, malignant
woman who had been her husband's ruin, the same articles being so full of mis-statements as to astonish her. In
fact, it was thus the knowledge of the book and the Blackwood article first came to her. Not long after a friend
wrote to Mrs. Stowe "*Will* you, *can* you, reconcile it to your
conscience to sit still and allow that mistress to slander
that wife,—you, perhaps, the only one knowing the real
facts, and able to set them forth ? "

Mrs. Stowe still waited for a refutation of the slanderous
publication, being aware that the facts of Lady Byron's
reasons for leaving her husband, were known in various circles in England.

As no friend came to her defense, Mrs. Stowe decided,
not without extreme reluctance, that it was her duty, to
publish what Lady Byron had so impressively confided to
her. She was at this time in impaired health, and was
under treatment, with her husband who was suffering with
a painful malady, at a celebrated private hospital in New
York city. Her younger sister, Isabella Beecher Hooker,
was her confidant and companion, and bears witness to the
painful struggle which Mrs. Stowe passed through, but at last
she dictated, from her couch, to this sister, who wrote as
she directed, the disclosure which fell like a thunderbolt
upon the literary and social world.

In the article, which speedily raised a storm of discussion
all over the reading world, Mrs. Stowe sarcastically reviewed
the statement of Byron's wrongs which was going not only
over Europe, but the length of the American continent,
rousing new sympathy for him and "doing its best to bring
the youth of America once more under the power of that

brilliant and seductive genius from which it was hoped they had escaped." She remarked, that only the strictest moralists seemed to defend the wife. Gentler hearts "regarded her as a marble-hearted monster of correctness and morality, a personification of the law, unmitigated by the gospel."

Mrs. Stowe outlined the facts which Lady Byron had given her, of the events of her courtship and married life (which are indeed interesting reading, and amply refute the charges made against Lady Byron, of impatience or heartlessness), and in a terse paragraph which electrified the world, disclosed the special reason why Lady Byron, after more than a year of sorrowful remonstrance, left her erring husband. It was in these words.

"From the height at which he might have been happy as the husband of a noble woman, he fell into the depths of a secret, adulterous intrigue, with a blood relation, so near in consanguinity, that discovery must have been utter ruin and expulsion from civilized society. From henceforth, this damning secret became the ruling force in his life, holding him with a morbid fascination, yet filling him with remorse and anguish and insane dread of detection."

Mrs. Stowe proceeded to show how Byron, when he found the wife whom he had married in answer to the entreaties of his friends, who was to serve as a cloak to his intrigues and dissipations, could not be deceived nor cowed into submission to his horrible infidelities, resolved to be rid of her.

He therefore inflicted upon her every cruelty possible from a drunken roué to whose brutality was superadded the inventive ferocity of a devil, until, with a child a few weeks old, she left his house and returned to her father's home never to return, never during her life to make public her terrible injuries. Henceforth, she lived for the daughter who grew up inheriting her father's brilliant talents with all of his restlessness and morbid sensibility. After her child's death, which followed a youthful career as a gay woman of fashion, Lady Byron devoted herself to wise philanthropies, inventing practical schools, managing with skill several institutions, which resulted in great benefit to artisans, seamstresses and other classes of laboring men and women, preserving always a silence, which in the light of the disclosure, appeared to have been not malignity, but Christian forbearance.

There could be no well founded doubt of the truth of Lady Byron's story, except upon the supposition that she was insane; that being so long "wrapped in dismal thinkings" had made her mad.

Mrs. Stowe, believed she was in her right mind, and gave unhesitating credence to the story. She had decided it was right to publish the story and she did it. Mrs. Stowe's sense of justice was through life, perhaps her strongest characteristic. When it fell to her to administer it, whether to the statesman, politicians and Christian people of the United States upon a constitutional wrong, or to the social world who were sympathizing with and falling under the influence of a man whom she knew to be false and unworthy to the core, she was inexorable and unbending as Fate, quite as stern and regardless of self as the figure who with bandaged eyes, holds the scales of good and evil balancing in her hand.

The cloudburst of horrified deprecation, invective and personal abuse of the woman who had been brave enough to tell the disgusting story, fell simultaneously upon both continents, and a single week sent forth a hailstorm of publications upon the Byron mystery.

Blackwood and the Quarterly Review thundered forth vehement salvos against Mrs. Stowe, making every accusation from falsehood to meddling, from ignorance to poor taste, and the Examiner, The Pall Mall Gazette, The Times, and hundreds of lesser organs, (for no one of the British journals felt itself too uninformed or inconsequential to take up the question) joined in surprise and indignation that an American woman should volunteer to disclose what Lady Byron's respected trustees had declined to make known.

Macmillan's came in for a share of the public execration, which, however under the unprecedented call for that number of the Magazine, it appears they bore with equanimity. The press of the United States, at one and the same time expressed their amazement at Mrs. Stowe, at The Atlantic, and at everything, perhaps, more than at the author of "Don Juan," of "Parisina," of "Manfred," and the rest, which give abundant proof of the poet's perverted instincts, displaying in their motives a moral insanity which makes his wife's story credible.

The New York Tribune discussed the controversy at length, trying to administer impartial justice to the memories of Lord and Lady Byron, but few representatives of even the American press, said a word in extenuation of the principle which actuated Mrs. Stowe, or the judgment which permitted her action. Upon that point, the Saturday Review in an otherwise exceptionally fair article upon the Byron controversy, stated its opinion with clearness, using terms which could not be mistaken for flattery to the intellectual abilities, judgment, taste or high motives of the author of " Uncle Tom's Cabin."

Mrs. Stowe, who had expected severe comment in certain foreign reviews, had not been prepared for the avalanche of adverse and unjust criticism that poured in upon her from American writers, who she thought should have trusted her judgment and right feeling. Upon one point they all agreed, which was in a demand for proof, a detailed account of her interview, and a summary of her reasons for the disclosure. Friends implored a justification of herself. The solicitors of Lady Byron, of whom until then, Mrs. Stowe had had no knowledge, wrote a personal letter inquiring by what authority she had published facts which were known to them, but which they had decided to suppress, and other calls which she could not ignore, came asking for reasons for her work, and proofs of the " True Story of Lady Byron."

As has been stated Mrs. Stowe was in impaired health, which, be it noted, she did not adduce as an apology for her disclosure, but afterwards mentioned as the cause of some minor inaccuracies, such as the misspelling of a name and miscalculating the period of the Byrons' married life by a few months, which were incident to her having to dictate the article. While she admitted to the critics, the inartistic effects of her astounding article as a literary production, she never for an instant, failed to stand by its statements and purpose. She soon published a card in the Hartford Courant saying that she had a more comprehensive statement in hand, which would be her complete *Vindication* of *Lady Byron*. It appeared early in 1870, being published by Fields, Osgood and Company, and was a " History of the

Byron Controversy from its Beginning in 1816 to the Present Time."

No one can judge fairly of Mrs. Stowe's relation to the unpleasant affair, until this book has been carefully read.

Without attempting to unravel the labyrinthine intricacies or discuss the contradictions of the maddening controversy, whose published details make a literature of its own it is our province to consider Mrs. Stowe's relation to the affair.   As to whether the horrid story was true, a question which several of the British reviews, even while condemning Mrs. Stowe's action yet decided in the affirmative, we have nothing to do, except so far as it involves her sincerity and high purpose.

Harriet Beecher Stowe believed the truth of Lady Byron's statement as she believed in her own existence.

It was fair to consider that if Lady Byron had any friends who had respect for her memory they would speak.

As they did not, Mrs. Stowe decided she could not leave the false history which was thus created, to stand uncontradicted.   She said in her book "Lady Byron Vindicated."

"I claim for my countrymen and women our right to true history. For years, the popular literature has held up publicly before our eyes the facts as to this man and this woman, and called on us to praise or condemn.   Let us have *truth* when we are called upon to judge.   It is our *right*.   There is no conceivable obligation on a human being greater than that of absolute justice.   It is the deepest personal injury to an honorable mind to be made through misrepresentation, an accomplice in injustice.   When a noble name is accused, any person who possesses truth which might clear it, and withholds that truth, is guilty of a sin against human nature and the inalienable claims of justice.   I claim that I have not only a right, but an obligation to bring my solemn testimony upon this subject."

The reviewers, some of the fairest of whom picked flaws and made criticisms so trivial as to scarcely do justice to their own comprehension of the great essentials of her manifesto, as well as the superficial readers of this generation, or the many who discuss the question from mere hearsay and blame Mrs. Stowe because they find the disclosure she made, revolting, should be reminded that *she did not re-open the controversy.*

It was done by Blackwood's Magazine in July, 1869, in an article recommending the Guiccioli book.

While Mrs. Stowe had not been formally constituted the advocate of Lady Byron (who evidently expected that her trustees would see justice done her memory, having put the facts into their hands to use at discretion), she had confided the story of her injuries to Mrs. Stowe without any restrictions, sure that her cause could be trusted to Mrs. Stowe's judgment and affection. The time came when Mrs. Stowe would have become an accomplice in injustice, had she withheld the knowledge confided to her. It should be considered that she was not, therefore, permitted by her strong moral sense, to preserve the silence which she would have preferred.

The author of "Guenn" a writer of rare discrimination and force, has said of a similar responsibility, " I believe it would be a better place, this cowardly, false world, if a few rare souls should spurn restraint and speak out plainly what they think. What crimes are not committed in the name of tact, refinement, discretion,—what sins of meanness and falsehood!"

Mrs. Stowe did not volunteer to uncover the mass of

26

moral corruption which her disclosure opened to the morbid curiosity of the world, nor did she create or tolerate it, any more than she precipitated slavery upon the United States or advocated the Fugitive Slave Bill, of 1850. It was forced upon her by the writer who re-opened the controversy, making Byron only a lesser god, suffering from the slanders of his wife, and his mistress (the last one), the true soul-wife, whom he missed in his marriage.

The eminent reviewer before referred to, who, said of Mrs. Stowe, " This is not the first time in Mrs. Stowe's literary career that her good intentions—that is, her weak judgment and passionate and undisciplined temper—have sown a crop only to be watered with blood and tears," failed, very naturally, perhaps, to comprehend her high conscientiousness, unworldly earnestness, honesty and far-sighted estimate of the relative value of mundane things.

Who shall say that justice done to an innocent woman, may not counterbalance in the eternities, the moral degeneration suffered by that class of humanity which gloated over the unpleasant details which were of necessity set forth?

Shall we decide that the sum total of depravity, absorbed by the public, which, in consequence of her statement, was inundated by a stream of abomination and a literature of nastiness which is absolutely unparalleled in the records of human depravity and sin, was any greater, than that which for a lifetime, had saturated society, in Byron's slanders against virtue, his shameless exposure of the sanctities of his married life to a host of ribald fellows at the Noctes Ambrosianæ Club and the pernicious influence of his immoralities, as set to graceful verse?

To the baleful influence of his seductive poems he added

the effect, direfully confusing to young and enthusiastic minds, of an injured genius, a beautiful sinner, whose follies were pardonable, because of his gifts, and his wrongs.

Mrs. Stowe's revelation, told of the perverted excess of a social sin, which was so instinctively revolting to human nature, that it carried its own antidote, and at one blow destroyed the glamour which Byron had contrived to throw about his sins, revealing him in all the unutterable loathsomeness of his moral condition. Had these considerations not more than turned the scales, there was always abstract right against wrong, justice to be done, and Harriet Beecher Stowe was impelled to choose her course, even if for the time it was necessary to bear aspersion and perhaps leave this action behind her, as a blot upon her fair fame upon earth.

It was greatness, to remove this principle from its worldly environment, and courage, to act conscientiously, with a premonition of the anguish she must inevitably endure. Mrs. Stowe suffered, walking with tears and bleeding feet among the sharp thorns of invective and misconstruction which sprang up with her seed of truth, but she never wavered, though carrying to her grave the memory of her wounds.

A few years before her death, the writer, then failing to realize what a pain it had been to her, once referred to the subject in conversation. Her face flushed deeply, but she raised her clear eyes with a sad smile, saying, "Yes; it was a hard thing to do. What a storm the critics did raise about it. But I shall never be sorry I wrote it. It was right, and the devil and all his angels could not make me sorry."

CHAPTER XIX.

"MY WIFE AND I; OR HARRY HENDERSON'S HISTORY." A
SERIAL IN "THE CHRISTIAN UNION." THE STORY OF A
YANKEE BOY, WHO GOES TO COLLEGE, ADOPTS LITERATURE
AS A PROFESSION IN NEW YORK, THE FRAMEWORK UPON
WHICH TO HANG MANY INTERESTING DISCUSSIONS. "PINK
AND WHITE TYRANNY." A SOCIETY NOVEL WITH AN
ADMITTED MORAL. "PALMETTO LEAVES." PICTURESQUE
AND SUGGESTIVE LETTERS FROM FLORIDA. "POGANUC
PEOPLE." THE LAST IMPORTANT WORK OF THE AUTHOR
OF "UNCLE TOM'S CABIN." AGAIN THE LOVES AND LIVES
OF PLAIN NEW ENGLAND FOLK. MUCH OF THIS STORY
AUTOBIOGRAPHICAL. AN INSTRUCTIVE ACCOUNT OF THE
RELIGION ESTABLISHED BY LAW IN NEW ENGLAND. MRS.
STOWE'S CHILDISH RELIGIOUS EXPERIENCES. THE CON-
VERSION OF ZEPH HIGGINS AT THE SCHOOL HOUSE MEET-
ING. ONE OF THE MOST INTENSELY POWERFUL AND
DRAMATIC SCENES EVER DEPICTED. THE CELEBRATION
OF THE SEVENTIETH BIRTHDAY OF HARRIET BEECHER
STOWE. A GARDEN PARTY AT THE HOME OF HON. AND
MRS. WILLIAM CLAFLIN AT NEWTONVILLE, NEAR BOSTON.

AT this period Mrs. Stowe's name was associated with
that of her sister Catherine in the publication of a work
called "The American Woman's Home," but we are
informed she was able to write very few of the pages which
pleasantly discussed domestic economy.

404

HOME OF HARRIET BEECHER STOWE, ON FOREST STREET, HARTFORD, CONN.

In 1870, Mrs. Stowe began a serial story in *The Christian Union*, to which her favorite brother had transferred his interest, called "My wife and I, or Harry Henderson's History."

It opened in a manner particularly felicitous, showing the author's progress in graceful expression and lightness of touch, in which she acknowledged that her aim was not so much the making of a story, as to promulgate certain ideas which such a vehicle enabled her to ventilate.

In the history of Harry Henderson, a plain Yankee boy from the mountains of New Hampshire, through his child-hood and youth, serious love affairs, and experiences as a Benedict, and a citizen of New York city, all the topics of the time were freely discussed. There is much that is tender and moving in the writer's sympathetic appreciation of the difficulties of "being a boy," and many reflections which emanate from her childish memories of her own father and mother, and brothers and sisters; as, for instance, when she describes the close and confidential companionship of Harry Henderson's parents, we receive an impression of the intel-lectual relations of her own father and mother.

"With her he discussed the plans of his discourses, and at her dictation changed, improved, altered and added; and under the brood-ing influence of her mind, new and finer traits of tenderness and spirituality pervaded his character and his teachings. In fact, my father once said to me, "She made me by her influence."

See Mrs. Stowe's estimate of real poverty, and the greatest evil following straightened means.

"But my father and mother, though living on a narrow income, were never really poor. The chief evil of poverty is the crushing

of ideality out of life—the taking away its poetry and substitu-
ting hard prose ;—and this with them was impossible. My father
loved the work he did, as the artist loves his painting and the
sculptor his chisel. A man needs less money when he is doing
only what he loves to do—what, in fact, he *must* do,—pay or no
pay.

"In the midst of our large family, of different ages, of vigorous
growth, of great individuality and forcefulness of expression, my
mother's was the administrative power. My father habitually referred everything to her, and leaned on her advice with a childlike
dependence. She read the character of each, she mediated between opposing natures ; she translated the dialect of different
sorts of spirits to each other. In a family of young children,
there is a chance for every sort and variety of natures and for
natures whose modes of feeling are as foreign to each other, as those
of the French and the English. It needs a common interpreter,
who understands every dialect of the soul, thus to translate differences of individuality into a common language of love."

Her estimate of the unselfish child love which a boy
often gives an infantile playmate is particularly sweet, and
her idea of its worthy reflex influence, tender and delicate
in the extreme.

Again, she whimsically sets forth one of the theological
encounters which were so familiar to her whole life.

"Uncle Jacob was a church member in good standing, but in
the matter of belief he was somewhat like a high-mettled horse in
a pasture,—he enjoyed once in a while having a free argumenta-
tive race with my father all round the theological lot. Away he
would go in full career, dodging definitions, doubling and turning
with elastic dexterity, and sometimes ended by leaping over all the
fences, with most astounding assertions, after which he would
calm down, and gradually suffer the theological saddle and bridle

to be put on him and go on with edifying paces, apparently much refreshed by his metaphysical capers."

She testifies unmistakably in favor of co-education, and the value of preserving religious exercises as a daily regime at college. Her ideas upon this point are worthy of notice.

" Now it is one peculiarity of the professors of the Christian religion that they have not, at least of late years, arranged their system of education with any wise adaptation to having their young men come out of it *Christians*. In this they differ from many other religionists. The Brahmins educate their sons so that they shall infallibly become Brahmins ; the Jews so that they shall infallibly be Jews ; the Mohammedans so that they shall be Mohammedans ; but the Christians educate their sons so that nearly half of them turn out unbelievers—professors of no religion at all

" There is a book which the Christian world unite in declaring to be an infallible revelation from Heaven. It has been the judgment of critics that the various writings in this volume excel other writings in point of mere literary merit as much as they do in purity and elevation of the moral sentiment. Yet it is remarkable that the critical study of these sacred writings in their original tongues is not in most of our Christian colleges considered as an essential part of the education of a Christian gentleman, while the heathen literature of Greece and Rome is treated as something indispensable, and to be gained at all hazards."

The recent discussion upon the desirability of a course of Bible study as a means not only of religious training but critical and scientific culture as well, in which T. T. Munger, Newton M. Hall and Samuel Hart have taken a prominent part, and the adoption of such a study as a new feature in the curriculum of Dartmouth and other colleges, testify to the wisdom and practicability of Mrs. Stowe's suggestion, made twenty years ago.

Her view of theological creeds, shows the stand she had taken early in life and found comforting to the end.

" You see, as to the theologies, I think it has been well said that the Christian world just now is like a ship that's tacking. It has lost the wind on one side and not quite got it on the other. The growth of society, the development of new physical laws, and this modern scientific rush of the human mind is going to modify the man-made theologies and creeds; some of them will drop away just as the blossom does when the fruit forms, but Christ's religion will be just the same as ever—His words will not pass away."

Mrs. Stowe makes Harry Henderson a journalist and an author, and thus opens a new field for her discussion. She demonstrates the moral responsibility of authorship, and the effervescent personality of Jim Fellows, the rattling reporter and book critic, whom we recognize as nearly related to Frank Russell, our sprightly acquaintance in "Dred," and Bob Stephens, Christopher Crowfield's bright son-in-law, is here intensified into one of the best characters she has ever drawn. His exposition of the methods and moving springs of journalism, and critical decisions upon literary works, must indeed have been decidedly quickening to the public pulse, and have caused some calloused consciences to twitch in an uncomfortable manner.

But now we begin to smile affectionately at the writer who has shown such Herculean strength upon great questions, for such trustfulness of the great metropolitan world as she evinces in the liberties allowed to her characters, would invite every species of social impositions, many of them perhaps more serious than any degree of drawing-room " buncoism " yet developed.

Harry Henderson meets his future wife in a Fifth Avenue stage, makes her acquaintance in a surprisingly unconventional manner, one which it may be conjectured the author would not have wholly approved outside of her manuscript, and without more ado than a polite word, accompanies her home, shielding her by his umbrella from the rain, and as a reward receives an unhesitating invitation to call! It was before the days of American chaperones, but even the more lax forms of society in that day, would hardly seem to have quite sanctioned the immediate confidence given to the hero.

There follows a glimpse of social life from the same very unworldly standpoint, but her young men and women are good, sound characters, who talk well, so well that we hardly believe in them. But of necessity they must do this in a work where they are employed as forms upon which to hang the ethical arguments, which are so execrated by the modern school of critics. There is no disguise about these pills of wisdom. True, they are pleasantly sugar-coated, but they are openly administered, with a spoonful of diversion to carry them down. And they are extremely wholesome and beneficial.

Ida Van Arsdel, the young woman philosopher, is a good character and says and does very sensible and stimulating things, embodying Mrs. Stowe's opinions upon the best possibilities for young women, who do not marry.

In the introduction to " The Illuminati " we find descrip-

tions and a discussion which resulted in considerable amusement to the public, and some heart-burnings among near
friends of the author. Many readers thought they saw in the
character of Mrs. Stella Cerulean,—Mrs. Stowe's own sister—Mrs. Hooker. She is set forth as "a brilliant woman
beautiful in person, full of genius, full of enthusiasm, full of
self-confidence, the most charming of talkers, the most fascinating of women" who "had one simple remedy for the
reconstruction of society, about whose immediate application she saw not the slightest difficulty," which was by giving the affairs of the world, forthwith into the hands of
women; who felt that those who claimed merely equality
for women were behind the age, women being the superior,
the divine sex.

This lady had recently allied herself with the woman suffrage movement, and one of its leading women, of whom
for specially aggravating reasons, Mrs. Stowe and most of
the friends of Henry Ward Beecher, strongly disapproved.
But this interpretation, which naturally followed the fact of
the estrangement between herself and this sister, Mrs. Stowe
afterwards disavowed. It was, however, a strong presentation of the extreme views then held and promulgated by
a certain class of hasty reformers, and a source of deep satisfaction to many conservative readers.

The depiction of Miss Audacia Dangereyes who marches
into the office of Harry Henderson and Jim Fellows, successfully enforcing a subscription to her paper, could point
to none other than Victoria Woodhull, and the scene shows
the results of notions such as she held, carried to their
logical extreme. The account of her interview with the

sprightly and imperturbable Jim Fellows, is richly humorous
and entertaining.

The sketch of Bolton, the noble, finely educated, home
loving fellow, whose life was darkened by an insane appetite
for stimulants, is drawn from the wells of bitter knowledge
and deep feeling, and appeals most powerfully to those who
know by terrible experience of the bondage of body and soul
into which human nature can fall, through this unnatural
appetite.

The progress of the hero and pretty bird-like Eva Van
Arsdel, from admiration to friendship and love, with the
various questions upon mercenary marriages which are
induced by the existence of a rich rival, and the relation of
social life to church affairs, permit all manner of discussion.
In the description of the match game of croquet, which considerably advances Harry Henderson's love affairs, we have
a bit of writing as fine, in its small way, as the Chariot
Race or the Naval Encounter of the slave-manned galleys,
of Ben Hur.

The loss of Papa Van Arsdel's money, gives Eva to
Harry, her true lover, and their marriage follows, with the
home-making in which Jim Fellows is the most competent
and ubiquitous assistant, and the story closes.

"My wife and I" and its sequel, "We and Our Neighbors," which continue the characters under new conditions,
and the discussions of those changing experiences, are not
great works, though they are full of homely wisdom which
perhaps may avail as much as brilliant genius, in the progress of civilization. In these latter books, the weightier
problems of life are left, and the writer drops into delight-

ful disquisitions upon every-day possibilities for good and pleasantness.

The burning inspiration of the earlier works of the author of "Uncle Tom's Cabin," glows tenderly now in the evening shadows, her stern opposition to great wrongs is softened and sweetened into less intensity in these essays upon social life. So, the pungent sharpness of the green age of the best fruit, is by time, matured and softened, taking on new and delicious flavors which are the fitting charm of waning vigor. These books were published by J. B. Ford and Co., in 1871 and 1873.

"Pink and White Tyranny," a story also to be classed among Mrs. Stowe's minor works, was published by Roberts Brothers of Boston, in the year 1871. It was termed a society novel and admitted to have a moral. As the title indicates, it is descriptive of the absolute power, seriously misused, of a pretty, frivolous woman, not only upon her unfortunate husband, but over society, which agreed that it was easier to succumb to her petulant sway, than to oppose her.

The heroine is one of Mrs. Stowe's butterfly women, and this time is a consistent character, full of whims and caprices which spring from unadulterated selfishness, which the prettiness and coquetry of the little sinner do not excuse, though her beauty and shallowness sufficiently account for her conduct. She comes through a career of flirtation, which though somewhat modified by modern restrictions, is quite possible in our society, to a marriage which is a natural result, when a great hearted, unsophisticated, wealthy, young man from a country town, comes in contact with a calculating and finished coquette.

Through different phases and experiences of social exis-

tence in a country town of Massachusetts, a season at Newport, and some festivities in New York, we are led with the
frail heroine, and the companionship of her friends, the
Follingsbees, whose vulgarity and pretentiousness are
cleverly shown, until her home and her husband are
neglected, and poor John Seymour turns to his sister for
consolation, eventually finding in his child, the comfort
he has missed in the frivolous and heartless wife.

It is forcibly set down, that in spite of his wrongs, John
Seymour bears with the spirit becoming a man, his disappointment in life, and the petty annoyances which amount
to tyranny in his wife, accepting his destiny, with no idea
of escaping from it, because he took his pretty wife as it
has transpired "for worse." We quote the author's moral—

"We have brought our story up to this point. We informed
our readers in the beginning that it was not a novel, but a story
with a moral; and, as people pick all sorts of strange morals out of
stories, we intend to put conspicuously into our story exactly what
the moral of it is.

"Well, then, it has been very surprising to us to see in these
our times that some people, who really at heart have the interest
of women upon their minds, have been so short-sighted and reckless as to clamor for an easy dissolution of the marriage-contract,
as a means of righting their wrongs. Is it possible that they do
not see that this is a liberty which, if once granted, would always
tell against the weaker sex? If the woman who finds that she
has made a mistake, and married a man unkind or uncongenial,
may, on the discovery of it, leave him and seek her fortune with
another. so also may a man. And what will become of women
like Lillie, when the first gilding begins to wear off, if the man
who has taken one of them shall be at liberty to cast her off and

seek another? Have we not enough now of miserable, broken-winged butterflies, that sink down, down, down into the mud of the street? But are women-reformers going to clamor for having every woman turned out helpless, when the man who has married her and made her a mother, discovers that she has not the power to interest him and to help his higher spiritual development? It was because woman is helpless and weak, and because Christ was her great Protector, that he made the law of marriage irrevocable. Whosoever putteth away his wife causeth her to commit adultery. If the sacredness of the marriage-contract did not hold, if the Church and all good men and all good women did not uphold it with their might and main, it is easy to see where the career of many women like Lillie would end. Men have the power to reflect before the choice is made; and that is the only proper time for reflection. But, when once marriage is made and consummated, it should be as fixed a fact as the laws of nature. And they who suffer under its stringency should suffer as those who endure for the public good. 'He that sweareth to his own hurt, and changeth not, he shall enter into the tabernacle of the Lord.'"

As usual, Harriet Beecher Stowe spoke for the enduring things of this life, and against the ephemeral ideas which come and go with every decade, sometimes indeed appearing to possess qualities which answer to reason, and seem to be confirmed by the logic of many instances, but which end, by receding to the background before the evident good to the greatest number, which Heaven-ordained laws and the facts of every-day life, are seen to demonstrate.

"Pink and White Tyranny" is written off-hand, and is full of the disillusions of the author's entrance into the story, in various philosophical observations to the reader. But we have learned to expect this from Mrs. Stowe and are always glad to see her thrust her head from behind the scenes and explain the play. Dickens had a way of stop-ping to pet his characters in the most artless manner, and Mrs. Stowe not only does this, but takes the reader into her confidence upon all questions, in a way that would be sur-prising, were it not so cordially done that it appears to be quite the proper thing, if a little unconventional.

Under the suggestive and attractive title of " Palmetto Leaves " was published in 1873, by (James R. Osgood & Co., of Boston), a collection of Florida letters written by Mrs. Stowe from her plantation at Mandarin, which had appeared in The Christian Union. A southern writer recently stated that her letters from her home upon the St. John's river, upon orange growing in Florida, as well as the open-ing for successful market gardening there, brought thou-sands of people to the state. She wrote of a " Flowery January," a " Water Coach and a Ride In It," " Mag-nolia " and " Yellow Jessamines ; " of " Florida for In-valids," and " Swamps and Orange Trees " in so vivid and picturesque language that thousands of readers felt and gratified a deep longing, for the soft atmosphere and luscious fruits and dazzling flowers of the South-land.

In answer to hundreds of letters which poured in upon her at Mandarin, she also wrote of more practical themes such as " Buying Land in Florida." " Our Experience in Crops " and " The Laborers of the South " in her own in-imitable and instructive style. This southern home was the romance of her mature life, the haven of her desires, which after a few weeks of frost and snow each year, would not be denied, and by January the family were usually *en route* for the winter home in the summer land, upon the silver St. Johns river.

In 1873 Mrs. Stowe prepared a set of sketches of women in Sacred History. It was a superb volume, which, in its plainest binding, sold for six dollars, and was illustrated with sixteen chromo lithographs, after paintings by Raphael, Batoni, Baader, Vernet, Delaroche, Portaels, Goodall, Koehler, Landelle, Merle, Devodeux, Vernet-Lecomte and Boulanger. It was a new departure in the history of book illustration, and its publishers, J. B. Ford & Co., of New York, were justly proud of the enterprise. The subjects treated were: 1, Sarah, the Princess; 2, Hagar, the Slave; 3, Rebekah, the Bride; 4, Leah and Rachael. These were selected from the Patriarchal Ages.

Those of the National Period were: 5, Miriam, Sister of Moses; 6, Deborah, the Prophetess; 7, Delilah, the Destroyer; 8, Jeptha's Daughter; 9, Hannah, the Praying Mother; 10, Ruth, the Moabitess; 11, The Witch of Endor; 12, Queen Esther; 13, Judith, the Deliverer.

The women of the Christain Era were: 14, Mary, the Mythical Madonna; 15, Mary, the Mother of Jesus; 16, The Woman of Samaria; 17, The Daughter of Herodias; 18, Mary Magdalene; 19, Martha and Mary.

Mrs. Stowe's affection for the Bible and its grand teachings, no less than her education and mental characteristics, made her peculiarly fitted to bring these historic characters out of the false and unnatural light in which they have appeared to many, showing them as real flesh and blood, human beings calling forth an interest and sympathy which is seldom felt for those who lived in those far-off times.

The book in its original form was so successful, it was thought well to enlarge the plan, and it was therefore put forth in quarto form in twenty-five parts, illustrated

THE WINTER HOME AT MANDARINE, FLA.

with the original sixteen chromo lithographs and nine more. The text also was enlarged by the introduction of selected poems bearing upon the subjects, from well-known writers.

Then, later, when this large and expensive work had had its natural course, the book was published in smaller form and called "Bible Heroines." The sale reached something like 50,000 copies.

Another work of religious interest was shortly after compiled by Mrs. Stowe.

It was entitled "Footsteps of the Master," and consisted of meditations upon the Life of Christ with appropriate poems, carols and hymns, original and selected.

It showed the author to be a devout student of theological lore and in its arrangement, in the order of the Church Festivals of the Christian Year, testified to her preference for the Anglican observances.

She had become attached to the Episcopal Church, largely through the influence of her son-in-law, and found a peculiar beauty and usefulness in its ceremonials.

This volume was also published by J. B. Ford and Co. having a good sale.

After a period of some years of waning activity, Mrs. Stowe began the writing of her last story, " Poganuc People." With it practically ended her remarkable literary career, which extended over twenty-five years of her mature life, and comprised more force and originality than the work of any other American woman. In the books just preceding the religious works above referred to, Mrs. Stowe had been upon unfamiliar ground, or one might say, promulgating themes that were not indigenous to the soil from which sprang her great "Uncle Tom's Cabin,"

"The Minister's Wooing," "The Pearl of Orr's Island" and "Old Town Folks." These must remain her distinguishing successes, when her other books are forgotten.

To this list of creations, which carry inherent strength and vitality in their very atmosphere, evincing a genius which George Sand described as " pure, penetrating and profound, one which fathoms the recesses of the human soul," she was about to add another, her last important work, embracing her own preferred themes, and those which took firmest hold upon the sympathies of her readers. As she began in the Mayflower, the first success of her girlhood, so she ended, in "Poganuc People," reproducing the loves and lives of New England folk, illuminating and throwing in relief as no other writer has done, the amusing peculiarities and the pure worth of homely character, which pertained to the immediate descendants of the Puritans.

" Poganuc People" returns to Litchfield, as the thoughts and memories of age turn again to scenes and impressions of childhood, and the story is largely autobiographical. We are again led into an old-fashioned kitchen of seventy years ago, and see through the eyes of an observant and sensitive child, the kind homeliness of " Nabby " the young woman who " helped " the minister's wife, and feel something of the interest which went out from the childish heart towards the festivities which were going on at that Christmas season at the Episcopal church, from which she was tacitly forbidden by her father, who was true to his Presbyterian principles.

The author's discussion of the state of religious affairs in Poganuc, affords an instructive idea of the condition of the church which was in existence in New England, and particularly in Connecticut, at this time. It is a picture that holds much that is properly a source of pride to Americans, for though it has of late become the fashion to pick flaws in the regime of the Pilgrim fathers, it is only little minds that can underrate the vitalizing force with which their system of church and state, imbued every character.

"The Episcopal Church in New England in the early days was emphatically a root out of dry ground, with as little foothold in popular sympathy as one of those storm-driven junipers, that the east wind blows all aslant, has in the rocky ledges of Cape Cod. The soil, the climate, the atmosphere, the genius, and the history of the people were all against it. Its forms and ceremonies were all associated with the persecution which drove the Puritans out of England and left them no refuge but the rock-bound shores of America. It is true that in the time of Governor Winthrop the colony of Massachusetts appealed with affectionate professions to their Mother, the Church of England, and sought her sympathy and her prayers; but it is also unfortunately true that the forms of the Church of England were cultivated and maintained in New England by the very party whose intolerance and tyranny brought on the Revolutionary war.

"All the oppressive governors of the colonies were Episcopalians, and in the Revolutionary struggle the Episcopal Church was very generally on the Tory side; hence, the New Englanders came to have an aversion to its graceful and beautiful ritual and forms, for the same reason that the free party in Spain and Italy now loath the beauties of the Romish Church, as signs and symbols of tyranny and oppression.

"Congregationalism—or, as it was then called by the common people, Presbyterianism—was the religion established by law in New England. It was the State Church. Even in Boston in its colonial days, the King's Chapel and Old North were only dissenting churches, unrecognized by the State, but upheld by the patronage of the colonial governors who were sent over to them from England. For a long time after the Revolutionary war the old *regime* of the State Church held undisputed sway in New England. There was the one meeting-house, the one minister, in every village. Every householder was taxed for the support of public worship, and stringent law and custom demanded of every one a personal attendance on Sunday at both services. If any defaulter failed to put in an appearance it was the minister's duty to call promptly on Monday and know the reason why. There was no differences of religious opinion. All that individualism which now raises a crop of various little churches in every country village was sternly suppressed. For many years only members of churches could be eligible to public offices ; Sabbath-keeping was enforced with more than Mosaic strictness, and New England justified the sarcasm which said that they had left the Lords-Bishops to be under the Lords-Brethren. In those days if a sectarian meeting of Methodists or Baptists, or an unseemly gathering of any kind, seemed impending, the minister had only to put on his cocked hat, take his gold-headed cane and march down the village street, leaving his prohibition at every house, and the thing was so done, even as he commanded.

" In the very nature of things such a state of society could not endure. The shock that separated the nation from a king and monarchy, the sense of freedom and independence, the hardihood of thought which led to the founding of a new civil republic, were fatal to all religious restraint. Even before the Revolutionary war there were independent spirits that chafed under the constraint of clerical supervision, and Ethan Allen advertised his farm and stock for sale, expressing his determination at any cost to get out of ' this old holy State of Connecticut.'

" It was but a little while after the close of the war that established American independence that the revolution came which

broke up the State Church and gave to every man the liberty of
' signing off,' as it was called, to any denomination that pleased
him. Hence arose through New England churches of all names.
The nucleus of the Episcopal Church in any place was generally
some two or three old families of ancestral traditions in its favor,
who gladly welcomed to their fold any who, for various causes,
were discontented with the standing order of things. Then, too,
there came to them gentle spirits, cut and bleeding by the sharp
crystals of doctrinal statement, and courting the balm of devo-
tional liturgy and the cool, shadowy indefiniteness of more æsthetic forms of worship. Also, any one that for any cause had a
controversy with the dominant church took comfort in the power
of ' signing off' to another. In those days, to belong to no
nhurch was not respectable, but to sign off to the Episcopal
Church was often a compromise that both gratified self-will and
saved one's dignity ; and, having signed off, the new convert was
obliged, for consistency's sake, to justify the step he had taken by
doing his best to uphold the doctrine and worship of his chosen
church."

The meeting of the village politicians in " the store," the
Doctor's sermon against the Popish observance of Christmas
day, Mr. Coan's answer, Election Day in Poganuc, and the
description of the daily arrival of the stage coach, are a
series of creations which have become classic, having only
one or two successful imitators in all the company of
American writers.

Hiel Jones the stage driver is unmistakably a New England Yankee, and one as well drawn, and deservedly popular, as Sam Lawson. He emphatically belonged to a social
and civic condition now many years gone by, but the preservation of this, his "counterfeit presentiment" is a historical boon to generations yet to come, who will have lived

too late, however to have the thorough belief in his personality, that comes to readers of to-day.

Hiel's courtship of spirited Nabby Higgins is vastly humorous and entertaining, and little Dolly's entrance into refined society among the dignitaries of Poganuc, shows the social condition of what composed the aristocracy of New England. A most worthy ascendancy of the fittest, it appears, though not in the least derogating from the honest common sense and native ability, of the less cultured citizens of the town.

An irresistible bit of humor in a subsequent chapter entitled "The Puzzle of the Town." This lay in so important a question as the situation of the school house. Its site was an inconvenient and unpleasant one, but it had been thus far impossible to obtain the unanimous vote of the citizens to move it to a more desirable place. Zeph Higgins, evidently a first cousin to "Uncle Lot" is doubtless one of the strongest depictions of the author who has presented to us so many clear cut and distinctive personalities. While earnestly desiring that the school house should be moved, he always managed through his unaccountable perversity, to defeat any measures taken to secure that end. To the intense amusement of the reader, Zeph Higgins at last resolves to take the affair into his own hands, and with his "boys" and several pairs of oxen, raises the school house from its foundations to his great sled, and moves it to the spot which every one prefers, thus settling the question, which he alone, has for years kept open.

Summer days in Poganuc, the excitement and patriotic burnings of the Fourth of July, the approach of dreamy autumn and later frosts, and the fascination and exhilarating joy of going a-chestnutting, all reflect scenes of Harriet Beecher's early youth and have a special charm and pathos in this last story.

The "apple bee" and the "wood spell" are retrospective views of the occasions in Lyman Beecher's household.

We all know the graphic power of Harriet Beecher Stowe, when dwelling upon themes which thoroughly engaged her sympathies. She has never failed when thus enlisted, to produce in the reader the emotions of pity, anger, or even hatred in the intensest degree. No less powerfully could she move at will the springs of tears or smiles, of overwhelming enthusiasm and uplifting joy, over fiery human experience which left pure gold in the place where had been a large admixture of dross. With all Mrs. Stowe's severe criticism of Theological doctrines, it must be noted that she never exhibited any of the sarcasm of religion which so seriously taints much modern fiction. It was a question she could not treat lightly, and though dealing a terrible blow at the dogmatism and austerity of the Puritans, she never failed to uphold and glorify the beauty of Christianity, in both spiritual and temporal lights.

Religious "revivals" have come to be regarded with a sort of tolerance by a large portion of intelligent moralists.

Even many people who consider themselves Christians, mildly deprecate the excitement and emotional upheavals which pertain to the stated periods, when mortals are made to realize in a special manner, their sinfulness and spiritual shortcomings. But it indeed must be a calloused heart which can read Mrs. Stowe's story of a revival in Poganuc, with its bearings upon diverse minds and different individualities of the parish, without feeling that this system had its beneficent influence, one which cannot be under-estimated without evincing considerable flippancy in the mind of the objector.

No one can read without emotion, the history of Zeph Higgins and the terrible discipline which he endured. He was a self-willed man, who considered all ceremonial religious observances as effeminate demonstrations, who rebelled at all ecclesiastical authority, who found any reverential attitude or words irksome to his perverse, ungraceful nature; who had a Spartan contempt for anything æsthetic, and all the scorn of beauty and cultivated expression which characterized certain rough stages of New England life.

He had quarreled with a friend, a fellow church member, and had forsworn on this account the church. He was one who cleaved to a quarrel with the tenacity and devotion, which we recognize as one of the strange problems of our human nature. He hugged and nursed his wrath as closely as if it made him happy, instead of embittering his very life blood.

Zeph Higgins found his ideal of all that was lovely, in his wife. When she gathered her children around her and went to church to pray for them and for him, he kept silence, because she, of all the others upon earth, was the only being he did not instinctively oppose. Mrs. Higgins, after a life of hard work and sacrifice, became ill, and after some weeks of sickness, died. The struggles and rebellion of the hard man, who having not the grace to accept blessings gratefully, lacked still more conspicuously the patience to bear with trouble, come home to the reader with crushing force, and one can with difficulty read through the pages which tell of the inevitable approach of death, and the stricken husband's wildly useless and miserable rebellion.

Will you merely read of a funeral in the old times? Then take some less powerful writer in hand. This one you must perforce attend, if you read. You feel the strange stillness, smell the close air, see through the gloom of the shrouded windows, the white wrappings which envelop the furniture and pictures. You hear through the ominous silence, the ticking of the kitchen clock, and hear the hoarse whispers of the " manager."

Then the solemn tones of the minister's voice as he reads and prays, and the quavering voices of the singers who put their heads together for an instant as they try to catch the key-note which is given under the breath of the leader. Then the old funeral hymn, "China," which has added new pangs to life and death in its mournful move-ment, seeming often an exquisite refinement of cruelty to the wrung hearts of the mourners, and all who must contemplate the end of this existence.

The going out of the coffin in the more or less clumsy hands of the bearers; their shuffling steps in the passage; the departure of the procession of vehicles to the last resting place; the knots of friends who remain to talk over the personal affairs of the bereaved family; the twos and threes of men in their best clothes who stand in the yard waiting for the women to go home; all come with vivid distinct-ness before the mind, and as long as the writer wills, we are spell bound.

The author gives her childish religious experience in the chapter called "Dolly at the Wicket Gate," and most ten-derly is it done.

Reader, are you "principled against revivals?" Then cease to follow the story here, for you will witness one in all its aspects, and much against your will perhaps, be wrought upon as if you verily heard the preacher's voice, and felt the silent influences of the occasion. Zeph Higgins again becomes the centre of interest. His unlovely desolation, his fretful misery and rebellious sorrow have served to almost deprive him of the sympathy of his family and friends; the sympathy which he so needs and longs for, and, as usual, perversely shuts away. Zeph has become specially intolerable, as he is now debating with himself whether he will take the first step towards reconciliation with his church, by going to the prayer meeting which is to be held in the school house near by.

In the scene that follows, one of the greatest Mrs. Stowe ever created, there is all of the realism of the modern school, with a spirit and subtle atmosphere pervading the painting, which lifts it into the sublime. Few representations in literature are more intensely dramatic than the description of this meeting in a New England school house. It proceeds to a climax, ever-growing in feeling, as poor cross-grained, contrary, Zeph Higgins, now broken and despairing in his grief rises to confess his faults, declares himself struck down by the Lord, and that he cannot be resigned.

His concluding words, "I ain't a Christian, and I can't be, and I shall go to hell at last, and sarve me right," call no attention to his quaintness of verbal expression, one is too much with him for that, but they do show in their spirit, that having come to this confession, he is at last setting himself right with his own soul; and that the next step, that of adjusting differences with his neighbors and becoming submissive to a Higher Power, will the easier follow. Let the author finish the chapter.

" And Zeph sat down, grim and stony, and the neighbors looked one on another in a sort of consternation. There was a terrible earnestness in those words which seemed to appall every one and prevent any from uttering the ordinary common-places of religious exhortation. For a few moments the circle was as silent as the grave, when Dr. Cushing said, 'Brethren, let us pray;' and in his prayer he seemed to rise above earth and draw his whole flock with all their sins and needs and wants, into the presence-chamber of heaven.

" He prayed that the light of heaven might shine into the darkened spirit of their brother; that he might give himself up utterly to the will of God; that we might *all* do it, that we might become as little children in the kingdom of heaven. With the wise tact which distinguished his ministry he closed the meeting immediately after the prayer with one or two serious words of exhortation. He feared lest what had been gained in impression might be talked away did he hold the meeting open to the well-meant, sincere but uninstructed efforts of the brethren to meet a case like that which had been laid open before them.

" After the service was over and the throng slowly dispersed, Zeph remained in his place, rigid and still. One or two approached to speak to him; there was in fact a tide of genuine sympathy and brotherly feeling that longed to express itself. He might have been caught up in this powerful current and borne into a haven of peace, had he been one to trust himself to the help of others; but he looked neither to the right nor to the left; his eyes were fixed on the floor; his brown, bony hands held his old straw hat in a crushing grasp; his whole attitude and aspect were repelling and stern to such a degree that none dared address him.

" The crowd slowly passed on and out. Zeph sat alone, as he thought; but the minister, his wife, and little Dolly had remained

at the upper end of the room.   Suddenly, as if sent by an irresistible impulse, Dolly stepped rapidly down the room and with eager
gaze laid her pretty little timid hand upon his shoulder, crying, in
a voice tremulous at once with fear and with intensity, "O, *why*
do you say that you can not be a Christian?   Don't you know
that Christ loves you?"

"Christ loves you!"   The words thrilled through his soul with
a strange, new power; he opened his eyes and looked astonished
into the little, earnest, pleading face.

"Christ loves you," she repeated; "oh, do believe it!"

"Loves *me*!" he said, slowly.   "Why should he?"

"But he does; he loves us all.   He died for us.   He died for
you.   Oh, believe it.   He'll help you; he'll make you feel right.
Only trust him.   Please say you will!"

"Zeph looked at the little face earnestly, in a softened, wondering way.   A tear slowly stole down his hard cheek.

"Thankee, dear child," he said.

"You will believe it?"

"I'll try."

"You will trust Him?"

"Zeph paused a moment, then rose up with a new and different expression in his face, and said, in a subdued and earnest
voice, "I will."

"Amen!" said the Doctor, who stood listening, and he silently
grasped the old man's hand."

In a few more pages, in which various characters are well
settled in life, and Dolly becomes a young lady, marrying a
distant cousin whom she meets during a visit to friends in
Boston, the story of Poganuc People closes.

The thin, wrinkled hands that laid down the pen with
its last word, never more took up any protracted labor.
The weary brain rested now, and in the years which

followed, dwelt only upon the themes of life which were new every morning and fresh every evening.

Mrs. Stowe was induced to furnish two short biographical articles for a work published by A. D. Worthington & Co., of Hartford, called "Our Famous Women." These were of her eldest sister, Catherine E. Beecher, and Mrs. A. D. T. Whitney whom she had familiarly known as one of her father's young parishioners in Boston.

In 1881 Houghton, Mifflin & Co., who had now obtained control of most her works, issued the "Pussy Willow" stories, and another collection called "A Dog's Mission" both of which are most attractive juvenile books.

The last notable event in the literary life of Harriet Beecher Stowe was the Garden Party given by Houghton, Mifflin & Co., in honor of her seventieth birthday. It was an event of absorbing interest to a large company of distinguished people who were present, and the great reading public who watched from thousands of English-speaking homes for an account of the occasion. This was given in a supplement to the Atlantic Monthly. From the facts there given and personal sources of information we are furnished this account.

Messrs. Houghton, Mifflin & Co., began some years ago a series of festivals to authors, who were contributors to *The Atlantic Monthly*. They gave first a Dinner to Mr. Whittier, followed by a Breakfast to Dr. Holmes; upon the approach of Mrs. Stowe's 70th birthday they offered a similar tribute to her. Mrs. Stowe assented to their proposal, and as Hon. and Mrs. William Claflin generously tendered their spacious and beautiful country home and grounds at Newtonville, near Boston, for the occasion, the season and the place and

Mrs. Stowe's well known fondness for *al fresco* pleasures, suggested that the festival take the form of a Garden Party.

The following invitation was sent to many persons in all parts of this country, and to several in Great Britain, eminent in letters, art, science, statesmanship, and philanthropy :—

Messrs. Houghton, Mifflin and Company request the pleasure of your presence at a Garden Party in Honor of the Birthday of

HARRIET BEECHER STOWE,

at " The Old Elms " (the residence of Hon. William Claflin), Newtonville, Mass., on Wednesday, June Fourteenth, 1882, from 3 to 7 P. M.

4 Park Street, Boston,
June 1st, 1882.

About two hundred guests gathered in response to this invitation.

Rev. Charles Beecher, Rev. and Mrs. Henry Ward Beecher, Rev. and Mrs. Edward Beecher, Prof. Calvin E. Stowe, Rev. and Mrs. Charles E. Stowe, Mrs. Mary B. Perkins, sister of Mrs. Stowe, Rev. and Henry F. Allen and his wife, who is the youngest daughter of Mrs. Stowe, Rev. Lyman Abbott, A. Bronson Alcott, Thomas Bailey Aldrich, Arlo Bates, Frances Hodgson Burnett, Rose Terry Cooke, Abby Morton Diaz, Francis J. Garrison, William Lloyd Garrison, Jr., Mr. and Mrs. Curtis Guild, Dr. Oliver Wendell Holmes, Mr. and Mrs. H. O. Houghton, W. D. Howells, Lucy Larcom, Mr. and Mrs. George P. Lathrop, Mr. and Mrs. George H. Mifflin, Louise Chandler Moulton, Charles C. Perkins, Nora Perry, Elizabeth Stuart Phelps, Abby Sage Richardson.

Mr. and Mrs. Horace E. Scudder, M. E. W. Sherwood, J. T. Trowbridge, Kate Gannett Wells, Mrs. A. D. T. Whitney, Anne Whitney, John G. Whittier, and many others of our American literary guild, formed a part of this famous Garden Party.

The day proved all that could be desired for such a festival. It was one of Nature's perfect June days, with the atmosphere exactly tempered and perfumed for a high holiday, such as this proved to be at Newtonville.

The hours from three to five o'clock were spent socially. On a stage under the shade of a great tent sat the most famous literary woman of the age, her sad sweet face framed in the gray hair which clustered in curls about her head. As guests arrived they were presented to Mrs. Stowe by Mr. H. O. Houghton, and then they gathered in groups in the parlors, on the verandas, on the lawn, and in the refreshment rooms.

At five o'clock they assembled in a large tent on the lawn, and after a song by Mrs. Humphrey Allen, Mr. Houghton gave an interesting address. This was followed by remarks from Henry Ward Beecher, in which he said that for many years after the publication of "Uncle Tom's Cabin" he was given credit, by many wise people, of having written the book. He said "the matter at last became so scandalous that I determined to put an end to it, and therefore, I wrote 'Norwood.' That killed the thing, dead."

Mr. Whittier was present, to the great satisfaction of all the company, but he excused himself from reading the poem he had written, which was read by Mr. Frank B. Sanborn.

Dr. Holmes, on being presented, described the circum-

stances in which he first read "Uncle Tom's Cabin," and
the deepening of his interest in it, so that he soon laid aside
the novel of Dickens which he had been reading, and gave
himself up wholly to "Uncle Tom's Cabin" until he had
reached the end. He then read his poem, full of his own
fine humor and pithy reflections—three verses of which are
here given,—

> " If every tongue that speaks her praise
> For whom I shape my tinkling phrase
>   Were summoned to the table,
> The vocal chorus that would meet
> Of mingling accents harsh or sweet,
> From every land and tribe, would beat
>   The polyglots of Babel
>
> Briton and Frenchman, Swede and Dane,
> Turk, Spaniard, Tartar of Ukraine,
>   Hidalgo, Cossack, Cadi,
> High Dutchman and Low Dutchman, too,
> The Russian serf, the Polish Jew,
> Arab, Armenian, and Mantchoo
>   Would shout, " We know the lady ! "
>
> Know her ! Who knows not Uncle Tom
> And her he learned his gospel from,
>   Has never heard of Moses ;
> Full well the brave black hand we know
> That gave to freedom's grasp the hoe
> That killed the weed that used to grow
>   Among the Southern roses."

Then followed the poems of Mrs. A. D. T. Whitney and
Elizabeth Stuart Phelps, the latter being read for her, by

Dr. Holmes. J. T. Trowbridge then read a poem, which was afterwards printed in the *Youth's Companion*, entitled "The Cabin."

Mrs. Allen, daughter of Mrs. Stowe, contributed a poem, which was read by her husband, Rev. Henry F. Allen.

Mrs. Annie Fields who was at this time in Europe, wrote a poem in honor of the occasion, which was then read, followed by the bright sonnet of Miss Charlotte F. Bates.

Speeches were made by Judge Albion W. Tourgee, Rev. Edward Beecher, Mr. Edward Atkinson and others. Mr. Atkinson described an interview between Professor Lieber and Senator Preston, of South Carolina, who was of the extreme type of Southern men before the war. "Uncle Tom's Cabin" had just appeared, and conversation turned upon it. The senator was strongly excited, and in reply to a question he said, "We have read Uncle Tom's Cabin, and I know it is true. I can match every instance in it out of my own experience."

Music by the Germania Band and the Beethoven Club, and songs by Mrs. Humphrey Allen at intervals during the speeches and poems, lent variety and enjoyment to the brilliant entertainment.

Mr. Houghton then stated that Mrs. Stowe had consented to say a few words, and as she came to the front of the platform her earnest face lighted with deep feeling, her speaking eyes looked kindly upon the company, all of whom she saw were warm with sympathy and love for her.

Many of them were veterans of the abolition "Old Guard," personally unassuming and "fanatical" as ever, but profoundly satisfied now that fulfillment of their hope had come.

Everyone rose by a simultaneous impulse of affectionate respect, and listened with eager interest while in her simple and unemotional manner, she spoke as follows :—

" I wish to say that I thank all my friends from my heart, —that is all. And one thing more,—and that is, if any of you have doubt, or sorrow, or pain, if you doubt about this world, just remember what God has done; just remember that this great sorrow of slavery has gone, gone by forever. I see it every day at the South. I walk about there and see the lowly cabins. I see these people growing richer and richer. I see men very happy in their lowly lot ; but, to be sure, you must have patience with them. They are not perfect, but have their faults, and they are serious faults in the view of white people. But they are very happy, that is evident, and they know how to enjoy themselves,— a great deal more than you do. An old negro friend in our neighborhood has got a new, nice two-story house, and an orange grove, and a sugar-mill. He has got a lot of money, besides. Mr. Stowe met him one day, and he said, 'I have got twenty head of cattle, four head of ' hoss,' forty head of hen, and I have got ten children, all *mine, every one mine.*' Well, now, that is a thing that a black man could not say once, and this man was sixty years old before he could say it. With all the faults of the colored people, take a man and put him down with nothing but his hands, and how many could say as much as that? I think they have done well.

" A little while ago they had at his house an evening festival for their church, and raised fifty dollars. We white folks took our carriages, and when we reached the house we found it fixed nicely. Every one of his daughters knew how to cook. They had a good place for the festival. Their suppers were spread on little white tables, with nice clean cloths on them. People paid fifty cents for supper. They got between fifty and sixty dollars, and had one of the best frolics you could imagine. They had also for supper ice-cream, which they made themselves.

"That is the sort of thing I see going on around me. Let us never doubt. *Everything that ought to happen, is going to happen.*" In those last words was condensed her living faith in the goodness of God and His working all things for the best. It was a belief which she never gave up, in the darkest hours of her life. It was the one conviction which enabled her to do her grand work. She had courage and its resultant attribute hope, which Wilkinson touchingly characterizes "that last obduracy of noble minds."

After Mrs. Stowe's remarks, Mr. Houghton felicitously expressed the gratitude of the company to Mr. and Mrs. Claflin for the kind courtesy which had, with rare generosity, given their house and grounds for the festival. The company then slowly dispersed, many gathering about Mrs. Stowe for congratulation and farewell.

Many letters of regret were received, but only four of them were read at the Garden Party.

These letters were placed in Mrs. Stowe's hands,—all of them expressing regret in not being able to be present to participate in the pleasures of the festival, and showing strong appreciation and admiration for her and the power-ful influence she had exerted throughout the land. Follow-ing are the names of some illustrious people from whom these letters were received:—R. B. Hayes, J. R. Lowell, George William Curtis, G. W. Cable, Thomas K. Beecher, Mary Mapes Dodge, H. M. Alden, Rebecca Harding Davis,

George Cary Eggleston, Wendell Phillips, Henry Cabot
Lodge, Rev. William H. Beecher, Rev. Phillips Brooks,
Prof. Alexander Agassiz, John Burroughs, Henry James,
Rev. Samuel Longfellow, Ernest Longfellow, and the
Misses Longfellow, Dr. E. W. Emerson, Judge Nathaniel
Holmes, Louise M. Alcott, Julia Ward Howe, Col. T.
W. Higginson, S. L. Clemens, Dr. Samuel Eliot, Hon. Carl
Schurz, Rev. Dr. C. A. Bartol, Rev. Edward Abbott, and
many others.

Rose Terry Cooke, her beloved friend and young co-la
borer in literature, especially that pertaining to abolition,
early New England Theology, and characteristic Yankee
thought and custom, has said of this occasion:

"Praise was showered upon her like incense; poems read
in her honor; and before her gathered a crowd of friends
with love and laud in every eye, on every lip; but it was
not for the praise of men to ruffle her serene countenance
or disturb the dreamy peace of her eyes, that seemed bent
upon some far away distance, where the babble of earth is
heard no more, but the silent welcome of heaven is ready
and waiting.

She received her ovation with the calm simplicity of a
child, and in a few words of gracious thanks and counsel,
dismissed her guests, when all their speech had been uttered,
and went out with her husband, her son and her grandchildren into the fresh June air, the young summer verdure,
and the crowding flowers, and away to her home and its
duties, as a saint to her cell, untouched by the hot breath
of flattery, unmoved by the loud plaudits of men, calm in
that mild consciousness of devotion and duty that is deeper
and dearer than this life's most earnest homage, or its richest gifts."

With this event ended, in effect, the public career of the author of "Uncle Tom's Cabin." The remaining years of her life were quiet and restful. She had leisure; the delicious ease and freedom from pressing work, for which she had longed so many burdened years.

She enjoyed the sweet do-nothingness which should come to all, in the afternoon of their lives.

She could indulge her desire—long suppressed in her laborious literary life—to read.

She could take precious mornings, all to herself, in the green fields and woods. She could stop by the way to call upon a friend. And, when her husband, bowed with the weight of years, became ill, needing tender care, she could give it to him, with the fullness and devotion which freedom from other duties permitted.

At last, when he had passed on, she could live in serene contentment, quietly awaiting her summons to follow him whither so many loved ones seemed to be drawing her heart and soul.

When her mind, from the weakening of its mortal casement, gradually became abstracted from her earthly surroundings, and it appeared, a year ago, that the call had come for her to enter the new life, the world paused, dreading to hear of the death of the grandest woman of the age.

Her wandering thoughts were full of the sublimities of the promised land where so many friends reached forth welcoming hands.

There she would be free from physical ills; there she would be young again; there would the vigor of her spiritual self be restored; there would she find the reward for her work here: but so strong was her sympathy with this world, so long had her thoughts and feelings been turned towards the weal and woe of humanity, that the thread would not be severed, and she still stands with reluctant feet near the brink of the river.

She is forgetful of the past. She no longer regards the future with intelligent anticipations. She is dimmed and deluded as to earthly concerns, yet holds with marvelous tenacity to her physical tenement.

It has been said *she died*, when her clouded intelligence appeared to go out under the fell stroke of apoplexy, but it still flashes up clearly at intervals, showing that she is merely imprisoned by bodily infirmities, until, her spirit finally released, the windows shall open toward Heaven, and her freed soul go home.

When Harriet Beecher Stowe laid down her pen, a great mental and spiritual force ceased to act. When she rested from work, an influence which has proved more pervasive and lasting than that of any other living writer, no longer thrilled upon the questions of the age.

When she had said her farewell to the world, in the few simple words at the Birthday Garden Party, there left the stage a woman who has marked an era; one who, superior to the ephemeral interests of humanity in general, and her sex in particular, dealt in principles; who looked over and beyond social and political conventionalities at eternal truths; and having received an immortal message spoke it, fearlessly—with pain often, but grandly, gloriously.

A genius she was, with high and peculiar gifts of nature and an intuitive power, which guided her unerringly to the ends to be achieved, but supporting it, was a conscientious-

HARRIET BEECHER STOWE IN HER OLD AGE.

ness that was sublime, a courage that was indomitable, a persistence that was irresistible.

To these qualities, must be attributed the prominence she held even over that mighty generation of her own family, which is now passing away. Among the tremendous influences which went forth from its array of orators, scholars and teachers, hers was strongest and most enduring.

To these forces, must be credited her political status, which is high among the illustrious company of American statesmen, not one of whom ever made so powerful a manifesto as her book against Negro Slavery, which marked an epoch not only in our national history but throughout the civilized world.

But for these, "Uncle Tom's Cabin," which a literary historian has recently declared "stands upon the top shelf, side by side with the 'Illiad,' 'Don Quixote,' 'Pilgrim's Progress,' and their half dozen peers," would never have been written.

But for these living fires, her knowledge of the old systems of New England theology, and observation of its effects upon human character, would never have found expression in "The Minister's Wooing"—a work whose literary merits alone, place her name with those of Irving, Bryant, Longfellow, Emerson, Hawthorne, Holmes, Lowell and Whittier, those great contemporaries who formed the first important and distinctive wave of native American literary talent.

It is stimulating, it is splendidly encouraging, to look through the eloquent beauty of her descriptions, through the tense fibre and rare strength of her arguments, through the melting tenderness and contagious humor of her philosophy, behind the almost unaccountable momentum of her literary power, to these moving springs. For back of the book was the mind and heart. Back of the work was the woman, brave, consistent and unassuming.

So, she leaves us not only the noble legacy of her written thoughts, but the priceless heritage of her personal example.

It is that of a well endowed life grandly lived.

THE END.

3477-6

www.ingramcontent.com/pod-product-compliance
Lightning Source LLC
Chambersburg PA
CBHW022009110726
47901CB00006B/1446